Conor's
over a mo
lower his he
to move.

"You don't know what you're saying, Olivia."

She gazed up at him with those damnable dark
eyes. "I know exactly what I'm saying. I want you to
make love to me. Don't . . . don't you want to?"

Did he want to? It would be a taste of heaven
itself. He closed his eyes, fighting what he wanted
with everything he had.

"Conor?"

He'd lost, and he knew it. So much for being
valiant and noble and doing the right thing. It had
been proven to him a long time ago that he wasn't a
hero anyway.

He opened his eyes. "Don't hate me for this
tomorrow, Olivia," he said, and cupped her cheeks,
tilting her head back as he brought his mouth closer
to hers. " For God's sake, don't hate me."

His mouth came down on hers before she could
reply. Her lips parted freely, and with that first taste
of her, he knew that there was no turning back.

"Funny and wrenching, heartwarming and
emotional, *Conor's Way* can't fail to make you
laugh and cry."
—PATRICIA GAFFNEY

"Laura Lee Guhrke perfectly captures
the Americana aura in *Conor's Way*.
A beautiful read!"
—*Romantic Times*

By Laura Lee Guhrke

Prelude to Heaven
To Dream Again
Conor's Way

Published by HarperPaperbacks

Conor's Way

 Laura Lee Guhrke

HarperPaperbacks
A Division of HarperCollinsPublishers

If you purchased this book without a cover, you should be
aware that this book is stolen property. It was reported as
"unsold and destroyed" to the publisher and neither the
author nor the publisher has received any payment for this
"stripped book."

This is a work of fiction. The characters, incidents, and
dialogues are products of the author's imagination and are
not to be construed as real. Any resemblance to actual events
or persons, living or dead, is entirely coincidental.

HarperPaperbacks   *A Division of* HarperCollins*Publishers*
                10 East 53rd Street, New York, N.Y. 10022

Copyright © 1996 by Laura Lee Guhrke
All rights reserved. No part of this book may be used or
reproduced in any manner whatsoever without written
permission of the publisher, except in the case of brief
quotations embodied in critical articles and reviews. For
information address HarperCollins*Publishers,*
10 East 53rd Street, New York, N.Y. 10022.

Cover illustration by Vittorio

First printing: April 1996

Printed in the United States of America

HarperPaperbacks, HarperMonogram, and colophon are
trademarks of HarperCollins*Publishers*

❖ 10 9 8 7 6 5 4 3 2 1

For John, of course.
Who else would put up with calls at
one o'clock in the morning Belfast time
to answer questions about Gaelic?
With much love, as always.

ACKNOWLEDGMENTS

Thanks to James Bowen, deacon of the Roman Catholic Diocese of Boise, for dusting the cobwebs off my knowledge of Catholic theology. Thanks also to all the folks at the Ruston, Louisiana, public library for going above and beyond the call of research librarian duty. Thanks to the real Carrie—Carrie Gibson—for being my inspiration when I created Carrie Taylor. Thanks also to Tip O'Connor for some much needed, last-minute assistance. Tip, best of luck with the young Irish writers. And a very special thank-you to the friends who keep me sane: Rachel Gibson, Jill Hill, Stef Ann Holm, and Sandy Oakes. Especially Sandy, whose insightful comments and ideas always help. Yes, Sandy, you can stop being cheerful and have that major depression now—the book's finished.

1

Northern Louisiana, 1871

When Conor Branigan ducked under the ropes and entered the ring, the men of Callersville knew he was just too pretty to be a good fighter. Women, of course, would have expressed a rather different opinion of the matter, but no women were there. As it was, the men of Callersville took one look at Conor's lean body and handsome face, and decided they had a sure winner in their local champion.

Conor paused in the center of the ring and responded to the boos and whistles that greeted him, the outsider, with an impudent salute just for show. Then he sauntered over to his corner of the ring and prepared to wait while the bookmaker's clerk took the last bets. His blue eyes scanned the rowdy Friday-night crowd without noticing any face in particular. After twenty towns and twenty fights in seventy days, all the faces looked the same—shiny with sweat, eager for the fight, and anonymous.

But Conor didn't mind that. Life on the boxing circuit suited him. If he won the fight tonight, he'd celebrate his victory by taking a hot bath, smoking a strong cigar, and sharing a bottle of good Irish with some carmine-lipped angel of mercy who asked for nothing more than a dollar bill and a kiss good-bye. Tomorrow, he'd move on to the next town and the next fight.

No ties, no family, no commitments. That was Conor's life now. And that was the way he liked it.

A round of cheers went up as his opponent entered the tent, and Conor turned to watch Elroy Harlan make his way through the crowd. The reigning champion of Jackson Parish and the odds-on favorite was a huge, hulking wall of a man who stepped into the ring amid the encouraging shouts of his friends and neighbors.

Conor figured that Elroy outweighed him by a good forty pounds, but he knew from experience the big ones were usually too slow. If Elroy had a build similar to his own, Conor might have been worried, but when Elroy moved to his own corner and scowled at him across the ring, Conor just leaned back against the ropes and gave the other man a deliberately provoking smile. Provoked men got angry.

"Irish son of a bitch," Elroy snarled.

Conor's grin widened. Angry men made mistakes.

Prizefighting was just a job, a way to make a living. It wasn't fun, but it was better than gutting fish in Boston or cleaning up horse dung in the streets of New York twelve hours a day for a pittance wage. It was better than swinging a sledgehammer under the hot sun on the railroad line. Conor worked only two nights a week, five months a year, and the rest of the time, he was free. He answered to no one, he needed no one. Yes, life on the boxing circuit suited him just fine.

"Getting a bit cocky, aren't you?"

Dan Sweeney's voice interrupted his thoughts, and Conor turned his head to give his manager a careless shrug. "I can't help it, Danny. Look at the man. I probably won't even have to hit him. I'll just dance around him until he's so dizzy, he just falls down."

Conor's style of boxing was something the two men had often joked about, but this time, Dan didn't laugh. Instead, he glanced around, then leaned closer, resting his forearms on the ropes between them. "Odds are in, boyo."

"And?"

Dan rubbed one hand across his jaw. "No surprise. Elroy's the heavy favorite. But all the bets on him have been small, each no more'n a dollar or two." Dan paused, then added, "On the other hand, a couple rich men are up here from New Orleans. Saw you fight at Shaugnessey's last spring, and they've bet the limit on you. Five hundred each."

"Then they'll be even richer pretty soon."

But Dan shook his head. "No, lad. The bookmaker had a wee talk with me, and he's made it clear he'd rather not pay out that kind of money, if you take my meaning."

Conor did. If Elroy won, the payouts would be many, but paltry, and the bookmaker would make a nice profit on the bets of the two men from New Orleans. If Conor won, only those two men would walk away winners, but the bookmaker would lose a lot of money. He met Dan's eyes and said it aloud. "He wants me to go down."

"Let's just say it'll be healthier for us all if Elroy wins this one."

Conor smiled again, a benign smile. "Over my dead body."

Dan scowled at him. "That could happen," he muttered. "Don't be stupid."

The referee beckoned Conor forward, indicating that the fight was about to begin, and Dan stepped back. Conor straightened away from the rope and moved toward the center of the ring as he unbuttoned his shirt. Dan was right. He'd never been ordered to go down before, but he knew if he defied the bookmaker, he was asking for trouble. He might make it out of the tent, he might even make it out of town, but he wouldn't get much further than that. Better to just let old Elroy sneak in a punch that would send him down to the floor. Easier. Safer.

Conor shrugged out of his shirt and tossed it to land in the corner behind him. Shocked murmurs rippled through the crowd at the scars that scored his chest and back, and Conor responded to the stares and speculative whispers as he always did. He ignored them.

But his outward calm was a deception. There were some who thought those scars were badges of valor and courage, but Conor knew the truth. He felt the old familiar hatred stir deep within him as he remembered the men who had given him the scars. Men who had stripped away everything he was, piece by bloody piece, until he had become what they wanted, until he had become the very thing he hated most. Now, he kept that hate buried deep, hidden by a cocksure smile and an arrogant confidence, but it never left him.

Some things never change, he thought, as he waited for the referee to signal the beginning of the fight. This wasn't Ireland, but there were still men who demanded his subjugation, men who wanted to own him, use him. Rebellion flared, sudden and hot.

The referee drew the line of powdered chalk in the dust. "Toe the line, gentlemen!" he shouted, and jumped out of the way. "No kicking, no gouging, no biting."

The rosary of the prizefighter. A litany Conor heard

twice a week from May to September. *Hail Mary*, he thought, and ducked as Elroy swung at him with a ham-sized fist. *And going down be damned.*

The fist sailed over his head. Conor straightened, then punched hard, left to the ribs, right to the jaw, left to the ribs again, but he jumped back before an answering blow could touch him.

He glanced at Dan, and saw the old man shaking his head. He knew that before the fight was over, Dan would be long gone, and he'd be facing the consequences of his choice alone. *Aye. Some things never change.*

Elroy swung again, but this time Conor wasn't quite quick enough. The fist slammed into his cheek, and he staggered back a step, seeing stars.

Jaysus, Conor, get out of the way. He could hear his brother Michael giving him instructions as if they were boys again, as if this were a field back home in Derry, not a sweat-scented tent in Louisiana, as if Michael were still alive. *Don't just stand there. When he's comin' for you, get out of the way.*

Elroy lunged again, fists flailing, and Conor took his brother's advice. He ducked to the left, hammered three punches in Elroy's gut, and danced out of reach. Then he spun full circle and heard the crack of bone against bone as his fist caught Elroy with an uppercut to the jaw.

Elroy stumbled, recovered his balance, and lifted his fist for an answering punch. But Conor wasn't there.

"What the hell?" Elroy muttered and looked around in confusion.

Conor gave a beckoning whistle, and the other man turned around just in time for the final blow. A groan of dismay went up as Jackson Parish's reigning champion hit the dirt with a resounding thwack. Conor hung back, shifting his weight from one foot to the other, breathing through his teeth, waiting to see if Elroy would rise to continue the fight. The other man tried, but he couldn't even get to his knees.

Conor claimed victory by raising one clenched fist in the air as Elroy was dragged out of the ring. Michael would have been proud.

But he knew his triumph would be short-lived, and the price for it would be dear. He walked to his corner and grabbed a towel. As he wiped the sweat from his face, he watched the losing bettors head for the exit. Only two men stopped by the bookmaker's table to collect their winnings, and Conor knew they were the two rich men from New Orleans.

As he'd suspected, Dan was gone. The promoter handed him the twenty-five dollars in prize money, and he tucked the folded greenbacks into a flap inside his boot, even though he knew the bookmaker's men would take it back, probably just before they beat the hell out of him.

Conor donned his shirt and buttoned it, grimacing at the pain that shot through his hands. He picked up the leather pack that contained everything he owned, slung it over one shoulder, and headed for the exit of the now empty tent.

He didn't make it that far. Three men stepped through the wide doorway, and Conor watched them move to stand side by side, blocking his path. The man in the middle spoke. "There's someone who wants to have a word with you."

"Indeed?" Conor's grip tightened on the strap of his pack, ready to toss it aside if the need arose, but he kept his voice casual. "That's a shame, for I'm just leaving."

"I don't think so." The man in the middle stepped forward, and the other two followed suit, walking toward him.

Conor could've taken any one of them, or even two, but with three against him, he knew he didn't have a prayer. Nonetheless, he couldn't make a run for it, so he dipped one shoulder, and the pack slid off to land in the dirt beside him. He kicked it out of the way, clenched his fists, and took a swing at the closest man, hitting him hard enough to send him sprawling back into the dust. But before he could make any further moves, the other two seized him.

He struggled against their hold, but he couldn't break free. The third man rose and stepped up in front of him. Conor knew what was coming. He lashed out with one foot, landing a kick square in the man's groin, but that brief victory was the last one he got.

The other man straightened, and Conor saw the fist coming toward his face. He tried to duck and failed. Pain exploded in a white-hot flash behind his eye just before the punch to his gut knocked all the wind out of him. The fists pummeled his face and body until he stopped struggling. When the other two men let him go, he sank to his knees. A kick in his kidneys sent him sprawling forward with his face in the dirt. He licked his lips, tasting blood and dust.

The two men who had been holding him moved to stand on either side. They began kicking him back and forth between them like a tin can, and Conor's body jerked in response. It didn't take long before he heard something crack, and he knew the sound was his own ribs breaking. He tried to crawl away, cursing his own stupidity. He should have taken the fall. When was he going to learn not to piss into the wind?

"Enough."

Conor felt himself rolled onto his back. He opened one swollen eye to find a lean, auburn-haired man he hadn't seen before standing over him. The man placed one polished boot on his throat, pressing down with his weight until Conor couldn't breathe.

"Let me introduce myself," the man drawled, speaking around the slender cheroot clamped between his teeth. "I'm Vernon Tyler. Now, you being a stranger and all, that name might not mean much to you. So I'd better explain how things are around here."

Vernon straightened and stepped back. Conor sucked in a great gulp of air that hurt his ribs as the other man took a puff on his cheroot and made a sweeping gesture with one arm. "I own most of this town, and most of the land around it, which I lease to local tenant farmers. I own the mercantile and the sawmill. I own the restaurant, the newspaper, and the hotel. What I don't own, I option. Most everybody around these parts works for me. I'm the boss, I'm the bank, and I'm the law. You understand me, boy?"

Conor managed to nod. He understood very well. The accent might be different, but it wasn't anything he hadn't heard before.

"Good. You cost me a good chunk of money tonight, and I don't take kindly to losing money. You ever cross my path again, boy, I'll snap you into pieces like a dry stick and use you for firewood." Vernon dropped his cheroot to the ground and crushed it into the dirt with one heel, then he reached down and stuck his fingers inside Conor's boot. Pulling out the money, he turned to the men who stood beside him. "Boys, take this sack o' shit and dump it in a field where it belongs."

One man grabbed Conor's ankles, another grabbed his wrists, and he felt his body coming apart like an overcooked chicken as he was dragged out of the tent to a wagon nearby and hefted into the back. He gritted his teeth and endured the pain without a sound. Crying out, showing pain, was the first step toward giving in.

The wagon lurched and started forward, heading out of town, every bump in the road an agonizing reminder of bruised muscles and broken bones. Conor closed his eyes and began to count backward from one thousand, a trick he'd learned a long time ago. Focusing on the inane task sometimes kept the pain at bay. *Nine hundred ninety-nine, nine hundred ninety-eight . . .*

He was in an open wagon in the Louisiana country-side, but in his mind, he was back in the Mountjoy. The summer breeze carried the scent of ripening peaches and blooming jasmine, but the dank, sour smell of prison overpowered their sweetness. *Eight hundred fifty-two, eight hundred fifty-one . . .*

The wagon hit a rut, sending Conor's body a foot into the air. He landed on his shoulder, hard, and it felt as if the prison guards had just snapped his arm out of its socket, then rammed it back into place again. He bit his lip until it bled, but he still made no sound. Four years and thousands of miles away, but this time he wouldn't give the Orange bastards the satisfaction of a scream.

Somewhere in the distance, he heard the rumble of thunder. He felt a drop of warm summer rain on his skin, but then it turned cold . . . the rain again, the damned Irish rain, carried by the winter wind through the one-foot square of window above his head. He pulled against the chains that held him to the wall of his cell, but he couldn't avoid the icicles that hit the back of his neck like tiny needles. *Seven hundred twenty-six . . .*

The wagon slowed. A push of somebody's boot, and he rolled off the back, landing on the dirt road with a thud. A fresh wave of pain shimmered through his body and he cried out, hating his own weakness, just before the blessed darkness overtook him. *Seven hundred twenty-five, seven hun . . .*

When he awoke, he was lying in the middle of a road in the middle of nowhere. He was alone, and it was morning. Closing his eyes, he lapsed back into unconsciousness.

Olivia Maitland needed a man. It wasn't just because she wanted to clear the south pastures and plant cotton next spring. It wasn't just because the fences were falling down and the back porch sagged. It wasn't just because the peaches would be ripe in two months and there was nobody to help her pick them.

No, the fact was, Olivia Maitland needed a man because the roof leaked like a sieve and she was afraid of heights.

She snapped the reins, but Cally was a stubborn old mule who intended to take her to town in his own good time, and he made no attempt to move faster. The slow pace only gave her more time to dwell on her problem. Olivia shifted her weight on the wagon seat and tried not to be impatient.

Maybe when she got to town she'd find that this time somebody had answered the advertisement. She'd used her egg money to put a help-wanted advertisement in the *Jackson Parish Gazette*, and she'd put up notices all over town, but that had been over three months ago, and she hadn't had a single reply. Of course, all she could offer was room and board, and that didn't make for much of an incentive. What few able-bodied men there were around Callersville could work at the sawmill for real wages or tenant farm for themselves.

A drop of rain hit the back of her hand, darkening the worn brown leather of her glove. Another drop fell, then another. Olivia glanced up at the heavy, gunmetal gray clouds overhead, and she wondered if she ought to turn back. It had rained during the night, and the road was already muddy. She might make it to town, but if another storm came down now, Cally would never be able to get her home.

Her trip was probably futile anyway. Stan had told her last time she was in town that she could no longer buy at the store on account, and she doubted asking again would accomplish much.

Olivia caught her lower lip between her teeth and stared at the rutted, curving road ahead. Times had been hard ever since the war, but since Nate's death the previous summer, times had gotten even harder. Nate had been old, cranky, and not always reliable, but he'd been strong for his age, handy with a hammer, and staunchly loyal. He'd also been there to help her bring in the harvest.

She had three girls to raise, hogs and chickens to tend, peaches to harvest come September, and there weren't enough hours in the day to manage everything by herself. Until Nate's death, she hadn't realized how dependent she'd become on the old farmhand or how much she would miss him.

She thought of her girls and wondered how she was going to provide for them if she couldn't get her peach crop to market. Perhaps she should never have taken them in when their parents died in '65. Perhaps they'd have been better off going to the orphanage if she couldn't take care of them properly.

All the burdens suddenly seemed so heavy, and Olivia felt much older than her twenty-nine years. "Lord," she murmured, "I could really use some help down here."

As if in reply, the rain began to pour down, and Olivia sighed. "I guess not."

She hunched forward on the seat and pulled her

broad-brimmed straw hat down lower over her eyes. It wasn't much to ask for, really. Just one man to help, a man who didn't mind hard work and didn't expect to get paid for it.

Olivia pulled on the reins slightly, guiding Cally around the sharp bend in the road. As the wagon rounded the curve, she noticed something lying directly in her path about two dozen feet ahead. She jerked hard on the reins, bringing Cally to a stop, and stared between the mule's ears at the man who lay sprawled in the middle of the road.

She should probably just turn around right here and head home. There were always nasty characters wandering the roads these days—had been ever since the war. Olivia toyed with the reins in her fingers, uncertain what to do. She was alone, and the man was a stranger.

Still, he didn't look like much of a threat just lying there like that. Keeping her gaze fixed on him, Olivia climbed down from the wagon. She hitched her faded brown skirt up enough to keep the hem out of the mud as she moved closer.

It was kind of hard to tell what he looked like, but Olivia knew he wasn't from around Callersville. His short hair was black, but caked with mud. His face was lean and clean-shaven, but swollen and darkened by purple bruises. There was a deep gash above his eye, and another on his chin. His clothes were torn and muddy. He didn't move as she came cautiously closer, and she wondered if he was dead.

But as she hunkered down beside him, she saw the rise and fall of his chest. No, he wasn't dead. At least, not yet.

She stood up and glanced around, but she saw nothing that might explain what this man was doing out here in this sorry condition. He was alone and didn't appear to have any belongings with him.

Suddenly he groaned, and she realized he must be in a great deal of pain. She couldn't just leave him here. If she could get him into the wagon somehow, she could take him back to the house.

Olivia stared down at the unconscious stranger, and she wondered if he knew how to patch a roof and pick peaches. Right now, he didn't look capable of much at all. She sighed and pushed back her hat, glancing at the dark skies above, blinking at the rain that hit her face. "Lord," she said heavily, "this isn't exactly what I had in mind."

2

Conor came awake reluctantly. He knew he was still lying in the road, and it was raining again. He also knew that everything hurt. Every part of his body ached, making him acutely aware that he was awake. He kept his eyes shut, willing himself back into unconsciousness, but it didn't work.

He heard a voice above him, a woman's voice. Turning his head sideways, he opened his eyes and found himself staring at the sodden hem of a dull brown skirt. The image blurred, and he blinked, trying to focus. After a moment, the image of the woman standing beside him became clear.

His gaze traveled upward, past the shabby dress and faded duster that disguised any feminine shape she might have had, to her face. But she wasn't looking at him. Her face was tilted skyward, and he heard her breathe a heavy sigh before she looked down and saw him awake and staring at her.

She didn't smile. She placed her hands on her hips,

small hands in a man's gloves. She pursed her lips and studied him from beneath the brim of a battered straw hat. "Well, now," she said in the slow, drawling voice of a Louisiana native, "you're in pretty sorry shape, mister."

Conor was in complete agreement with that assessment of his situation.

She met his eyes. "You out here 'cause you tried to rob somebody?"

He tried to shake his head and winced at the pain that small movement caused. He swallowed hard. "No."

"Somebody rob you?"

"You might say that."

"Mmm." She turned away, and he thought she was going to leave him there. He was certain of it when he watched a wagon pulled by a sorry-looking mule roll past him. But she brought the wagon to a halt and jumped down again, her boots making a splash as she landed in a puddle.

She walked back over to him. "Think you can make it into the wagon?"

Conor nodded and started to sit up, but intense pain sliced through his midsection. He groaned and fell back into the mud. The woman moved to help him, but he told himself he didn't need her help. He drew a deep breath, set his jaw, and rose to his feet without assistance.

But before he could take a step toward the wagon, everything around him started spinning, and his knees buckled. She was at his side in an instant, wrapping an arm around his hips and bracing her shoulder under his to prevent him from falling. She staggered a little beneath his weight, but she kept him on his feet. "Proud, aren't you?" she commented, and Conor had no idea if it was a compliment or a criticism.

He leaned on her heavily as she helped him to the wagon. It was only a few feet, but it seemed like miles to Conor. When they reached the back, he waited a moment to catch his breath, then lifted himself into the wagon, falling back to hit the floorboards with a thud, his legs still dangling over the edge. He closed his eyes and fell back into unconsciousness.

Olivia walked to the front of the wagon, climbed in, and snapped the reins. Poor Cally floundered in the mud for a second, but he soon found his feet, and she turned the wagon around, heading for home.

As abruptly as it had begun, the rain stopped, and she was grateful. Cally would be able to get them to the house without too much trouble.

She thought of the battered man in the back of her wagon. What was she going to do with him? Olivia had tended enough wounds during the war to know he had several cracked ribs and was probably bleeding inside. It would be weeks before he was on his feet, and when he was, he'd walk on down the road.

Olivia turned her head and looked at him. He was unconscious again. She cast a rebellious glance in heaven's direction. Next time she asked God for a man, she'd be a lot more specific about what she wanted.

"Is he dead?" Carrie's hushed voice piped up in the silence and was immediately followed by a disgusted sound from her older sister.

"Of course not," Becky said, with all the superiority that came from being fourteen and the oldest. "We wouldn't be tendin' him if he was dead, would we?"

"I guess not." Carrie watched from the doorway as Becky and Olivia bent over the stranger on the bed. Her younger sister, Miranda, stood beside her, wide-eyed and silent. Chester, the family's sheepdog, had given the man a suspicious sniff, then positioned himself between the bed and the two girls in the doorway, knowing strangers were not to be trusted.

Olivia pulled off her hat and tossed it onto the chair that stood in one corner of the room, then peeled off her sodden duster. It landed atop the hat. Rolling up her sleeves, Olivia cast a glance at the young girl opposite.

"How is he, Mama?" Becky asked.

"I'm afraid it's pretty bad, honey. He may be bleeding inside."

"Should we roll him off the board?"

They had found a long wooden plank in the barn to use as a makeshift stretcher, enabling them to get him out of the wagon and into a bedroom on the first floor of the house. They had laid him on the bed, board and all. He had let out a groan or two, but he had not awakened.

Olivia stared down at him and frowned thoughtfully, considering Becky's question. "I don't think so," she answered. "Some of his ribs are cracked, and it'll be easier for me to bind them if we leave him as he is for now."

To bind his ribs, she had to get his shirt off. The shirt was spattered with blood and torn in so many places, it wasn't worth mending. She grabbed the edges of his collar and gave the white linen a hard yank. Buttons went flying and the shirt came apart in her hands. "Dear God."

"What is it, Mama?" Carrie spoke again, stepping through the doorway as if to have a look.

Olivia held up one hand to stop the child, and Carrie came to a halt just inside the door. She then glanced at Becky, who was staring in astonishment at the vivid scars across the man's chest.

"Becky, go to the kitchen, and take the girls with you," she ordered, wanting them out of the room. "Take Chester, too. Put the kettle on to boil. Unhitch

Cally and put him in the barn. Bring the water to me when it's boiling, and a pail of cold water from the pump. Can you do all that?"

"Yes, ma'am." Taking her sisters by the hand, Becky ushered them out of the room. Never far behind the girls, Chester followed.

Olivia stared down at the man. Despite his present condition, he was strong and well muscled, as if used to hard work. Once his injuries had healed, maybe he'd be willing to stay for a while. Maybe he'd be able to help her with the farm. Maybe God had answered her prayer after all.

She leaned closer and studied his scars, which were visible despite the black hair that covered his chest. She recognized the marks of burns, whip lashes, and bullet wounds. But still others were jagged, as if his skin had been ripped open. She had occasionally seen the scars of cruelty on black slaves, she'd seen the scars of battle on Confederate soldiers, but she had never seen anything like this.

She traced one white line from his collarbone to his shoulder with the tip of her finger, wondering what had been done to him. Terrible things, she knew, and a wave of compassion ran through her.

When she pressed a hand to his forehead, she felt the heat of a slight fever. By nightfall, it would be worse. He stirred in sleep and shook his head restlessly, then muttered a string of curses. Olivia snatched her hand back, appalled, knowing he must be a very bad sort of man to utter such words, even in sleep, and she knew she'd been mistaken. God would never send her such a man to help her. The other way around was probably closer to the truth.

She left the room to gather the items she needed. First, she picked comfrey leaves in the garden, trying to remember everything Old Sally had told her about medicinal herbs. She wished the other woman were here now, but like Nate, like her family, Old Sally was gone.

She had Becky steep the comfrey in boiling water, instructing her to place jars of the liquid in the well to cool. Then she collected scissors, iodine, bandages, and rags. By the time she returned to his room, the man was tossing in the bed, as if tormented by some violent nightmare.

Olivia walked to his side and set her supplies on a nearby chair. When she felt his forehead again, she was alarmed by the heat. She hadn't been gone long, but his fever had gotten much worse. No wonder he was delirious. His ribs could wait. The first thing she had to do was get him out of his wet clothes.

Becky entered with a bucket of cold water and brought it to Olivia, then left the room again. She returned moments later with the kettle of steaming water. Olivia pointed to the thick rug at the foot of the bed. "Put it there," she instructed. "I'll—"

"Bastards!" the man shouted, his fist slamming the harmless pillow beside him. "Bloody fucking bastards!"

She glanced at the fourteen-year-old girl who stood by the foot of the bed. Becky's gaze was fixed on the man, her mouth open in horrified awe.

"Becky," she said sharply, and the girl looked up. "Go on out and get the girls some dinner," she added in a softer tone. "I'll stay here."

"Won't you need my help?"

She gave Becky a reassuring smile. "I'll do fine. It's almost noon, and I need you to feed the girls some of that stew I started this morning."

Becky gave the man in the bed one last curious glance, then departed, leaving Olivia alone with her tormented patient.

Moving to the foot of the bed, Olivia pulled off his boots and immediately encountered a problem she hadn't thought of before. There was no way to get his trousers off. They were still wet and he was a big man, too heavy to lift or move by herself.

She finally had to use her scissors to cut the trousers off at the sides, a painstaking and difficult task, since he wouldn't lie still. One brief glance at his nakedness and she hastily looked away, covering the lower half of his body with a sheet. Life had changed a great deal since the war, but there were some proprieties that were always observed. Even after her father's accident, when she'd done practically everything but eat his food for him, bathing him was something she had not done. Nate had taken over that particular task. Even during the war, when she'd tended wounded soldiers at the makeshift hospital in Vienna, she'd never caught so much as a glimpse of an unclothed man. The matrons had not allowed it. She was an unmarried woman, after all.

No one would know.

Her one quick peek at him had told her nothing at all. One wouldn't mind seeing with one's own eyes what was always so carefully hidden.

No one would know.

Olivia bit her lip. She glanced at the open doorway, then she lifted the sheet and took a much longer look, astonished by what she saw. But when she heard her mother's horrified voice censure her all the way from heaven, she quickly lowered the sheet, blushing hotly. Curiosity was indeed a wicked, sinful thing.

In one of the pockets of his trousers, she found ten greenbacks, but nothing else. She set the money on the washstand and consigned the pieces of his trousers to the rag bag, along with the tattered remnants of his shirt. She wrapped his broken ribs with stout linen, cleaned his cuts with iodine, and applied compresses soaked in the cold comfrey tea to his bumps and bruises. By sunset, she was exhausted, but she knew her work was far from over. His fever was still alarmingly high, and she had to bring it down.

Throughout that night and the two nights that followed, she tended him. She sponged his face and chest with cool water. She forced water and willowbark tea into him one spoonful at a time. She tried to soothe him, but her soft voice close to his ear only seemed to make him worse, and she kept out of his way when he raged. She tried to catch a moment or two of rest during the infrequent times when he seemed to be at peace.

He spoke, sometimes in a whisper, sometimes a shout, but always incoherently and seldom with tenderness. Most of what he said was unintelligible to her, since he spoke in an odd foreign tongue she did not recognize. But sometimes his words were in English, and she caught wild mutterings about guns and amnesty, a place called Mountjoy, and a man named Sean Gallagher.

By the dawn of the fourth day, his fever had still not broken. Olivia dipped her rag in the bucket of cold water beside her chair, for perhaps the hundredth time, and wrung it out, watching him and wondering again what horrors he dreamed about. Suddenly, he lashed out with one arm, and Olivia jumped out of the way, watching as he knocked over the china figurine on the bedside table. It teetered, then fell. Olivia made a grab for it, but the china statue fell off the table and hit the floor, smashing into pieces.

Olivia stared down at the fragments of what had been a shepherdess. It was one of a pair that had belonged to her great-grandmother, brought from the woman's native Scotland and passed down for three generations. Since the war, Olivia had been forced to sell nearly everything of value to make ends meet, but she had not been able to part with the pair of figurines. The delicate shepherdess had survived travel, time, war, and poverty, only to be destroyed by a violent man's dreams.

Olivia felt for the chair behind her and sank into it wearily. She stared at the broken pieces around her feet, too tired even to sweep them up, and she fought back the sudden urge to weep.

Conor didn't need to open his eyes to know that he was no longer lying in the road. He caught a luscious scent, an enticing mixture of freshly baked bread, hot coffee, and clean sheets that told him he was in either heaven or somebody's house, and heaven wasn't likely. The thought of fresh bread made him realize how hungry he was. He inhaled deeply, an action that sent a wave of pain through his midsection and made him feel as if iron bands were wrapped around his torso. His hunger vanished.

He opened his eyes, blinking against the bright sunlight that filled the room. Pulling back the sheet, he saw that someone had removed his clothes and bound his ribs. He frowned, unable to remember anyone doing such a thing. He remembered the fight and the men who'd beaten him, but everything after that was a blur of distorted yet familiar images—people dying, Sean's murder, blood and guns and prison guards, Delemere's voice in his ear, and a strange woman bending over him. Oh, Christ. He'd been having the dreams again.

He remembered the woman. She had found him in the road, and he'd gotten into her wagon. He must be in her house. He lifted his head and caught a glimpse of a plain and colorless room, but then everything began to spin. His head fell back against the pillows.

"Mornin'."

He turned his head at the sound. Seated in the chair near his bed was a little girl of about nine, her short legs dangling over the edge of the seat. She kicked them idly back and forth as her blue eyes watched him.

Conor licked his dry lips, a movement that made his jaw throb. "Hullo," he answered, his voice cracking on the word. God, he was thirsty.

The girl continued to study him as if he were some strange and curious insect. "Why do you shout so much?"

"Shout?" Dazed and groggy, he tried to understand what she was talking about.

"All the time. We can hear you through the windows." She frowned accusingly. "You keep us awake at night."

Conor suddenly realized what she meant. He was dismayed that this little girl had overheard him in the throes of his nightmares. God only knew what he'd been saying. "I must have been dreaming."

Her frown disappeared, and she nodded with understanding. "Nightmares. I have those, too. Don't worry. Mama says you don't have to be scared of nightmares 'cause they aren't real."

The girl's mama didn't know what she was talking about. His nightmares were very real indeed. "How long have I been here?" he asked.

"About three days, I reckon."

"Three days?" He stared at her in astonishment, unable to remember anything about the past three days.

The girl tilted her head thoughtfully. "What's 'wanker' mean?"

"What?" Startled by the question, he wondered what other choice epithets he'd blistered this wee one's ears with. "A lass your age shouldn't know such words as that, I'm thinking."

"It's a bad word, isn't it?" She was obviously delighted. "I've never heard that one before."

The comment was so outrageous, he couldn't help grinning, but acute pain shot along his jaw, and his grin disappeared as quickly as it had come.

"I'm Carrie," she went on. "Who are you?"

"Conor."

"Who were you shouting at in your dreams?" she asked.

He turned his head and stared at the ceiling. He closed his eyes and thought briefly of prison guards and British landlords. "No one important."

"You called them all sorts of names."

He tried to deny it. "I never did."

"Yessir. You said they were bloody bas—"

"Carrie!" A female voice caused Conor to lift his head, more slowly this time, and he recognized the woman with the wagon. "That will be quite enough," she told the child. "You know I told you not to come in here."

"But I wanted to see him, Mama."

"Breakfast is ready. Go on out to the kitchen."

"But—"

"Out," the woman ordered, pointing to the open doorway behind her.

Carrie gave an aggrieved sigh. "Yes, ma'am." She slid off the chair. "Good-bye, Mr. Conor."

Giving him a wave of farewell, she walked to the door. "I just wanted to have a look," she added in an injured tone, and left the room.

The woman began walking toward him, and Conor studied her as she approached. The first thing that struck him was her drabness. Her dress was brown, the color of muddy water, and buttoned up to her chin. Her hair was brown and curled in a simple bun at the base of her neck. She reminded him of a plain brown moth.

But when she halted beside the bed and he got a good look at her face, he found himself revising his opinion. Her eyes were brown, too, so dark and soft, they reminded him of chocolate, and were surrounded by thick, absurdly long lashes. She had fine-textured skin the color of fresh cream. And there were tiny lines at the corners of her eyes that told him she was a woman who smiled often. But she did not smile at him.

"I'm Olivia Maitland," she said.

"Conor Branigan," he returned, wishing she'd give him something to drink. He was so thirsty.

"Well, Mr. Branigan, you've caused quite a stir round here." A slight frown marred her forehead. "I hope your vocabulary isn't quite so colorful when you're awake."

The prim disapproval in her voice was tempered by her soft, drawling accent. Nonetheless, it grated on him, making him feel defensive. He put on his mask and smiled at her, even though that smile made his jaw hurt like hell. "'Tis indeed," he said with practiced carelessness. "I curse and shout all the time, don't you know."

She looked as if she believed him. "I won't have such language in front of my girls," she said, leaning closer to press a hand to his forehead.

Her skin felt deliciously cool against his. He caught the scent of vanilla and cloves on her hand, and he felt the sharp pang of hunger again. "Remind me of that next time I'm asleep, and I'll try to restrain myself."

She had the grace to blush, an action which softened the sternness of her frown and quite spoiled the effect. "You still have a fever," she said and drew her hand away. "You also have several cracked ribs and some severe bruises. Whoever beat you up did a mighty fine job of it." She gazed at him steadily, as if expecting an explanation.

He had no intention of giving her one. "Where are my clothes?"

"In my rag bag. What's left of them, anyway."

She saw his puzzled frown, and her blush deepened. "I had to cut them off of you," she said and turned to the table beside his bed. "I couldn't get them off any other way."

This woman had undressed him. An interesting notion, he thought, his gaze skimming the profile of her body, pausing for a thorough study of each feminine curve along the way. Not that there was much to see. The high collar and long sleeves of her dress revealed little, but he noticed a small waist and generous hips, and he felt a pang of regret. Too bad he'd been unconscious at the time.

She lifted a rag out of the bucket of water on the table and wrung it out, then turned back around and dabbed his cheeks with it. He licked his dry lips, savoring the feel of the cool water on his face. "What about my pack?"

She paused. "I didn't find anything with you. Except some money." She waved the rag toward the washstand across the room. "I put it over there."

He'd left his pack in the tent, he remembered. Damn. There was a bottle of good Irish whiskey in there, and he could have used it now. He glanced up at the woman and wondered if she might have a wee drop in the house, but he instantly rejected that idea. Women like her didn't drink, or if they did, they didn't admit it.

The woman leaned over the bed again and pressed the wet rag to his forehead. "I've wrapped your ribs," she said. "But it will take about six weeks for them to heal. I think you might also have some internal bleeding. Do you have any family I should notify about your injuries?"

He closed his eyes. "No," he said flatly. "No family at all."

She straightened and dropped the rag back in the bucket. "I'll bring you some tea for the fever."

Tea sounded . . . acceptable. He watched her remove the bucket from the table and set it on the floor. Then she left the room, returning several moments later carrying a tray. On the tray were a chipped china teapot that had obviously seen better days, a matching cup, and a flat tin pan. She set the tray on the table, then picked up the pan and set it on the floor beside his bed. "If you need to relieve yourself," she explained.

She picked up the cup and stepped closer to the bed. Blowing into the cup to cool the tea, she stared down at him over the rim, her eyes studying him without revealing her conclusions.

After a moment, she tested the temperature with the tip of her finger, nodded as if satisfied, and bent over him. "Drink as much as you can."

He lifted his head slowly, gritting his teeth against the pain, and her free hand curved behind his neck to provide additional support as she pressed the cup to his lips. He inhaled and felt his insides twist at the noxious smell. He pulled back slightly. "Jaysus, what sort o'tay is this?"

"Please, don't swear, Mr. Branigan. It's willowbark tea, and you've had plenty of it over the last few days. It's for the fever."

"Hell with the fever," he muttered, staring with distaste at the cup beneath his nose and the pale green liquid within. "This stuff will kill me."

"I know it smells bad. It tastes worse. But it helps with the pain and keeps your fever down."

He shot her a doubtful glance, but he allowed her to tip some of the tea into his mouth. He swallowed until nearly half the foul stuff was gone. She was right, it tasted even worse than it smelled. But the simple act of swallowing also hurt his ribs, and keeping his head up made him dizzy. His head began to throb and his stomach clenched. He was going to throw up. *Jesus, Mary, and Joseph.*

He gagged, and the tea came right back up, all over her hand, the cup, and himself. Almost violently, he pushed her hand away, then sank back into the pillows and wiped one hand across his mouth. He squeezed his eyes shut and willed his stomach to stop retching. God, he hated this—the weakness, the humiliation, the utter helplessness of it. "Told you so," he croaked.

He felt the woman slide her other hand from behind his head to smooth back the hair from his forehead. "You're not going to die, Mr. Branigan," she said in the gentlest tone he'd heard her use. "You're too ornery for that."

3

Conor Branigan's fever broke late that night, a fact for which Olivia said a grateful prayer. He fell into a dreamless slumber, and she was able to catch a few hours of uninterrupted sleep herself before dawn.

She rose at sunrise, washed and dressed, then started breakfast. When she looked in on him again, he was still sleeping peacefully. After waking the girls, she left Becky in charge of getting the younger ones up, then went out to do the morning chores.

When Olivia returned to the kitchen, the girls were already there. Becky had finished making breakfast for her, and all three girls were seated at the table. Chester lay on the floor, waiting for any stray scraps one of them might sneak to him under the table. Olivia set the pail of eggs she'd gathered from the henhouse on the wooden counter and washed her hands, then ladled a bowl of cornmeal mush from the pot on the stove.

"How is Mr. Branigan, Mama?" Becky asked.

"He's much better," she answered and sat down at the table. "His fever's broken."

"Is he the one who's goin' to stay and help us like Nate used to?" Miranda asked.

"No." Olivia was dismayed by the very thought. "He certainly is not."

"Where do you suppose he got all those scars?" Becky asked.

"I don't know," Olivia answered, and wasn't sure she wanted to find out.

"Well, I like him," Carrie said. "It's fun to watch him while he's asleep. Can I go see him after breakfast, Mama?"

"No," she answered sharply. "I've told you not to go into his room."

"Why not?"

"Because he has a filthy tongue and a vile temperament. I want you to stay away from him." She glanced at Miranda. "You, too. Is that clear?"

They nodded and fell silent. Olivia returned her attention to her breakfast, relieved to let the subject of Conor Branigan drop. She stared down at her bowl, thinking about the day ahead. Now that the man was doing better, Olivia knew she had to make another trip into town.

She had chickens and hogs, so she never lacked for meat, and her own garden provided more than enough vegetables; but there were many necessities she just couldn't get anywhere but the mercantile. She was nearly out of flour and cornmeal, and molasses was running low.

This time, she would take with her all the fresh eggs and three dozen jars of the spiced peaches she'd put up last fall. If Stan Miller would no longer let her buy on credit, she might be able to barter for what she needed to see them through until harvest.

Olivia felt a sudden burst of anger. Vernon owned the store, and she knew Stan was following his orders. It was standard practice to give credit until the harvest, and she knew what Vernon was doing. Just one more way to make things harder, one more way to break her down and persuade her to sell her land. Olivia set her jaw stubbornly. It wasn't going to work.

"Can I go out and play, Mama?"

Miranda's voice broke into her thoughts, and Olivia looked up. She glanced at the child's bowl. "You haven't finished your mush."

The girl made a face that clearly said why. Olivia couldn't help smiling at the sight of Miranda's round face scrunched into a ridiculous expression of distaste.

Olivia glanced at Becky and Carrie and noticed their bowls were also half full. Her smile faded. She wanted to give her girls so much more than mush for breakfast and made-over dresses and hard work. She thought of her own childhood, of all the things taken for granted, of the security that came with money. It was a life her girls had never known, and probably never would. But love counted for a lot, and no one could love these girls more than she did.

Olivia rose to her feet, pushing back her chair. "Tell you what. If I'm not mistaken, there's a tin of maple syrup in the pantry. How about I pour some of that on your mush along with some butter?"

Her suggestion was rewarded with shouts of enthusiasm. Olivia went to the pantry and brought out the can she'd been saving. Maple syrup was one of their favorite things, and she'd intended to keep it for a special occasion, but she supposed that special things didn't always have to be saved for special occasions.

She added a spoonful of syrup and a dollop of butter to each bowl, and the girls finished their mush without further complaint. As Olivia watched them, she wished she could solve all their problems so easily.

An hour later, Olivia hitched Cally to the wagon for another journey into town. She climbed into the wagon, giving Becky instructions. "Be sure to look in on Mr. Branigan every half hour or so. He'll be asleep most of the time, but if he wakes up, try to get some more of that willowbark tea into him, or if he won't drink it, at least plenty of water. And some of that broth I've got simmerin' on the stove would be good, too."

Becky nodded, and her pretty face took on a serious expression at the responsibility of being in charge. "All right, Mama."

"I'll be back before noon." Olivia snapped the reins and Cally moved out of the yard. "And keep the girls out of his room," she shouted over her shoulder before the wagon rounded the side of the house and started down the oak-lined lane that led to the main road.

Callersville was a small slip of a town on the road from Monroe to Shreveport, a place where people sometimes passed through but seldom stayed, where porches sagged and dogs slept in the shade, where old men whittled and young widows quilted and honeysuckle bloomed. Olivia had been to New Orleans and Baton Rouge a few times. One summer, her father had taken the whole family to Mobile to visit her aunt Ella and uncle Jarrod. But most of her life had been spent right here in Callersville. Olivia gazed at the yellow jasmine and blue lupines that grew wild along the road, and knew she wouldn't have it any other way.

She passed Tyler's Sawmill and Lumberyard, turned at the Baptist church, and pulled into the center of town. She came to a halt in front of Tyler's Mercantile, which was situated between Tyler's Restaurant and Tyler's Barber Shop. The man just had to have his name on everything, Olivia thought, jumping down from the wagon. As if everybody round here didn't already know he owned just about every building in town.

She picked up her basket of eggs from the wagon seat and mounted the steps to the mercantile. She nodded to Jimmy Johnson and Bobby McCann, who sat on the bench by the open door pulling a hefty chunk of saltwater taffy between them, and she was surprised to note that for once they didn't seem to be up to any mischief. Maybe it was just the heat.

She entered the store, relieved to discover that it was Lila Miller who stood behind the counter today. "Mornin', Lila," she greeted, setting the basket on the wooden counter and pushing back her hat.

The woman gave her a smile. "Olivia! Missed you in church Sunday."

"I had some things come up at home and couldn't get into town," she answered. "How are you?"

"I'd be fine, if it weren't for this heat." Lila tucked a loose strand of dark hair behind one ear, propped her elbows on the counter, and fanned herself with a copy of *Godey's Lady's Book*.

Olivia glanced around, but Lila's husband was nowhere in sight. The only other person in the store was their fifteen-year-old son, Jeremiah, who was stocking shelves with cans of Borden's Condensed Milk.

The boy nodded to her. "Mornin', Miss Olivia. How's Becky?"

She smiled back at him. Jeremiah and Becky were friends, and she knew there would come a day when they would probably be more than that. Becky was too young yet for courting, but when the time came, Jeremiah would make a fine husband. "She's fine, Jeremiah. I'll tell her you asked about her."

The boy grinned with obvious pleasure, and Olivia turned back to Lila. "Stan gone this mornin'?"

Lila nodded. "Went to Monroe. Did you need to see him?"

"Not really," Olivia answered and gestured to the basket of eggs. "I need supplies, and I was hoping I could barter for what I need. I've got some of my spiced peaches out in the wagon, too."

The eyes of the two women met across the counter, and Olivia knew that Lila was thinking about the day the lists came in from Gettysburg and how they'd cried together, Olivia for her two brothers and Lila for her eldest son. Things like that counted for more than Vernon would ever understand.

Lila straightened and set aside her magazine. "Now, I was here when Vernon went over the books with Stan, and I heard him say no more credit for you. But," she added, her blue eyes innocently wide, "I don't recall him sayin' a word about not taking goods in trade."

Olivia returned the conspiratorial smile Lila gave her. "Thank you. I've got three dozen jars of peaches and two dozen eggs."

Lila made a sound of appreciation. "Heavenly, your peaches. We'll have no problem selling them."

"I need flour, rice, cornmeal, and molasses. Is this enough to trade?"

The two women negotiated the barter, quickly agreeing on how much Olivia could get for her eggs and her peaches.

"Wagon's out front," Olivia said.

"Jeremiah," Lila called to her son, "fill the sacks and load them onto Miss Olivia's wagon. Get her a barrel of molasses, too. And bring in that crate of her peaches."

Jeremiah went to do as his mother asked, and Lila

turned to Olivia. "Got some new dress patterns in. Care to have a look?"

Olivia hesitated, tempted, but before she could reply, two men entered the store.

"Mornin', ladies," Grady McCann and Oren Johnson said in unison, doffing their hats as they approached the counter.

Olivia nodded to them. "Saw your boys out front. Looked like they were enjoyin' that saltwater taffy. Hope I don't find a piece of it stuck to my wagon seat when I go back out there."

"Now, Olivia," Grady said, in a placating voice, "you know they was only havin' a bit of fun."

"Hmm." Olivia picked up the *Godey's Lady's Book* and began flipping through it. "I'm not sure God takes kindly to taffy in the church pews, Grady, particularly when a mess of it ends up on the backside of Mrs. Tucker's dress." She shot him a wry glance, remembering how poor Lisbeth Tucker had tried in vain to stand up for the hymn two Sundays before. She added good-naturedly, "'Course, it did make the service more excitin'."

The two men laughed. Everybody around Callersville knew that Reverend Allen wasn't the sort of preacher to put the fear of God in a body. He just put everybody to sleep.

Olivia looked over at Oren. "How's Kate doing?"

The man beamed at the mention of his wife's name. "She's fine. A bit hard for her with all this heat, but she's holding up all right."

"Think this one's going to be a boy or a girl?"

"Well, I'm kinda hoping for another son, Liv. I love my daughters, but I think sometimes Jimmy feels outnumbered."

"What can I do for you boys?" Lila asked, diverting the men's attention.

"Need a new pair of boots," Oren said.

"Pound of eightpenny nails for me," Grady added.

As Lila showed Oren the boots and measured out nails for Grady, Olivia studied the fall fashions in *Godey's*. The harvest dance would be coming up in September, and she wanted so badly to make Becky a pretty dress to wear. Things like that were important to a young girl.

"That was some fight the other night, wasn't it, Oren?" Grady's voice intruded on her thoughts, and Olivia glanced up, curious.

"I've never seen anything like it," Oren replied. "Couldn't believe the way that Irish feller did it." He swung a fist in the air enthusiastically. "All that dancin' around and then, slam! Knocked Elroy clean off his feet."

Olivia froze at Oren's words, hugging the magazine to her chest, as the two men began to discuss the incident. "What fight?" she asked.

The two men stopped talking, glanced from her to each other, then down at the floor, looking suddenly uncomfortable.

"It was a prizefight," Grady explained reluctantly, pointing to an announcement still tacked to the wall. "Circuit boxers. They travel from town to town, fighting the local champion, or challenging all comers. It depends." He saw her frown and toss down the magazine. "Now, it's nothin' to get riled about, Liv. It's just a bit of fun."

"It's gambling, Grady, no getting around it." She looked at the notice from a few days before, at the names printed there plain as day, and felt a sudden unreasoning anger. She'd had almost no sleep the past four nights for tending that man, a man who'd cursed a blue streak in front of her girls, broken her great-grandmother's china shepherdess, forced her to miss Sunday services, and thrown up on her; a man who hadn't given her so much as a thank-you. All that because he was a traveling prizefighter who made his sinful living off gambling and violence?

Olivia turned on her heel and strode toward the door.

Jeremiah came in carrying her crate of peaches. He took one look at her face, and hastily stepped out of her way.

"Wagon's loaded, Miss Olivia."

"Thank you, Jeremiah," she replied, through clenched teeth, as she marched past him and out of the store, contemplating a little violence of her own.

Conor was so battered and weary that he longed for sleep, but the wee girl's words about his dreams made him tense and edgy. Three years of trying to forget, but he could not forget. Three years of running, but he couldn't run away from himself. Every time he thought he had, the dreams came back. He closed his eyes and concentrated on the present—the tantalizing smell of freshly baked bread that drifted through the open door and the feel of the soft mattress beneath him. He drifted back into a light sleep.

A soft sound woke him instantly. He opened his eyes, and for the second time in as many days, he found himself the subject of a little girl's scrutiny. Not the impudent lass who liked to hear him curse. No, this one was even younger, with a round face, brown hair, and big blue eyes. She was looking at him over the top of the footboard like a solemn baby owl peering over the edge of the nest.

Beside her, also staring at him over the footboard, was an enormous sheepdog, the biggest he'd ever seen.

The dog looked him over, then uttered a low, unfriendly growl, his opinion of Conor obvious. Well, it was an English sheepdog, after all. Conor wondered what the animal would do if he growled back. Probably jump over the footboard and take a piece out of him. Deciding he'd been injured enough, Conor turned his attention back to the child.

"Well, now," he murmured, his voice soft, as if he might startle her away. "Who might you be?"

Her eyes got even wider, but she didn't answer.

"Miranda, where are you?"

The voice caused the child to glance over her shoulder, and Conor heard footsteps approaching. He followed the child's gaze to the door as yet another girl appeared, this one a blonde of about fourteen.

How many daughters did Olivia Maitland have? he wondered, as he watched the older girl enter the room. He was starting to lose count.

She stopped just inside the doorway and glanced at him, meeting his eyes for only a moment before she looked away and noticed the wee girl at the foot of the bed. "Miranda, you know you're not supposed to come in here," she chided in a whisper. "Mama said so."

The little girl hung her head, caught in the act. "Sorry, Becky," she whispered back. "He was asleep."

The older girl crossed the room and took Miranda by the hand. "I'm sorry, Mr. Branigan," she murmured. "She didn't mean to wake you."

"It's all right," he answered, unable to remember the last time anybody had cared about disturbing his sleep. The girl started to turn away, but his voice stopped her. "Becky, is it?" When she nodded, he went on, "I don't suppose you might have any tay about? Real tay, I'm meanin', not that foul green stuff your mother's been tryin' to give me."

A tentative smile lifted the corners of her mouth. "We get it whenever we're sick, too. Awful, isn't it?"

"Terrible. Would you be able to make me a cup of real tay? I've a powerful thirst."

"I'd be happy to." She paused then added shyly, "Are you hungry? I'll bring you some soup."

"An angel of mercy, you are indeed," he said, smiling at her. "Thank you, love."

She blushed at that. "I'll b . . . bring it quick as I can," she stammered, and hastily retreated, pulling little Miranda with her. "C'mon, Chester."

The dog hesitated, looking from him to the girl and back again. He uttered another growl as if telling Conor he'd better behave himself, then he followed the girls out of the room. That dog definitely did not like him. But then, he'd always heard dogs were excellent judges of character. Perhaps there was a lesson in that.

The two girls and the beast had scarcely departed before he heard a door slam in the distance and more footsteps coming down the hall toward his room. He watched as Olivia Maitland stepped through the doorway. She marched to the bed, placed hands on hips, and frowned down at him, her brown eyes no longer soft. "You're a prizefighter," she said, with such loathing she might as well have accused him of being the devil himself.

"I am indeed." She looked so appalled, so full of self-righteous indignation, he couldn't help tweaking her tail a wee bit. "Damn good at it, I am. You should come and watch me sometime."

"I suppose men place bets on you, gambling away their hard-earned money, don't they?"

"Of course they do, God bless 'em."

Her full lips pressed into a disapproving line, and she turned away. "Did the Lord give men no sense at all?" she muttered under her breath, and began to pace. "Up four nights running, tending a man who makes his living with his fists. A man who curses in front of my girls. Sinful."

He didn't think now was the time to point out he hadn't exactly cursed *in front of* her daughters, and he certainly hadn't done it on purpose.

She glanced up at the ceiling. "I won't have him here. I won't."

He watched her resume her pacing back and forth across the rug, muttering to herself, and he wondered if perhaps she were touched in the head.

"Prizefighting," she repeated, still pacing. "And gambling."

He could have added several other sins to the list, but he didn't want her to have apoplexy. Instead, he remained silent.

She stopped wearing out the rug and turned to glare at him. "Is that how you got all those scars?"

His eyes narrowed. "Of course. I always get scars like this when I'm punched in the gut."

The sarcasm wasn't lost on her. "How then?"

Damn her questions and her curiosity. He lifted his head and glared right back at her, all the defiance of a lifetime in that look. "Prison."

Stunned, she stared at him, horror dawning in her eyes. "Prison?" she whispered. "I don't understand. What did you do?"

"Does it matter?" He flung back the sheet, uncovering his chest. "I got exactly what I deserved."

Her face went white. She swallowed hard and lowered her head, murmuring something softly under her breath. It sounded like a prayer.

"Don't pray for me, Mrs. Maitland," he said harshly. "There's no one listening."

4

FUATHAÍM
County Derry, Ireland, 1846

Men with crowbars were in the yard. Conor was eleven years old, old enough to know what that meant. The housewreckers had come. He stopped at the edge of the clearing, the two precious trout he'd poached out of the landlord's stream that morning clutched in his hands. He watched, sick with fear.

His mother stood before the hated man on horseback, and Conor could hear her anguished pleas. But the landlord's agent looked down at her with an impassive face and did not seem to hear. He signaled to the men behind him, who started forward, armed with their crowbars and ready to do their job.

Pleading had failed, so the keening began.

His mother started the lament with a piercing shriek that set everyone shivering, even the housewreckers, who'd seen it all before and had come prepared to face it yet again. Moira Branigan was the finest keener from Ballymagorry to Ballygorman, and everybody knew it. Just the week before, her wails of grief had accompanied her own beloved husband to the hereafter, wails so loud people all along the River Foyle knew that Liam Branigan had died.

The housewreckers stopped and looked away, suddenly hesitant, for they were Irish, too. They'd lost their own homes in this same way, their own wives and daughters had keened, and even the desperate need for a job was not enough to make them go forward.

Conor shivered as well, watching his mother. Though feverish with the typhus that had already killed her husband, she tore at her clothes and wailed with all the strength of her grief and despair. Behind her, huddled together in bewildered fright, his sisters echoed their mother with mournful cries of their own.

But even this wild symphony evoked no compassion from the landlord's agent. He barked an order to the men, and once again they began moving toward the cottage.

She fell to her knees before the agent's horse, arms upraised in supplication, invoking every office of the Saviour, asking for the intercession of the Blessed Virgin, calling on every pleading of the saints, using all her remaining strength for prayers, reproaches, and pleas for mercy. The housewreckers walked past her.

Conor heard another cry, this one of outrage, and suddenly his brother appeared out of nowhere. Michael raced across the yard to the doorway of the cottage and blocked the entrance, feet apart, fists clenched. Michael was fifteen and the man of the house now; he was ready to fight.

Conor wanted to fight, too, but he was scared. He knew he ought to be brave, like Michael, but he wasn't, and the thought made him hot with shame. He stood alone, hidden behind a tree and clutching the string of fish, hating the housewreckers, hating himself even more for being helpless and afraid.

The housewreckers dragged Michael away from the door, rewarding his defiance with a blow that sent the lad sprawling into the dirt beside his kneeling mother. Two men entered the house. Michael tried to rise and follow, but Moira stopped him. She wrapped her arms around her raging son and keened even louder.

In less than a quarter of an hour, the housewreckers demolished what had been his family's home for generations. Using ropes, crowbars, and brute force, they pulled the cabin apart like a walnut shell and reduced it to a pile of stone, timber, and thatch. Because of Michael's brief rebellion, the agent had it set afire, but the fire destroyed little. Most of the furniture and clothing had already been sold to buy food. Conor stared at the blazing fire, and his fear hardened into fury.

An open carriage passed by, slowing for a moment to watch this roadside scene, and Conor recognized Lord Eversleigh, the new landlord, and his companion, Reverend Booth. Recently arrived from London, titled and wealthy, Eversleigh had purchased the land by auction and had been welcomed by the people of Dunnamanagh one month before in the desperate hope that he would be their saviour, when it seemed even God had abandoned them to the famine. One week later, the evictions had begun.

Conor tore his gaze from the rich Englishman in the carriage to stare at the burning pile of rubble that had been his home. When he looked back at the road again, the carriage was in motion, driving on as if nothing out of the ordinary had happened.

The hard, hot anger suddenly burst within him, shattering like glass into shards of bitterness and hatred. He dropped the fish he was forbidden by law to catch and ran after the carriage. Beyond reason, he had no coherent thought, no goal, no plan. All he had now was *fuathaím*. Hate.

He caught up with the carriage as it slowed for a bend in the road and he ran beside it, using sheer determination to keep pace as it rolled past bare meadows, meadows dotted with piles of blackened stone where other cottages had once stood, where families like his had once lived and other children like him had once played—meadows that were empty now.

"We'll give you no money," Eversleigh called to him with a dismissive wave of his hand, as if Conor were nothing more than a troublesome fly.

"Not a farthing," Booth added from his place beside the viscount.

Conor said nothing, he asked for nothing. He simply refused to be ignored. He continued to run beside the carriage, matching its speed, keeping pace with the rich Englishmen it carried.

They passed St. Brendan's, where two dogs fought in the weed-choked churchyard over the carcass of another. When they turned onto Dunnamanagh Road, Conor knew he'd run at least two miles. But he did not stop. He did not slow down. He cast a sideways glance at the carriage, and he knew he had the landlord's attention. Eversleigh was watching him in silent fascination.

Without warning, a cramp seized Conor's empty belly, and he stumbled. His strides faltered, his pace slowed. With a cry of rage and despair, he watched the carriage move ahead, but he would not concede defeat. Regaining his balance, he pushed himself harder, until he was once again parallel with the coach. Not giving in was the only thing that mattered.

"By God, is the child mad?" Eversleigh shouted to his companion. "What demons possess these Irish?"

"They're all mad, sir," Booth replied.

Over and over, they told him he would get no alms from them. Conor ignored them. He stared straight ahead and continued to run. Sweat ran down his face and soaked the swallowtail coat he wore—the only garment he owned. With every stride, the sharp pebbles in the road cut his bare feet until they bled. His heart pounded as if it would burst right through his chest. He could hear his own desperate rasping breaths, he felt the ache in his side, and he thought sure he was going to run until he dropped dead. But, by the Holy Mother, if he died, he'd do it on his feet, not begging on his knees or cowering in fear behind a tree. Not now, not ever again.

Finally, Eversleigh could stand it no longer.

"Stop the coach!" he cried, tapping the driver's shoulder with his gold-tipped walking stick.

Slowly the carriage rolled to a stop, and Conor stopped with it. He doubled over, shaking, his hands on his thighs to keep from falling, and stared down at the red smears on his feet. He drew in great gasps of air, unable to get enough to fill his lungs. He licked his lips, tasting the salty tang of sweat. After a moment, he forced himself to straighten. Lifting his head proudly, he met the eyes of the man who had just destroyed his home and made his mother a beggar.

Eversleigh was the first to look away, unable to hold his gaze, and Conor knew the sweet taste of triumph. He'd beaten them. He'd won.

The landlord turned to his companion. "I suppose I ought to give the boy something."

The reverend shook his head and frowned in disapproval. "My lord, you're much too generous. He'll make bad use of it, I'm afraid."

"Yes, I know," Eversleigh answered, reaching for his money purse. "But well earned in this case. He was entertaining to watch." He stretched one arm out of the carriage, holding a coin toward Conor, who made no move to accept it. "Take it, boy," he urged, leaning closer.

"Don't touch him, sir!" Booth cried sharply. "Infested with all manner of vermin, he is."

Eversleigh dropped the coin and snatched his arm back in horror, realizing the child had lice.

Conor lifted his gaze from the coin in the dust and once again met the landlord's eyes. In their depths, he saw a combination of revulsion and pity. Slowly, he bent and retrieved the coin, intending only to spit on it before he tossed it back in the man's face.

He couldn't do it. The coin was a sixpence—not enough to buy even one of the gold buttons on the land-lord's coat, but enough to feed Conor's family for a week. Survival was more important than pride, and Conor knew he'd been a fool. He thought he'd won, but he had not. There was no way to win.

His fist curled tightly around the precious coin. He offered no thanks. He said no prayers. He did not bless the Englishman for his generosity. He simply walked away without a word. In his mind, he saw his burning home, and in his heart, he damned the man to hell.

5

Prison. Olivia felt sick. She had a criminal staying right here in her house, sleeping under her roof. She closed the door behind her, but she couldn't close her thoughts to the man on the other side. What on earth had she been thinking, plucking a stranger out of the road and bringing him home as if he were harmless as a stray puppy?

Prison. Why? What had he done? Robbery? Murder? She shivered, remembering the cold, defiant blue eyes that had challenged her with that one word. A dangerous man, with eyes that told her he was capable of anything.

I got exactly what I deserved.

Olivia turned away from the door. She walked down the hall and headed for the kitchen, trying to banish her apprehension. Right now, the man couldn't even stand up. Whatever he'd done, he wasn't in any condition to do it now, and by the time he was, she'd make certain he was far away from here.

When she entered the kitchen, Becky was there. She

took one look at Olivia's face and walked to her side. "What's wrong, Mama?"

Olivia came out of her reverie with a start. "Nothing," she answered and took a deep breath, gathering her thoughts. "Where are the girls?"

"Miranda's in the parlor, playing with her dolls. Chester's with her, of course. Carrie wanted to go see Mr. Branigan, but when I told her she couldn't, she took a book and went down to the orchard in a huff."

She gestured to a tray on the counter and the teapot that rested beside it. "I was just going to take Mr. Branigan some tea and something to eat." She smiled. "He said he wanted real tea, not that awful green stuff."

Olivia did not return her daughter's smile. "Thank you, honey, but I'll take him his meals. I don't want you going in there."

"But why not?"

She looked into Becky's innocent face and could find no way to explain her fear. "I just don't want you around him. Why don't you set the table for dinner? I'll go find Carrie."

"But it's noon. Shouldn't we take Mr. Branigan something to eat?"

"I'll do that when I get back," Olivia answered, and walked out the back door. She walked down the path to the orchard in search of Carrie, but her thoughts were not on her daughter.

She wanted him gone. When she'd found him in the road, she'd been certain God had answered her prayer—sent her someone to help with the harvest, someone who might stick around long enough to repair a few fences or fix her roof, someone strong, steady, and reliable. Instead, He'd sent her Conor Branigan: prizefighter, gambler, sinner. Criminal.

In the lane leading down to the orchard, she stopped

and leaned against a huge oak tree. "Why?" she asked aloud. "Why have You sent this man to me?"

She usually found comfort in speaking to God this way. Some people may have thought it odd, even presumptuous, to talk to God as if He were a friend, but Olivia had never thought of God as a gray-bearded wise man floating on a heavenly cloud. She'd always imagined God to be much closer than that.

But He didn't seem close now. Her question hung in the air, unanswered, and Olivia sank down to the soft earth beneath the tree, afraid and bereft.

Even as she wondered what she was going to do with him, Olivia knew there was nothing she could do. The man was seriously injured. Regardless of who he was or what he had done, she couldn't just dump him back in the road.

In her mind, she could still see the scars that marked him. She could not even begin to imagine how or why, but it didn't take imagination to know he was a man who had endured great pain, both of body and spirit. Dear God, what had happened to him in prison?

Olivia wondered why she should care. He was a criminal. He thought prayers were a waste of breath and gambling was something to be proud of. He probably drank, too.

I got exactly what I deserved.

"Why?" she asked again with a touch of desperation. "The man's been in prison. Why did You send him to me?"

It was not God who answered.

"Mr. Conor's been in prison?"

Olivia looked up and found Carrie staring down at her from between the branches of the tree. She should have known. Carrie had a knack for being where she wasn't supposed to be and hearing what she wasn't supposed to hear. "Carrie, for heaven's sake!" she cried. "What are you doing up there?"

Carrie held up the book in her hand as an explanation, but she refused to be diverted from the fascinating news. "Mr. Conor was in prison?" she asked again. "How come?"

Olivia didn't like her daughter's fascination with their dangerous guest. Nor did she like the fact that Carrie climbed trees. "I don't want to talk about it. Please come down from there."

Carrie pulled off her reading spectacles and put them in the pocket of her dress. She then tucked her book under one arm and climbed down from the tree, moving with the agility of long practice. Olivia stood up and watched nervously, but she knew Carrie wasn't nervous. Unlike her mother, the child wasn't afraid of heights. Her blue calico dress went flying up as she jumped to the ground, revealing her white cotton drawers.

Olivia drew a deep breath of relief. "Carrie, if you're going to climb trees, try not to show your drawers," she scolded. "It isn't ladylike."

"I'm not a lady, I'm a little girl," Carrie answered smugly, and brushed bits of bark from the backside of her skirt. "What'd he do?"

"I don't know, and I don't care." Olivia took her daughter's hand in hers, and they started back to the house. "I want you to stay away from him."

"You don't like Mr. Conor, do you, Mama?"

"No."

"Why not? Because he was in prison?"

Because he has the coldest eyes I've ever seen. "Yes."

"But you don't know why he was in prison. Maybe he didn't do anything wrong. Maybe it was all a mistake."

"You're so young," Olivia murmured.

Carrie didn't understand that comment, but it didn't matter. "Maybe he's like that man in the book you read to us. Remember? Edmond Dantes. He got put in prison, and he didn't do anything wrong. He—"

"Carrie, that will be enough!" Olivia said sharply, her patience at an end. She stopped walking. Turning to the child, she said, "That was just a story. In real life, men who have been in prison are not nice men."

"But Mama, you're always saying a good Christian doesn't judge," Carrie replied. "A good Christian always tries to find the good in others."

Olivia didn't like her own lectures thrown back in her face, especially by her nine-year-old daughter. "It's not that simple."

"Why not?" Carrie looked up at her. "Aren't we good Christians, Mama?"

Olivia looked into her daughter's eyes and sighed, not fooled by the deceptive innocence in their depths. Sometimes, Carrie was just too clever for her peace of mind.

Carrie, of course, wasted no time in announcing the news to her sisters the moment she walked into the house, and Olivia found herself inundated with their questions and comments. Was she going to let him stay? Was he really a bad man? Maybe he was a train robber. Did he know Jesse James? Did they let him out of prison, or did he escape? Maybe he was wanted.

Olivia put a halt to their speculations. "He's going to stay until his ribs are healed, then he'll be on his way. Until then, I want all of you to stay away from him." With that, she dished out soup and bread to them, and when they were finished eating, she sent them out to weed the garden.

Olivia dumped out the now cold tea Becky had made and set the kettle of water on the stove to make a fresh pot. Conor Branigan continued to invade her thoughts as she waited for the water to boil, his mocking voice and bitter words reminding her that he was not what she'd prayed for.

Carrie was so fascinated by him, and that disturbed her greatly. He wouldn't be in any condition to leave for at least six weeks. She couldn't keep the girls away from him for that long, especially Carrie.

Olivia looked up. Through the window, she could see the girls in the garden. Becky was doing exactly what she'd been asked to do, industriously pulling weeds. She was such a good girl, she tried so hard to help.

Olivia could see Miranda's head over the tops of the tomatoes. She was staring at one of the plants, probably watching some grasshopper devour the crop. She couldn't have killed it—she got upset watching Olivia swat a fly.

As for Carrie . . . Olivia watched her picking strawberries, eating about half of them as she went. She'd try to deny it later—with red juice all over her face. Olivia smiled. Carrie really was the most precocious child.

Aren't we good Christians, Mama?

Her smile faded. She'd always tried to be. She'd always believed herself to be charitable and fairminded. But now, when her lofty principles were put to the test, she found that it wasn't so easy.

The kettle whistled, and Olivia turned away from the window. Carrie was right. She should find out the whole truth before she started making judgments. She ladled out a bowl of soup and poured a cup of tea, then set both on the tray along with a slab of corn bread, and took the tray to his room.

She found him sleeping peacefully when she entered his room, undisturbed by nightmares. She moved toward him, uncertain how to proceed. Now that she'd decided to confront him, she was loathe to postpone it.

She set the tray on the table and hesitated by the bed, studying him. His cuts were healing and his bruises were fading. He needed a shave, she realized, noting the black shadow across his jaw. It made him look even more disreputable, and yet, sleeping quietly like this, he didn't seem like a criminal. He seemed like a tired man who had traveled far and suffered much and had finally found a place to rest. Suddenly, she wished he could have been the kind of man she needed.

"Why?" she whispered. "Why were you in prison?"

Almost as if he'd heard, his eyes opened, and he saw her standing there.

Flustered, she took a quick step back and gestured to the tray. "I've brought you something to eat."

"If it's that foul green tay you've brought me, take it back," he murmured, his voice sleepy and definitely sulky. "I'll not have it. If you had a bit of whiskey, now, that would be different."

Whiskey. She was right. He drank, too.

"This isn't a hotel, Mr. Branigan," she reminded him tartly as she fetched a pillow from the armoire in the corner. "You take what you get around here. And you'll find no spirits in this house."

"That doesn't surprise me. And you don't have to call me Mr. Branigan, you know. I have a first name."

Olivia had no intention of using it. She came back to the bed. "Can you sit up?"

He did. He gritted his teeth and sweat broke out on his forehead as he pushed himself to a sitting position. She shoved the pillow behind him.

She reached for the cup and pressed it to his lips. "Drink it slow," she ordered. "No sense having it come right back up again."

He flashed her a rebellious glance over the cup, not liking the reminder of yesterday. But he obeyed her, sipping slowly until the tea was gone.

She set aside the cup. Then she picked up the tray

and sat down carefully on the edge of the bed to feed him the soup.

Conor hated this. He watched her dip the spoon into the bowl, her other hand cupped beneath it to catch any dribbles as she brought it to his lips. He hated being fed as if he were a helpless baby, but he knew he was too weak even to grab the spoon from her hand. He swallowed the soup, feeling his body respond to the nourishment even as his mind rebelled against his own weakness.

As she continued to spoon soup into his mouth, a long-buried memory suddenly surfaced, and he was back in Derry. He was a boy again, and the Quaker lady from the Religious Society of Friends was feeding him Soyer's Soup, that watery, meatless concoction declared by the British government to be adequate for the starving masses. She'd had brown eyes, too, he remembered, eyes that apologized for the lack of real food, eyes soft with compassion. Pity.

He fought back, struggling against the memory, trying to send Soyer's Soup and that scared, hungry lad back to the past where they belonged.

"I think you and I should have a little talk."

If Olivia had suddenly drenched him with a bucket of water, she couldn't have pulled him out of the past more effectively. Conor eased his aching body back down to a prone position and donned his armor of pretended indifference. "Weather's fine today. A bit hot, I'm thinking, but not too bad."

She set the spoon in the empty bowl and studied him thoughtfully. He knew she was trying to read what was beneath the surface.

"Why were you in prison?" she asked. "What did you do?"

But Conor was very good at hiding what he didn't

want people to see. He'd been doing it for so long that sometimes he could even fool himself. He smiled at her. "None of your bloody business," he said politely.

"You're in my house, Mr. Branigan, and that makes it my business."

"Not for long. The minute I'm able to walk out of here, I will."

That did not seem to appease her. She glared at him. "That's at least six weeks away. Until then, you're in my house and in my care. I think I have the right to know what sort of man I've got under my roof."

She'd taken him into her home. She'd nursed him and fed him, and he ought to be grateful. Guilt assailed him and he took refuge. "What do you want me to say—that I was wrongly imprisoned, that I was an innocent man, that I am lily-white and pure?" His voice mocked her, mocked himself.

"Tell me the truth."

He almost laughed. Was she really so naive? He opened his mouth to give her a lie, a lie plausible enough to end her damnable probing into his dark, shadowed corners. The truth wouldn't satisfy her anyway.

"I have three children," she said.

Conor knew a sucker punch when he got one. The lie died on his lips.

Those brown eyes regarded him without blinking, as the eyes of a wild doe might watch a hunter approach, wise and wary, with a hint of fear. Oddly, that bothered him. He'd told her about prison because he'd wanted to shock her, to shatter her self-righteous indignation. He had succeeded, it seemed. She was afraid of him, afraid for her children. "Christ," he muttered.

He looked away, feeling unexpectedly awkward. Staring at the cracks in the white plaster ceiling, he told her part of the truth, the unimportant part. "I was arrested for attempted robbery and treason against the British Crown. I was convicted of the attempted robbery, but not the treason, and I spent fourteen months in a Dublin prison, then I was granted amnesty and released. I'm not going to steal your silver or murder you in your bed, Mrs. Maitland."

He didn't expect that simple statement to satisfy her. He steeled himself for more questions, questions he had no intention of answering.

But she didn't ask them. She rose to her feet and said, "Thank you for telling me. You're welcome to stay until your injuries have healed. However, I'd appreciate it if you would refrain from swearing."

With the tray in her hands, she walked toward the door, but paused in the center of the room to glance at him over one shoulder. "By the way," she added, "it's Miss Maitland. I'm not married. Never have been."

With that unexpected pronouncement, she turned and walked away.

Vernon was in his office at the sawmill when Jimmy Johnson brought him the telegram. He tossed the boy a picayune for his trouble, and Jimmy caught the five-cent piece in his hand. "Thanks, Mr. Tyler."

The boy pocketed the coin, then left, whistling, as Vernon unfolded the telegram. He read the short missive, crumpled it in his fist, and shoved it into his pocket. Rising to his feet, he crossed the room and opened the door. Over the roar of saws, he shouted, "Joshua! Get your butt in here."

Vernon resumed his seat behind his desk just as his foreman entered his office. "What is it?" Joshua Harlan asked as he shut the door behind him.

"I just got a telegram from New York. My father-in-law wants an immediate report on the situation."

"What do you suppose that means?"

"His investors are probably getting antsy about the railroad, is all. Hell, none of us thought Olivia would be so damned stubborn about this."

"You're sure there's no way to go around her place?"

Vernon yanked open a drawer and retrieved a surveyor's map. He slapped it down on the desk. "If you can find a way to lay track around Peachtree without going straight through Choudrant Bayou or dynamiting through the mountains, would you kindly tell me what the hell it is?"

Joshua didn't bother to look at the map. "Sorry," he muttered, sinking into a chair. "Stupid question."

Vernon jabbed one finger at a point on the map. "Any way you look at it, Peachtree is smack-dab in the way. Olivia's got to sell that land."

"She's already told you flat-out she won't sell. What do we do now?"

Vernon reached into the box on his desk and pulled out a cigar, but he didn't light it. He drummed it against the desk top, thinking of all the work he'd done during the past four years, all the money he had spent, and all the plans he had made. They had to get that railroad built.

When he'd married Alicia Jamison in '63, he'd promised her daddy they could make millions down South after the war. He'd known even then the Confederacy was doomed and there would be plenty of opportunities. He'd come back to his hometown in '67 just the way he'd always known he would, as a wealthy businessman. He'd used Hiram Jamison's money to buy every piece of land and every business that he could get his hands on, taking advantage of the hard times and low land prices. Now, he controlled the lives of the same people who had once looked down their noses at him. Not a day went by that he didn't savor the satisfaction of that.

But Vernon had bigger ambitions. He and Hiram had purchased all the land for a very good reason. They were going to build their own railroad, with track running all the way from Monroe to Shreveport. Surveyors and engineers had already told him that for geological reasons it wasn't possible to bring the railroad through Callersville, but Vernon didn't care. He planned to build a whole new town. He already had the site picked out, six miles to the north, right at the edge of Olivia Maitland's peach orchard, and right on his proposed railroad line. The only thing that stood in his way was Olivia's stubbornness. Damnation. She could ruin everything.

He thought of the day eleven years ago when her daddy had laughed at him, throwing his request to court Olivia back in his face and firing him for even daring to make it. Even after so many years, he could still hear Samuel Maitland's drunken laughter, and it still rubbed him raw.

"What are you going to tell Mr. Jamison?"

Vernon came out of the past. "The truth. That I have everything under control." He bit off the end of his cigar and spit it into the brass cuspidor beside his chair. "I'll get Olivia to sell me that land somehow."

"How?"

"I'll have a little talk with her about it at church on Sunday, up my price, and see if that persuades her," he said, lighting the cigar. "If she still won't sell, we'll just have to use some stronger methods of persuasion."

Joshua looked up, his pale gray eyes meeting Vernon's green ones over the desk. "If it comes to that, I better get a nice chunk of money."

"If it comes to that, you will," Vernon promised. "You will."

6

Conor wanted out of bed. Endless hours of lying here with nothing to do but sleep, think, and stare at the walls was driving him stir-crazy.

He wanted out of this house. The knowledge that his private torments and shameful secrets had been heard by three innocent little girls and their puritanical mother appalled him. He didn't know how much he had revealed about his experiences in the Mountjoy, but whatever they'd heard was too much.

If one of his bad spells was coming on, he wanted to deal with it in his own way. Alone. Here, there was no boxing ring to act as a physical outlet. There was no anonymous hotel room where he could take refuge, no whiskey to numb his brain, no beckoning road to provide a means of escape.

The only distraction was her. Olivia Maitland, who brought him trays of soup and emptied his bedpan and said nothing about the nightmares that had kept her daughters awake those first few days. She tried to feed him and he rebelled, refusing to be coddled like a babe. After that first meal, he fed himself, fighting the exhaustion of his efforts.

He wondered about her statement that she'd never been married. He tried to imagine starchy Olivia Maitland in the role of a scarlet woman and failed utterly. Those girls were adopted, no doubt about it.

As if sensing his restlessness, Olivia brought him some books. He didn't tell her they wouldn't be much good to him. He did not know how to read, he'd never gone to school. Schools and books were for rich Protestant children with tutors. Reading was something he'd never thought much about, but as he flipped through the pages of one of the books and stared at the unintelligible words, he suddenly wished he knew how. Not that it mattered, of course. Reading wasn't important to a man who made his living in the boxing ring. He set the book aside.

Restless, frustrated, and bored, afraid to sleep and unable to do much else, he began to long for something to distract him. On his seventh day in bed, his desire for a distraction was granted. Carrie paid him a visit.

When the door opened and he saw her standing there, he was so glad for the company that he didn't care how many of his secrets she knew.

"Mornin', Mr. Conor," she greeted him in a whisper.

Leaning back in the doorway, she took a look down the hall, then she stepped inside his room and shut the door behind her. "I'm not supposed to be in here," she confessed in a normal voice. "Mama said."

"I wouldn't want you to get in trouble."

"That's okay. I've been in trouble lots of times."

He remembered their first conversation, and her announcement did not surprise him. He grinned.

She walked across the room to the end of the bed

and leaned over the footboard, studying him. "I thought you might be lonesome."

Lonesome didn't even begin to describe it. "Thank you."

"I hate being sick," she told him. "There's nothing to do. I don't have to go to school if I'm sick, but that don't matter. If you're sick, you can't do anything fun anyway."

He thought about all the drinking, card-playing, and women he was missing, and he couldn't agree more.

"You like to go fishing?" she asked abruptly.

He thought about all the fish he'd stolen out of the landlord's streams back home. There were severe penalties for those who were caught, but he had never been caught. And he and Michael had taken a great deal of pleasure in stealing Eversleigh's precious trout. "I love it."

That seemed to make her happy, and she smiled. "What about climbing trees? Ever do that?"

"I've climbed many a tree in my time, lass."

"Do you know how to whistle?"

He pursed his lips and gave her a few bars of "Pop Goes the Weasel."

She laughed. "I like you, Mr. Conor," she said. "You'll do just fine."

Do for what, he didn't know.

Carrie's smile faded. She tilted her head thoughtfully to one side and frowned as if she were trying to work something out in her head. "Mama doesn't like you, though. She says you're not nice 'cause you were in prison. She says you got a filthy tongue and a vile temperament. What's 'temperament'?"

"It means the kind of person you are."

"Oh." She straightened and turned to lock her hands together around the bedpost. She leaned back, swinging to and fro. "But vile means bad, and I don't think you're bad. You shout awful loud, though. The first night you was here, you was screaming there were orange men everywhere." She stopped swinging and looked at him around the bedpost with a frown. "Men aren't orange, Mr. Conor. 'Less they're painted. Were they painted, like Indians?"

"No," he answered. "Just British."

He knew a nine-year-old American girl knew nothing about British Protestant orange and Irish Catholic green, but his brief explanation seemed to satisfy her nonetheless.

"Carrie!"

Olivia Maitland's voice floated to them through the open window. Carrie frowned in consternation and let go of the bedpost. "I got to go."

She walked to the door, but she paused with her hand on the knob and looked back at him again. "You got any little girls?"

"No."

"Boys?"

"No. I don't have any children."

"No wife neither?"

"No."

She smiled at him and opened the door. "That's good. A man can't have a wife if he's already got one, can he?"

For a moment, he didn't understand what she meant. The door closed and realization hit him. He sank back into the pillows with a feeling of dread.

Oh, Christ. He knew he had to get out of this house.

That afternoon, Conor tried to get out of bed. He managed to get his legs over the side, and that was all. Too weak and in too much pain to go any further, he gave up.

The next day, he gave it another go, but his knees buckled the moment he tried to stand, and he fell right back into the bed. Despite the softness of the mattress, it was a bone-jarring experience that left his ribs aching for hours. But it gave him something to do. He occupied his time cursing Vernon Tyler for having him beaten, and himself for being stupid enough to allow it.

He thought about Dan and wondered where the old man was now. Probably back in Boston, searching the docks for another Irish lad fresh off the boat with no money and plenty of anger. It wouldn't take him long to find one.

Conor pressed a hand to his ribs and winced. Even if he managed to get out of bed, it'd be weeks before he could walk out of here, another month before he'd be in any condition to fight. There was no point in rushing things. But then he remembered Carrie's words about wives and kids, and decided he didn't care. Even if he had nowhere to go, he wanted out of here.

Frustration, restlessness, and boredom motivated him to try again the following morning. He moved to lie sideways across the mattress with his feet on the floor. He then worked his way to the foot of the bed, grimacing at the pain that radiated through his body with every inch he moved. He gripped the footboard, took three quick breaths, and jerked himself to a sitting position.

Christ, it hurt. He made a desperate grab for the bedpost. Clinging to it like a lover, he waited until the pain had ebbed to a dull ache before going any further. Then he pulled himself off the bed.

Nine days after his body had been pummeled to mush, Conor stood on his feet—clutching the bedpost and holding on for dear life—weak, bruised, and bare-ass naked in the morning sunlight. That was how she found him.

"Merciful heavens!"

He glanced up to find Olivia standing in the doorway with a breakfast tray in her hands, shocked at the sight of him wearing nothing but a swath of linen bandage around his ribs. Hell, he didn't know why she should be shocked. She'd stripped off his clothes; she must have seen him naked, bruises and all. Although, perhaps not, he amended, studying her expression. She'd probably kept her eyes closed the whole time.

She backed out of the room, blushing and staring down at the tray in her hands. She mumbled an apology and something about finding him some clothes, then rested the tray against her hip to pull the door shut with her free hand.

Just for fun, he might have remained standing there until she returned, but his legs were shaking like jelly. He eased himself back down onto the bed and collapsed, pulling the sheet over his body so her maidenly sensibilities wouldn't be offended. He wanted his breakfast.

After a few minutes, he heard a light tap on the door, then it opened just a fraction. He heard her voice through the opening. "Mr. Branigan?"

"Yes, Miss Maitland?"

There was a long pause, then she said, "Have you . . . that is, are you . . . "

He knew perfectly well what she was asking, but she sounded so tentative, he couldn't resist having her on a bit. He pretended not to understand. "Am I what?"

Another long pause, then, "Are you decent?"

Now that was a question for debate. His stomach growled, and he decided to stop teasing her. "No, but I'm safely under the sheets."

The door opened wider, and she peeked at him. Satisfied that he was speaking the truth, she entered, but she wasn't carrying his breakfast tray this time, much to Conor's disappointment. A large basket was hooked over one arm, and she carried a basin of steaming water in her hand. Draped over one shoulder were several garments. "I've brought you some things."

Her acute embarrassment aside, there was something different about her today. She looked softer somehow, prettier. Instead of wearing her hair in a plain coil at the nape of her neck, she had it swept up in a soft and intricate puff that looked ready to tumble down at the slightest provocation. The battered hat had been replaced by an absurdly small bonnet of yellow straw and white ribbon. The collar of her plain gray dress was still far too high for his taste, but she had softened it with some sort of white, lacy thing that draped her neck and shoulders. He approved of the change.

"How pretty you look! You should wear your hair like that all the time."

The blush in her cheeks deepened at the compliment, but she did not look at him. "That wouldn't be very practical," she answered, setting the basin and basket on the table beside his bed. "I'm afraid the hogs and chickens wouldn't be impressed."

He grinned at that. "So why is today different?"

"It's Sunday. I'm taking the girls to church. You'll be here alone until this afternoon." She slid the clothes off her shoulder. They landed in a pile beside his hip. "I've brought these for you. I hope they fit."

The linen underdrawers and shirt and gray wool trousers were of fine quality, the clothes of a wealthy gentleman; but the once-white linen had yellowed with age, and all the garments smelled musty, as if they'd been packed away. He wondered who they belonged to.

He glanced at Olivia, but she still wasn't looking at him. She was studying the contents of her basket with great fascination, her cheeks still pink. "I've brought your boots," she said, holding up the pair for him to see before she bent to place them on the floor beside the table. "I've washed your socks, and they're in here, too. I've also brought soap and water so you can wash, and I thought you might want to shave, so there's a shaving kit," she added. "And a mirror. And a toothbrush. And some soda. I—"

"Olivia." He interrupted her rambling as his stomach growled again. "Would you happen to have any breakfast in that basket?"

She made a vexed exclamation and dropped the shaving kit back in the basket. "Your breakfast! I forgot all about it." She shot him an apologetic glance. "It's probably stone cold by now. I'd better make you a new one."

Seizing on the perfect excuse he'd given her, she departed in a rush.

After she'd gone, Conor turned his head and gazed longingly at the steam rising from the basin. Hot water, a toothbrush, a razor. Heaven on earth.

He sat up and reached for the water, but his tired body rebelled at even that small exertion. Water sloshed over the sides of the shallow basin as he pulled it onto his lap. He brushed his teeth and washed as best he could, moving with agonizing slowness. By the time he had lathered his face and picked up the razor and mirror, his hands were shaking with the effort.

He held the mirror up only long enough to get a good look at his bruised and battered face, then his arms fell to his sides and he leaned back against the headboard, exhausted and frustrated.

Damn. He couldn't do it. He'd worn himself out just standing up, and now he couldn't even shave. But when he heard a knock on the door, he forced himself to lift the mirror and try again. He had started this, he was going to finish it.

Olivia entered the room with his breakfast, realizing

with only a glance that he had overdone it. She took one
look at him, noticed how his hand shook as he brought
the razor to his cheek, and instantly forgot her earlier
embarrassment. She hastened to his side and set the tray
on a nearby chair. "Here, let me help you," she offered,
leaning across the bed to take the razor from him.

He jerked his hand back to prevent her. "I can do it
myself. I don't need any help."

He sounded so grouchy, she bit her lip to keep from
smiling. She straightened and stepped back to let him
have his way. During the past few days, she'd done a lot
of thinking about Conor Branigan and what he had told
her, and she had reached the conclusion that his explanation about prison had been the truth. During his
delirium, she hadn't understood most of what he'd said,
but he'd muttered something about treason, and she
knew by his scars and his nightmares that he must have
been severely punished, possibly even tortured. He had
grit, she admitted, watching him struggle. Grit and
pride.

He managed two strokes with the razor before he cut
himself. "Bloody hell!" He dropped the mirror to press
a finger to the cut on his chin.

"It's very hard for you to accept help from anyone,
isn't it?" she asked softly. "Why?"

He glared at her, and she knew he hated questions
almost as much as he hated being fussed over. She
ignored his scowl and moved to stand beside him again.
"Let me do it."

He shook his head.

"You'll never get your strength back if you push
yourself too hard," she pointed out, and she knew she'd
won with that argument. He let her take the razor and
the basin of water.

"Lean back," she ordered. She set the basin on the

table, then sat down on the edge of the bed. "Leave this to me."

She tilted his head to the opposite side for a better angle, and brushed the razor down his cheek, scraping away stubble and soap carefully.

"I don't know that I trust you with a razor in your hand," he said when she paused to rinse the blade. "Sure and you're thinking to mend my sinful ways by slitting my throat."

She grasped his chin and tilted his face upward. "The thought occurred to me," she said, beginning to shave beneath his chin. "But then we'd end up in hell together for eternity," she added, "and I don't much fancy that."

"Which don't you fancy?" he countered wryly. "Hell or me?"

Her hands stilled for a moment, and the sight of him leaning against the bedpost flashed through her mind. "Stop talking," she admonished, firmly pushing the vision away, "or I will end up slitting your throat."

He obeyed without argument, and she resumed her task, feeling him slowly relax. His eyes closed, his breathing deepened, and it pleased her that, despite his words, he trusted her to that extent. She studied his face as she worked, and she couldn't help thinking again that he was a very handsome man. If only he weren't so wicked.

"There," she said, and leaned back to survey her handiwork. "All done."

He opened his eyes, and she handed him the mirror. "Not bad," he was forced to admit, rubbing a hand across his jaw.

"I used to shave my father," she said. "After his accident, he couldn't do it himself."

"What happened to him?"

She took a deep breath. "It was just after the war. He fell off a ladder and broke his back." She stood up and turned to rinse the razor one last time. "He died about six weeks later." She paused and looked at Conor. "He never liked accepting help either."

Conor handed her the mirror. "Thank you," he said quietly.

"You're welcome."

He smiled at her, and she decided that maybe he wasn't such a wicked man after all. She turned to put the razor back in its case.

"Olivia?"

She glanced down at him. "Hmm?"

He gave her a lazy look from beneath thick black lashes, and his smile widened into the devil's own grin. "I don't suppose you'd care to help me get dressed, love?"

Carrie was fidgeting, and Olivia couldn't blame her. As a preacher, Reverend Allen was a sore disappointment to the people of Callersville, but the old fellow was so nice, nobody had the heart to tell him so. His monotone voice droned on, accompanied by the buzzing of several flies and the soft snoring of Ellie Hathaway, who was ninety years old and known to doze off about midway through the sermon. "Carrie, sit still," Olivia admonished in a whisper to the child beside her.

"I can't," Carrie whispered back. "My foot's asleep."

Olivia sighed. Giving up, she turned her attention back to the sermon, but the reverend went on talking about Eve and the serpent in one long, unbroken sentence, and she soon found her mind wandering to something much more interesting and much less pious than the sermon.

Conor Branigan. She could see him as clearly as if he

were sitting before her now, handsome as the devil, stubborn as a mule. She could see the exhaustion in his face and the determination in his eyes as he'd tried to shave. She could hear the low, almost seductive pitch of his Irish voice and smell the clean, pungent fragrance of shaving soap. She could still feel the heat of his skin against her fingers.

For heaven's sake, she was in church. Olivia felt herself blushing with shame as she remembered that fact, and she quickly lowered her head, hoping no one was watching her. He must be the devil, to make her think such things, especially in church. She closed her eyes, but instantly she pictured him again, leaning against the bedpost, and she quickly opened her eyes. She glanced around, desperate for something to occupy her attention.

To her left, Miranda was asleep, her head resting against Becky's shoulder. Becky was listening to the sermon, or at least trying very hard to do so. Jeremiah Miller sat beside her, as he always did.

Olivia glanced to her right and noticed that Carrie was still fidgeting, tapping her feet together.

Across the aisle, Jimmy Johnson and Bobby McCann were playing the rock and scissors game, much to the chagrin of Bobby's mother. They were obviously no more interested in the sermon than she was. Jimmy's mother was absent, of course, confined by pregnancy to her home and garden, a custom Olivia privately thought was rather silly. Since the Lord had designed women to have babies, she doubted a pregnant woman in church would have offended Him much.

Olivia watched the two boys, and she supposed the rock and scissors game was better than saltwater taffy in the pews. They wouldn't dare, not with the Chubb sisters right in front of them.

The Chubb sisters were the moral backbone of

Callersville, spinster ladies who knew the proper etiquette for every situation, who still believed that unmarried women under thirty-five never went about unchaperoned, and who staunchly refused to acknowledge that the war had ended their way of life.

Olivia knew she didn't rate very high in their estimation. She went about unchaperoned all the time. They had strongly advised her against adopting the Taylor girls, as she was an unmarried woman and such a course of action would not be proper. Olivia had ignored their advice, and had endured their looks of censure and sighs of disappointment ever since.

She had shamelessly advertised for an overseer, a breach of propriety that had been the talk of quilting parties for weeks. Ladies, Martha Chubb had informed her, did not advertise for farmhands. *Of course not*, Olivia thought acidly. Ladies wore gloves to protect their white hands, and ate tiny sandwiches with the crusts cut off, and never bothered about how the fences got fixed or the crops got harvested. "What would your mother say about this, Olivia?" was their favorite phrase, a phrase that always made her squirm.

She looked at the Chubb sisters, thought of Conor Branigan, and shifted guiltily in her seat. Not wanting to think about it, she turned her gaze toward the front of the church. Vernon Tyler sat in his usual place, the very front pew, his Yankee wife beside him. Olivia forced herself not to grind her teeth. The hypocrite. Everybody knew he ran the cockfights out of an abandoned barn down Longstraw way and the prizefights out of a tent in Jackson Field. He made a hefty profit on the betting, but a chunk of that money ended up in Reverend Allen's collection plate every Sunday, so there were very few sermons on the evils of gambling.

She was a fine one to talk. She had a man staying in

her house who made his living off gambling. A sinful occupation, prizefighting. His image flashed through her mind again, the flex and play of sculptured muscles in the morning sunlight. He was probably very good at it.

People suddenly began standing up, and Olivia realized they were standing for the final hymn. Hastily, she got to her feet and opened her hymnal, holding it low enough for Carrie to see it, too.

"Mama," Carrie whispered as people began to sing, "you're on the wrong page. It's hymn eighty-nine."

Olivia turned to the proper page without replying. She sang along with the rest of the congregation, she bowed her head for the benediction, but all the while, the only thing she heard was Conor's voice murmuring, *I don't suppose you'd care to help me get dressed, love?*—and she knew why Eve had listened to the serpent.

7

After church, *Olivia* headed straight for the wagon, her girls in tow. She smiled and nodded to acquaintances as she passed, but didn't stop to chat with friends as she usually did. Flustered and embarrassed, she felt people only had to look at her to know the shameful thoughts she'd had in church.

"Olivia!"

She halted, wincing at the sound of Martha Chubb's voice. Knowing she couldn't escape, she turned around, pasting a smile on her face. "Good morning, Martha." She nodded to the other woman. "Emily."

"It's good to see you back in church, Olivia," Martha said. "Missed you last Sunday. We were a bit worried about you, dear. Everything all right at Peachtree?"

Olivia stared at Martha Chubb, Callersville's greatest gossip, and the ramifications of having Conor Branigan in her home suddenly hit her. She had a man—a stranger, a prizefighter—staying in her house. It was one thing to advertise around town for a farmhand to work her place—not approved of, but toler-ated. Farmhands lived in separate quarters. She couldn't very well make a man with cracked ribs sleep in the barn, but what would people say if they knew he was sleeping in her house?

"Nothing to worry about," Olivia answered Martha's question, striving to sound casual as she invented a lie that might satisfy the other woman's curiosity. "Carrie was feeling a bit poorly, I'm afraid. Nothing serious—"

"But, Mama," Carrie interrupted, looking up at her in confusion. "I'm not the one who's been sick. It's—"

"Oh, there's Lila Miller!" Olivia interrupted before Carrie could say another word. "I need to speak with her. Come along girls." She gave the Chubb sisters a nod of farewell and ushered Carrie and Miranda toward the mercantile, where Lila had just gone inside. A glance over one shoulder told her Becky was following.

"Mama, you lied," Carrie said in amazement as they crossed the dusty street. "You lied to the Chubb sisters."

Olivia stepped onto the wooden sidewalk and came to a halt. With a quick glance around to make sure no one was within earshot, she leaned down. "We'll talk about it some other time," she said in a low voice. "Now, you girls mind me. Not a word about Mr. Conor to anyone. Understand?"

They all heard the hard edge in her voice. "Yes, ma'am," they murmured in perfect harmony.

"Good." She turned to her oldest daughter. "Becky, I've got to talk with Lila for a minute. I want you to take the girls to the wagon and wait for me there. And remember, not a word."

Becky nodded and took the two other girls to the wagon. Olivia turned and walked in the opposite direc-tion. She paused at the open door of the mercantile and knocked on the jamb. Lila was behind the counter, her back to the door as she pushed a bolt of brightly colored calico into place on one of the shelves. She turned at the sound of the knock. "Afternoon, Olivia. You know the store's closed Sundays."

"I know," Olivia replied as she walked to the counter, "but I saw you head over this way, and I was hoping you'd let me look at those new dress patterns you offered to show me the other day. I want to get some ideas."

"Going to make yourself a new dress?" Lila asked, bending down to retrieve a wooden box from beneath the counter.

"It's not for me," Olivia answered, sorting through the box of Butterick patterns until she found some appropriate for young girls. "I want to make Becky a dress for the harvest dance."

Lila smiled with understanding. "That's right, she's fourteen now. She'll be needing a long dress." Her smile faded, and she sighed. "Of course, it's not anything like it was before the war, when we were debutantes." Realizing what she'd said, a contrite expression crossed her face. "Liv, I'm sorry."

"Don't fret about it." Olivia stared down at the pattern in her hand, remembering the lavish balls of her girlhood, trying not to care how few of them she had attended, trying not to care that she'd never had a coming-out ball. "Besides, you're right. Things aren't like they used to be."

Glancing up, her gaze scanned the bolts of fabric lining the shelves. "Could I see that blue muslin up there?" She pointed to the shelf just above Lila's head, with no idea of where she'd get the money to buy the fabric.

"It's a fine one," Lila said, pushing aside the patterns to unroll a length of fabric across the counter. "Very pretty."

"Blue is Becky's favorite color," Olivia said, her fingers rubbing the sky-blue fabric wistfully. "She would look lovely in this."

"If you're goin' to buy that, I hope you have the cash to pay for it."

Olivia heard Vernon's voice, and she knew there would be no sky-blue muslin dress for Becky.

She turned, shoulders square as she faced him. He was still an incredibly handsome man, whipcord lean with thick chestnut hair. She could recall how fine he'd sat a horse in the days when he'd been overseer at Peachtree. Many a time, she'd sat at her window, a painfully shy girl, withdrawn and plain, spinning secret romantic daydreams as she'd watched him ride through the orchards and cotton fields.

But the handsomeness that had fired her romantic imagination as a girl no longer held any appeal. Olivia silently blessed her daddy for refusing to allow Vernon to court her so long ago, even though she knew that slight had wounded Vernon deeply and still hurt him to this day. "Good morning, Vernon."

The man glanced past her as he stepped through the doorway and entered the store. "Lila, the store's closed today. You shouldn't be in here working. Why don't you go on back to the church and visit with your friends?"

Lila didn't need to be told twice. Taking her cue, she started for the door, giving Olivia an apologetic glance as she passed.

"And close the door behind you," he added.

The bell over the door jangled as Lila departed.

Vernon crossed the room to stop a few feet in front of Olivia. "Saw you come in here. I just thought I'd see if you might've reconsidered my offer."

"No, Vernon. I haven't."

He stepped closer. "Now, Olivia," he said in a smooth, persuasive voice, "you know Peachtree's too big for you to manage by yourself."

"I don't know. I'm managing just fine," she lied.

"Really? Finally found some man to run it for you?"

She thought of Conor Branigan. "No," she admitted.

"Well, now, that's a surprise, with the generous salary you're willing to pay. Three meals a day and room and board to boot." He laughed softly. "Why a man'd have to be out of his mind not to accept an offer like that."

Olivia stepped back, hitting the counter behind her. She lifted her chin. "I'm not selling my land. Not to you or your Yankee friends."

"Maybe you ought to reconsider. There'll come a time when you won't be able to pay your taxes, and I'll pick up Peachtree real cheap. I'll get that land sooner or later."

Olivia knew he was probably right. All he had to do was wait for one bad year, one year when her peach crop failed. She wouldn't be able to pay the outrageous Yankee taxes, and Peachtree would be put up for auction. But, until then, she was going to fight him tooth and nail. "Well, Vernon, I reckon it'll have to be later."

"Be reasonable, Olivia. I've been more than fair. A dollar an acre is a right generous offer." He patted his breast pocket. "I've got a quitclaim deed and a bill of sale all written up. You'd just have to sign it."

"How convenient," she murmured. "But I'm not signing anything."

"Five hundred dollars is a lot of money. You could move into town, get yourself a nice little house, and still have enough left to buy them orphans of yours some decent clothes. You could have a much easier life, Olivia."

"How nice for me. And what about the town? Nothing kills a town faster than a railroad built six miles away. You build that railroad and Callersville dries up."

"If I could bring it through the town, I would. But the surveyors have told me that won't work. Besides, what do you care? If you sold your land to me, you and your girls would be taken care of."

"What about my peaches? You want to put that railroad of yours right through my orchard."

"Don't you understand? I've made you a good offer. You'll have enough money that you won't need that orchard. They're just a bunch of trees."

"No, Vernon, you're the one who doesn't understand. You never have. Peachtree is my home."

"I want that land." His voice hardened. "I always get what I want."

"Not always, Vernon," she answered gently, meeting his narrowed gaze with a look of pity. "Not always."

That reference to her father's refusal of his marriage suit so long ago and the pity he saw in her eyes brought a proud and angry flush to his face. "Your daddy," he said contemptuously, "was nothing but a worthless drunk."

"He was not worthless. He was a good man."

"Olivia, honey, your daddy was a drunk, and everybody knew it. His brain was so pickled with bourbon, he would have run Peachtree into the ground long before the war if it hadn't been for me."

"That's not true."

Vernon leaned closer to her. "He may've thought I was just poor white trash, but he was no better—afraid of his own wife, trying to hide his bourbon from her, too drunk to know what he was doing and too stubborn to let his sons or his overseer handle things. Well, your daddy died a drunk, your brothers are gone, I'm the one who's got money now, and all the pride in the world won't feed them girls of yours. You might as well accept my offer now." He paused a moment, then added softly, "I can make things easy for you, Olivia. Or I can make them a whole lot harder. It's your choice."

Olivia wasn't going to let him bully her. "Do whatever you like. But you'll never get Peachtree."

The door of the store opened, causing the bell to jingle. Vernon stepped back from her as an elegantly dressed woman entered the store.

"Vernon?" Alicia Tyler came toward them. She laid a proprietary hand on her husband's arm.

He glanced at his wife. "I told you to wait in the carriage."

A slight frown marred the woman's lovely forehead. "I don't appreciate waiting when I'm forced to sit out in the hot sun," she answered, and glanced at Olivia. "Have you finished your business here?" she asked.

The question was directed at Vernon, but it was Olivia who answered. "Yes, quite finished." Her gaze left the woman and returned to the woman's husband. "Not in a million years, Vernon."

She stepped around the couple and walked toward the door, her shoulders rigid, her back straight. Drunkard or not, Daddy would have been proud.

Despite his intention not to spend any more time lying in bed, Conor's first effort to remedy the situation had exhausted him, and he slept most of the day. It wasn't until sundown that he regained the strength to get up again.

Dressing was a slow and difficult process, but Conor

managed it by sheer determination. He put on the clothes Olivia had brought him, then left the room where he'd spent the past nine days. A dim hallway led him into a foyer of high, coved ceilings, a foyer wide enough for two Derry cottages to fit within it.

Just walking the short distance down the hallway left him weak and a bit woozy, so he paused in the foyer for a moment to catch his breath. As he did so, he studied his surroundings. He stared at the curving staircase that led to the upper floors and realized that Olivia Maitland's home must have been quite beautiful once. But the ecru wallpaper was peeling, the blue staircarpets were worn to threadbare patches, and the parquet floor was scratched and dull. When he gripped the newel of the staircase to steady himself, the ornamental wooden ball that capped it came off in his hand.

He thought of Olivia's drab dresses and chipped teapot, her dilapidated wagon and her sorry-looking mule, and he realized that the war must have taken just about everything she had. But he also knew the wealth that had once been here had been built on the backs of slaves.

He couldn't help comparing it to Ireland; he couldn't help remembering all the blood and sweat his own people had spilled so that rich British landlords could have velvet carpets and curving staircases. He found it hard to mourn the loss, but he understood how difficult it must have been for Olivia to watch her way of life disintegrate around her.

But his way of life had disintegrated long ago, and Conor forced away his memories of home. *Let it alone,* he thought, and carefully put the wooden ball back in its place.

In the distance, he could hear voices, and he followed the sound to the back of the house. Olivia and the girls were in the kitchen, seated around a table, having their evening meal. Chester lay in a nearby corner, obviously waiting for his share.

"Are you going to make me a cake for my birthday, Mama?" Miranda asked, as Conor paused in the doorway to the kitchen, inhaling the delicious scent of fresh bread and fried chicken.

His gaze caught on Olivia and lingered there, watching as she reached out to brush back a lock of Miranda's hair with a soft and loving gesture. "Of course I am, sweetie."

They were a family. Something stirred inside him, something long-buried and half-forgotten that constricted his throat and twisted his guts. Instinctively, he moved as if to turn away.

Chester lifted his head and let out a low growl. The talking suddenly stopped and all of them looked up to find him in the doorway.

"Mr. Branigan, you're on your feet again." Olivia rose from her place at the head of the table and gestured to the food. "We were just sitting down to supper. I was going to take you in a tray, but since you're up, maybe you'd like to join us?"

A chorus of enthusiastic agreement from the girls followed.

Olivia turned to her oldest daughter. "Becky, would you set a place for Mr. Branigan, please?"

Conor did not step forward. He hesitated in the doorway, uncomfortable. He didn't belong here, he was the stranger, the outsider who looked in.

But then Carrie jumped up and came over to him. She grabbed his hand and pulled him toward the table. "You can sit next to me," she announced, gesturing to the empty chair beside her own with all the majesty of a queen bestowing a favor upon her favorite knight.

Left without a choice, Conor pulled out the offered chair as Becky left the table to fetch him a plate.

"I see the clothes fit," Olivia commented.

Conor turned so that she could see where both shoulder seams of the shirt had ripped apart. "They do now."

He turned back around in time to see her smile. It caught him by surprise, and he realized that he'd not seen her smile before. He had thought her to be passably pretty at best, but when Olivia Maitland smiled, some undefinable shift of light and shadow occurred, some subtle rearrangement of her features took place, and she became suddenly beautiful. It was an unexpected and magical transformation.

He was staring at her. He quickly looked away, and realized Becky was standing beside him with a place setting. He sat down, and Becky put a plate and utensils before him. Once she had returned to her chair, Olivia spoke again. "Becky, it's your turn. Would you say the blessing?"

"Perhaps Mr. Conor would like to do it?" Becky suggested, smiling at him across the table.

Conor froze in his chair, staring at the laden table. Memories of a girl's grateful, whispered blessing flashed vividly across his mind, and he felt suddenly suffocated. *Thank God for food?* He wouldn't do it. He couldn't. The words would choke him.

"I'm not really hungry." He rose to his feet so abruptly it hurt. "I think I'll go outside and get some fresh air." He turned his back and walked out of the kitchen as fast as his battered body would take him, leaving Olivia and the girls staring after him in bewilderment.

8

OCRÁS
Derry, Ireland, 1847

"*Tá ocrás orm*, Conor," Megan murmured.

"I know. I'm hungry, too." Conor sat down beside his little sister and wrapped her emaciated body in the ragged blanket he'd stolen, glad he'd found it, not caring that he'd taken it off a body still warm. He was long past caring about things like that.

She leaned back against the brick wall of the alley with her head on his shoulder. "Did you find anything?"

He hesitated, his hand at the pocket of his coat, unwilling to bring out what he'd found in the fish market. But Megan looked up at him, and the moonlight plainly showed the ravaged hollows in her once-round cheeks. He pulled out the fish scraps and held out the largest piece to her.

Megan lifted her eyes to heaven and whispered a

grateful blessing on the food, made the sign of the cross, then stuffed the fish into her mouth.

But her stomach was unable to tolerate the putrid fish after a week of nothing at all. She turned her head to the side and vomited what had taken Conor hours to find. Too weak to sit up any longer, she curled into a ball beside him with her head on his lap. "I'm sorry," she whispered miserably.

Conor swallowed hard. "It's all right. Just go to sleep. I'll find something better tomorrow."

But there wasn't anything better, and both of them knew it. Conor ate slowly, fighting back his own nausea with every bite, and thought about the ships he'd seen sailing out of Lough Foyle that afternoon—ships bound for England, ships he knew were loaded with Irish butter, grain, pigs, and poultry that would soon grace the tables of rich British households.

His mouth watered. He closed his eyes, picturing those ships, and he forced himself to stop thinking about *ocrás*. He focused his thoughts on only one emotion, the one emotion that had kept him alive this long. *Fuathaím.*

"I can't see." Megan's frantic whisper interrupted his thoughts, and she groped for his hand. "Conor, I can't see."

Fear gripped him. "I can't see either," he lied. "'Tis black as pitch out here."

"No. There was a moon, but I can't see it now. I think I'm dying."

"No, you're not. You're only nine. How would you know if you was dying?"

"You'll be all alone now. I'm sorry."

"You're not dying," he answered roughly, jerking the blanket up around her shoulders. "Stop blathering on about it like a peahen."

"I'm scared, Conor. There's no priest for confession." Her voice became weaker with every word she spoke. "If I don't confess my sins, I could go to hell."

Conor didn't tell her both of them were already there. "You haven't committed any sins, and you'll not go to hell, Megan. I promise. I've never broken a promise to you, have I?"

"No."

"Well, then. You're not going to die, and if you was to die, sure and the angels'd be waiting at the gates of heaven to greet you."

"That would be nice." Her fingers entwined with his, then tightened with a strength he didn't know she possessed. "Make me another promise."

"What?" He looked down into her pale face, watched with frantic denial as her eyes slowly closed. He suddenly wished he'd told her about the ships. He wanted to grab her and shake her, he wanted to shout at her to think about the housewreckers, her sisters, and Michael. Anything that would make her hate as he did, make her want to live for vengeance as he did.

But Megan wasn't like him. She couldn't hate anybody. It just wasn't in her.

"Please don't let the rats get me," she whispered, letting go of his hand. "Or the dogs. Find a graveyard and bury me proper in the ground. Promise."

He felt as if hands had closed around his throat, choking him. "I promise."

Megan died that night. Conor decided he hated God almost as much as he hated the British, and it was hate alone that gave him the strength to keep his promise.

9

Olivia found him on the front veranda, sitting on a bench and staring into the twilight. Lost in thought, he didn't seem aware of her presence, and she took a moment to observe him unnoticed.

He was such an unpredictable man, with moods that could change quicker than the weather. She recalled how he'd jumped up from the table and hightailed it out of there when Becky had asked him to give the blessing, and she could find no explanation for his abrupt exit.

She walked toward him, and he glanced up as she approached, but his expressionless face gave her no clue to what he was thinking. "I saved a plate for you," she said. "When you want it, just let me know."

He didn't reply.

She sat down on the bench beside him. "I'll get a few more of my brother's shirts out tonight and see if I can't piece them together into a shirt that'll fit you."

That caught his attention. "These clothes belonged to your brother?"

She nodded. "Stuart. He died in the war." She paused, then added, "So did my brother Charles. Both of them were killed at Gettysburg."

A long silence fell between them, and she was surprised when he spoke. "I'm sorry about your brothers," he said, without looking at her.

She was surprised. Sympathy was the last thing she would have expected from this man. "Well, that was eight years ago," she murmured.

Leaning back, she studied the gnarled oak trees, gardens, and lawns that had once made Peachtree a place of beauty and grace. The oak trees were shapeless now, the gardens overgrown, the lawns unkempt. "You know, when I was a little girl, my brothers and I used to sleep out here on summer nights. Sometimes, I find myself thinking about those days, and I get to missing my brothers, and I come out here with my pillow."

She looked over at Conor. "Sounds silly, doesn't it?"

"No." His lips tightened slightly, and he looked away, staring out at the gardens. "It isn't silly at all."

He fell silent, and she wondered if perhaps she ought to just go back in the house and leave him be. But then he spoke again. "When I was a lad, my brother, my sisters, and I all slept in the hayloft."

He'd never mentioned his family before. In fact, when she asked him, he'd said he had no family. Curious, she turned toward him, wanting to know more. "In the loft? You didn't sleep in the house?"

"Well, an Irish cottage isn't like what you've over here. At home, the barn is part of the house, with the loft over the top." He glanced over at her and grinned. "Hay makes for great pillow fights."

She laughed, noting the mischief in that smile. "Most of them started by you, I reckon."

"I never did. It was my brother, Michael, who always

started it." He laughed softly. "He was my older brother, and I wanted so much to be like him. Everything he did, I had to do. The result was that we were always in trouble, the pair of us. He taught me how to box when I was barely eleven."

She caught the yearning in his voice. "You must miss him very much."

His smile vanished, and he looked away. "I miss him every single day."

Olivia knew he was a private man, but she was unable to stop herself from asking questions. "Where is he now? Still back in Ireland?"

He stiffened, and she thought he wasn't going to answer her question. When he finally spoke, his voice was so low, it was almost a whisper. "The famine hit Ireland when I was eleven. When I was twelve, I watched a British landlord's men beat my brother to death with sticks." He paused, then added, "For stealing one of their cows."

She was stunned, but she didn't show it. "What about your sisters?"

She could almost see a wall close in around him, shutting her out. Conor looked over at her, and it was as if their brief moment of companionship had never been. "They died," he answered in a voice that chilled her. "They starved to death."

The sun was just peeking over the horizon the following morning when Olivia went down to the orchard. Although the sky to the east was tinged with the delicate pink and gold of a gorgeous sunrise, she didn't notice its beauty. Olivia walked amid the peach trees, still preoccupied with the troubled thoughts that had kept her awake much of the night.

Lord, he was a hard man. Hard and bitter, with a wall around him a hundred feet high. But once, he'd been a boy who had pillow fights with his brother and sisters, who had gotten into mischief. He'd been a boy who had watched his brother beaten and his sisters starved, a boy who'd grown up only to be tortured in prison. No wonder he was bitter.

In her mind, she relived again that moment when he'd told her about his family, his voice so calm, his eyes so cold. He still carried the scars, and her heart ached for him.

Olivia leaned against a tree, staring with unseeing eyes at the trees along the next row. Caught up in her thoughts, she didn't notice anything odd at first, but when she did, she straightened abruptly, and thoughts of Conor Branigan's past fled from her mind.

The leaves of one tree were wilted. She walked over to the tree to examine it more closely, but she couldn't find anything wrong. She saw no sign of insects or disease that could be responsible. But the tree was ailing. She couldn't figure it out, until she glanced down and saw a gash in the bark. Frowning, she bent down for a closer look.

Olivia ran her hand along the cut that circled the entire trunk, dismayed. This tree had been girded with a knife, to prevent water and nutrients from reaching the leaves. It was dying.

She turned away and began looking for other trees that might have been damaged in the same way. Within minutes, she found half a dozen more.

Who would do such a thing? Even as she asked herself the question, Olivia knew the answer. Vernon was behind this. She recalled their conversation after church the day before, and his words of warning. *I can make things easy for you, Olivia. Or I can make them a whole lot harder.*

She stared down at the fatal wound at the base of one of her trees, and she noticed the cigarette butts that were scattered around it. She bent down and pinched one between her thumb and forefinger, holding it up with a thoughtful frown. The two Harlan boys and their father all smoked cigarettes. And all of them worked for Vernon over at the sawmill. Maybe Vernon had given them another job on the side. She dropped the cigarette back in the dirt.

She'd known Vernon all her life, she knew he was full of big talk. After returning from up North two years after the war, he'd bought up just about every piece of land round these parts, and most of the businesses in town as well. Now he wanted Peachtree.

So far, she'd been able to hold her own against him. She had refused his offers to buy her out, she had ignored his threats to force her out. She knew how he'd always felt about her and how deeply her refusal to defy her father so long ago had wounded him, but she'd never dreamed he would do anything like this.

She felt certain Vernon was behind the damage to her trees, but there was no way she could prove it. Vernon was powerful and he had powerful Yankee friends. She left the orchard and walked back toward the house, firmly banishing her worry. Slashing her trees was a warning, meant to shake her up, intimidate her into selling. It wasn't going to work.

When Conor awoke, he found a pitcher of fresh water and two neatly folded shirts outside his door. He bent down, one arm around his sore ribs for support, and scooped up one of the shirts. Olivia had promised to piece together some shirts that would fit him, and she had. He discarded the torn shirt from the day before and donned one of the new ones. It fit perfectly.

He used the water in the basin, then left his room, following the scent of something sweet and luscious to the kitchen. Olivia was there, standing at the kitchen table, using a spatula to scoop what looked like sweet biscuits off a tin sheet and onto a plate. "Whatever it is you're making," he said from the doorway, "I want a taste of it."

Olivia glanced up at him and smiled. "You're as bad as the girls," she said, "always wanting the cookies right out of the oven."

He walked to her side and grabbed a "cookie," as she called it, off the plate. She gave him a warning look, and began to drop spoonfuls of dough onto the sheet.

"Where are the girls?" he asked, taking a bite of the cookie.

"They went over to the Johnson place for the day to visit."

He finished the cookie and reached for another, but she snatched the plate away. "Cookies are no breakfast for a grown man," she told him sternly. "Give me a second and I'll fix you a real breakfast."

"Thank you." Conor sat down at the table and watched as she moved about the kitchen, vaguely remembering the last time a woman had offered to make him breakfast. Somewhere in Maryland, he thought it had been, or maybe Virginia, and she'd come to one of his fights. Afterward, she had approached him with a whispered offer of herself for supper and eggs for breakfast. He'd taken her up on the first part of her offer, but not the second. After it was over, she'd fallen asleep and he'd left town. She had smelled of cologne and tobacco, and she'd had red hair and a pink silk dressing gown. Funny how he could remember details like that, but he couldn't remember her name.

He watched Olivia, and it struck him how different she was from the redhead in pink silk. Olivia Maitland was a woman who wore dresses buttoned up to her chin. A woman who smelled of cloves and vanilla and had eyes like chocolate. *Good enough to eat*, he thought, and wondered what the hell was wrong with him.

Women like her were not for men like him. He vastly preferred easy redheads who took his money and left him his freedom, women who didn't give a damn if he swore and whose names he didn't have to remember, women who didn't need what he couldn't give and who didn't have daughters who wanted a daddy.

Olivia walked over to the table and set a plate of food in front of him. He stared down at it for a moment, then looked up at her. "What's this?" he asked curiously, pointing to one side of his plate.

"Grits," she answered. That did not enlighten him, and she seemed to realize it. "I don't suppose you've ever had them, but here in Louisiana, we eat grits all the time. They're delicious."

He continued to eye her with some skepticism. "I'm not sure I trust the opinion of a woman who makes me green tay," he said, and picked up his fork.

"Well, if you don't like my cooking, you can do it from now on."

He grinned at the challenging lift of her chin. "I'd be happy to. But I'm afraid we'd all starve."

She laughed and walked away, leaving him to his breakfast. But Conor noticed her watching him as he lifted a forkful of grits to his mouth and he knew she was waiting to see what he thought of them. He took a bite, and he wondered why anybody, in Louisiana or anywhere else for that matter, would eat them. A person might just as well eat buttered wallpaper paste. But food was something Conor never took for granted. "Delicious," he said.

Pleased, she gave him that astonishing smile, a smile well worth a few mouthfuls of wallpaper paste.

"You wouldn't say that if you'd come round here about eight years ago," she said, pouring him a cup of coffee. "Old Sally—she was our cook—had died, and I started doing all the cooking. I'd never cooked a meal before in my life. My mama never thought it was an appropriate skill for a young lady of quality," she added with a wry smile.

"My first meal was a disaster," she confessed, as she brought the cup of coffee to him. "Thank goodness my grandmother collected recipes and wrote them down in a journal. If I hadn't found that journal, I would never have learned how to cook."

While Conor ate his breakfast, Olivia finished baking cookies. When he pushed back his plate and rose from the table, she did not miss his grimace of pain.

"Ribs still pretty sore, I imagine?"

He didn't reply, but he didn't have to. She walked over to the pantry to get her medicine box. "I've got a camphor liniment that'll do wonders."

"Don't bother. I'm fine."

"It's no bother," she replied, and emerged from the pantry with a fresh roll of binding and her medicine box. "I want to have a look at your ribs anyway to make sure they're healing properly," she said, crossing the kitchen to stand in front of him, "and I ought to put a fresh binding on them."

She set the box and the roll of linen on the table beside her. When she turned toward him, Conor shook his head. "There's no need to make a fuss. I told you, I'm fine."

"You're not fine. You're a man with cracked ribs,

and I know they're causing you pain. So kindly remove your shirt, and don't argue with me."

She was certain he was going to refuse, but in the end, he didn't. "Too bad they don't allow women in the military," he muttered as he unbuttoned his shirt. "With you on their side, the Confederacy might have won the war."

She shot him a wry glance as he tossed the shirt aside. She opened her box and removed a bottle of liniment, then she turned to him and laid one hand against his ribs, pushing gently with her fingers.

"Ouch!" he cried, leaning away from her. "Jaysus, stop poking me!"

"Don't swear at me, if you please." She moved her hand and pressed again, feeling him wince. "They seem to be coming along well enough, although I think it'll be several more weeks before they're completely healed."

She unfastened the pins and began rolling the long swath of linen that supported his injured ribs away from his body. The task forced her to slip her arms around his waist, and the intimate contact made her acutely aware of him, aware of sinew and muscle and solid masculinity. It was an unexpected feeling that robbed her of the ability to breathe, and brought back the memory of him standing naked by the bed. Something warm and aching spread through her limbs, making her want to lean into him. Her hands fumbled and she dropped the binding. It unrolled as it fell to the floor.

"Oh, dear." She retrieved the swath of fabric from the floor and set it on the table, then reached for the bottle of liniment. She pulled out the cork, poured some of the liniment into the palm of her hand, and began rubbing the pungent oil gently into the bare skin of his torso.

She heard his sharp intake of breath, and she paused to glance up at him. "Did I hurt you?"

"No," he answered, but his voice sounded strained, his breathing slightly uneven. A tiny muscle worked at the corner of his jaw. "No. You didn't . . . hurt me."

She tried to finish her task quickly. Though she kept her gaze fixed on her hands, they refused to work properly, and her movements were hopelessly awkward. She finally managed to pin the fresh binding in place.

"All done," she said, but instead of stepping back as she knew she ought, she remained where she was. Her hand flattened against his side, and she could feel the heat of his skin through the linen. "Does that feel all right?"

He didn't answer, and she looked up into his face.

His eyes were smoky blue, almost tender against the harsh planes of his face. His lips curved slightly, the corners touched with amusement. She lowered her hand, flustered, and stepped back.

He caught her wrist. "Don't stop now, love," he murmured, his thumb brushing back and forth across her palm in a slow caress. "Sure, I was beginning to enjoy it."

He smiled at her, a heated, knowing smile. She jerked her hand away and ducked her head, her gaze skimming his body as she looked down, catching at the buttoned flap of his trousers. She stared, realization washing over her in a hot flood, and she felt herself blushing with mortification. She backed away from him, then turned and fled.

Conor watched with both amusement and chagrin as Olivia retreated out the back door, his body still tingling with arousal. Christ, what did she expect when she touched him like that? He might not be in the best of shape, but he wasn't dead.

He recognized innocence when he saw it, but he also recognized desire. And curiosity. It was rather a revelation to discover that underneath Olivia Maitland's prim and starchy exterior, there was a real woman. "I'll be damned," he murmured.

He donned his shirt, took a pull from his cup of cold coffee, and left the house. He didn't know where he was going, but it didn't matter. There really wasn't anywhere to go.

Olivia was on her knees in the garden. She did not look at him as he passed, but kept her eyes on the cucumbers she was picking as if it were a fascinating task. Her cheeks were still burning.

One more second, and he would have taken her up on what she hadn't even known she'd been offering. One more second of her hands on him with her face lifted unknowingly for a kiss, and his cracked ribs and her fluttering innocence be damned. It was obvious that she had no idea of the game she was playing, no knowledge of the stakes.

Conor remembered Carrie's words, and he reminded himself that the stakes were bloody well too high. But he could still feel the touch of Olivia's hands, a touch that soothed and aroused at once, a touch that was both innocent and provocative. He knew that if she touched him like that again, he was going to make it clear what kind of fire she was playing with, and he'd enjoy every minute of it.

During the days that followed, Olivia avoided Conor as much as possible. The incident in her kitchen had been embarrassing and awkward. But it didn't matter that she took such great pains to avoid him. Her mind insisted upon reliving the mortifying incident over and over, and every time she thought of his smoky, half-closed eyes and his low, seductive voice, her knees went stupidly weak.

It was her own fault. She should not have touched him in such an intimate fashion. Looking back, she had no idea what had possessed her, for she had been unable to stop herself. It was as if Olivia Maitland, plain, God-fearing spinster, had undergone an extraordinary transformation beneath that intense blue gaze and become a sort of shameless Delilah.

Every time she thought of it, her acute embarrassment came flooding back, along with an odd, breathless excitement that she was certain could not be anything but wicked. As a result, she kept her demeanor scrupulously stiff and formal whenever she was around him.

One morning about a week after he'd gotten on his feet again, Conor woke and went out to the kitchen to find her and the girls on the back porch, giving Chester a bath. Buried to the elbows in soap suds and trying to keep Chester from bolting out of the washtub, she was too busy with her task to be embarrassed by Conor's presence.

Sopping wet and looking pitiful, the dog didn't even bother to growl at Conor—and surrounded by four females, it didn't seem like the poor mutt had any chance for escape. Conor leaned one shoulder against the doorjamb to watch, feeling some measure of satisfaction that Chester was so miserable.

"All right, girls," Olivia said, "let's rinse him off. He's not going to like it, but we've got to have him nice and clean in time for the party."

"My birthday party," Miranda added.

Conor watched as Olivia bent down to Miranda's eye level. "That's right," she said, smiling at the child. "But you know how Chester hates water. So you hang on to him good and tight, okay?"

"Okay, Mama." Miranda dug her two small fists into Chester's wet, soapy coat. "I've got him."

Conor grinned, watching her. Chester was about twice her size. If he chose to make a run for it, wee Miranda wouldn't have a prayer.

Olivia straightened and reached for the bucket of water by her side. "All right, girls. Here we go. Hang on to him."

Chester didn't give them the chance. As Olivia raised the bucket over his head, the dog jumped out of the tub, easily breaking free of the grip the three girls had on him. In the process, he jostled Olivia's arm and sent a cascade of water down the front of her dress.

Chester paused long enough to shake, sending a spray of soap suds in every direction, then he took off, escaping down the porch steps before anybody could grab him. The girls immediately went after the dog, Olivia groaned in dismay, and Conor burst out laughing. It hurt his ribs like hell, but he couldn't stop it.

Olivia whirled around at the sound of his laughter and studied him in some surprise. "Well, that's a sound I never thought to hear," she murmured.

"What?"

"You laughing." She tossed aside the empty bucket and brushed a wet strand of hair out of her eyes. "I was beginning to wonder if you knew how."

"I know how." As he spoke, he realized he couldn't remember the last time he'd laughed—really laughed, not the cynical, mildly amused kind, but genuine, spontaneous laughter. He knew it had been a long time ago.

His gaze lowered, and his smile faded. Her dress, soaking wet, clung to her in a most provocative way, and he took a moment to appreciate the shapely figure beneath the drab brown dress, thinking about the way she'd touched him that morning seven days ago, and wondering how he could get her to do it again.

He looked into her face, watched her lips part and her eyes grow wide, and knew she was thinking about that morning, too. He took a step toward her, and she took a step back. He saw that wary look come into her eyes again, a look that was anything but encouraging. He took another step toward her just as a laughing shriek rang out.

He glanced past her toward the yard, and what he saw there caused him to grin again, forgetting her apprehension. "You'd best get some fresh water," he advised. "You'll be needing it, I'm thinking."

Olivia blinked, staring at him blankly. "What?"

He pointed to the yard, and Olivia glanced over her shoulder. Chester, his wet coat now caked with mud from the dusty yard, had been pinned to the ground by the girls, but in the process, he'd managed to make them as muddy as he was.

"We got him, Mama!" Miranda cried, releasing her grip on the dog to wave at her mother with one mud-encrusted arm. "We got him!"

Olivia groaned again, this time in defeat.

But she wasn't defeated for long. She sent the girls to the swimming hole with a basket of sandwiches, an easy way to get the mud off of them.

As for Chester, she decided that she wasn't going to let a dog get the better of her. She fetched fresh water from the well and a length of rope from the barn. With a rope fastened to his collar, that tethered him to the porch rail, there was no escape for poor Chester, much to Conor's amusement.

"He doesn't much care for baths, does he?"

She jumped back as Chester shook himself, spraying her still-damp dress with another shower of water and valiantly trying to slip free of the rope around his neck. "No," she answered. "He never has liked water. I think some farmer round here tried to drown him when he was a pup." She glanced over at Conor. "They do that sometimes, sad to say. When I found him, he was hurt, and I figured some fox might have taken a nip or two at him before he got away. I couldn't just leave him hurt like that, so I brought him home."

That comment did not surprise Conor at all, and he found that he and the dog had something in common.

When Olivia had finished bathing the dog, she rubbed his thick wet coat with a towel to absorb most of the water, but she had no intention of letting him go rolling around in the dirt until he was completely dry. She untied the rope, grabbed him firmly by the scruff, and led him into the house, where she finally let him go. Freed from the torture at last, Chester raced out of the kitchen.

"I think he's gone off to hide," Conor commented from the doorway.

"He'll be back when the girls come home," Olivia answered, and turned toward the stove. "At least he'll be out of my way while I bake a cake."

"So, it's wee Miranda's birthday today, is it?"

Olivia nodded. "She's six today, and she's so excited about it because this year she gets to go to school with Becky and Carrie." As she spoke, Olivia opened the stove and began stoking the coals. "We're giving her a party this afternoon."

Olivia fixed him breakfast, and as he ate, he watched her mixing ingredients in a pan, reading aloud from the dog-eared journal beside her. "Place over a low fire and stir until thick, adding eggs one at a time," she murmured, and took the pot over to the stove.

After a few moments, she paused in her stirring and made a sound of vexation. "Would you mind taking a peek at the recipe there, Mr. Branigan, and tell me how many eggs I'm supposed to add?"

He didn't answer, and when she glanced over her shoulder at him, she suddenly realized why. He was staring down at the open journal on the table.

Olivia lifted the pot from the stove so the pudding wouldn't burn and carried it with her to the table. He pushed the journal toward her without looking up, and she glanced down at the recipe. "Three eggs," she murmured absently, and looked back at him. He was staring down at the table as if he found it fascinating. "You can't read, can you?" she said gently.

He kept his gaze fixed on the blue and white plaid tablecloth. "No."

"And all this time I was bringing you books, thinking it'd help pass the time. Why on earth didn't you tell me?"

He didn't reply to that, but he didn't have to. She knew the answer by the way he wouldn't look at her. Olivia stared at his lowered head, and she realized again what a proud man he was. "I could teach you to read, if you like," she offered, trying to sound casual.

"No."

"It's not that difficult, really. You could—"

"No."

"Mr. Branigan, there's no shame in not knowing how to do something. The shame's in being afraid to try."

"Afraid?" He lifted his head and his eyes were suddenly dangerous. "Woman, you have no idea what I'm afraid of, or what I'm ashamed of. So don't pretend that you do."

He glared at her, trying to stare her down with all that cold defiance. It was a look she was beginning to understand, a look meant to intimidate and keep people from getting too close. She decided to ignore it.

"You know, my roof's in pretty poor shape," she said, and resumed stirring the pudding. "Been leaking for nigh on two years now. A year ago, I sold two hogs and bought all the materials so that Nate, my farmhand, could fix it for me; but he died last summer, and the roof never got fixed. Now, I've got pans and tin cans all over my attic floor to catch the water." She sighed. "I know I ought to get up there and fix it myself, but I just can't bring myself to do it. And I feel ashamed of myself for being a coward."

He stared at her, clearly wondering what she was rambling on about.

"You see, I'm scared of heights." She lifted the spoon and watched vanilla pudding dribble slowly from it into the pan. "Always have been. My mama said it was because my brother Charles held me out over the rail on the upstairs veranda when I was three. I don't remember that, but to this day, I can't bring myself to walk on that veranda. Mama said he was only teasing, like boys do, and he didn't know I was really scared or that I could've been hurt. Of course, after my daddy fell off that ladder six years back, I was even more afraid of heights. So I just can't get up the nerve to fix that roof."

She dropped the spoon back in the pot and looked at him. "We all have our fears, Mr. Branigan, and our weaknesses, and things we're ashamed of."

She turned away, but she added softly, "But if you ever decide you want to learn to read, you let me know. I'd be happy to teach you."

"I won't be here that long."

Olivia set the pan on the stove, knowing that what he said was true. A few weeks from now, he'd be gone. The thought of his departure should have brought a feeling of relief. It didn't, and Olivia truly didn't understand that at all.

10

Conor was not a family man. Birthday parties for little girls were beyond his experience. When the girls returned from their swim, and Olivia sent them upstairs to change into dry clothes for the party, he decided it was a fine afternoon for a walk, and disappeared out the back door.

Beyond the dusty yard and well-tended garden, the mule and a very pregnant cow grazed in a pasture surrounded by a wooden fence. A pitiful excuse for a fence, to be sure. It leaned drunkenly inward, and a good many of the slats were broken. At the end of the pasture stood a barn and chicken coop, their weathered gray wood obvious beneath peeling red paint.

He could see several more outbuildings that were in no better condition than the barn, flanked by deserted cabins. Beyond the buildings, he could see an orchard of fruit trees. With the exception of the garden and the orchard, everything spoke of neglect.

Conor made it as far as the barn before his body

gave out. Feeling light-headed, he sank down into the knee-high grass to rest for a moment, and leaned back against the rough wood of the barn wall.

Weakness. He despised it. He thought of all the times in his life when he'd been helpless, all the times he'd vowed never to be helpless again; and yet, here he was, without the strength to walk more than a few dozen yards. His fault.

The dizziness passed and Conor opened his eyes, staring across the yard at the back porch of Olivia's house. From this distance, he could see how it sagged in the middle, as if ready to collapse. The house wasn't in much better shape, he realized, his gaze traveling to the roof.

If the roof was leaking so badly that she had tins all over her attic floor, it had to be fixed soon or the whole thing was going to rot and cave in. Given Olivia's fear of heights, he doubted she'd get around to it. People didn't face their fears, they ran from them. He knew that better than anybody.

He thought of how she'd offered to teach him to read. A nice, pointless offer. He didn't need words to bring another man down in the ring. Besides, what he'd told her was true. He wouldn't be here long enough to learn to read. In a few weeks he'd be back on the road, free and far away from here.

A door banged and the sound of laughter interrupted Conor's thoughts. He glanced at the porch again and saw the girls come running down the steps, that mangy dog Chester right behind them.

"C'mon, Mama!" Miranda called impatiently over her shoulder. "Hurry!"

Olivia emerged from the house, carrying a handkerchief, and joined the girls in the yard. Conor watched as she tied the handkerchief over Miranda's eyes, then spun her around three times.

Blindman's bluff. His sisters had played that game many a time. He watched as little Miranda tried to catch one of the others, but they danced out of reach and her efforts were in vain, until Olivia stepped into her path. It didn't escape Conor's notice that she allowed herself to be captured.

"I got you, Mama!" the child cried, tearing off the handkerchief.

"You sure did," Olivia agreed, accepting the blindfold from her daughter. She tied it over her eyes, and the game began again.

As Conor watched Olivia playing games and laughing with her girls, he felt every single ache and pain in his body. More than that, he felt old. He wasn't old, he told himself—he was only thirty-four. No, wait, this was 1871. He was actually thirty-six. Where had the time gone?

Olivia and the girls had formed a ring of joined hands and were singing "Ring-Around-The-Rosy," their voices painfully out of tune. The song ended and they all fell to the ground, laughing.

Conor felt a sudden longing, a bittersweet mixture of desire and regret for all he had missed. It was a sensation so unexpected and so unwanted that it startled him, and he shoved it away before it could take hold.

What the hell is wrong with me? he wondered, watching as they stopped their game, brushing dust off their skirts as they moved toward the porch. The last thing he wanted was a family. Prisons didn't have to have stone walls and iron bars. He rose to his feet, intending to move farther away, where he couldn't hear their laughter.

But Carrie caught sight of him standing by the barn door. "Mr. Conor!" she cried, waving to him from the porch. "Come and have cake with us."

He turned away as if he hadn't heard, but of course, that didn't work. Carrie came running, calling his name, Miranda right behind her—and Conor knew there was no escape. He sighed and turned back around to face them.

Both girls skidded to a halt in front of him. "We're going to have cake now," Carrie said and grabbed his hand. "C'mon."

"It's my birthday cake," Miranda added, seizing him by the other hand. "Pudding cake. You have to have some."

He didn't have any idea what pudding cake was, and he didn't really want to find out. Despite the insistent tugging of the two girls, he didn't move. Miranda continued to pull at him, but Carrie did not. Instead, she let go of his hand and stared up at him. Her lower lip began to tremble. "Don't you like us?"

Conor knew perfectly well when he was being manipulated by feminine wiles, and he couldn't help grinning. She did it rather well, too, considering she was only about nine. Give her a few years, and this lass was going to be a heartbreaker. He allowed himself to be led toward the house.

Olivia and Becky were in the kitchen, and both of them looked up as he was dragged into the room by his captors.

"I see you've decided to join the party, Mr. Branigan," Olivia commented, as she looked up from the bowl of cream she was whipping.

"I didn't have much of a choice in the matter," he told her ruefully.

"So I see."

He didn't miss the laughter in her eyes or the tiny smile that curved the corners of her mouth. He suspected she knew exactly how uncomfortable he felt, but she made no comment.

She resumed her task, stirring cream rapidly with a whisk, as Becky dribbled in spoonfuls of sugar. The other two watched with growing impatience, until finally Olivia set the whisk aside. She turned to Miranda. "Well, Birthday Girl, do you want to help me cut the cake?"

Miranda gave her mother a delighted smile and nodded. She turned toward the ring-shaped yellow cake that stood on the table. Olivia moved to stand behind her and showed her how to hold the knife. "Not so big," she admonished, laughing, as Miranda started to slice the cake. "If you want a second piece, you can have one after supper."

Her hand over her daughter's, she guided the child in slicing the first piece. After five wedges had been cut from the cake, Olivia placed them on plates and slathered on a generous spoonful of jam, then Becky spooned whipped cream over them. Miranda took the first plate and brought it over to Conor, holding it out to him with both hands.

He glanced down at the slice of yellow cake with its center of vanilla custard and its topping of peach jam and whipped cream. Now he knew what pudding cake was: trifle without the rum. He thought the lack of rum a shame.

"Thank you," he said as he accepted the plate, wondering how he was going to eat the confection. She'd forgotten to bring him a spoon.

"Are we going to play more games, Mama?" Miranda asked as she walked back over to her mother's side.

"If you like," Olivia replied. "How about charades?"

This suggestion was greeted with shouts of enthusiasm.

"You'll play charades with us, won't you, Mr. Conor?" Carrie asked, her mouth full of cake. "Please?"

Conor glanced out the window and wondered where he might find a suitable hiding place as the other two girls joined in, pleading and cajoling.

Conor looked at Olivia, but she proved to be no help whatsoever. "Charades it is, then," she said as she crossed the room to hand him a spoon.

He shook his head. "No. Absolutely not."

"You don't have to if you don't feel up to it." She glanced toward the three girls, and he followed her gaze across the kitchen to find three pairs of imploring blue eyes fixed on him.

Conor played charades. He felt like an idiot, but he did it anyway.

Conor Branigan continually surprised her. Olivia plucked another stocking from the pile of mending she and Becky were working on and glanced at the man seated across the library playing checkers with Carrie. Miranda sat beside him on the sofa, and he repeatedly asked the child for advice on how to move his pieces, so that she wouldn't feel left out.

Given the way he lived, prizefighting and moving from town to town, Olivia suspected he wasn't used to being around children. But he had a way with them nonetheless.

"I win!" Carrie declared, taking Conor's last checker.

"Now, how'd you manage that?" Conor shook his head in pretended bewilderment and glanced at the child beside him. "We had her surrounded."

"That's okay," Miranda told him. "We beat her twice."

Carrie began rearranging the pieces on the board. "Let's play again."

"Not tonight," Olivia said firmly. She set her mending aside and rose from her chair. "It's bedtime."

She ignored the pleas and protests. She endured one, and only one, round of good-nights to Mr. Conor, then ushered all three of them upstairs.

"Did you have a fun birthday, honey?" she asked Miranda, as she knelt down before the child to help her pull her long white nightgown over her head.

"It was the best one I've ever had, Mama."

"I'm glad." She hugged the child and stood up. "Say your prayers."

Miranda did, and when she had finished, Olivia tucked her into bed. She kissed the child good-night, put out the lamp, and headed for the door, but Miranda's voice stopped her. "Mama, do you think Mr. Conor will be here for my next birthday?"

She didn't know what to say except the truth. "No, honey."

"Why not?"

"Because Mr. Conor has his own life to go back to. He can't stay with us forever. Now, go to sleep."

She left Miranda's room. Chester was curled up in the center of the hall, and Olivia stepped over him to enter Becky's room.

Becky was sitting at her dressing table, brushing her hair, and Olivia walked over to stand behind her. "How about if I do that?" she suggested. "It's been a while since I brushed your hair for you."

Becky handed over the brush, and Olivia began pulling it through the girl's long blond hair. She was nearly done before Becky spoke.

"Mama, do you think I'm pretty?"

The question was so abrupt and anxious that Olivia paused in her task. She met her daughter's eyes in the mirror. "I think you're very pretty."

"As pretty as Cara?"

Cara Johnson was Becky's best friend, and Olivia could still remember what it felt like to be fourteen and have a beautiful best friend, how gawky and insecure it had made her feel.

"Yes," she answered. "As pretty as Cara. You look like your mother."

"I do? I don't really remember what she looked like."

"She was beautiful. Sometimes, I was so jealous of her."

"You were? But you were her best friend."

"Just because you're best friends doesn't mean you don't feel jealous," Olivia answered and resumed her task. "I've been thinking about the harvest dance. I can't afford to make you a whole new dress, but I thought maybe we could find one of my old dresses that could be made over for you to wear."

"Really?" Becky turned her head and looked up at her. "There's a blue one that's really nice."

Olivia smiled. "There is, hmm?" she teased. "And how would you know that, miss? Been looking through my chest and playing dress-up, have you?"

Becky nodded. "I like the blue one a lot."

"We'll see what we can do."

"What are you going to wear, Mama?"

"Oh, I don't know." The brush hit a knot, and Olivia worked carefully to untangle it. "My gray one, I suppose."

"That's nothing special. You wear that one every Sunday, and you wore it to the dance last year. You should wear something special. What about that red silk that's in the chest? You would look beautiful in that, Mama, you really would."

The red silk. It was dark claret red, she remembered,

and she'd worn it once, a long time ago. "I'd forgotten all about that dress," she murmured.

"We could make it over for you," Becky said, "just like we're going to do with mine."

"We'll see." Olivia ran the brush through Becky's hair one last time to be sure the knot was gone, then she set the brush aside and planted a kiss atop her daughter's head. "There. All done."

"Thank you, Mama."

"You're welcome. Now, say your prayers and get to sleep."

She left Becky's room, noticing that Chester was no longer lying in the hallway. She wondered where the dog might have gone, but when she entered Carrie's room, she knew. The room was empty. Carrie had probably gone back downstairs, and Chester had followed her. Olivia let out an aggrieved sigh and wondered what new excuse Carrie had dreamed up to postpone bedtime. Probably something to do with Conor Branigan.

She turned around and marched back downstairs, fully prepared to give Carrie another lecture on bedtime stalling. But the sight that met her eyes as she entered the library brought her to an abrupt halt, and she stared in astonishment.

Conor was sitting in one of the overstuffed chairs by the fireplace and Carrie was sitting on his lap, dressed in her nightgown and wearing her reading spectacles. Her bare feet dangled over the arm of the chair, and her head rested in the dent of Conor's shoulder. With one arm wrapped around the child, he was looking down at the open book she held in her hands, listening as she read aloud. Chester lay sleeping on the floor nearby, oblivious to the man he'd been growling at for over two weeks.

Olivia blinked, not quite able to assimilate the sight. This was Conor Branigan, prizefighter and ex-convict, the same man who a few hours before had to be dragged like a recalcitrant mule to a little girl's birthday party.

"'. . . and this time it vanished quite slowly,'" Carrie read, "'beginning with the end of the tail, and ending with the grin, which remained some time after the rest of it had gone.'" She paused to turn the page and caught sight of her mother standing in the library doorway. "Mama!"

Conor glanced up at her, then immediately away, but Olivia didn't miss his grimace of pain as Carrie wriggled on his lap.

The child held up the book. "I'm reading Mr. Conor a story."

"I see that," Olivia answered, stepping into the room. "But Mr. Conor happens to have cracked ribs. Sitting on his lap is not helping them heal."

"Oh!" She immediately slid off of Conor's lap and gave him an apologetic look. "Was I hurting you? You should've said something."

"Not to worry, *mó paisté*," Conor told the child. "I'm all right."

Carrie turned to her mother. "See, Mama? He's all right." She moved to sit on the arm of the chair with her book, but Olivia's voice stopped her.

"I seem to remember telling you that it was bedtime."

"But I'm not sleepy. Why should I have to go to bed if I'm not sleepy?"

"Upstairs," Olivia ordered, pointing to the doorway. "Now, young lady."

"But I haven't finished the story. Alice just met the Cheshire Cat."

Olivia was not impressed. "Caroline Marie, I mean now."

Conor put a hand on Carrie's shoulder. "You'd best do as your mother says before both of us get into trouble."

"Okay, Mr. Conor," she immediately agreed, and so obediently that Olivia nearly groaned. The child held out her book to him. "You can borrow it as long as you want. That way, you can finish the story yourself."

"Thank you."

"The best part's when Alice meets the Queen of—"

"Carrie!" Olivia started forward threateningly, and this time, Carrie obeyed.

Olivia led her daughter up the stairs, and Chester followed them. The dog resumed his post in the center of the hall, and Carrie paused to give him a good-night pat before entering her bedroom with her mother. "Mama, after today, does this mean we don't have to stay away from Mr. Conor anymore?"

Olivia wondered when she'd lost the battle. But she was forced to admit that Carrie had understood instinctively what she had not: Conor Branigan was no dangerous criminal. He was a hard man, true, and he'd lived a hard life. She'd heard him use language vile enough to peel paint off walls. But he hadn't uttered a single foul word in front of the girls all day. Not one. He'd played charades, he'd played checkers, he'd let Carrie read him stories.

She knelt down in front of her daughter. "Only if you promise not to hurt his ribs by jumping up and down on his lap like you did."

Carrie nodded earnestly. "I promise."

"And," Olivia added, "if you promise not to sneak downstairs after your bedtime."

"I won't."

"Good." Olivia straightened. "Now, I want you to say your prayers and get into bed."

The child made no move to comply, and Olivia wondered if she was again trying to postpone bedtime.

"Mama, does God always answer prayers?" Carrie asked as she looked up at her mother.

There was an earnest sincerity about her expression that told Olivia the question wasn't just another stalling tactic. "Always," she answered. "Why?"

"If you ask God for something, and you pray really, really hard, will God give it to you?"

Olivia suspected the child's questions were leading somewhere, and with Carrie, that could mean trouble. "Not necessarily," she answered cautiously.

Carrie pondered that for a moment, then she said, "Even if you're good? Even if you eat all your greens at supper, and say your prayers every single night, and go to bed when you're supposed to?"

Olivia would never use the Lord as a way to make Carrie eat her vegetables or go to bed on time. But just now it was very tempting. "Even then. God may not think what you're asking for is right for you."

"But it doesn't hurt to ask, does it?"

"No, sweetie, I suppose it doesn't hurt to ask."

Carrie pressed her palms together and closed her eyes, frowning with earnest concentration. But Olivia noticed that the child didn't say her prayers aloud as she usually did, and she wondered what Carrie was up to.

"Why all these questions about God anyway?" she asked when the child opened her eyes. "Is this about that pony you've been wanting all year?"

Carrie shook her head. "Oh, no, Mama, I don't want a pony anymore."

Olivia pulled back the sheet, and Carrie jumped into bed. "What is it, then?" she asked, pulling the spectacles gently from Carrie's face to lay them on the bedside table.

Carrie didn't answer, and it was obvious that she didn't want to tell. "I was just wonderin' about God, is all," she said so innocently that Olivia's suspicions heightened.

"I see." She decided to let the matter drop, knowing the child would eventually blurt out what she wanted so badly that she'd promise to eat all her collard greens to get it. "Why don't you wonder about God tomorrow?" she suggested. "It's time to get some sleep."

She kissed the child good-night, turned out the lamp, and left the room.

Conor was still in the library when she returned downstairs, standing by the bookshelf with Carrie's book open in his hands. He was staring down at the page, frowning with such fierce concentration that he didn't notice Olivia until she moved to stand by his side.

He slammed the book shut and shoved it between two others on the shelf. "She asked me to read her a story. What was I supposed to say? I told her it would be better if she read the story to me. I felt like an idiot."

She laid a hand on his arm. "No reason to feel that way. Carrie had the opportunity to learn to read. You didn't. That's all."

Conor stiffened beneath her touch and pulled away. He crossed the room and turned his back to her as he studied the faded cabbage-rose wallpaper surrounding the fireplace. Olivia watched him in uncertainty, not quite knowing if she had said the wrong thing. He was such a solitary man, complicated and inscrutable. She wished she understood him a little better.

"Does that offer still stand?"

The unexpected question startled her. The rigid set of his wide shoulders told her how it had cost his pride to ask. "Of course."

Bending down, she pulled Becky's slate and slate pencil from the lowest shelf, then walked to his side. He turned as she approached.

She wrote on the slate, then held it up so he could see what she'd written. "*A*," she said. "That's the letter *A*."

"*A*." He stared at it for a moment, then the corners of his mouth lifted in a wry smile as he looked at her. "Like 'Alice.'"

She smiled back at him. It wasn't much of a basis for understanding, but it was a start.

Later that night, while everyone else slept, Olivia took a lamp and went up to the attic. She opened the cedar-lined chest that contained all her old clothes, the silk and muslin dresses, the hoop skirts, the lacy undergarments, and delicate slippers of the days before the war, when she'd never dreamed of slopping pigs and mucking out chicken coops.

She pulled out the blue silk gown Becky had mentioned and examined it. It had a neckline modest enough for a young girl, and would do very well if she took up the hem a bit. It had a musty, cedar smell, but soaking it in potato water would take care of that. She set the blue silk aside.

The red silk evening dress lay beneath it. She unfolded it and walked to the dust-covered cheval glass that stood in one corner. She held the dress against herself, smiling at the outrageously full skirt, trying to remember how she'd ever been able to get through a doorway wearing this dress. But then, she'd only worn it once, to a ball at Taylor Hill. Daddy had been drinking all day, she remembered, and he'd been particularly obnoxious that night. He'd brought their evening to an abrupt end by tossing a glass of bourbon into Jacob

Taylor's face and being coldly asked to leave the premises. They had never been invited back.

Olivia stared at her reflection in the dim light, and all the girlish resentment she'd pushed deep down inside flared up with sudden, bright intensity. She thought of all that she had missed, the beaux, the barbecues and balls that she'd never attended because of Daddy's drinking and overbearing possessiveness. No young man in the four parishes, even the ones of good families and impeccable backgrounds, had been given permission to court her. Not that there had been many.

She understood her father's fear of loneliness had been the reason behind it. He had been terrified that she would marry and go away. Stuart and Charles had tried to reason with him on her behalf, but their attempts had come to naught. Away at university most of the year, there had been little else they could do.

Olivia draped the red silk over one arm and fingered the skirt of practical brown cotton she wore. Now, her father and brothers were dead, but it was too late. She was twenty-nine. She was an old maid. She looked like one, she dressed like one, she even thought like one. She'd long ago given up on the romantic dreams of her girlhood, but sometimes she wondered. . . .

Olivia held the red silk in front of her again, thought of Conor Branigan's smoky blue eyes, and wondered wistfully if it was too late for an old maid to find a little romance.

11

The reading lessons began the following evening after the girls had gone to bed. That was Olivia's suggestion, suspecting Conor might not want the girls to see him learning to read. They wouldn't have laughed at him, but she knew he would be uncomfortable if they watched him reciting the alphabet.

She began by writing all the letters on Becky's slate. Holding it up so that both of them could see it, she pointed to each letter, making the sound then asking him to repeat it. He had an excellent memory. Within half an hour, Conor was able to repeat all twenty-six letters perfectly.

"Very good," she said, smiling at him across the kitchen table. "These letters represent all the sounds we make to form words. Before you can learn to read, you have to memorize all of them. Now, I expect you to repeat these letters to yourself at least a hundred times before tomorrow's lesson."

He groaned. "It's like the rosary. I always hated the

rosary. Hail Mary, full of grace, over and over, until the Blessed Virgin herself was probably sick of hearing it."

Olivia didn't know anything about the rosary, but she got the idea.

He grinned at her. "My brother and I used to make up different words for it, and I was terrified that one day I'd blurt out the wrong ones by mistake." His grin faded. "At least I don't have to say it anymore."

"Why not?"

He didn't answer for a long moment. "I was excommunicated from the Church five years ago," he finally said, "for being an insurrectionist, a rebel, and most important, for being an inconvenience."

"I don't understand."

He gave her a pitying glance. "The tangled web of Irish religion and politics too confusing for you? It really comes down to power in the end. Catholic cardinals who want to keep control of our souls, the British government that wants to keep control of our country. Conor Branigan and his troublesome friends in the way, defying the lot of them, stirring republican sentiments, and upsetting the power structure. What's the result? Excommunication and prison for me, and a fine example set for all those disgruntled Irishmen who might dare to whisper the hated word 'rebellion.'"

Although she knew nothing of the Catholic religion and less about Irish politics, Olivia understood disillusionment and the death of dreams. She heard both in Conor's voice. "I'm sorry."

"Sorry? For me?" Disbelief and anger warred in his expression.

"No. Not for you. I'm sorry for the loss of your faith."

"Don't be. I lost my faith before I was twelve years old."

"That can change. It's never too late."

Suddenly his grin returned, impudent and taunting. "Trying to redeem me, Olivia?"

She stiffened at his mockery. "No, Mr. Branigan. I'm not that optimistic."

He nodded approvingly. "Very wise of you, love. I've got many sins on my soul, most of them far more enjoyable than defying parish priests and British laws, and I intend to rack up plenty more of them before I die."

"Have you no convictions?" Olivia asked in disbelief. "Isn't there anything you believe in?"

"No." He fell silent, but after a moment, he spoke again, all mockery gone from his voice. "I betrayed everything I believed in," he said flatly. "Because of that, I'm already destined to burn. So what difference will a few more sins make?"

The following morning, Conor was up early enough to see the sunrise—not an unusual sight for him since sunrise was when he typically went to bed. But during the past two and a half weeks, it seemed as if he'd done nothing but sleep. He was unaccustomed to so little physical activity, but it was more than that. He could feel the restlessness growing within him, the need to move on.

He found fresh water and clean towels outside his door so he knew Olivia was awake. So were the girls. He could hear their chatter all the way down the hall.

But when he entered the kitchen a short while later, he found it empty. On the table were the full plates of an untouched breakfast. Conor frowned, wondering where Olivia and the girls had gone.

He wandered outside and found all of them in the barn. The girls were huddled in the opening of one of the stalls and when he stepped inside, Carrie ran to him. "Princess is in trouble," she said and grabbed his hand, looking up at him with beseeching eyes. "You can help her, can't you, Mr. Conor?"

She pulled him toward the stall. Olivia was kneeling in the straw beside the pregnant cow he'd noticed the day before. The cow was in labor, and he could tell by Olivia's anxious face that there was indeed a problem.

"What's wrong?" he asked.

"I think the calf's breech." She pushed the calf's feet back into the womb and reached inside to turn the calf around. But she couldn't manage it, and she sat back on her heels, panting. "Oren told me, if the hooves come out pointing down it's breech, and I have to turn it, but I can't."

In her agitation, she wiped her hands on her skirt instead of her apron. "I've tried three times. It's too big."

Conor heard the desperation in her voice and the hint of panic. He began rolling up his sleeves, glad that for once he could make himself useful. He entered the stall and knelt down beside her. "Move over," he ordered. "You're not strong enough, lass. Let me do it."

She eyed him dubiously. "Do you know anything about cattle?"

"Olivia, Irish butter is known to be the best in the world. Where do you think we get it from? Chickens? I grew up on a farm. Move over." He patted her hip, and she hastily scooted sideways, almost as if his touch burned her. Another time, he might have a go at finding out if it really did.

He glanced up at the girls, who stood watching silently outside the stall, their expressions fearful. "Becky, take the girls up to the house," he instructed. "Then bring me some soap, water, and clean towels."

"Is Princess's baby going to die?" Miranda asked.

"Not if I can help it, *mó cailín*. Go with Becky, now."

Becky took the other girls out of the barn. Conor glanced at the calf's feet which were once again protruding from the womb, due to the insistent pushing of its mother. "It's breech, all right. And it's a big one. I'll have to turn it around. Let's just hope it doesn't get stuck coming out."

"I've never birthed a cow before. Babies, yes. Hogs, puppies, but this is my first time with a cow. What do we do if it gets stuck?"

"I'll have to pull it out," he answered.

Becky returned with a crock of soap, a bucket of hot water, and an armful of clean towels. "How is she?" the girl asked as Olivia rose to take the items from her.

Conor looked up. "We're going to be out here awhile, I'm thinking."

"You'll save the calf, Mr. Conor," Becky said. "I know you will."

"I'll do my best."

Becky left the barn again, casting one last glance over her shoulder before she departed. Olivia sank down into the straw beside Conor, who was inside the cow up to his elbows. "How can I help?" she asked.

He shook his head. "You can't, love."

The minutes went by. Olivia watched as Conor worked to turn the calf around. He wasn't doing his cracked ribs any good, and she knew he must be in pain, but he did not show it.

By sheer strength, infinite patience, and only one or two curses, Conor finally got the calf in the correct position. With some strong tugging on his part, the newborn was pulled from its mother's body and jumped to its feet.

Olivia looked at Conor with relief and gratitude. "Thank you."

She leaned back against the side of the stall and watched the calf take a step toward Conor to butt his head against the man's hand with a soft moo.

"A hero," she murmured. "Who would have thought?"

He shot her a wry glance. Pushing the calf toward its mother, he fell back against the side of the stall beside her. "Don't let it get around. I have my reputation as a wicked sinner and prize bastard to think of."

She heard the defensiveness in those words. She studied his hard profile for a moment. "I don't think you're half as wicked as you pretend to be," she said softly.

"Aye, well, that's the thing about pretending." Pushing himself to his knees, he reached for the bucket of water then plunged in his arms elbow-deep to rinse off the blood. "If you do it long enough, you make it the truth."

Olivia's words turned out to be prophetic. Conor became a hero.

The girls were absolutely delighted by the calf, but it was Conor who received their devoted attention for the rest of the day. After a late breakfast, they insisted on taking him all around the place. They showed him everything, from the privy, which he'd already discovered on his own, to the swimming hole, which he hadn't. They dragged him through the orchard, they showed him how to slide down the haystack behind the barn. It felt good to be on his feet, but by the time Olivia rang the dinner bell, he was exhausted.

Olivia must have sensed it. After dinner, she sent the girls out to clean the henhouse. "It'll keep them busy until sundown."

"I'm glad to hear it." He eased back in his chair. "They're lovely girls, all of them. But they're wearin' me out."

She laughed as she set a basket of mending on the kitchen table and sat down. "Already? It's only been half a day."

"'Tis an injured man I am," he reminded her. "I'm not up to this yet."

"Mmm." She threaded a needle and pulled a skirt out of the basket, a skirt of faded gray. "I have a feeling that won't make any difference."

"Probably not," he agreed. "They'll probably have me climbing trees before the day's out."

She lifted her head and frowned at him. "You do, and I'll have your hide. I didn't spend four days and nights putting you back together so you could fall out of a tree a few weeks later and crack your ribs all over again."

"Worried about me?"

She sniffed. "Not at all. I'm just tired of trays and bedpans is all."

That was probably the truth. Now that he was up and around, he could see how much work she had to do each and every day, and he knew he'd only added to her burden. "I never have said thank-you for what you did for me."

She began pulling the needle back and forth through the fabric. "No need. Most folks would have done the same."

Conor doubted it. Most people would have just ridden on. But he was beginning to realize that Olivia's cloak of propriety protected a very soft heart. He wasn't used to it, that softness, he didn't trust it. The world was so full of hard knocks and jagged edges.

He studied her with her head bent over her sewing.

Her hair was braided today, rolled at the back of her head, and secured with a bow of green ribbon. He was glad she had taken his words to heart and changed the way she wore her hair. The light from the kitchen window behind her shot glimmers of red through the delicate tendrils at her neck. Her hair fascinated him because it looked so soft, as soft and thick and luxurious as sable.

"Why aren't you married?" he asked, then wished he hadn't.

She paused in her sewing. "Didn't have much of a chance," she answered without looking up. "My mama died when I was fourteen, and it hit my daddy pretty hard. My brothers, too. There . . ." She hesitated, then went on, "There wasn't time for barbecues and parties and the like."

Conor got the feeling that she'd originally started to say something else, but had changed her mind. He wondered what.

"The war came when I was nineteen, and of course, all the local boys joined up to fight," she went on. "Nowadays, there aren't many men left round here. We lost so many, and the ones that came home who didn't have wives already took a look around, and decided things had to be better out West."

He could understand that. It sounded a lot like Ireland after the famine. "Don't you ever think that, Olivia?"

She looked up. "What? That things might be better someplace else?" She shook her head. "No, never. This is my home." She tilted her head to one side and her eyes softened dreamily. "There's nothing prettier than the hills all green in the spring, and nothing smells sweeter than wild honeysuckle in the summertime. Besides, most folks who think things are better someplace else are just running away from something, and they usually find that whatever they're running from is still with 'em when they get there."

Her words hit him like a punch. "You're a wise woman, Olivia."

"No, Mr. Branigan. That's not wisdom. Just common sense."

He studied her face, seeing the contentment of her expression. 'Twas a rare gift indeed that she had. The ability to be happy. He envied her that. God, how he envied her. "Somehow, I don't think there's anything common about you," he murmured.

"You must feel that way, too. I know you miss Ireland, I can hear it in every word you speak. Don't you ever want to go home?"

Want it? Conor closed his eyes. He could see the mist rising over Derry fields, every shade of gray and green. He could hear the mournful melody of Irish whistles and *Uilleann* pipes. "'Tis not a question of wanting," he said dully, opening his eyes. "I can't go home." He shook his head and looked down, frowning at his hands. "I can't ever go home again."

That afternoon, Vernon received another telegram from New York, this one far less patient and far more demanding than its predecessor. He smothered a curse and glanced at his wife, who sat in the chair beside him.

The shafts of sunlight through the lattice wall of the gazebo formed a crisscross pattern on her apple-green dress, but a frothy lace parasol shielded her face from the rays, while the fan in one hand and the glass of cool lemonade by her side helped her deal with the stifling heat she hated so much. "Well?" Alicia asked. "What does it say?"

He forced himself to smile. "I think your father

misses you. He's insisting that we not postpone our annual visit."

"How delightful. No doubt he wants to know how this railroad you two dreamed up is coming along," she answered, slanting him an innocent look.

"If that's the case," Vernon answered, careful to keep his irritation from showing, "I don't see why he's insisting on having me go all the way up there. He wants me to meet with the investors, he says. It's such a waste of time, nothing but shaking hands and making small talk. I can't afford to be away just now."

"Well, I shall be grateful for the change of scene. It's bad enough to be stuck here in this dull little backwater, but to be forced to endure this heat passes all bounds. I don't see why we can't live in New York anyway. At least then we could go to Newport in the summer."

"You know why. Alicia, this isn't going to be a backwater forever. I'm going to build a new Atlanta right here. You just have to be patient."

He could tell she was not pacified by that promise. His wife might look as luscious as a spoonful of whipped cream, but Vernon knew she possessed the same iron will as her father when it came to getting her own way. "It seems to me we've had this talk before," she said. "Several times now."

The reminder that this railroad scheme was already four years in the making made Vernon want to grind his teeth. But he did not. Alicia was watching him, clearly expecting a reply. "I know how much our annual trip to New York means to you, and I know how much you miss your father," he said. "We'll go if you want it so badly."

She smiled. "Thank you, darling. And I'll try to be more patient."

He took her hand in his. "You've been wonderful. I don't how you manage to put up with me."

"Because you are my husband, and I love you," she answered, a touch of warmth creeping into her voice. "We'll leave in the morning."

She rose and left the gazebo. Vernon watched her cross the expansive green lawn toward the antebellum mansion her daddy's Yankee money had paid for, and he couldn't help wondering what his wife really felt about him. It only mattered because Hiram worshiped the ground his daughter walked on, and Vernon knew if he didn't keep her happy, he'd be in a heap of trouble.

He leaned back in his chair and stared down at the telegram. Alicia was getting more impatient with each month that passed. More important, so was her father. He knew this waiting game with Olivia had to end soon.

An image of Olivia as a child flashed through his mind. She'd always been a shy girl, and there had been times when he'd actually felt sorry for her. He remembered the time her cat had been caught in a fox trap, and how he'd helped her get it out, and how she had looked up at him with worshipful gratitude in her brown eyes.

He'd watched her grow up, and for a while, he'd thought that maybe he'd marry her. She came from one of Louisiana's oldest families; she could have given him the respectability he craved. Samuel Maitland's money had made it all even more appealing.

He'd wanted to court her; he'd offered to marry her. And Samuel Maitland had laughed at him. Laughed. A corrosive anger rose within him at the galling memory, burning away any notions of being softhearted about Olivia.

Vernon scowled and crushed the telegram in his hands into a ball. He now had all the wealth, respectability, and power he'd ever wanted, and nothing was going to take those things away from him, especially not memories of a time when he'd had a stupid hankering for Samuel Maitland's daughter. That was all in the past, he told himself firmly. Once he got back from New York, he would do whatever he had to do to force her out.

While Conor spent the afternoon taking a much-needed nap, and the girls cleaned the chicken coop, Olivia took a walk through her orchard. She cleared away the fallen leaves and rotting fruit from the half-dozen trees that were dying; but as she worked, her mind was not on Vernon and his petty, obvious schemes to intimidate her. Instead, another man, a man more complicated and far more compelling, dominated her thoughts.

During their reading lesson that evening, Olivia watched him out of the corner of her eye as she poured tea for both of them. He was seated at the kitchen table, bent over the slate, frowning with intense concentration. Dissatisfied with his first awkward attempts at writing, he'd been practicing on that slate for several hours, writing the alphabet over and over.

Olivia was surprised to discover that, beneath his surface impudence, Conor was extremely disciplined, and even was a perfectionist.

She thought about his comment that afternoon that he couldn't go home, and she wondered what he had meant by that. He obviously missed his homeland a great deal. She also wondered why a man who could be both gentle and patient when dealing with her pesky nine-year-old daughter's stalling tactics at bedtime would choose to make his living hitting other men in a boxing ring.

She brought the two cups of tea to the table and set one before him.

He glanced up briefly. "Thanks."

She took a seat across the table, watching as he wrote on the slate, and she smiled when he made an exclamation of frustration and rubbed out the line of *G*s he had just written.

"You know," she murmured, "sometimes it's possible to try too hard."

He looked at her across the table and saw her smile. He tossed down the slate pencil with a sigh. "You're right. It's time for a break."

She shook her head and pulled the slate away from him. "No, it's time to stop for this evening. You've done enough for one night. Drink your tea."

Deprived of the slate, he had no choice. He leaned back in his chair, taking a swallow of the tea she had made. It was hot and strong and sweet, just the way he liked it. "This is very good tay, by the way."

"Thank you. My aunt Ella sends it to me. She knows I'm fond of it."

"Sends it? Where does she live?"

"Boston. My uncle Jarrod has a position there in a bank. They moved there from Alabama after the war."

He took another sip of tea. "Boston was where I landed when I came to America." He smiled. "Fresh off the boat, I was, so poor I didn't even have lint in my pockets."

Olivia laughed, and he gave her a frown of mock censure. "Don't you be laughing, lass. 'Tis no less than the truth."

"Of course," she said gravely, trying to assume a serious expression.

"So, there I was," he continued, "standing on the docks with my pack over my shoulder, when this grizzled old Donegal man came up to me. His name was Dan Sweeney. He said I looked a strong, strapping lad, and he asked if I wanted a job. I said I did, and he took me to this pub in Boston's Irish district. When we got inside, he pointed to this hulking brute and said, 'He's the champion, undefeated for a hundred and twenty fights running. Think you can send him down to the floor?' I said that would be no problem at all. Everyone in the pub laughed at that. They thought I was crazy."

Conor paused and grinned at her across the table. "They all bet against me. Ten minutes later, they weren't laughing anymore, and I had five dollars in my pocket. Only in America an hour, and I decided this was a fine country, indeed. A few months later, Dan and I started touring the boxing circuit."

"You've seen a great deal of the country, I imagine."

"I like to roam."

Olivia tried to understand how that might appeal. "I guess it must be exciting, in a way, traveling from place to place," she said. "But doesn't it become a bit tiresome after a while?"

"No. Dan and I travel the circuit five months a year. The rest of the time, I'm on my own. I'm free to go where I want, when I want."

"It sounds like a lonely life," she said softly.

His lips tightened, and he looked away. "Sometimes," he admitted.

Olivia studied his hard profile, thinking about what he had told her about his brother and sisters, and her heart went out to him.

When she'd first seen Conor lying in the road, he had seemed like the answer to her prayer. But his appalling language and frank confession about prison had convinced her she'd been mistaken. The past two days had given her reason to think again, and Olivia suddenly found herself in a quandary.

What if she asked him to stay on?

He was not what she would have chosen for a hired

hand. He was irreverent and caustic, cynical and sinful. He cursed, he drank, he was a hard man.

Yet, she was coming to realize that he might be what she needed. He seemed to have no obligations that would force him to leave. The way he'd handled the birth of the calf told her he knew about farm animals. He was strong, he was capable of hard work. Maybe he'd be willing to stay.

Her decision made, Olivia broke the silence that had fallen between them. "Mr. Branigan, I've been thinking about what you did with Princess and her calf, and I thought . . . that is, I was wondering if you might consider staying on after your ribs have healed."

"What?" He seemed startled. "Stay here?"

"Yes." She took a deep breath. "I could use some help around here, and you said yourself that you don't have a home of your own to go back to."

He stared at her in disbelief. "Are you offering me a job?"

"I've been wanting to hire someone to work on my place for months now," she went on in a rush, "but I haven't been able to find anybody. I'll need help bringing in my peach crop come September. I want to plow the south pastures and plant cotton in the spring. If I had two cash crops, there would be less risk. And someday, I'll put in another orchard. Pears, maybe."

"I make twenty-five dollars for every fight I win, and I usually win. What are you offering?"

Dismay clouded her face. "I can't afford to pay wages. My peaches bring in enough to pay the taxes on my farm, with only a bit left over for living on. But I can give you room and board. I know it's not much to offer, but at least you'd have a home, a place to hang your hat."

Conor didn't tell her a home was the last thing he wanted. A place to hang his hat meant facing the past, looking to the future. He couldn't do it. All he knew how to do was get through the days, one by one.

"The fact is, Mr. Branigan, that I can't run this farm by myself. I need someone to help me."

She looked up, staring at him with those soft brown eyes. She needed him, she was asking for his help. It was the kind of look that was both imploring and proud, the kind of look that could stir a man's conscience, provided he had one. Conor didn't, of course. He slowly shook his head. "No. Thank you for the offer, but I can't stay."

She bit her lip and looked down at the table. The silence lengthened as he stared at her lowered head, and he suddenly felt like a bastard. His defenses came up.

"I like my freedom," he said. "I like to be able to pick up and move on when I choose."

"It wouldn't have to be permanent," she said without looking up. "You would be free to leave whenever you wanted to, of course."

"Right. What if I felt like leaving the week before your harvest? Or in the spring, just before you wanted to plant that cotton of yours? Do you think I wouldn't feel obligated to stay?"

She didn't answer.

Irritated with her for needing his help, and angry with himself for feeling guilty about refusing to give it, he shoved back his chair and rose.

"I won't be tied down. I'm no good at commitments, I'm not dependable, and I'm not staying here. I can't. I'm sorry."

He strode across the kitchen to the back door without a backward glance, but he could feel her gaze follow him.

"I understand," she murmured as he walked out the door, but he knew she didn't understand at all.

12

NEAMH
Belfast, Ireland, 1862

    Conor leaned sideways, and the light brush of air against his cheek was the only part of the punch that touched him. He responded with a hard-knuckled right that sent Angus O'Farrell stumbling backward into the tables and chairs of the pub.

Laughing, the onlookers pushed Angus back into the open space that served as a boxing ring, hoping for a bit more sport than that, but Conor wasn't going to give it to them. Not tonight. Mary was waiting.

He could see her lovely face peeking through the doorway of McGrath's, and he decided it was time to stop tormenting poor O'Farrell. He evaded Angus's last swing, and hit him again, sending the fighter from Carrickfergus to the floorboards. The crowd gave a groan of disappointment that it was over so quickly. Conor made his way to the bar amid approving pats on the back, and grabbed his shirt, yanking it on but not bothering to button it.

He leaned against the bar, blood pumping through him like the pistons of a steam engine. He felt alive in every part of himself and genuinely happy for the first time in years.

He accepted a shot of paddy and a pint of ale from Colm McGrath, who looked even more grim than usual. Colm was sweet on Mary and knew that Mary was outside waiting for Conor. But Colm also knew that Conor's boxing brought people into the pub and made him money. The two men had been friends almost from the day Conor had arrived in Belfast seven years before, but Mary had changed that.

Conor downed the paddy and slammed the glass on the bar. He chased it with a long draught of the ale, but didn't finish the pint. No drink was worth keeping an angel waiting.

He made his way toward the door, pausing to shake hands with poor O'Farrell, who was slumped over a pint and looking a wee bit dazed still. Conor waved good-night to the lads and stepped out into the street.

She was right beside the door, and he pulled her into his arms for a quick, hard kiss, then glanced around for someplace more private. "Come on."

He put her arm through his and led her around the corner, down the side street, and into the alley behind McGrath's.

They turned to each other. He cupped her face in his hands, pulled her close, kissed her. The touch of her lips sent waves of pleasure through him, and he could tell by her response that she felt it, too. But it wasn't enough. He slid his hands down to her waist and pulled her closer; he opened her mouth with his and deepened the kiss.

Mary was a good Catholic girl, but Conor had already made her forget everything the priests said. More than once. They played a dangerous game, and the fires of passion had gotten out of control. More than once. But neither of them could stop it. He broke the kiss with a groan and a desperate gasp for air. "We can go to my flat," he said raggedly. "My mate's gone to England. Football tour."

"I can't." Her hands closed over his forearms, and for the first time ever, she pushed him away. "Not tonight."

Something in her voice caught him, tugged at his heart. Dread seeped into him like the chill of a damp Belfast winter. "Mary? What's wrong?"

She shook her head and drew a deep, steadying breath. "Nothing," she said and gave him a reassuring smile. "I just can't tonight. That's all. I'm sorry."

"It's all right, lass. I'll survive the night without you. If I get drunk enough."

He took her hand in his, and they leaned back against the brick wall of a tenement dingy from years of accumulated coal dust. Silence fell between them as they both tried to bank the fires inside themselves.

"I watched you fight," she said. "You're very good at it, you know."

He shrugged. "It's a job. That's all."

"You already have a job. Boxing is much more than that."

He did not reply, and both of them were silent again. In the distance, drunken laughter floated to them from McGrath's, mingling with the hacking cough of a flax mill worker from the broken window above their heads. Mary was right. Being a carpenter was his job, but boxing was something else. "'Tis the challenge of it, I suppose. The competition."

"That's not it," she murmured with a shake of her head. "There are things inside you, Conor, feelings that rage and seethe and strive to get out, passions that drive you that I don't understand, that I can't reach. You're seeking something, and I don't know what it is. Sometimes, you frighten me."

Startled, he looked at her, and he saw the apprehension in her face. He turned and reached out to touch her cheek, pale and translucent in the moonlight. "Christ, Mary, what does that mean? You afraid of me? I love you, lass. I'd never hurt you."

He brushed his thumb across her lips, felt her tremble. "No, it's yourself you hurt," she said against his hand. "I heard about the meeting."

Conor lowered his hand and looked down at the ground between them. "It was all just talk. You know how it is. A few pints and all the lads get worked up, start singing about dear Ireland with tears in their eyes and start talking freedom. It's harmless enough."

"The Brotherhood isn't harmless, and you know it. If you follow the Fenians, they'll destroy you."

"You've been listening to Father Keenan again."

"Irish Republican Brotherhood." Her voice rose, suddenly filled with an anger so unlike her. "It sounds sane enough, but it's not."

"And this is?" He made a sweeping gesture with his arm, his own anger rising at the dung heaps, urine, and raw sewage of the Belfast slums surrounding them, Catholic and Protestant ghettos that were the bastard children of Britain's industrial revolution.

Mary refused to look at the squalor. "The Church will excommunicate you," she whispered. "You'll be barred from *Neamh*."

Conor looked into her lovely face. Sweet Mary, who worried more about the destination of his soul than he ever would. "Mary," he murmured, curling the tendril of hair at her cheek around his finger, its beauty a sharp, sweet contrast to the bruises on his hand. It was the hair of an angel, a gloriously rich mixture of red and gold that when loose could cover him like sunlight. He pulled her closer. "Mary," he said against her lips, "*Neamh* is not where I'll be going when I die. You're the closest thing to heaven I'll ever see."

She gave a tiny sob against his mouth and pulled back. "It doesn't have to be that way."

"What would you have me do? Put the British yoke on my shoulders and work their stolen land like some dumb, mindless animal? Or toil in the factories they've built, live in the wretched slums they've made, and pretend that I'm very happy to be a subject of the Crown?"

"I'd have you make a life for yourself, man. A hearth, a home, a family. I'd have you leave the past behind and think of the future."

To Conor, it was the same thing. "I can't forget. I won't forgive."

"I know," she said on a soft sigh of resignation and pain. She turned and sagged back against the wall. "But you can't win this fight, Conor. They'll break you." She paused, then added softly, "I can't bear to watch it happen. Not to you."

From the pub, the drunken laughter faded away, and a song began.

I wish I had you in Carrickfergus, if only for nights in Ballygrand. . . .

Angus had obviously recovered enough from his defeat to raise the lads in song.

I would swim over the deepest ocean, the deepest ocean, to be by your side.

"Colm asked me to marry him."

Six words, and the world opened beneath his feet.

He felt himself falling into a dark abyss. "What did you say?"

Straightening away from the wall, she faced him. "Are you going to stay in the Brotherhood?"

He looked into her face, and he knew what she was thinking. "Mary, don't. For God's sake, don't make me choose."

"I have to, Conor!" she cried. "I can't live with the uncertainty. I can't spend my nights pacing the floor, wondering if you're going to come home, knowing that one night, you won't." She paused and took a deep breath. "If you stay in the Brotherhood, I'm going to marry Colm. It's that simple."

He felt all his joy slipping away, leaving him more empty than he'd ever thought he could be. He should have known this would happen; he should have seen it coming. He'd thought he could have both, but he could not. Even O'Bourne, who had recruited him into the Brotherhood two years before, had warned him that women and causes did not mix. He hadn't believed him then. He looked at Mary, pale and resolute, and he believed him now.

He had to say something. "Colm's a fine man."

"You're not even going to try to stop me, are you?" she asked. There was no surprise in her voice, but there was pain. He heard it, he felt it, but he could not ease it.

Colm was a good man. He wasn't. Colm could offer Mary something. He couldn't. Colm owned a pub, the only business in a Belfast slum that ever prospered. He had enough money to support her, to give her the hearth, home, and children she wanted. She would always know that at dawn Colm would be lying beside her, not dead in some alley or ditch with a British bullet in him. Life was hard enough, and she deserved at least that much. Conor knew he could never give it to her.

He couldn't give it to any woman. He'd been a fool to ever dream otherwise.

His lips tightened and he shook his head, a movement that tore his heart in half. "No," he answered. "I can't give up what I believe in, Mary. Not even for you."

"I love you, Conor." She reached up and touched his cheek. "Good-bye," she murmured, and stood on tiptoes to kiss him quickly, then she turned away. "God bless."

He watched Mary as she walked down the alley, picking her way carefully on the cobblestones that were slick from years of accumulated filth. Mary, who was a slender and graceful flower that had somehow grown out of the Belfast dung heaps. Mary, who was the only truly good and beautiful thing in an evil and ugly world. She paused at the corner, and he thought for a moment she would turn and look at him one last time. But she went on, disappearing from his view, and he had the sick feeling he had just thrown away his only chance at heaven.

13

During the next few days, Olivia said nothing more about her offer of a job or Conor's refusal. She continued teaching him to read, and he made rapid progress. He also grew stronger with each passing day. He began taking walks every morning, each one longer than the last. The girls sometimes accompanied him, but often he went alone.

The girls' worship of Conor did not lessen as the days passed, but only seemed to strengthen with time, forging a bond that worried Olivia. She knew the closer they got to him, the harder it was going to be when he left. Yet, without a father, the girls had missed so much, and when she watched them together, she just couldn't bring herself to put a stop to the friendship.

She was fiercely protective of her girls, but she knew she couldn't always protect them from heartaches. They would be disappointed when he left, but they would get over it. And she'd find someone else to help her, someone steady and stable, someone God-fearing and hard-working who didn't swear, didn't drink, and didn't have smoky blue eyes that made her weak in the knees.

Olivia lifted the ax in her hands and brought it down toward the log on the stump in a clumsy swing. The blade sank into the wood far enough to get stuck, but not far enough to split the log. It didn't matter that she chopped wood nearly every day, she never got any better at it.

Asking him to stay was a stupid idea anyway, she thought as she began working the blade free. It was for the best that he was leaving soon. She and the girls didn't need his help. They were managing just fine. Olivia reached for the wedge, jammed it into the crack she'd made in the log, then straightened and glanced up at the sky overhead. "Just fine," she repeated aloud. "We don't need him."

She pushed back her broad-brimmed hat and glanced around, her gaze lingering on the dilapidated barn, the crooked fences, and weathered outbuildings. Even in the soft light of dawn, they looked old and tired.

Her shoulders slumped. Suddenly, she felt as worn and weary as her surroundings. It didn't make any difference what she wanted. Conor was leaving. That choice was not hers to make.

She had made her choice a long time ago. She looked at the garden surrounding her, seeing the overgrown rose arbors, misshapen boxwood hedges, and battered gazebo for what they were: the pathetic vestiges of what had once been a beautiful and gracious plantation.

She could remember her mother giving cotillions in this garden—a graceful figure moving amid the crowd in a cloud of apricot silk. Olivia looked down at the dull gray skirt and the heavy leather work gloves she wore, and she sighed. What would her mother say if she could see Olivia now?

She'd be scandalized to see her daughter wearing a man's gloves and chopping wood, when she had been born and bred to play the piano and host garden parties. But after her mother's death, there had been no music, there had been no parties in this garden.

She could remember when all the slaves had departed in '63. Only Nate had stayed on—dear, dependable Nate. She'd given him twenty acres of prime land for his own farm, but she knew he hadn't stayed because of that. Twenty-one then, she had watched the other slaves go, and she had realized the truth she'd been shielded from all her life—that slaves weren't happy being slaves, that up-country white folks didn't care what happened to the plantations, and that the beauty and grace of her childhood had been a false and fragile existence all along.

She could remember the anguish that had etched deeper into her father's face with each passing year—a man lost without his wife, bereft without his sons, bewildered without his way of life, trying to drown the pain in Kentucky bourbon, and later, cheap moonshine.

Olivia could picture him on the day they'd heard Lee had surrendered at Appomattox—high on a ladder only a few feet from where she was now, waving a bottle and singing "Look Away, Dixieland," at the top of his lungs, before he came crashing down amid the camellias, his back as broken as his spirits.

She and Nate had tended him for those six agonizing weeks, watching his life ebb slowly, relentlessly away as he refused to eat, refused to bathe or shave himself, wanting only to die, and hating her and Nate for keeping him alive. They had buried him in the family plot beside her mother, beside the wooden markers Nate had made for her brothers' graves.

She had wandered through her empty house and her empty days, aimless and lost, clinging to the remnants of her faith and trying to find a purpose to her life. Her family was gone, and she had no one. Nate was a staunch and loyal friend, but he could not replace the family she had lost. Then, that summer, the girls had come to live with her, and she had found the purpose she'd been seeking. Now, she had a new life, made from the ashes of the old.

Conor's words came back to her like an echo. *I like my freedom.*

Well, soon he would have all the freedom he wanted, and she would go on as she always had. If she didn't find anyone to help her, she'd carry on without help.

Peachtree might not be a gracious plantation anymore, but it was hers. She was going to hang on to it, even though that meant she'd have to fix her own roof and pick her own peaches. When the time came, she prayed she'd find the courage to do both. Olivia lifted the ax and went back to work.

There were a few things Conor just couldn't tolerate, and watching a task being done wrong was one of them.

He stared out the kitchen window that looked out on the side of the house, watching Olivia's pathetic attempts at log-splitting, and he felt that irritating and inconvenient prick of conscience. He knew how hard she worked; he knew how difficult things were for her. He couldn't stay, but hell, he was healthy enough now to split a few logs. It was the least he could do.

He went outside and rounded the corner of the house to the woodpile.

Olivia looked up as he approached. "Mornin'. You're up early."

He studied her as she clumsily swung the ax again, missing the log altogether, and he shook his head. It was a wonder, indeed, that she didn't chop her foot off. He walked to her side.

"What are you doing?" she asked as he took the ax from her hand.

"I can't stand it." He gently pushed her a safe distance away. "I just can't stand it. The way you chop wood is a disgrace, it is, indeed."

"What are you talking about?" Olivia asked, watching as he walked back over to the stump.

He looked over his shoulder at her and smiled, an instant of dark blue eyes and wicked humor, then turned and swung the ax, hitting the log dead center. Two more quick blows of the ax, and the log split, falling away from the stump as two pieces of firewood. He looked over at her again, his features as seriously innocent as a schoolboy's.

"Show-off," she accused; but she smiled as she pulled several pieces of wood and kindling from the small stack she'd already chopped, and walked away.

The girls weren't up yet, and the house was quiet, except for the steady, measured sound of the ax. Olivia pulled off her gloves and started a fire in the stove with the wood she'd brought in, but as she made breakfast, she couldn't help watching him through the open window.

His profile to her, he worked at a steady pace, without wasted effort. She thought of her own clumsy attempts, of how long it took her every morning to do what he did so effortlessly.

He paused and set down the ax. Unbuttoning his shirt, he pulled it off then tossed it aside. He wiped the sweat from his brow with one forearm, balanced another log on the stump, and resumed his task. Olivia noticed the flex and play of his muscles as he worked, fascinated by the chiseled contours of his broad back and shoulders, and the strength in his arms as he swung the ax. He moved with a masculine grace and strength that were fascinating to watch. That warm aching feeling returned, and she leaned against the counter, breakfast forgotten.

A sound above her head startled Olivia out of her reverie. She glanced up at the ceiling and heard the sound of footsteps. The girls were up.

Olivia shook her head, chiding herself. She didn't have time for idle daydreaming. She turned away and began to set the table, forcing herself to concentrate on that rather than the intriguing view out of her window.

Carrie was the first one down the stairs. "Mornin', Mama," she said, and immediately caught sight of Conor through the window. She ran to the counter and hoisted herself up, her feet dangling in the air. "Mornin', Mr. Conor!"

"For heaven's sake, Carrie, don't shout," Olivia remonstrated. She watched as Conor laid down the ax and walked to the window.

"Good morning, *mó cailín*," he said to the child, and rested his forearms on the sill. "Why don't you come on out here and help me stack this wood for your mother?"

Carrie glanced at Olivia over one shoulder. "Can I, Mama?"

Olivia nodded, and Carrie slid down from the counter. She raced out the back door, and within moments she and Conor were stacking wood, side by side. Olivia watched them together and again felt a pang of uncertainty. Perhaps she should put a stop to things now and send Conor Branigan on his way.

When Becky came down with Miranda a few minutes later, she sent them out to feed the chickens and bring in the eggs, then she made a pan of corn bread, listening to the conversation going on outside.

". . . and Bobby McCann said I couldn't go fishing with them 'cause I'm a girl." Carrie's voice rose indignantly. "I don't know what that's got to do with it. I've caught bigger fish than Bobby plenty of times."

"You know how to fish?" Conor asked.

"'Course I do. Nate taught me."

"Nate? Your mother's farmhand, wasn't he?"

"He lived down by the creek, and we used to go fishing all the time. But he died last summer."

Olivia heard her daughter's heavy sigh, and she knew what was coming. She walked over to the window and watched as Carrie hung her head.

"And now I don't have anybody to go fishing with," she ended, so forlornly that Olivia felt a pang of guilt. Second to climbing trees, fishing was the child's favorite pastime, and there had been little time for Olivia to take her.

Conor knelt down to Carrie's eye level. "We'll have to go sometime," he said.

Carrie's sad expression immediately vanished. "Really? When? Can we go today?" Her voice rose eagerly with each question.

"We'll ask your mother. She and your sisters may want to come along."

"Becky and Miranda don't know how to fish."

"Well, then I guess we'll have to teach them, won't we? Besides, we're bound to get hungry, and I'll bet your mother would bring along a fine picnic basket." His voice rose slightly. "Maybe some of that fried chicken of hers, and that blackberry pie she makes that's so good."

He looked over his shoulder at Olivia and grinned, making it plain he knew she had been listening to every word.

"I'll think on it," she called back, and turned away from the window.

In offering to take Carrie and her sisters fishing, Conor got more than he bargained for. Miranda couldn't bear the thought of drowning those poor little worms, and refused to fish until he had convinced her that they didn't feel a thing and were very happy living inside of catfish. Becky couldn't seem to keep her line from tangling in every tree in the vicinity or getting it wrapped around every log and rock in the water. Carrie just wanted his attention. Between the three of them, he was quite busy.

Olivia sat on the grass in the shade, and she couldn't help laughing as she watched him race back and forth along the bank of Sugar Creek, moving from one girl to another, with Chester constantly getting in the way. Just as he'd toss out his own line and get comfortably settled, one of them would need help. He baited their hooks, disentangled their lines, replaced their lost sinkers; and he never got the chance to catch a single fish of his own.

After about two hours of this, he called a halt. He walked over to Olivia's side and sank down beside her, leaving the girls to fend for themselves. But they didn't want to continue fishing without him, and after pleading and cajoling failed to move him, they wandered off, taking Chester with them, giving Conor at least a few moments of peace and quiet.

"Bobby McCann must be a smart young lad," he mumbled, falling back into the soft grass with a groan.

Olivia laughed. "Don't tell me that Conor Branigan, prizefighter, is worn out by three girls—again?"

He turned his head and looked up at her. "I told you before, Olivia, I'm an injured man."

"Un-uh," she said, with a shake of her head that told him she didn't accept that excuse. "That was a week ago. Besides, I saw you chop all that wood this morning. You'll have to come up with something better than that."

"All right." He sat up and reached for the picnic basket. "I'm weak from lack of food," he said, flipping back the lid.

He began rummaging in the basket. "Fried chicken. Brilliant idea, that. Blackberry pie. Another brilliant idea." He lifted a loaf of bread and inhaled the fresh, mouth-watering scent of it, then he glanced at her.

"When I was in prison, this is what I missed the most."

Olivia stared at him. "Bread?"

He nodded and closed his eyes, savoring again the scent of the loaf in his hand. "Fresh bread and butter," he said dreamily. "And hot water. I missed that almost as much."

He reached into the basket for a knife and the lump of butter she'd brought, then unwrapped it from its covering of damp cloth. He tore a piece of bread from the loaf and spread a thick coating of butter over it. "When I was in prison, we got bread, but—" He stopped abruptly, not wanting Olivia to know about the bread, not wanting her to know that they'd told him to beg like a dog to get it, and he had.

"What?" she prompted. "You got bread, but . . . ?"

"But it wasn't like this," he said instead. "It was dark and coarse and stale. That first morning I woke up here, the smell of fresh bread was the first thing I noticed, and I thought for a second the angels had made a mistake." He looked up and gave her an impudent smile. "Sent me the wrong direction, you know."

"Is that what you think heaven smells like?" she asked, leaning back with her weight on her arms. "Fresh bread?"

He took a hefty bite from the piece in his hand. "Absolutely," he answered, his mouth full of bread. "I'm convinced of it."

"I guess everybody has their favorites."

He leaned closer to her. "What's your favorite, Olivia?" he asked teasingly.

She thought about that for a moment. "Well, I'm rather partial to pralines, myself. I know there just have to be pralines in heaven."

"What are pralines?"

"A sort of candy."

He watched as she closed her eyes and licked her lips as if savoring the remembered taste. He could not move, he could only stare at the upward curve of her mouth and the exposed, creamy skin of her throat, his body taut.

"Pecans," she drawled in that languid voice that sent a jolt of pure lust through him. "Butter, brown sugar."

She opened her eyes. He felt certain his thoughts must be written on his face, but she only smiled at him, seemingly unaware. He struggled for something to say. "You'll have to make them."

"Oh, the girls will love that. I haven't made pralines for quite a while."

The girls. A nice, safe topic. He asked the first question that came into his head. "How did they end up living with you?"

Olivia sat up and turned to look out at the creek. "Their mother, Sarah, was my best friend. She died in '65, and I took the girls in."

"What about their father?" Conor asked. "Did he die in the war?"

"Yes." She sighed, looking out at the creek. "His brother couldn't pay the taxes on their place, so he put it up for auction and went out West." She looked over at Conor, her eyes dark and sad and hauntingly lovely. "He didn't want the girls. He didn't want the responsibility."

Conor understood what made a man shy away from responsibility. He'd struggled through madness and desperation; he'd experienced hopelessness and grief; he understood those demons well. But to let them take hold when there was family who needed you was unforgivable. If the demons ever got him, Conor wanted no one left behind who cared enough for him to suffer for it.

"If I hadn't taken the girls in," Olivia went on, "they'd have been sent to the orphanage, since there was no kin who wanted them. I couldn't bear the thought of Sarah's girls in an orphanage. I had this big house. It just seemed like the right thing to do."

"You've a soft heart, Olivia."

She shook her head. "I needed those girls as much as they needed me," she said, a catch in her voice. "I was alone, I had no family left, and I was so lonely. I love those girls, Mr. Branigan. They're my girls, now."

He looked into her eyes, as soft and dark as melted chocolate, and he wondered what his life might have been like if somebody, anybody, had done that for him when he was a lad. Maybe he'd have found the contentment he saw in Olivia, maybe he'd have found peace, maybe he wouldn't have betrayed everything he valued. Maybe.

Conor knew it was futile to think of what might have been. He'd made his choices, and he had to live with them now. It was too late for anything else. It was just too late.

*   *   *

They had their picnic and did some more fishing, then Conor took a nap while Olivia and the girls played tag with Chester.

By the time they packed up the gear and walked back toward the house, the sun was just beginning to set. It was a glorious summer evening, with a slight breeze that kept the heat from being unbearable.

Olivia walked in front along the well-trodden path, the picnic basket hooked over one arm, picking wildflowers for the supper table with Miranda and Becky. Carrie and Conor followed, Carrie proudly clutching the string of catfish, most of which were hers.

When they reached the orchard, Olivia paused. "I'm going to stop a minute and have a look at the peaches," she told her daughters. "You girls go on up to the house and get cleaned up for supper."

They walked on ahead. "Carrie, you be sure and put those fish right in a bucket of water," she called. "And you girls put away those fishing poles Mr. Conor made for you."

Conor lingered to walk through the orchard with her as she inspected the ripening fruit.

"I've noticed there aren't any other peach orchards around here," he commented.

Olivia smiled and patted the trunk of one tree with her hand. "My daddy planted this orchard when I was thirteen. It was for my mother. Daddy used to call her 'Peaches' because she loved the fruit so much, and he renamed this plantation Peachtree for her." She looked over at Conor, and her smile widened. "Everybody thought he was crazy to waste good acres on anything but cotton. But Daddy, well, he always did things his own way. As it turned out, these trees were a blessing."

"Why is that?"

Olivia faced him, leaning back against the tree. "After the war, Daddy died, and I had no income. I needed money desperately. The Yankees came in and started running things, and taxes went sky-high. All the slaves were gone, of course, so there was no one to till the fields or plant cotton except me, and I couldn't do it by myself."

She gestured to the trees all around them. "But the orchard was already well established. After my mama died, my daddy lost all interest in the orchard, so I had been taking care of it, grafting new trees, having them pruned, and seeing to the harvest. It's my mother's legacy, and I felt it was important to preserve it. Now, this orchard gives me a good cash crop nigh on every year without too much work. It's a crop I can manage myself." She shot him a wry glance. "Well, except for picking time, of course."

"'Tis a bit hard to pick peaches when you can't climb a ladder."

"Nate used to do it for me, before he died." She gave an irritated sigh and looked up at Conor. "It's such a bother, being afraid of heights. I hate it. It's a weak and silly fear."

"What are you going to do this year, Olivia?"

"I don't know." She turned her face away, too proud to ask for help again. To her disgust, her voice was a bit shaky when she added, "Do it myself, I imagine. The girls will help me."

She straightened away from the tree without looking at him, and they walked through the rest of the orchard in silence.

At the edge of the orchard, he stopped walking and glanced back at the peach trees. Olivia also came to a halt, wondering why he had stopped.

He looked over at her. "How long?" he asked abruptly.

Bewildered, she stared back at him, not understanding the question. "What?"

"How long until they're ripe?"

"About a month."

They stared at each other, and she watched him frown at her almost as if he were angry. He raked a hand through his hair. "I'll stay long enough to help you bring your crop in," he said, walking past her before she could recover from her surprise enough to reply. "Then, I'll be moving on."

Olivia stared after him as he walked away, so astonished that it wasn't until he was out of earshot that she realized she hadn't even said thank-you.

That evening after supper, while Olivia and the girls went through the ritual of Saturday-night baths, Conor sat at the kitchen table with slate, pencil, and dictionary, writing down all the words he could think of that began with *C*, using the dictionary to look up the words he could not spell. After an hour of this, Conor decided his first conclusion about reading had been right all along. He didn't need to learn how.

After the girls were in bed, Olivia took her own bath, donned her nightgown and wrap, then went down the back stairs into the kitchen to check on his progress one last time before going to bed. She found him looking through the dictionary. "How's it going?" she asked.

He looked up, glaring at her in exasperation. "This dictionary doesn't have 'kitten' in it."

"Yes, it does," she said, smiling. "You'll find it under *K*."

"That doesn't make sense."

She laughed and sat down across the table. "Mr.

Branigan, you'll find a lot about the English language that doesn't make sense."

"Knowing the British, that doesn't surprise me."

"No political discussions, if you please," she admonished sternly, tapping the table with one finger. "Think of words that start with *C*."

Conor bent back over the paper again. "If 'cat' starts with *C*, 'kitten' ought to start with *C*," he grumbled.

Olivia choked back another bubble of laughter. Trust Conor always to have an opinion. She studied him as he wrote on the slate, his handsome face serious and intent, his attention focused on his task.

Though he'd been reluctant to learn to read at first, once he'd committed himself to the task, he was relentless. He asked innumerable questions, and he never seemed to forget the answers. But he also tended to be impatient and overly critical of his own efforts.

Though he was dissatisfied with his progress, Olivia knew he was progressing quite rapidly. In less than a week, he had memorized all the consonants and vowels and had begun learning simple words. A week from now, he would begin reading and writing simple sentences. A month from now—

In a month, he would leave. The peaches would be in, and he would go away. She was truly grateful that he was staying long enough to help her with her harvest, but as she studied him across the table, she wondered what it would be like when he no longer sat here with her in the evenings, when he had gone, and all she had was the memory of his presence.

Desolation suddenly swamped her, and she realized she would have nothing tangible to show he had been here at all. Like the Cheshire Cat in Carrie's story, he would vanish, and only the memory of his smile would remain.

He straightened in his chair with a sigh, bringing Olivia's attention back to the matter at hand. "Give me all the words starting with *C* that you have," she instructed.

He set aside his pencil. "'Cat,'" he said, reading from the slate before him. "'Cot,' 'cut,' 'call,' 'cost,' 'corn,' 'cold.'" He paused a moment. "'Kiss.'"

He looked up at her, and their gazes locked across the table.

"'Kiss' starts with a *K*," she whispered.

"Does it, now?" His gaze lowered to her lips. "Fancy that."

Olivia felt a sudden rush of anticipation and denial, pleasure and panic. Her pulse beat frantically in her ears like the rhythm of a runaway train. She lifted her hand as if to touch her mouth, then jerked it back.

The corners of his mouth lifted in a ghost of a smile, and he did what she'd almost done; he reached out and traced the line of her lips with the tip of his finger.

A quivering began deep inside her. Her lips parted, and she knew she should speak, should protest, should pull away. But she remained motionless and silent, awash in the sensation of his featherlight caress.

Was this carnality, she wondered, this raw ache, this intense pull? *He knows of this,* she thought, watching his gaze follow the deliberate motion of his finger back and forth across her lower lip. *He knows all about it.*

His hand moved to span her jaw, caress her throat. Then, slowly, he pulled away, leaving her in the aftermath of the sensations he had created, bereft and dazed and still waiting for a kiss that never came.

"'Tis getting late, I'm thinking."

Slowly, the low sound of his voice penetrated, and she found herself getting to her feet. "Of course," she mumbled. She rose, staring down at the table, her cheeks burning, unable to look at him.

"Tomorrow, we can go on to words beginning with *D*," she said. She shifted her weight from one foot to the other. "I don't know what made you decide to stay another month to help me bring my crop in. But I want you to know that I'm very grateful, and if there's any way I can repay you—"

"Go to bed, Olivia."

She obeyed the terse command, fleeing from the kitchen without a backward glance. But alone in her room, after she'd crawled into bed, she lay there with one arm around her pillow and her hand pressed to her lips, trying to relive that moment when he had touched her.

No man had ever touched her in such a way. Even Vernon had never dared to touch her like that. She thought of all the silly, whispered speculations she and Sarah had indulged in as girls. After Joe had begun courting Sarah, she'd confessed to Olivia that Joe had actually kissed her in the gazebo at Taylor Hill, but when asked to describe it, she had been unable to do so. "You'll find out, Olivia," she had whispered, with a secretive smile, a blush, and a delicious little shiver. "You'll find out."

But that was a long time ago, and Olivia was still waiting. Somehow, those intervening years had just slipped away. Somehow, moonlight and magnolias and kisses in a gazebo had never come her way. They had been denied her by the needs of her grieving father, kept from her by the turbulence of war, pushed aside by the priorities of day-to-day survival.

She thought of Conor, and longed for what had passed her by.

Olivia hugged her pillow tight. He was only staying a month, she reminded herself. And she knew she would never find out what Sarah had been talking about.

14

Troubled by vague and shadowy dreams during the night, Conor awoke feeling edgy and restless. Although it was barely dawn, he dressed and went for his morning walk.

He could not remember the specifics of his dreams the night before, but they unnerved him nonetheless. Vague whispers of the demons echoed in his mind, reminding him that they were still with him.

He walked, concentrating on the inane task of putting one foot in front of the other. He wanted to keep walking forever, away from this place, away from the past, away from himself.

But he could not. He'd made a promise to Olivia that he would stay until her harvest, that he would help her bring in her peaches. It was the first promise he'd made to anyone in a long time, and it was already smothering him.

Conor walked until the sun was up, until the restless feeling was gone. He turned and began retracing his steps toward the house. But as he passed the barn, another voice intruded on his thoughts, a voice that even raised in frustration was soft and drawling.

"Cally, you stubborn old mule, come back here!"

Conor walked around the corner of the barn and found Olivia there, standing beside a gaping hole in the pasture fence. She didn't see him. Hands on hips, she was watching the mule, who was trotting away from her across the yard and who obviously had no intention of returning to the confines of the pasture.

"Ornery," Olivia muttered as she started after the mule. "Just plain ornery."

Conor grinned and leaned one shoulder against the side of the barn as he watched her chase the mule around the yard, the skirt of her gray Sunday dress whipping behind her in the warm breeze. He knew she was trying to get the animal headed in the right direction, but Cally clearly had other ideas.

"Need some help?" he called as she paused for breath.

She turned around. "How long have you been there?"

"Long enough." He approached her, still grinning.

Olivia did not return his smile but gestured to the mule, who had paused about a dozen feet away. "Cally broke through the fence again. Darn mule, always getting loose."

She frowned at the animal. "I never should have bought you in the first place. I should have just let Elroy shoot you."

Cally tossed his head, not the least bit intimidated. He pawed the ground with one hoof as if beckoning her to continue the chase.

"Elroy?" Conor asked, pausing beside her. "Elroy Harlan?"

"How did—" She broke off, realizing the answer to her own question. "Elroy's the one you fought in that boxing match," she said, a note of disapproval creeping into her voice.

"At least I won the fight," he pointed out. "Elroy didn't even last one round."

She sniffed, unimpressed. "I'm not surprised he's been doing that boxing. He needs the money, I imagine. He used to own the land across Sugar Creek, but he lost his farm a few years back. Mean old coot, Elroy," she added. "Cally used to get out of his pasture and go runnin' off. One day, I saw him chasing Cally through the woods with his shotgun, yelling he was going to shoot him. He would have done it, too. I couldn't let that happen, and I told Elroy I'd take the mule off his hands. Paid two dollars for him, too." She shook her head and glared at Cally. "I think I got cheated."

Conor leaned closer to her. "If you go around the other side," he said in a conspiratorial whisper, "we'd have him surrounded."

She nodded. "All right, but don't be surprised if he manages to get away from both of us."

Fifteen minutes later, a disgruntled Cally was back inside the pasture, and Conor was examining the fence. "'Tis no wonder he got out," he told Olivia. "These boards are so loose, it'd only take a bit of pressure to pull the fence apart. Look."

He reached over the fence, made a fist, and slammed it against one of the boards. The nails holding the board to the fence posts popped out, and the board fell to the ground. "All the mule had to do was kick it once or twice."

"I know the fence is in pretty poor shape, but it seems like every time I nail one board back in place, another one comes down."

"Mama!" Becky's voice called from the back porch. "If we don't hurry, we'll be late for church."

Olivia glanced across the yard at her daughter. "I know, honey," she called back. "I've got to hitch the wagon first."

Conor pushed the board he'd knocked down back in place. "If you'll get me a hammer and some nails, I'll fix this fence while you're at church."

His offer seemed to surprise her. "You will?"

"Since I'll be staying another month, I might as well have something useful to do."

She smiled at him, that astonishing smile that always caught him off guard. "Thank you, Mr. Branigan."

"I do have one stipulation to make," he added. "Stop calling me Mr. Branigan. I have a first name."

She eyed him thoughtfully. "Does this mean we're becoming friends now?"

He looked out over the pasture. It had been a long time since he'd stayed anywhere long enough to have friends. "I guess it does," he admitted.

But as he watched her walk away, he admired the sway of her hips and remembered the softness of her mouth beneath his finger, and he thought friendship sounded a wee bit tame.

After Sunday services, Olivia would have taken the girls straight home, but Oren Johnson stopped her just outside the church. "Do you have a minute, Olivia? I wanted to talk with you."

"Certainly." She looked around for her daughters. Becky was standing on the church steps talking to Jeremiah, Miranda was enduring a round of cheek pinching from the Chubb sisters, and Carrie was huddled in a circle with Jimmy Johnson and Bobby McCann, concocting some form of mischief, she was sure.

"Becky," she called, but she had to repeat her daughter's name twice before Becky's attention was diverted from her friend. "Keep an eye on the girls. I'll be back shortly."

Becky nodded and turned back to Jeremiah as Olivia followed Oren away from the church along the dusty main street.

"I already told you that you could buy Princess's calf, Oren," she said, laughing. "You don't have to worry that I'll sell him to somebody else."

Oren shook his head. "This isn't about that calf, Olivia." He stopped and turned to her. "Has Vernon been making you any more offers about Peachtree?" he asked in a low voice, glancing around to make sure no one else was within earshot.

She nodded. "Just two weeks ago, he asked me again if I'd sell. I refused, of course. Why?"

"Has he been threatening you?"

"No. Not overtly." She met Oren's somber gaze. "The day after I refused his last offer, some of my peach trees were girded. It killed them, of course. I found some cigarette butts there, and I thought maybe it was the Harlan boys."

"It could have been them. Elroy and his boys work for Vernon."

She sighed. "It's so hard to believe."

"Why? Vernon's a greedy son of a—" He broke off at her disapproving frown. "Sorry, Liv. He's greedy. You know that."

"I know. But I've known Vernon all my life, and he wasn't always like that. He was kind to me when I was a girl, he was even sweet on me. I don't like thinking he would do something like this."

"Olivia, he might do even worse if you keep refusing to sell. You know how bad he wants that railroad deal, and you're the only one who could spoil his plans."

Oren glanced around uneasily. "I think Vernon's getting some pressure from his father-in-law to get this land thing settled."

"What makes you think so?"

"Vernon got a telegram two and a half weeks ago, and another one last week," he answered. Olivia instantly understood how Oren knew about the telegrams. His son worked at the telegraph office.

"Both telegrams were from Hiram Jamison," Oren went on. "That's why Vernon and his wife left for New York unexpectedly. They weren't planning to go this year, but for some reason, they changed their minds. They'll be gone about six weeks, according to his wife."

She couldn't help smiling. "Oren, you hear more gossip than Martha."

He grinned back at her. "Kate's sister is one of the maids over at Vernon's place, you know."

It was no wonder that news around Callersville became common knowledge within a day. It was more amazing than the telegraph itself.

Oren's grin faded. "If Vernon's father-in-law is getting impatient and starts putting the pressure on, Vernon could get nasty. Maybe you ought to move into town for a while."

Olivia shook her head. "I can't do that. I've got peach harvest in a month. Besides, nothing is going to happen until Vernon gets back."

"I wouldn't be too sure about that, Liv. Joshua and his brothers are still here to do Vernon's dirty work." He tugged on the brim of his hat. "Kate and I worry about you and the girls being out at Peachtree alone."

But she and the girls weren't alone. Olivia thought of Conor, and she thanked the Lord he had decided to stay another month. "We'll be fine. Vernon won't do anything to hurt me or my girls, or order Joshua to do so."

"I hope you're right," Oren answered.

"Thank you for telling me all this."

"No need. That's what neighbors are for. I'm just glad my land isn't on Vernon's proposed route for that railroad. Be careful, Liv."

They parted company at the church, and Olivia looked around for her daughters, but Miranda was the only one she found. The child was still hemmed in by the Chubb sisters. Deeming Miranda to be fine for the moment, if not exactly happy, she left the child there and went in search of the other two. Carrie's absence did not surprise her, but Becky's did. She had told her oldest daughter to watch the other two, and Becky was such an obedient girl. Leaving her sisters was so unlike her.

She went in search of Carrie first. She had a sneaking suspicion that she would find her daughter getting into mischief with Jimmy and Bobby, and when she found the trio kneeling in the dirt behind the church, around a game of marbles, her suspicion was confirmed. She gave all three of them a hide-blistering lecture about marbles on Sunday, and ended the game, much to Carrie's dismay. "I was on a roll, Mama," she protested, as Olivia dragged her away and left the boys to gather their marbles without her. "I was winning."

"Caroline Marie, if I've told you once, I've told you a thousand times, no marbles on Sunday. Shame on you for being so blasphemous."

Carrie tried, she really tried, to look penitent. She hung her head, she shuffled her feet. Olivia sighed. "Have you seen Becky?"

"She went for a walk down by the creek," Carrie answered, pointing to the nearby woods, "but she said she'd be right back."

"A walk?" Olivia repeated in surprise. It wasn't at all like Becky to go for a walk when she'd been told to watch her sisters. "Carrie, I want you to go find her while I fetch Miranda and bring the wagon around."

Carrie turned and ran toward the woods in search of Becky. Olivia retrieved poor Miranda from the clutches of the Chubb sisters, then walked with her across the street to where she'd left the wagon. Miranda climbed into the back, and Olivia drove the wagon to a point just past the church, where she had a clear view of the woods that surrounded Sugar Creek.

She and Miranda waited about five minutes before Becky and Carrie emerged from the woods and came running for the wagon. Carrie climbed into the back with Miranda, and Becky stepped up onto the wagon seat beside Olivia.

"Sorry, Mama," she said breathlessly without meeting Olivia's gaze.

"Becky, I'm surprised at you," Olivia chided gently as she snapped the reins and the wagon started down the road, "leaving your sisters alone like that. What on earth were you thinking?"

"I didn't intend to be gone that long," Becky mumbled. "And they weren't alone. There were people all around."

"That isn't the point. I told you to keep an eye on them."

"Well, how could she?" Carrie piped up. "She was too busy swappin' spit with Jeremiah Miller down by the creek."

"Carrie! You brat!" Becky wailed as Olivia jerked hard on the reins and brought the wagon to a stop.

She looked over at her oldest daughter and watched the girl blush to the roots of her hair. "Is that true?" she asked.

Becky ducked her head and squirmed on the wagon seat. Her embarrassment confirmed her sister's comment, even before she mumbled, "It was just one."

Olivia was dismayed.

She glanced at the two girls in the back, then over at Becky again. "We'll talk about this when we get home," she said tersely, and snapped the reins, sending the wagon into motion again. The trip home was a long and silent one. Even Carrie had nothing to say.

Conor noticed tension in the air the moment Olivia and the girls walked in the house. He had finished with his task of pounding nails into the rickety old fence, and was now working on what Olivia called his "homework," in preparation for his next lesson. He looked up from the slate as they came in, and one look at Olivia's face told him something was definitely amiss.

"Carrie," Olivia said, "you and Miranda go out to the garden and dig up a bucket of those sweet potatoes while Becky and I have a little talk. And cut me a few bunches of collard greens, too." She glanced at Conor. "Mr. Conor will help you."

Conor rose and followed Carrie and Miranda out the door, wondering what was going on. It didn't take him long to find out. They hadn't dug more than two sweet potatoes before Carrie gave him all the details, summing up the story with the words, "Becky's in big trouble."

"Mama's not happy," Miranda added.

Conor could well imagine. He remembered the first time his own mother had caught Michael in the hayloft with Maud O'Donnell and the furor that had ensued. Michael's punishment had been swift and severe. The willow switch, the questions, and the recriminations, followed by confession to Father Donovan and endless hours on his knees doing penance. Conor remembered how humiliating the questions had been, and how futile the punishments. Michael hadn't stopped fondling Maud, he'd just become better at not getting caught. Had his mother been alive when he began enjoying that particular activity, Conor knew he would have suffered the same fate Michael had. He also knew his mother's punishments wouldn't have stopped him either.

"Why do people want to kiss anyway?" Carrie asked, interrupting Conor's thoughts. "Seems like a silly thing to do, if you ask me."

Conor grinned. "Someday, you may not think so."

Carrie frowned at him, clearly skeptical. "Boys are okay," she admitted grudgingly. "They like to do all the fun things, like marbles and fishing and stuff. But I don't think I'd want to kiss one," she added doubtfully.

Conor dug up another sweet potato, brushed the dirt off, and added it to the pail. "So you think boys do fun things, do you?"

She nodded. "Jimmy's daddy built him a tree house last year, but he won't let me go up there. They said that's boy stuff, so I'm not allowed. If I had a tree house, I'd let them go up in it. Why won't they let me?"

Conor thought about that for a moment. "Maybe they think you ought to be playing with your girlfriends, doing girl things."

"You mean, like dolls?" Carrie's nose wrinkled with distaste. "Yuk!"

"What's wrong with dolls?" Miranda asked. "I like dolls."

"Boring," Carrie stated, dropping another sweet potato in the pail. "I think kissing would be boring, too. I can't understand why Becky would want to kiss

Jeremiah anyway. Last summer, she didn't even like him. She said he was skinny, and his voice was all weird."

"Maybe she's changed her mind about him," Conor suggested. "Maybe she likes him now."

"Guess so. But you'd have to like a boy an awful lot, wouldn't you? I like Bobby, but if he ever tried to kiss me, I'd slug him."

Conor studied the wee girl on the other side of the sweet potatoes, and he could well imagine the merry chase she was going to put Bobby McCann through someday. He almost pitied the poor lad.

While Carrie was talking with Conor about Becky's transgressions, Olivia was trying to deal with them. She studied her oldest daughter across the kitchen table, noting the girl's resentful frown and closed expression, and she had the feeling she wasn't dealing with them very well.

"This is not fair!" Becky cried. "Carrie's always getting in trouble, and you never say anything to her."

"That's not true."

"Yes, it is. She sneaked up and spied on me, then tattled to you. But you didn't say anything about that."

"I will deal with Carrie later," Olivia answered. "But right now, we are not talking about her. We are talking about you. I asked you to keep an eye on your sisters, and you disobeyed me. What if something had happened? What if Miranda had wandered off and gotten hurt?"

"Miranda didn't get hurt."

"But she could have. Anything could have happened, and you weren't there. Becky, I count on you to help me with the girls. I need you to be responsible."

"Why do I always have to be the responsible one?" Becky burst out. "Why do I always have to be the good girl? 'Becky, watch the girls.' 'Becky, bring in the eggs.' 'Becky, do this. Becky, do that!' I'm sick of it!"

Olivia stared at her daughter's flushed and angry face, too stunned to be angry in return. Never, not once in six years, had the girl ever raised her voice to Olivia, and she couldn't quite take in the fact that it was happening now. "I didn't realize you felt that way," she managed.

"Well, I don't want to be the good girl anymore," Becky went on defiantly. "I don't want to be bossed around and told what to do. I'm fourteen, and I'm old enough to think for myself."

She looked into her daughter's rebellious face, and she knew that this was something they had to discuss. But she was completely at a loss about how to do it. "Honey, you may think you know what you're doing, but you don't."

Becky's face hardened into even more stubborn lines, and Olivia knew she'd said the wrong thing. She cleared her throat and began again. "Becky, I love you, and because I do, I worry about you. Kissing is . . . "

Her voice trailed off, and she looked at her daughter with both misery and embarrassment. Lord, this was hard to talk about. How could she explain the facts of life to an innocent fourteen-year-old when she was just as innocent at twenty-nine? How could she caution Becky on matters that she had only the vaguest knowledge of herself? Her own mother hadn't been there to talk with her about kissing and boys.

She leaned forward, clasping her hands together on the tabletop, and made another attempt to discuss the situation rationally. "Becky, kissing is something a girl of your age should not be doing. It can . . . " *Lord, give me strength.* "It can lead to other things."

"How would you know?" Becky lashed out, as if she

could read Olivia's own private thoughts. "You never
had any beaux."

Olivia swallowed past the lump of hurt in her throat.
"That's true—"

"Just because you never had any beaux is no reason I
can't."

"I'm not saying you can't have any beaux. I'm just
saying that you're not old enough for that yet. You're
only fourteen. There's plenty of time. When you're sixteen—"

"Sixteen?" Becky railed. "That's two whole years!
What if there's another war and all the boys go off to
fight. I'll be an old maid."

She sounded so painfully dramatic, it almost made
Olivia want to smile. "Honey, there's not going to be
another war. And, believe it or not, two years is not that
long."

"Two years is forever!"

"I know it can seem like it, but it isn't."

Becky's stubborn expression did not soften, and
Olivia decided it was time to be firm. "You are not old
enough to go for walks with a boy, and certainly not
unaccompanied. That sort of thing can ruin a girl's reputation. As for Jeremiah, I thought he was a nice, polite
boy, but this incident is forcing me to revise my opinion. I think it would be best if you didn't see much of
him from now on."

"What do you mean?" Becky jumped up so fast, her
chair went skidding backward. "What about when
school starts? Jeremiah and I always go over to the
store and have peppermint sticks after school."

"I know." Olivia also rose to her feet. "I think it
would be best if that stopped for a while."

"And I think you're mean and hateful!"

Olivia felt her own temper flaring. "That was

uncalled for, Rebecca Ann," she said sharply. "This issue is not open for debate. For the time being, you will not be going anywhere with Jeremiah. I intend to discuss the situation with Lila, and make sure this does not happen again."

"What?" Stunned, Becky stared at her. "You can't. I'll be completely humiliated. Jeremiah will never speak to me again."

"Under the circumstances, I find that a blessing."

Becky's face crumpled into misery. "How could you do this to me?" she burst out. "I hate you!"

She ran out of the kitchen, sobbing, and slammed the door behind her.

Olivia jumped at the sound. She leaned forward, pressing her fingertips to her forehead, feeling defensive, angry, and very worried. There were times when being a mother was a very trying thing.

When Conor opened the back door and looked in, Olivia was standing at the kitchen counter, with one arm wrapped around a bowl and a spoon in her other hand. She was savagely stirring the contents of the bowl, and she barely spared him a glance.

"Is it safe?" he asked from the doorway.

"I don't know what you mean." She slammed the bowl down on the counter and reached for the canister of flour.

"The way Becky went flying out of here, I thought it might be a war all over again. I sent Carrie and Miranda after her, just to make certain she doesn't do something dramatic and stupid, like run away from home."

She began measuring flour into the bowl and didn't reply.

He entered the kitchen and set a pail of sweet

potatoes on the pie safe beside the door. He closed the door, then leaned back against it and studied her across the kitchen. He hadn't seen her this angry since she'd found out he was a prizefighter. She got angry about the oddest things. Prim and proper, starchy Olivia. "So, what's to be poor Becky's fate, then?" he asked.

Olivia shoved the canister of flour back in its place and began stirring the dough in the bowl. "I suppose Carrie told you everything."

"Every fascinating detail."

She bristled at that. "I'm glad you find it fascinating. When you have daughters of your own, I pray they give you no end of trouble."

Conor grinned. "Sure, that's the mother's curse," he said blithely. "When I was a lad and got into mischief, my mother always ended her lecture with the words, 'Conor, my son, when you have children of your own, may they give you half the grief you've given me.'"

She continued to stir the contents of the bowl and did not reply.

"What are you going to do?" he asked.

Olivia stopped taking out her anger on the cookie dough. "I'm going to make certain this doesn't happen again," she said, reaching for an egg. She cracked the egg against the side of her mixing bowl with unnecessary force. "I'm going to talk with the boy's mother."

"What?" Conor stared at her back in disbelief. "Have you no heart at all, Olivia?"

She tossed aside the broken pieces of eggshell, and whirled around. "What?"

"Talking to his mother." Conor shook his head. "How embarrassing for the lad. Talk to him, if you must, but leave his mother out of it."

"He should be embarrassed," Olivia replied hotly. "He should be ashamed."

"Why? The lad was only stealing a kiss from a pretty girl behind the church. 'Tis harmless enough, I'm thinking."

"Kissing is not harmless," she shot back. "It can lead to—"

He folded his arms across his chest, and looked at her with one raised eyebrow, waiting for her to finish.

She pressed her lips together and turned away. "Becky's too young for that sort of thing," she said, cracking another egg into the bowl. "She's only fourteen."

"It was just a kiss. How old were you when you got your first kiss, Olivia?"

She began stirring again and didn't answer. He studied her rigid back and thought of that morning when she'd rubbed that liniment into his skin, and how his response to her touch had shocked her. He thought of last night when he had touched her lips and she had looked at him with wide, dazed eyes. He wondered if Olivia had ever been kissed in her life. Suddenly, he wanted an answer to his question. He wanted it badly. "How old, Olivia?"

"I don't think that's any of your business."

"And I don't think you've ever been kissed."

"I have, too." She picked up a bottle of vanilla and yanked out the cork. She dumped a spoonful of the brown liquid into the bowl. "Twice," she added, slamming the bottle down. A spray of vanilla spilled onto her hand and across the wooden counter.

He laughed out loud. "Twice? Two whole times?"

The egg came flying at him before he knew what was happening—but Conor was a prizefighter. He had quick reflexes, and he knew how to duck. The egg sailed over his head and hit the door with a splat.

White, yolk, and broken shell slid toward the floor. He whistled, then straightened, and grinned at her. "Good aim, but too slow. Care to take another shot?"

"Must you always be so mocking?" she demanded, her voice shaking with anger.

He began walking toward her, watching as she took a step back and hit the counter behind her. He stopped a foot in front of her and spread his arms wide. "Well, go on, then. I'm ready."

"What?"

"You've been kissed twice. Give me the benefit of your expertise. Show me how it's done."

"I will not!"

He studied her shocked and outraged expression and nodded slowly. "Just as I thought. Not a single kiss to your name."

She lifted her chin and scowled at him. He responded with a wicked smile, and waited.

"All right, then," she said, unexpectedly rising to the challenge of that smile. She stood on her tiptoes, touched her lips to one corner of his, and moved back again, so quickly that he almost missed the whole thing. "There."

"You call that a kiss?" He shook his head. "Olivia, I don't know what that was, but it wasn't a kiss."

She flushed pink, and a pained expression crossed her face. "There's no need to make fun of me. Not all of us have your . . . your . . . "

"My what?"

"Your capacity for sin," she snapped.

"Kissing is a sin, is it?"

"I'm sure it would be, the way you would do it."

He threw back his head and laughed. "God, I hope so."

She didn't share his amusement. "You know all about it, of course. No doubt you've kissed lots of women."

She started to turn away, but he lifted his arms to brace them against the counter, trapping her. He leaned closer, inhaling the scent of vanilla. "My fair share," he murmured. "Would you like me to show you how to do it properly?"

Her face took on a hint of panic, but she tilted her head back and met his eyes. "No, Mr. Branigan," she answered primly. "I would not."

He grinned. No woman could stick her nose in the air better than Olivia. "Afraid my sinful ways might corrupt you?" He bent his head until his mouth was an inch from hers. "After all, you might like it."

"I doubt it."

That was too much. He couldn't let that comment pass unchallenged. "'Tis doubting me, you are?" He touched his lips to one corner of hers. "I'm not sure you know enough about it to judge."

He tilted his head slightly and kissed the other corner of her mouth. "The main thing about kissing," he said, his lips brushing lightly over hers with each word, "is not to think about it too much."

He closed his eyes, savoring the vanilla scent that enveloped them both. He felt her lips tremble beneath his, but she did not move. He felt her stiffen, but she did not push him away. He ran his tongue across her closed lips, tasting, coaxing, until she yielded, until her mouth opened beneath his with a wordless sound of surprise that gave him the answer to his question.

He'd only been teasing, thinking all of this just a game, but suddenly it wasn't a game at all.

He deepened the kiss, and his body leaned into her, pressing her back against the counter. The aggressive move must have startled her, for he felt her hands come up as if to push him away. He would not let her. He captured her hands, lacing his fingers through hers and drawing their joined hands downward as he savored the softness of her mouth. Her brief resistance disappeared and her hands relaxed within his.

He let go and reached behind her head, pulling away the pins until her hair came down. The pins scattered across the counter and the floor as he buried his fingers in her hair and wrapped its thick strands in his fists.

Something told him he ought to stop, that this little game he'd started with her had already gone too far. He tore his lips from hers, intending to break it off before he lost what few wits he had left, but she made a tiny sound, a fluttering, purely feminine mixture of innocence and invitation. His last vestige of reason dissolved.

He trailed kisses across her jaw, along the line of her throat above the pristine white collar, to her ear. Pushing back her hair, he nibbled on the soft skin of her earlobe and felt her shiver. He tightened one hand in her tangled hair and slid the other down to her waist, then wrapped his arm around her and pulled her tight against him, feeling every soft curve of her body where she was pressed against him.

Her hips shifted against his weight, and he shuddered at the jolt of pure pleasure he felt. He wanted to take her down to the floor, he wanted to feel her move like that beneath him, he wanted to feel her thighs wrap around him.

His hand left her hair and slid down between them to open intimately over her breast. He kissed her again, not a tender kiss this time, but a kiss hard and demanding. As he tasted her mouth, he moved his thumb in a slow circle over her breast, and felt her response through the layers of fabric.

She broke the kiss with a desperate gasp for air. Somewhere past the roar in his ears and the lust that coursed through his body, he heard her say his name.

Permission or protest, he didn't know which. But somewhere within that whispered plea, he found a glimmer of sanity.

Christ, what was he doing? He jerked back, breathing hard, shocked by the hot, driving force inside him that had nearly taken her on a kitchen floor. He let her go and stepped away, his body still pulsing with frustrated arousal. He stared into her wide, startled eyes, striving for equilibrium. Years of will and discipline, years of rigid control and tightly leashed emotions, all of it nearly shattered with a kiss.

"On second thought," he muttered, "maybe you should have a talk with that boy's mother, after all."

He turned away and walked out of the house, breathing deeply of the sultry summer air, but he could not escape the luscious scent of vanilla.

15

When Becky came back to the house about two hours later, her eyes red and her face all puffy from crying, Olivia felt as mean and hateful as Becky had accused her of being. She also felt like a self-righteous hypocrite.

She watched her daughter walk straight through the kitchen and up the back stairs without even looking at her. "Dinner's almost ready," Olivia called after her.

"I'm not hungry," was the stiff reply that came back down. A moment later, she heard the door of Becky's room slam shut.

Olivia sagged against the counter, staring down at the plank floor and the one small hairpin still lying there, and her cheeks heated with guilt. She bent down and retrieved the pin, then pushed it into the coil of hair she had pinned back in place. She could still feel Conor's fingers pulling her hair down, tangling through it, tearing away all the staunch morality and virtuous ideals of a lifetime in the space of three heartbeats.

Only a few minutes before, she'd been giving her daughter a lecture on propriety. What a hypocrite she was.

Dinner was excruciating. Becky stayed in her room, Carrie and Miranda kept up a constant stream of chatter, and Conor acted as if nothing out of the ordinary had happened. She rather resented that.

She could still feel the heat of his mouth everywhere he had kissed her, she could still feel the weight of his body pressing her against the counter. Just the memory of it flustered her, made her feel restless and strange. And very, very guilty.

She chanced a look at him across the table as he and Carrie talked about tree houses, of all things, and she wondered how he could behave as if that kiss had never happened, how he could act so calm, so nonchalant about it all.

But then, by his own admission, he'd kissed lots of women.

Olivia pushed back her plate and rose. She prepared a tray and took it up to Becky's room, leaving Conor and Carrie to their talk of tree houses.

There was no answer when she knocked on Becky's door, and when she gently pushed it open, she found her daughter lying on her stomach in the center of her bed, her face buried in her pillow. She didn't look up when Olivia entered the room.

"I thought you might want something to eat."

"Go away," Becky mumbled from the depths of her pillow.

Olivia set the tray on the washstand and walked over to the bed. She sat down on the edge and reached out, touching Becky's shoulder. She felt her daughter stiffen, but she did not pull her hand away.

"I think we need to talk," Olivia said, rubbing Becky's shoulder gently. "I know that you probably don't feel much like talking now, but I have something to say, so you can just listen for now."

She paused for a moment, then she said, "I was very upset when I found out what happened this afternoon because you're my daughter. It's hard for me to think of you growing up. To me, you're still a little girl."

Becky sat up. "I'm fourteen. My mother married my father when she was only a year older than I am."

"That's true." Sarah had been about two months pregnant at the time, and her father had almost shot Joe in a duel, Olivia remembered. But she didn't tell Becky that. She fought back the protective panic that rose within her and took a deep breath. "Do you want to marry Jeremiah?"

A change came over Becky's face. Suddenly, she looked very bewildered and very vulnerable. "I don't know," she whispered.

"Honey, Jeremiah is the first boy that's come along. He's the first boy you've had feelings for. But there will be others. I think you know that," she added gently. "That's why you're unsure."

"He wanted to kiss me," she mumbled, ducking her head to stare at her hands. "And I wanted him to. I was curious. I wanted to know. . . ." Her voice trailed off into silence, but she didn't finish.

Olivia bit her lip. She understood perfectly.

Becky looked at her anxiously. "Was that wrong, Mama?"

Here was the perfect opportunity to give the appropriate mother's lecture. But Olivia thought of Conor Branigan, and she couldn't do it. "What do you think?"

"I don't know! I feel so confused."

She wrapped an arm around Becky and pulled her close. "I know just what you mean."

Olivia held her daughter for a long time, stroking her

hair and letting her think. She waited until Becky pushed away and sat up again before she spoke.

"Why don't you and I make a deal?" She reached out and brushed a wisp of hair gently out of her daughter's eyes. "I promise you that I will trust you. I will not forbid you to see Jeremiah. The two of you can continue to sit together at church and have peppermint sticks at the mercantile all you like. I will not say anything to Lila about this. In return, you promise me that you will not violate my trust in you. You won't walk with him alone. No more kissing down by the creek. If you want to go walking with him after church, I will accompany you."

"Mother!"

"Mind, I'll probably see lots of herbs and wildflowers to pick along the way, so you two will probably walk much faster than I will." She watched her daughter smile. "Is that a deal?"

"Deal."

"Good. Now, why don't you have some dinner? Then we'll go up to the attic and see if we can find a dress for you to wear to the harvest dance."

"Can Jeremiah take me to the dance?"

"Of course," Olivia answered. "In two years or so."

Conor could not sleep. He lay in bed, thinking of her, of how she had melted against him with all that soft yielding, how his own desire had flared in response, sudden, hot, and so intense, his body still ached with it.

Never had he lost control like that with a woman. For those few moments, he'd lost himself in her, forgetting everything. A lifetime of struggle to keep passions in check, a lifetime of suppressing all the hate and love and fear that raged within him, a lifetime of swallowing his pride and lowering his eyes and pretending indifference. A lifetime of control lost. Forget the prison guards at Mountjoy—they'd stripped away his control in bloody pieces, with much harsher weapons—but losing control to a woman whose only weapons were chocolate-brown eyes and soft, full lips was a shattering experience, indeed. In a kitchen, for God's sake, in broad daylight, where any one of the girls could have walked in and seen them.

Fatal to be vulnerable, fatal to need her, fatal to want her.

But he did. He wanted to touch her again; he wanted to lose himself in her softness and warmth again. The conflict was like anarchy inside him.

And she had no idea. Olivia was not the kind of woman he could easily tumble and conveniently leave behind. She was innocent. Very proper and completely innocent. He could still see her staring at him in shock, wide-eyed, with her fingers to her lips, tendrils of her long brown hair stirring in time with his harsh and labored breathing.

Through the window, he heard the incessant chirp of crickets and the low grumble of bullfrogs. The air was hot and sultry, there was no breeze at all, and the room felt suffocating. He rose from the bed, knowing he had to do something; he had to find a way to take his mind off her. A month of this, and he was going to be insane.

He never should have promised to stay. He should have just ignored the pleading look in her eyes yesterday, the proud lift of her chin, the catch in her voice that reminded him that somewhere, lost amid the guilt and the self-loathing, he still had a conscience.

He should have just walked on. A conscience was a damned inconvenient thing.

He pulled on his trousers and boots, took the lamp, and went outside. He stood on the porch, leaning against the rail and staring into the black emptiness beyond the lamplight.

Discipline. Control. Pride. They were his armor, they were all he had. So painfully won, so easily lost.

He remembered Mary's words from long ago. She'd been right about him. She had sensed the passions that seethed beneath the surface; she'd seen behind his mask, and it had frightened her. She had known that prizefighting wasn't just a job. The boxing ring was his outlet, his way of releasing passions in controlled increments, like a teakettle letting off steam. He'd always used sex the same way. But not with Olivia.

He picked up the lamp, walked down the steps, and crossed the yard to the barn. He found a stout length of rope and a burlap sack of oats that he guessed weighed about a hundred pounds.

He tied one end of the rope securely around the sack and tossed the other end over a rafter, then he pulled the sack up until it hung in the air at just the right level. He secured the contraption by slipping the rope end through a knot hole in the stall behind him, bringing it over the top, and tying a stout bowline knot. Not a very challenging opponent, he supposed, but it was the only one he had.

He threw a few quick jabs in the air, just to get a feel for it again, then he faced the sack, hauled back his right arm, and let fly with a good hard punch, sending the sack swinging away.

Too slow, he thought. He was out of practice. If he punched like that when he went back into the ring, even Elroy Harlan might be able to beat him. As the sack came swinging back toward him, he struck it again, this time with his left fist. Then his right, then his left, then his right.

He focused all his attention on his burlap opponent,

ignoring the twinges of lingering pain in his ribs. He kept the sack swinging for over an hour. Sweat rolled down his body, the muscles of his arms and back started to burn, but he did not stop. He kept practicing his punches until he couldn't lift his arm for one more.

He wrapped his arms around the sack to still its swinging, then he sank to the floor, breathing hard. His blood was pumping, his muscles were burning.

He took down his makeshift punching bag, coiled the rope and put it back where he'd found it, picked up the lamp, and left the barn. He walked the perimeter of the house a few times, until his body had cooled and his heartbeat resumed a normal rhythm, then he went back to bed.

But all his efforts proved futile.

His body still ached with wanting her; he could still feel the warmth of her body, and he knew the tension in him wasn't the kind that could be relieved by going a few rounds with a burlap punching bag.

Olivia woke the next morning to the unmistakable thump of footsteps above her. She stared up at the ceiling, still half-asleep, and she wondered if Becky had gone back up to the attic this morning to look at dresses again. She rose and went upstairs, but there was no one there.

She heard the sound of footsteps again, coming from the roof overhead, along with a strange squeaking sound. What on earth? She went downstairs and out the back door, then halted abruptly at the sight that met her eyes. In the yard were stacks of wooden shingles and sheets of tin—the materials she'd bought last year to fix the roof. And right beside the porch steps, a ladder leaned against the house.

Olivia raced down the porch steps and into the yard, far enough out to get a good look. She turned around.

Conor was up on her roof, straddling the peak and stripping away shingles with a hammer. Olivia pressed her hands to her cheeks and stared up at him, stunned.

Though it was just past sunrise, she could tell he'd been up quite a while. His shirt was off. She could see it hanging over the top of the chimney.

He was fixing her roof. A sudden gust of wind whipped Olivia's tangled hair across her face. She pushed it back and watched as Conor tore away another shingle and tossed it. He caught sight of her standing in the yard and froze as the shingle fell to the ground a few feet in front of her.

He was fixing her roof. She repeated it in her head over and over, like Conor's hated rosary, but she still couldn't quite believe it. The absurd prick of tears stung her eyes.

She lifted one arm to wave and realized that she was standing out here in her nightgown.

Oh, Lord. Olivia ducked back into the house and shut the door. But she couldn't resist having another quick peek out the window to stare at the stacks of shingles in her yard, just to be sure she hadn't imagined the whole thing.

She wrapped her arms around her ribs and closed her eyes. In her mind, she saw him on her roof, sitting astride the peak as if it were a horse. Windblown, perhaps, and definitely battle-scarred, but no less like a white knight out of a storybook, coming to her aid. She murmured a heartfelt prayer of thanks.

Christ, have mercy. She just wasn't going to make things easy on him, was she? Conor jammed the claw end of the hammer under another shingle and pried it loose. The only reason he was out here at this ungodly hour of the morning was because thoughts of her had kept him awake all night. Then what did she do? Come prancing outside in her nightgown with her hair all loose and tumbled, and the sun behind her. He'd been able to see the silhouette of her body beneath the gown, the shapely curves of her thighs and hips. He'd probably spend the rest of the goddamned day imagining it.

He'd bet all his money, all ten dollars of it, that prim white nightgown had pearl buttons all down the front. He thought how easily pearl buttons could slip free. "Bloody hell," he muttered, and pried away another shingle.

If he had any brains at all, he'd leave now, before things got out of hand, before he let his body do his thinking for him.

Conor paused, staring down at the hammer in his hands. He couldn't leave yet. He'd made a promise, and he intended to keep it even if it killed him. A few more glimpses of her in that nightgown and it probably would.

Determinedly, he pushed delectable visions of her out of his mind and turned his attention back to the task at hand.

He heard the back door slam, and he glanced down as Olivia and Carrie came out into the yard. He was relieved that this time Olivia was properly dressed. For the first time, he was rather glad she wore dresses buttoned up to her chin.

Carrie waved at him. "Mornin', Mr. Conor," she called up to him.

"Good morning, *mó cailín*," he called back.

"How come you're fixing the roof?"

"It needs fixing, don't you think?"

"I reckon! It leaks somethin' awful. Mama has all sorts of cans up in the attic for the water."

He glanced at Olivia. In one hand, she carried a cup, while she grasped a handful of skirt in the other, trying to prevent it from flying up in the stiff breeze. She'd pinned up her hair, he noticed. He imagined seeing her with her hair spread across a pillow, imagined her hair like silk in his fingers, and he quickly looked away. He'd better not think about that.

"Mornin'," she greeted. "You're sure up with the sun."

He wondered what she'd do if he told her why. Instead, he gestured to the roof. "Since I'm going to be here for a bit longer, I thought I'd have a go at fixing this roof of yours."

Olivia smiled up at him. "I appreciate it. Thank you." She held up the cup in her hand. "I'll make breakfast in a bit, but I thought you might want a cup of tea."

He set down the hammer and rose to his feet, hunched over to keep his balance.

"Be careful," Olivia admonished.

"Not to worry," he answered. "I've no intention of cracking my ribs again." He moved carefully along the sloping roof to the ladder, then he climbed down. Olivia handed him the cup of tea.

"Can I help you fix the roof, Mr. Conor?" Carrie asked.

"Carrie," Olivia said before he could reply, "you're not going up there."

"But, Mama—"

"No."

Conor noticed Carrie's crestfallen expression. He smiled down at her. "I'll be needing some nails. Might you be willin' to find me some?"

"You bet." She started toward the toolshed, but Olivia put a hand on her shoulder, stopping her.

"Chores, first," she said firmly.

"But I want to help Mr. Conor. He said I could." She

turned to Conor for assistance. "You said I could, didn't you?"

"Later," she said firmly, forestalling any reply Conor might have made. "Those chickens won't feed themselves."

"But I don't want to feed the chickens. I want to help Mr. Conor."

"Now, young lady." She turned Carrie in the direction of the barn. "And don't forget to bring the eggs in so I can make breakfast."

Carrie gave a dejected sigh and looked up at her. "You're no fun, Mama," she said sadly. "You're just no fun."

Olivia wasn't impressed. She pointed to the barn. "March."

Carrie walked away, feet dragging, shoulders slumped.

A low chuckle behind her caused Olivia to turn. "What are you laughing about?" she asked.

"I'm not sure if that lass will grow up to be an actress or a confidence swindler."

Olivia didn't much like either option, but she couldn't help smiling. "I know. I love that child, but she can be quite a trial on occasion."

"I'll bet." He lifted his cup and took a swallow of tea.

She studied the masculine hands wrapped around the delicate porcelain cup, remembering the first nights he'd spent in her home, and how those hands had lashed out in violent dreams, smashing her china shepherdess and punching her pillows. She remembered also the extraordinary feel of those hands in her hair, spanning her waist, touching her lips, and she wondered how a man's hands could be both strong enough to pound another man's body in a boxing ring and yet gentle enough to make her knees go weak when he touched her.

"It's going to take some time for me to fix this roof, I'm thinking."

His voice startled Olivia out of her reverie, and she realized she'd been staring. She lowered her head, glancing at the tools and wood around her feet. "I see you found the shingles."

He nodded and took another swallow of tea. "In that old shed back there," he said, gesturing to the dilapidated shack where Nate had kept all his tools.

Since Nate's death, Olivia hadn't gone poking around in that old toolshed. There were rats in there, that was all she knew, and it was enough to keep her out. "It's very nice of you to do this," she murmured.

"As I said, it gives me something to do." He swallowed the last of the tea and held the cup out to her. "Besides, this will help me get back into fighting condition."

She took the cup from him and turned to walk back into the house, feeling suddenly melancholy. She'd asked God for help, and she had gotten what she'd asked for. Conor was fixing her roof, and he was going to help her with her peach crop. He was going to stay one more month. That ought to be enough.

But now it wasn't. Olivia felt ashamed of herself for wanting more.

Hard work had its rewards. By late afternoon, Conor knew he had to be the most pampered carpenter in Louisiana. Becky brought him cool water from the well at least half a dozen times; Miranda brought him some of Olivia's fresh-baked cookies; Carrie brought him the nails he'd requested and hovered nearby for the rest of the day, fetching any tool he might happen to need, entertaining him with her lively chatter. If Conor had received this much feminine attention back in Ireland, he might have remained a carpenter for the rest of his life.

It was a hot, sultry summer day, and the heavy clouds that began rolling in during the afternoon brought no relief. He glanced up at the clouds, and he wiped another stream of sweat from his brow, stared down the huge section of roof he'd just finished patching, and figured it probably wouldn't be a very good idea to start on another section today.

He glanced down at his pint-sized assistant. Her calico dress stuck to her as if it had been glued on, and her cheeks were flushed bright pink from the heat. He set down his hammer and climbed down from the roof. "Carrie, my darlin', I think it's time for a trip to that swimming hole."

"Yea!" Carrie dropped the can of nails and grabbed his hand. "C'mon!"

"Wait a second, lass." He pointed to the can of nails and its spilled contents. "Is that where those belong?"

She bent down and scooped nails back into the can, then set it on the edge of the porch. "Better?"

"It'll do for now. Let's go find your mother and sisters."

Conor and Carrie found them in the kitchen, and from the look of things, only Miranda would be able to accompany them for a swim. Becky, wearing a blue silk dress, was standing on a chair, and Olivia knelt on the floor beside her, pinning up the hem. Miranda, seated at the kitchen table, was munching cookies as she watched.

"Carrie and I decided it was just too hot to do any more work." He glanced down at the child beside him. "Didn't we, moppet?"

Carrie nodded. "Yep. We're goin' swimming."

"Would you lasses care to come along?" Conor asked.

"I'll go," Miranda said, sliding off her chair; but Becky and Olivia both shook their heads.

"Not today," Becky told them. "Mama's making over a dress for me."

"I see that. And a lovely one it is, too. What's the occasion?"

Olivia pushed in another pin and glanced up at him. "Every September, the town holds a harvest dance. It's been done every year since the end of the war, and it's become something of a tradition."

"Mama's going to wear her red silk, aren't you, Mama?"

"Yes," she answered, and pushed in another pin. "If I can narrow the skirt a bit."

"Red?" Conor imagined seeing her in some color besides the awful browns and grays she usually wore. "I'd like to see that," he murmured softly. "Red's my favorite color."

Olivia did not comment on that. She pushed in the last pin and rose to her feet. "All done, honey."

Becky ran her hands down the sides of the skirt. "Oh, Mama," she breathed. "I love it. Thank you."

"You're welcome. Come down from there, and we'll make sure the hem's straight."

Becky jumped lightly down from the chair and turned a slow pirouette. She came to a halt facing Conor, her blue eyes shining. "What do you think, Mr. Conor?"

He smiled at her. "You look beautiful."

She blushed prettily and ducked her head, smoothing the blue silk. "Really?"

"Really. You'll have lads standing in line, you will, indeed."

"Just one lad, I hope."

He shook his head. "Pity, that," he told her. "My mother once told my sister Brigid that finding a husband was like buying a bonnet."

Becky laughed at that. "A bonnet?"

He nodded. "She said you look around, you try on a few, you don't buy the first one you see." He winked at her. "Take your time, lass. That's a bit of my mother's advice for you."

Olivia shot him a look of gratitude over her sewing basket. "Becky, go on upstairs and change out of the dress so we can get started on it. Mind the pins."

Becky went upstairs, and Conor took Carrie and Miranda down to the swimming hole, leaving Olivia alone in the kitchen. She picked up the tape measure, rolling it around in her hand, and she silently blessed Conor for his bit of Irish wisdom.

Becky was right. She wasn't a little girl, and Olivia knew she couldn't make her daughter's choices for her anymore. All she could do was hope Becky made the right choices for herself.

The pounding of horses' hooves and the rattling sound of a wagon floated through the open windows. Olivia dropped the tape measure into the sewing basket and left the kitchen. In the parlor, she pulled back a lace curtain at one of the windows to see who was coming up the lane.

It was Oren Johnson in his wagon, driving his team of grays at a speed that told her something was very wrong. She ran to the front door and down the steps as Oren turned the wagon into the gravel drive before the house and brought the team to a stop.

"Olivia, thank the Lord you're here."

"What is it, Oren? What's happened?"

"It's Kate." He pushed back his hat, and she could see the worry in his face. "The baby's coming."

"What? She's not due for a month."

"I know, but it's coming, and she's having a hard time. Doc Morrison's over in Choudrant Parish until Sunday. Measles outbreak over there. Can you come?"

"Of course. Let me get some things and tell Becky. Sit tight for a second. I'll be right back."

Olivia turned and raced back up the steps. "Becky!" she cried, heading for the kitchen. "Becky, come down here, quick!"

She grabbed a basket out of the pantry. Into it, she stuffed a handful of cotton batting, her medicine box, and two towels. Becky came into the kitchen as she was grabbing her hat.

"What is it, Mama? I thought I heard a wagon in the drive."

"Kate Johnson's having her baby, and Doc Morrison's away. I've got to go over there right now." Olivia jammed her battered old hat on her head as she headed for the door. "I don't know how long it's going to take, honey. Can you take care of getting everybody supper?"

"Of course," Becky answered, following her out the front door. "When will you be back?"

"I don't know. If it gets late, don't worry. Just put the girls to bed for me, all right? And don't wait up for me." She jumped up in the wagon beside Oren, and the wagon lurched forward, moving out of the drive. "I'll be back as soon as I can."

Becky stared down at the chessboard, trying to figure out what her next move should be. Conor sat opposite her at the kitchen table, and he could tell from her puzzled frown that she didn't know what to do.

He didn't advise her. He had her trapped, but he had

also left her one way out. He wanted to wait and see if she would figure it out for herself.

A roll of thunder sounded outside, and the rain began to pour down. Conor settled back in his chair and listened to the rain drum against the windows as he waited for Becky to make her move.

"Mr. Conor?"

He looked across the table at her. "Hmm?"

"Do you really think finding a husband is like buying a bonnet?"

He grinned. "I don't know, lass. I'm not in the market for either."

She laughed. "All right, switch it around then. Do you think finding a wife is like buying a hat?"

"I suppose it is, in a way. But being that I'm not a marrying man, and I don't wear hats, it's hard to say."

She studied him with her pretty, earnest face. "Don't you ever want to marry? Have a family?"

He was saved from answering by another voice.

"Becky?"

Both of them looked up to find Carrie standing in the doorway, barefoot and in her nightgown.

Becky frowned at her. "Carrie, you're supposed to be in bed. Mama said."

Her sister ignored that. "You better come quick," she advised. "Miranda woke up."

"Oh, no!" Becky groaned, and jumped to her feet. She ran out of the kitchen, leaving Conor staring after her in puzzlement.

Obviously, he'd missed something. "What's wrong with Miranda?"

"She doesn't like thunderstorms," Carrie explained. "She's scared."

Conor rose and followed Becky upstairs, Carrie beside him.

He entered Miranda's bedroom right behind Becky
and found Miranda huddled next to Chester on the bed,
making odd little hiccuping sounds.

Becky ran to the bed and put an arm around her sister. "It's okay, Mandy," she said with a hug. "It's okay."

Conor could tell that Miranda was terrified. He
looked at her, a round little ball of frightened misery.
Another crack of thunder sounded, lightning flashed,
and she buried her face against Chester's thick fur with
a whimper.

Something in that tiny, helpless sound sliced through
Conor's layers of protective armor and cynical indifference in an instant. Without thinking, he crossed over to
the bed and reached over Becky's lap, plucking the
frightened child out of the sheets, oblivious to Chester's
protective snarl.

Miranda immediately curled her arms around his
neck and heaved a little sob of relief, seeking comfort
and needing him to provide it. It had been a long time
since anyone had needed Conor Branigan, a long time
since anyone had turned to him for comfort. He froze.
Now that he was in this situation, he realized how completely inadequate he was to deal with it. He was not a
family man.

The thunder came again and Miranda snuggled
closer, clinging to him and trembling. He tightened his
hold and held her securely with one arm as he lifted his
free hand to rub her back in soothing circles.

"Well, now, what's this, *mó paisté*?" he murmured
into her hair. "You're not scared of a wee thunderstorm, are you?"

He heard her mumble something, and he pulled back
enough to look into her round, frightened eyes. "It's
just a lot of rain, love," he said gently, brushing back
the hair from her face. "It likes to put on a big show,

that's all, shouting and carrying on. Any time you hear that thunder shout at you, you shout right back."

Some of the fear left her eyes, and she nodded. "That's what you do when you have bad dreams, isn't it?"

Conor's lips twisted wryly. "Something like that," he admitted.

"And then you're not scared?"

"Mr. Conor's not scared of anything!" Carrie told her sister stoutly. She looked up at him, worship clearly shining in her eyes. "Are you?"

He wanted to laugh at the irony. He wondered what Carrie would have said had he told her the truth—that he was very scared of a great many things.

"No, moppet. I'm not scared of anything." He reached down and wrapped an arm around Carrie with a growl, then lifted her like a sack of potatoes. She laughed, grabbing his shirt in her fists to hang on.

He glanced over at Becky and gave her a grin. "If I'm not mistaken, love, there's still a whole plate of pecan butter cookies from yesterday just waiting to be eaten."

She grinned back at him. "Let's go."

Becky led the way downstairs with the lamp, and Conor followed her, carrying his two young charges. Chester walked beside him, and Conor got the feeling he was finally going to be tolerated by the grouchy old mutt.

In the kitchen, he set Carrie on her feet, and she immediately went into the pantry and brought out the plate of cookies.

"Why don't we go into the library?" Becky suggested as she poured apple cider for all of them. "It's much more comfortable in there."

Conor glanced at the straight-backed kitchen chairs, shifted Miranda's weight to one hip, and thought that was probably a good idea. "Come on, then. We might as well be comfortable. Carrie, bring the cookies. Becky, love, bring the lamp."

They settled into the comfortable cushions of the sofa in the library. Miranda curled up on his lap. Carrie snuggled against his side. On his other side, Becky leaned against him with her head on his shoulder. Chester flopped down to the floor at his feet.

"Tell us a story, Mr. Conor," Miranda murmured, snuggling against him to rest her cheek on his chest.

A story. *Oh, Christ.* He tried to think back to the stories the *seanachaie* had told when he was a lad, before the famine, before music and laughter and stories around the peat fire had vanished from his life.

"Once upon a time," he began, "there was a young lad by the name of Cuchulain, who lived in the grand court of the king. One night, he heard the baying of a hound, and he knew it was the Hound of Ulster, the great, savage beast that wandered the plains and terrorized all the wee children. All the other children shivered with fright when they heard that sound, but Cuchulain was a brave lad, and he wasn't afraid. The next morning, he went out to have a game of hurling with his friends—"

"What's hurling?" Carrie interrupted.

"It's an Irish game played with sticks and a leather ball."

"How do you play it?"

Conor started to explain, but Miranda nudged him impatiently with her elbow. "Forget that. What happened next, Mr. Conor?"

"While the children were playing," Conor went on, "the beast came upon them. It was a massive animal with wild green eyes and jaws like the devil. All the other children screamed with fright and started to run, but Cuchulain told them to stop and get behind him, which they did. The beast came straight toward them, running across the field with teeth bared, ready to tear all of them to pieces."

"Wasn't Cuchulain scared at all?" Miranda asked.

"No, lass. He was very brave, and he faced the hound squarely. He took his hurling stick and hit the ball. His aim was true, and the hurling ball struck the beast with such force that it fell, slain upon the field. And that was how Cuchulain killed the Hound of Ulster and saved the children. Cuchulain was so courageous and fair that he went on to become the high king of all Ireland."

"That was a good story, Mr. Conor," Becky said, reaching for a cookie from the plate on the table before them. "Tell us another one."

"'Tis very late. The three of you ought to be in bed, I'm thinking."

A flood of protest was his reply.

"I don't want to go back to bed," Miranda told him.

"Me neither." Carrie added, reaching for another cookie.

"Can't we wait up for Mama?" Becky asked, and her sisters nodded agreement.

Conor glanced from one hopeful face to another. "You girls realize your mother's not going to be happy to come home and find that none of you are in bed?"

All of them nodded again, smiling.

Conor sighed. "Right."

He settled Miranda more comfortably on his lap and started to tell them of "Cuchulain and the Courtship of Emer," but halfway through the tale, he realized that he wasn't getting any questions this time. He glanced down at the girls around him and found that all three of them had fallen asleep.

Conor realized that the story itself didn't matter. It

was the closeness they wanted, the sound of a voice to lull them into sleep.

But Conor did not sleep. He listened to the thunder, trying not to remember all the times his sisters had curled up beside him in dark alleys and roadside ditches in the rain. After Michael's death, it had been his responsibility to take care of them, to find food, to find shelter. They had trusted him, they had counted on him. He had failed them.

Tá ocrás orm, Conor. He could hear the plaintive voices of his sisters on the wind; he could see their tears in the rainfall. He struggled to blot them out, he tried to prop up the barriers that kept the disjointed fragments of his past at a tolerable distance. He didn't want to hear the voices now, not when he was awake, not when the girls were so near. *Tá ocrás orm, Conor . . . I think I'm dying . . . tell us.*

A loud crack of thunder rattled the windowpanes. Miranda snuggled against him with a tiny sigh, and his arm tightened around her. She felt so small in the crook of his arm, vulnerable and fragile. He glanced at Carrie curled up beside him like a kitten by the fire. He could feel Becky's hair tickle his neck. He tried to focus on those things, not the voices that echoed through his brain.

There were times when he wanted so badly to silence the voices and demolish the dark dreams permanently; but somehow, he had never been able to take the final necessary step. He'd thought about it plenty of times, savored it like an upcoming holiday, contemplated the countless ways he could do it. Yet, when the moment came, something always stopped him. Suicide was the final sin, the one he could not bring himself to commit.

Survival was his greatest talent. Famine, typhus, dysentery, bullets, knives, beatings—he had survived them all because dying would be giving in; suicide would be the ultimate capitulation.

Hate and anger were what had kept him alive. He had fed on them for so long, they were the only emotions he recognized, the only ones he still knew how to feel.

And yet, right now, surrounded by the warmth of the three precious girls who were using him as a pillow, hate seemed very far away, crowded out by things unknown and yet familiar, impossible things. Love. A feeling of belonging. A sense of peace.

He closed his eyes. It was all an illusion. He didn't belong anywhere. He didn't know what love was anymore. And peace . . . Christ, what was that?

So Conor sat listening to the rain and stealing a few moments of trust and affection he did not deserve from three wee girls who were not his. And he reminded himself at least twice that night that he was not a family man.

16

FENIANS
Belfast, Ireland, 1865

When Conor met Sean Gallagher for the first time, he wasn't sure if the man was the full-blown revolutionary genius others thought him to be, or just an old man full of piss and wind.

Conor had heard of him, of course. Gallagher was something of a legend, a follower of O'Connell, and later one of the leaders during the rebellion of '48. He had seen the inside of many prisons as a guest of the Crown, and had suffered any number of indignities at their hands. He was now a member of the Brotherhood's hallowed inner circle. But after two hours in this small, cramped room above McGrath's, listening to the man drone on like a *seanachaie* about hundreds of years of subjugation and injustice, and tell the same stories he'd heard all of his life, Conor began to wonder if the man ever stopped talking long enough to have a revolution.

Talk, talk, talk, he thought. *We Irish are so good at it.*

Nonetheless, Conor leaned back in his chair and listened, keeping his impatience hidden, remembering the words of O'Bourne just the night before. "Gallagher is the kind that keeps the spirit alive. Many a man can talk brave enough in the pub after a few pints, but Gallagher'll keep their anger high after the porter's gone, lad. And he knows what he's doing. Remember that."

O'Bourne was a captain in the Brotherhood, leader of Belfast's small republican circle. His goal was to organize the Brotherhood in Belfast, to find recruits, safehouses, and escape routes, and to establish Belfast as a cornerstone of the Fenian movement. Conor and the half-dozen other men in this room had been carefully chosen, their backgrounds exhaustively checked, and their Fenian sympathies closely examined. Most of them were like Conor, without home or family, with a fire in their bellies and no one to grieve if they died for the cause.

Gallagher was up from Dublin to inspect O'Bourne's recruits, and select a handful of them for some kind of mission. Out of the seven men in this room O'Bourne had recommended, Gallagher would choose two. Conor wished he'd stop giving a dissertation on Irish history and get on with it.

"Some of you may be asking yourselves why we're wasting our time sitting here talking about fighting for freedom when all those who have come before us have failed." Gallagher leaned forward, palms flat on the table before him. "Those of you who are waiting to see Ireland rise and throw off the British yoke in our lifetime will wait in vain. Don't expect our people to come pouring out into the streets to follow us down the freedom road. They won't. They've been subjugated too long."

He paused to let the words sink in, then he went on, "We are trying to fight a war with limited support, limited funds, and centuries of fucking bad luck. So, why bother? What do we have that gives us any hope of being free?"

Gallagher straightened, and his hands clenched into fists at his sides. "We have one thing the British can never conquer with their armies and their governments, one thing they can never capture with their laws and their prisons. We have the will to fight. As long as there is one man to sound the battle cry for freedom, one man to spit in the eye of tyranny, one man who refuses to be subjugated, the British will never truly conquer us. And that is why they not only hate us, they also fear us. No matter what happens, remember that, because that is what will save our land and our people in the end. Our refusal to be broken."

His gaze slowly circled the room, and Conor knew they were being assessed. Gallagher was deciding who had barroom courage and who had the real thing, who would break and who would not, who could give his life for Irish freedom and who could only boast about it.

"The Brotherhood is your family now, lads. You have no other. Take a good look at the other faces in this room. Outside this circle, trust no one. And remember, I've nothing against a bit of skirt from time to time, but for Christ's sake, if you take off your pants, that doesn't mean open your mouth."

Conor didn't have to worry about that. He was celibate as the Pope himself these days. He thought of Mary, and his heart twisted with pain. She'd married Colm a week after their conversation outside McGrath's. Seven months later, she was dead, and the child she'd been carrying had died with her. His child. Over two years in her grave now, and he still felt the pain. *Let it alone*, he thought, and forced away memories of her, forced himself to concentrate on Gallagher and the cause. That was all that mattered now.

"Spies are everywhere," Gallagher went on, "and many of them come dressed in petticoats." He reached into the pocket of his greatcoat and pulled out a revolver. He held it so that all the men in the room got a good look, then he cocked the gun. "Informers will pay with their lives," he said, as his arm made a slow sweep around the circle of faces, "and the hearthstone of hell will be their bedrest forever."

The gun paused at Conor's chair, and the eyes of the two men met over the barrel. All the other men in the room ducked instinctively as Gallagher pulled the trigger. All but one.

Conor didn't flinch, and the hammer fell with a harmless click.

Gallagher laughed low in his throat. "He's a cool one, is our Conor," he said, and set the gun on the table.

Conor knew that he'd just passed the test and decided it was time to get to the point. He straightened in his chair and asked the vital question. "What do you want us to do?"

Gallagher's lips moved in a twisted imitation of a smile. "I've got one thousand rifles sitting in a New York City warehouse, courtesy of our American cousins in *Clan na Gael* and I want you to help me smuggle them into Ulster starting three months from now."

Conor decided Gallagher deserved his reputation as a full-blown revolutionary genius.

17

Olivia was bone weary. She slumped in the wagon seat and pulled her hat low against the pouring rain, exhaustion settling over her. Oren sat beside her in the wagon, and neither of them spoke as he drove the wagon down the muddy lane toward Peachtree. Olivia was too tired to talk, and though Oren was now a father for the sixth time, he was still a man of few words.

She thought of Kate's tired but exultant face as she'd held her newborn son, and Oren, looking so proud he could bust, giving his wife a smacking kiss right in front of her. It warmed the heart, it truly did, to see them so happy like that after sixteen years of marriage. *It must be lovely to be married,* she thought, and drifted off to sleep.

The jerking stop of the wagon woke her. Olivia grabbed her basket and jumped down without waiting for Oren to help her. "You make sure Doc Morrison has a look at Kate and the baby as soon as he gets back."

"I will," he answered. "Thank you, Olivia, for everything."

He climbed back into the wagon seat and snapped the reins. The wagon rolled out of the drive as Olivia ran for the shelter of the veranda. She pulled off her muddy boots, then entered the house.

The house was quiet, but dim light spilled into the foyer from the library. *Conor must still be up,* she thought as she set down her basket and her mud-encrusted boots. He had waited up for her. A warm glow began inside her at the thought and made her smile.

After removing her rain-soaked hat and duster, she crossed the foyer to the library and smiled at the sight that met her eyes. Conor was sitting on the sofa, wide awake, with the girls piled around him and over him like a pack of wolf cubs in a den, all three of them cozy, comfortable, and asleep. Chester, also sound asleep, lay across Conor's feet.

Conor glanced at her over Miranda's head. "Don't you dare laugh," he muttered and turned his face away, looking almost embarrassed.

Olivia covered her mouth and shook her head. "I wouldn't dream of it. Are you comfortable? You look . . . rather smothered."

He glanced down at the children around him. "I do seem to be trapped at the moment."

Still smiling, she studied him. "You make a nice pillow."

He lifted his head and looked at her, his eyes silver-gray in the lamplight. The momentary embarrassment was gone, replaced by something else, something almost predatory. His lashes lowered as his gaze ran down the length of her in a slow, speculative perusal, from her wet hair to her sodden hem and stocking feet. "You think so, love?"

Olivia couldn't help but envision it, an inviting picture of tousled bedclothes and him. She froze with sudden awareness and an acute, overwhelming shyness. She wished she could say something clever in return, something flirtatious, but she felt hopelessly inadequate to the task. She'd never been any good at flirtation.

The sound of their voices woke Carrie. She lifted her head to find Olivia standing there. "Mama?" she mumbled sleepily. "We waited up for you."

"I see that," Olivia answered, relieved by the distraction. "But it's way past your bedtime." Walking over to the sofa beside Becky, she laid a hand on the girl's shoulder and shook her gently. "Becky, wake up."

Becky opened her eyes and lifted her head from Conor's shoulder. "Mama, you're home," she said with a yawn. "Did Mrs. Johnson have her baby?"

"Yes, she did. A boy, and they're doing just fine." Olivia turned to Conor, who rose and handed Miranda over to her. "Thank you," she murmured, taking the child in her arms. "I hope they weren't any trouble."

"How much trouble could they be? They all fell asleep, and right in the middle of one of my best stories."

Picturing it, she wished she'd been here. It would have been wonderful to see him telling stories to the girls just the way any father might do. But Conor wasn't their father. Not even close.

"Well, good night." She looked away. "Sleep well."

"I'll try," he answered, a hint of irony in his voice she didn't understand.

The girls bid Conor a sleepy good-night, and Olivia led them out of the library. She stopped in the foyer to light a lamp, then took the girls upstairs. "Go to bed," she whispered to Becky and Carrie as she paused in the hallway outside their rooms. "I'll tuck you in after I put Miranda in bed."

"I'm too old to be tucked in, Mama," Becky whispered back.

Olivia smiled. "Well, I can still come in and say good-night, can't I?"

"I suppose," Becky admitted, and went down the hall to her own room.

Olivia turned to Carrie. "You, too, miss. In bed you go."

For once, Carrie did not try to come up with any excuses. She went into her room without a single protest. Nonetheless, Olivia waited until she saw Carrie crawl into bed before she went into Miranda's room. She pulled back the sheet and gently laid the child in bed, trying not to wake her, but she woke up the moment Olivia let her go.

"It's still raining, isn't it, Mama?" she mumbled, opening her eyes.

Olivia sat down on the edge of the bed, thinking that Miranda must still be afraid. "Yes, but the thunder's stopped now, honey."

"I was scared," the child admitted. "But Mr. Conor says the thunder's just shouting at everybody, and next time the thunder comes and shouts, I should shout right back. That's what he does when he has bad dreams."

"He told you that?" Olivia was astonished that Conor would admit such a thing, especially to the girls. "I think it's a good idea. How about we do that next time?"

"Okay." Miranda snuggled down into the mattress. "He told us a story. It was real good, Mama." She gave a huge yawn. "I wish Mr. Conor could tell us stories every night." Her eyes slowly closed.

Olivia leaned down and kissed her daughter's cheek. "So do I, sweetie," she said softly. "So do I."

Olivia was exhausted, but sleep eluded her. She kept changing her position, punching her pillow, and rearranging her bedcovers, but she simply could not sleep.

Finally, she decided that a cup of tea would do her a world of good and got out of bed. She pulled on her wrap and left her room. But as she started down the back stairs, she noticed light spilling through the doorway of the kitchen below.

Conor was still awake? Olivia hesitated on the landing, wondering if perhaps she should forget the tea and go back up, but in the end, she didn't. She continued on down the stairs to the kitchen and found him hunched over the table, writing on the slate. He looked up as she entered the room.

"I couldn't sleep," she explained. "Couldn't you sleep either?"

"No."

"I thought I'd make myself a cup of tea. Would you like one?"

He didn't answer, and she walked over to the stove. She stirred the banked coals to life, added kindling, and put on the kettle to boil.

Neither of them spoke, but she watched him out of the corner of her eye as she made a pot of tea—hunched over the slate, forming letters with care.

"Practicing your penmanship, I see," she said, as she brought two cups of tea to the table.

He took the cup she offered him and sat back in his chair. "Yes, though I don't know what good it will do me, being a prizefighter."

"Prizefighting," Olivia murmured thoughtfully. She rested her elbows on the table, her fingers curled around the cup in her hands, studying him over the rim. "Why do you do it?"

He shrugged. "It's a way to make a living."

"There are plenty of other ways to do that."

"Indeed," he said lightly. "But most of them involve work."

Olivia wasn't fooled by that glib comment. She'd seen him work, and she knew laziness wasn't the reason. "Haven't you ever thought about taking up another profession? Something less . . . violent."

"Like what?" He looked across the table at her, and a shadow crossed his face. "A man doesn't need to know how to read to know the signs in the windows all say, 'No Irish need apply.'"

"Don't you ever feel like settling down in one place, having a stake in something more permanent than tomorrow's fight?"

He met her eyes. "I told you, I like to roam. I'm not the settling-down kind, Olivia. I like my freedom."

She'd known that the first moment she'd looked at him. "You could have a farm of your own. There's plenty of land out West to homestead. Free for the taking, so they say."

He shook his head. "I'm no farmer."

"What's wrong with being a farmer?"

He didn't answer for a long moment. "My father was a farmer," he finally said, "and his father, before him. We grew potatoes like everyone else. You see, there was so little land available to us—most of it being held by British landlords and put into grain that got shipped to England. Potatoes were the only crop we could grow that could feed our people on what little land we had. The potatoes fed our families; they fed our animals; they paid our land rents. They were everything to us. We couldn't survive without them. Then the *ocrás* came. The hunger."

His unwavering gaze was focused on her, but she knew he didn't see her. In his mind, he saw his homeland. "One mornin' when I was eleven years old," he said slowly, "I woke up to the sound of my mother screaming. I ran outside to see what it was all about, and I saw her standing with my da and my brother, pointing to the *clochan* where we stored our crops. She was sobbing and saying something about the potatoes. I ran to the *clochan* just as my da opened the door. The smell hit us. . . . Mother of God," he whispered, "it was like nothing of this earth, that smell."

He paused, but Olivia said nothing. She simply waited, afraid that if she spoke he would retreat behind that wall of his again—afraid he would make some glib comment to change the subject, and never tell her the rest.

"My da and Michael went into the *clochan*," Conor went on. "They told me to wait outside, but I didn't. I followed them. I saw them leaning over the bin where we'd put the healthy new potatoes from the fields just the day before. My da looked at me as I came in, and for the first time in my life, I saw fear in his face. I knew something horrible had happened."

He frowned, looking suddenly bewildered, like a child who didn't quite understand that a cruel joke had just been played on him. "I peered over the top of the bin, and I couldn't see any potatoes. The bin was full of this slimy mush that smelled like sulfur and looked like porridge. Black porridge. Sure, I thought I was looking into the bowels of hell."

His description was so vivid, Olivia could see that bin, smell that smell, as if she were there with him.

"We took a bit of the stuff and fed it to one of the pigs," he went on. "The pig died, and we knew it was the blight. We went out and tried to dig the potatoes that were still in the ground, but it was too late. Overnight, all the plants had withered and the potatoes had turned black right in the ground. Everywhere, it was the same, and that putrid sulfur smell hovered over the land like a thick fog. To this day, I can smell it."

She felt a queer shiver dance along her spine at the way he told the story, his voice so flat, so completely devoid of emotion.

"Within a month, there wasn't a potato left in all of Ireland. Within six months, our people were dying of starvation and disease, dying by the thousands. People in our village were dying so fast, there weren't enough coffins. They had to be buried in mass graves, just piled in with a bit of dirt thrown over to protect their bodies from the rats."

Olivia felt sick. She pressed her hand over her mouth, listening in anguished silence, her heart breaking for him.

Conor swallowed hard. His voice lowered to a hoarse whisper. "My father was the first in our family to die. The blight broke him, and the *fiabhras dubh* killed him. That's the black fever—typhus you call it. My mother keened for three days, so great was her grief. The typhus killed her as well, a week later. She died in a ditch because the landlord evicted us from our home and burned it down."

Conor looked at her and his gaze was glittering hard. "I will never be a farmer," he said, his voice filled with such passionate intensity, it startled her. He rose from the table and walked to the doorway that led into the dining room. He paused there, looking back at her over one shoulder. "I will never be tied to a piece of land. Nor to a woman, nor to a home, nor to a family, nor to a church. Nor to a way of life. Not ever again."

Olivia watched him through a blur of tears, despising the futility of it. For there was nothing she could say to comfort a man whose family was long dead; there was no balm to heal wounds that scored a man's soul; and there was no way to make a man believe in the ties that bind.

*   *   *

Conor couldn't escape the demons. He tried to run from them, but he couldn't run fast enough. Never fast enough. They kept pace with him, speaking in low, coaxing murmurs. He couldn't outrun them, because they spoke to him from inside his own head. He stopped running and sank to his knees. He clamped his hands over his ears, but he could still hear them.

If he were stronger, he could blot them out; he could crush his skull like a walnut shell and that would be the end of it. He pressed his hands hard against his head, but he wasn't strong enough. Never strong enough.

Orange. The hated color was everywhere, all around him. Flames of hell, orange sashes, hot pokers. The demons pulled his hands away and strapped him down. He felt the pain as they yanked his arm and twisted it, dislocating his shoulder again. He smelled his skin burning. He screamed.

Tell us, they murmured. *Tell, tell, tell . . .*

He did.

Conor awoke from the dream like a drowning man breaking the water—wet, disoriented, and gasping for air. He sat up, cradling his head in his shaking hands, feeling the sweat of panic on his face.

"Sweet Jaysus," he moaned. "Oh, shit, oh, shit."

He lifted his head and stared at the wall opposite his bed, trying to find reality in the pattern of morning sunlight through lace curtains. The dreams again.

When he'd first gotten out of prison, the nightmares had haunted him for months, but they had become less frequent with each passing year. He hardly ever had them anymore—until he came here. When he'd first woken up in this house, he knew he'd been having the dreams. But once he'd gotten better, they had gone away. Now they were back. *Not again*, he pleaded. *Not here.*

The door of his bedroom swung inward, hitting the wall with a bang and disturbing the lacy pattern of sun and shadow. Olivia took one look at his face and started toward him, her eyes wide with alarm. "Conor?"

Olivia. He focused on her, on the sunlight that fell over her in swirls and rosettes. She reminded him of the stained-glass Madonna in St. Brendan's, as one-dimensional and unreal as all the rest.

"No." His voice was only a fierce whisper, but it stopped her. "Leave me alone."

She didn't move.

Behind her, he could hear more footsteps. "Mama? Is he all right? Is he dreaming again?"

The girls. He couldn't let them see him this way. "Get out of here!" he ordered, gratified that this time he was able to shout. "Keep them away from me!"

He saw her bite her lip and hesitate. "Are you all right?" she asked.

He laughed, a harsh, choked sound. "Fine. Bloody well fine, thank you for asking."

She backed out of the room, still watching him with those soft doe eyes, as if she were the wounded one. The door closed between them, shutting her out, and he drew a long, deep breath of relief.

Conor disentangled the sheet and rose from the bed. He walked to the washstand and lifted his gaze to his reflection in the oval glass. His face was deathly pale, his eyes were bloodshot, his jaw was blue with beard shadow. He looked like hell, but that's what happened to a man who slept with the demons.

*   *   *

Olivia sent the girls out to pick blackberries. She didn't want them around Conor just now. She put on the kettle, knowing that he'd want hot water to shave and bathe. She also put on a pot of strong coffee. Worried and bewildered, she wondered what more she could do for him. He had made it plain that he didn't want her there, that he didn't want her help.

She'd been in the garden, but she had heard him through the open window of his room, and she'd realized he was having those dreams again, the violent memories of a man who had lived through horrors she could not even imagine.

The kettle began to whistle, and she poured steaming water from it into a pitcher and took it to him, setting it beside the closed door. She heard no sound from inside, and she knocked. "I've brought you some hot water, if you want it," she said, and retreated back down the hall before he opened the door.

Back in the kitchen, she started his breakfast, trying to keep busy, but the sounds she'd heard through the window still echoed in her mind, and her heart twisted with compassion. She lowered her face into her hands. Lord in heaven, she'd heard him sob like a child. That sound had frightened her far more than all the curses and shouts.

She lifted her head at the sound of footsteps and turned quickly toward the counter so that Conor wouldn't see her face when he came in. He wouldn't want her sympathy or her concern, and just now she doubted she could hide them. She began cracking eggs into a bowl as he entered the kitchen.

"Good morning." His voice sounded hoarse and a bit wobbly.

"Morning," she answered and grabbed a fork. She

glanced at him over one shoulder as she began whipping eggs. He'd shaved, she noticed, and he looked a bit better, though still drawn and incredibly weary. She wanted to tell him that they were only dreams, that someday they would go away, but she knew he wouldn't believe her. "I've got breakfast for you," she said instead.

He pulled out a chair from the table and sat down. "Where are the girls?"

"I sent them out to pick blackberries," she answered, pouring the beaten eggs into the cast-iron skillet heating on the stove. She glanced at him again. "They'll be gone all morning."

"Thank you. I didn't want them to see—" He broke off, and a fleeting expression crossed his face that she thought might be shame.

Understanding swamped her. He was a man who hated any sort of weakness. She took a step toward him, but stopped, reminding herself that he would not welcome compassion or sympathy. She watched as he leaned one elbow on the table and cradled his head in the palm of his hand. "Headache?" she asked.

"No." He straightened. "'Tis just a bit tired I am this mornin'."

An understatement if she'd ever heard one. She poured a cup of coffee for him and brought it to the table. "That ought to help."

"Thanks."

She returned to the stove and spooned eggs, fried potatoes, and biscuits onto a plate for him. "Eat," she ordered, setting the food in front of him. She walked away and began cutting vegetables for gumbo. Though she pretended to be occupied with her task, she watched him from the corner of her eye.

He stared down at the plate for a long moment, then picked up his fork. He began to eat his breakfast, but he didn't finish it. With the plate still half full, he pushed it away.

"Not hungry?" she asked.

"No." He shoved back his chair and rose. Without another word, he walked out the back door, wanting only to get away.

The barn door was open. He took refuge there, in the cool shadows that smelled of hay and dust. The summer breeze whistled through the open doors, stirring the straw at his feet, whispering to him like the prison guards in the Mountjoy, like the ghosts of his family, like the wind through the ruins on rocky Irish cliffs.

Peace, damn it all; he wanted peace. But he knew there was no peace for him, not in the touch of a gentle woman or the green hills of Louisiana she talked about. It was too late for that. He'd sold his soul to the demons; he'd betrayed everything worth believing in, only to make the pain stop.

That was the joke, of course. It never stopped.

He knew a bad spell was coming. The dreams were only going to get worse. When he was on the road, moving from town to town, he could stay ahead of them. With enough women and enough whiskey, he could drown them out. When he could go into the ring, when he could fight, he could keep them at bay with his fists. If all of that failed, he could find a room somewhere, a place where no one knew him and no one cared to, where he could bolt the door and fight his demons alone.

Here, he could do none of those things. He had to leave.

"All right, Vernon, tell me what is going on with the railroad deal."

Alicia hovered unseen outside her father's study, listening intently. She had been excluded from their meeting, of course, but that hadn't stopped her. The door of the study was slightly ajar, and she leaned closer to the opening as her husband began to explain the situation to her father.

Alicia Jamison Tyler knew her papa was a clever businessman. He had tripled his already substantial fortune turning out cannons and guns for the Union Army during the war. He seldom invested unwisely, and he would not hesitate to abandon a venture if it failed to produce results. Vernon knew it, too, and promptly launched into explanations.

Alicia heard a sound behind her and turned her head sharply, but the maid who crossed the hall at the opposite end didn't even see her, and Alicia resumed her eavesdropping. She knew next to nothing about this railroad deal, since Vernon never told her anything, and she had a vital reason for wanting to know the true facts of the situation.

"Let me get this straight," her father said. "We've got all the land we need, except one small piece. We can't go around it, and we can't get the owner to sell. So, this one woman could ruin everything we've planned?"

"Yes, but I guarantee—"

"Spare me your guarantees, Vernon," the other man said coldly. "I've been hearing them for a long time now. Several of my closest business associates have invested money in this venture, and it's getting harder and harder to explain the delays to them, which is why I've sent for you. While you are here, you will be meeting with my associates to reassure them that this railroad is not simply a figment of my imagination; and you will spend the next few weeks making a favorable impression on them. They want results, and you are going to be the one to look them in the eye and tell them their money has been wisely invested."

"Yes, sir."

"I want to start building that railroad by autumn. Put on some pressure and get the Maitland woman to sell."

"I'll telegraph Joshua immediately and have him go out to her place with a higher offer. Joshua can be very persuasive."

"Good. I don't have to remind you, Vernon, that a great deal of money is at stake here."

"No, sir. I want this deal to go through, not just for the money, but because I want to prove to you that I can do it. I am Alicia's husband, and I want to be the one to provide for her future."

Alicia rolled her eyes. She knew such statements pleased her father, but she had her own vision of her future, and that vision did not include living in a one-horse town in Louisiana. She hated everything about the place—she hated the heat, and the snakes, and the dreadful people who were so hostile just because she'd been born north of the Mason-Dixon line; but mostly, she hated being so far from her father and her friends. She was so lonely there. She'd been patient with Vernon because she loved him, but her patience was wearing thin.

She pasted a bright smile on her face and pushed the study door wide. "Really, Papa," she chided as she crossed the room to her father's side, "I think you're awful to make Vernon sit here in this stuffy little office and talk business when we've just barely arrived."

"I'm sorry, sweetheart," Hiram said, "but Vernon and I have a great deal to do while he is here."

"Business?" she said with a pout. "But I was hoping

to spend some time with you myself. I see you so rarely."

Hiram wrapped an arm around her waist and gave her an affectionate squeeze. "I promise, we'll have time together. I want to take you to the symphony. I know how much you've missed it."

"Oh, I would love that! Can we go to Newport as well?"

The two men exchanged glances, but neither of them spoke, and Alicia pressed her advantage. "Just for a few weeks. Please, Papa."

He gave in, of course. "All right, then. We'll go to Newport. We can invite my associates there for a weekend meeting."

"Thank you, Papa."

He smiled at her. "You know I can't say no to you."

She laughed and bent to kiss his cheek. She knew. In fact, she was gambling her future on it.

The girls returned with enough blackberries for a dozen pies, but Olivia made only two. She spent the afternoon turning the remaining berries into jam, and she kept the girls busy helping her.

She deliberately kept herself busy so that her thoughts would not dwell on Conor, but his tormented face haunted her just the same.

She had no idea where Conor was or what he was doing, but by late afternoon he still hadn't returned, and her relief at his absence began changing to worry. She decided she'd better go in search of him.

She'd seen him go out to the barn, and that was where she began looking. But she did not find him there. She checked all the other outbuildings, she searched the gardens, and she walked through her orchard again, calling his name until she was hoarse, but after an hour, she still hadn't found him.

Worried now, she paused at the edge of her orchard, trying to think where to look next, but she knew she had looked everywhere. Maybe he had walked to the road and some farmer on the way to town had given him a ride.

No, he couldn't have left just like that, without even saying good-bye. But even as she thought it, she knew he could. He probably had.

Olivia sighed and leaned back against a tree. He was a loner, a man who didn't want the company of anyone, at least not very often and not for very long. A man who had built a wall around himself to keep people at a distance. A man filled with pain who could snarl like a wounded animal, but who could soothe away a little girl's fear of thunderstorms.

What horrible memories did he relive in his dreams? But she knew. Starvation and death, prison and torture, treason and amnesty, guns and someone named Sean Gallagher. He said that he'd betrayed everything he believed in, he said that his scars were exactly what he had deserved; Olivia didn't care what he had done. Whatever it was, she would not believe it bad enough to deserve what had happened to him in prison.

She began walking back toward the house. She walked slowly, her thoughts spinning in futile circles.

"You can catch the stage in Callersville." The farmer looked over at Conor, who sat beside him on the seat of a wagon filled with turnips. "Stage'll get you as far as Monroe, and from there you can take the train anywhere you want to go."

But Conor knew he could not. Six dollars would not

get him to Boston. Perhaps, if he could get a ride as far as Monroe, he could find a pub that might take him on for a round of boxing and pay him enough to get train fare.

But even as he thought it, he saw Olivia's face in his mind, and her eyes held him with that look. That look that pleaded for help even as her pride refused to let her ask for it again. His promise came back to him, mocking him.

I'll stay long enough to help you bring your crop in.

It was a broken promise now. That was why he never made promises, because he knew how lousy he was at keeping them.

He drew a deep breath, and the dust churned up by the wagon wheels razed his suddenly dry throat, choking him. His own promise suffocated him.

What if he went back? He closed his eyes. It was only a month. He could handle that, couldn't he? One month.

He thought of his first few months in Boston, three years ago, and his dirty room at Polly Keane's. He thought about the day Hugh O'Donnell, the head of *Clan na Gael*, had asked him to help get American money for the Irish cause. Hugh had claimed Conor would be the perfect man to get Irish-American hearts breaking and wallets opening, because he was such a heroic figure. That night the dreams had come again, and he'd almost laid Polly out when she tried to wake him, because he'd thought she was a prison guard.

He could remember the way Polly's whores had looked at him afterward, how they had stepped back warily as he passed them in the hall, and how they had whispered about him behind their hands. But his reputation had caught up with him, and after they learned he was a Fenian who had survived torture in the Mountjoy, their fear had changed to an awe-tinged respect. That's when he'd left Boston, unable to bear how they had made his shame into something glorious, how rumor made a man a hero when he was nothing but a fraud.

I'll stay long enough to help you bring your crop in.

He couldn't stay. He'd made Olivia a promise, and he couldn't keep it.

He saw her eyes again, and guilt washed over him in a smothering wave. He hadn't even finished fixing her roof. He thought of her trying to go up on that roof and finish the job herself. *Damn, damn, damn.*

Conor straightened on the seat. "Stop the wagon."

"What?"

"I said, stop the wagon."

The farmer yanked hard on the reins and brought the wagon to a halt. He watched Conor jump down, and he shook his head in bewilderment. "Mister, I thought you wanted a lift to town."

"I changed my mind," Conor replied, certain he was going to regret his sudden attack of scruples. He always did.

18

It was nearly dark by the time Olivia returned to the house. The girls were in the kitchen, and they looked up hopefully when she walked in. "He didn't come back here?"

"No, Mama," Becky answered, pulling a pan of corn bread from the oven. "I've finished making supper."

Olivia glanced at Carrie and Miranda, and saw their disappointed faces.

She crossed the room and put an arm around Becky's shoulders. "Thank you, honey. We'd better eat."

They did, and the supper table was unusually quiet.

It was Miranda who finally broke the silence, voicing aloud the question that was on all their minds. "Did Mr. Conor run away from home, Mama?"

"Mr. Conor wouldn't do that!" Carrie cried, dropping her spoon into her bowl of gumbo with a splash and giving her younger sister an indignant scowl. "He wouldn't leave without saying good-bye. I know he wouldn't."

Olivia reached out and put a comforting hand on Carrie's arm. "I know you like Mr. Conor, but he might have left. This isn't his home, remember."

"We should look for him," Carrie said. "He might have fallen or something. He might be hurt."

"I looked everywhere," Olivia answered gently. "Besides, it's dark out now. We can't go searching for him in the dark." She saw Carrie's crestfallen expression and added, "We'll look again in the morning."

After supper, she put all three of her gloomy daughters to bed. She went into the kitchen and put the iron on the stove to heat. She might just as well get some work done, and there was always plenty of ironing. She knew she wouldn't be able to sleep yet. Not until he came back. If he came back.

It was silly. As she worked, she told herself that he was probably halfway to Shreveport by now, and she ought to be glad. He was a man who didn't need anyone, who could easily pick up and move on without so much as a backward glance. Besides, the girls had become far too attached to him. She was glad he was gone.

A noise outside had her flying for the door with a cry of relief. She flung it open, ready to lay into Conor Branigan for worrying them all to death. But there was no one there.

Olivia stepped outside. Walking as far as the porch steps, she peered into the blackness beyond the square of feeble lamplight that shone through the kitchen window. But she could see nothing. He hadn't come back.

She turned to go back into the house, but a movement in the shadows caught her eye. She froze, watching as a man emerged from the darkness, stepping into the pool of light surrounding her porch. It wasn't Conor.

"Evenin', Olivia." Joshua Harlan moved closer, his gait a bit unsteady. Planting one boot on the bottom step, he grabbed the rail and grinned up at her. The wad of tobacco in his cheek bulged out.

That grin sent a tiny shiver of apprehension dancing along her spine, and she remembered Oren's admonition to be careful. All the Harlan boys were bullies, and she knew by his slurred speech and unsteady movements that Joshua was drunk. But she met his gaze squarely, remembering the days when his family had lived just the other side of Sugar Creek and all the times when Joshua and his brothers had teased her, and pulled her hair, and tried to intimidate her. It had worked back then, but it didn't work anymore. "Evenin', Joshua. Bit late for a walk, isn't it?"

He shrugged and thrust his other hand into the pocket of his trousers. "Nice night for it, though. Wouldn't you say?"

"No, I wouldn't. Too hot and humid, if you ask me." She folded her arms across her ribs. "What do you want, Joshua?"

He turned his head and spit, sending a stream of tobacco juice across the dirt. "Vernon's gone on business for a few weeks, but he asked me to drop by your place while he was gone and see if you might have changed your mind."

How often did she have to repeat her answer before they accepted it? "No, I haven't."

"He also told me that he's willing to up his offer by another hundred dollars."

"The answer's still no. You tell Vernon it doesn't matter how much money he's offering, I'm not selling my land."

He nodded, moving the wad of tobacco to his other cheek. "I'll tell him." He glanced back over one shoulder in the direction of the orchard. "How're your peaches doing these days?"

She stiffened. "My peaches are just fine, Joshua. You tell Vernon that, too."

She turned to go back in the house, but she'd only taken two steps before he caught her by the arm, swinging her around to face him. "Now, I'm mighty glad to hear that. They're right fine trees, and it'd be a shame if anything happened to 'em. A fire, for instance."

She tried to yank her arm free. "Let go of me!"

"A fire could ruin your whole crop." His grip tightened. "Why don't you just sell that land now?"

"I said no, Joshua, and I mean it." She raised her free arm to hit him, but he caught her wrist. Shoving her back against the door of the house, he leaned closer. "I think you'd be smart to take Vernon's offer. Real smart."

The smell of moonshine and tobacco made her want to retch. She turned her face away. For the first time in her life, Olivia felt truly afraid of Joshua, and she had no idea what to do.

But before she could decide, she was suddenly free. Joshua let out a yelp of surprise as he was hauled away from her, and Olivia turned her head just in time to see Conor wrap an arm around the smaller man's throat from behind.

"I don't think she's interested, boyo," Conor said through clenched teeth, yanking Joshua's arm and twisting it back. "Shall I be needin' to tell you what the word 'no' means, lad?"

He jerked the pinned arm higher up Joshua's spine, and the other man let out a squeal of pain, shaking his head in answer. Olivia watched in shocked relief as Conor hauled him to the edge of the porch and trapped him against the rail. He grabbed a fistful of Joshua's shirt with his left hand, then drew back his right arm and slammed his fist into the other man's face.

Olivia heard the awful crack of bone against bone, and she winced at the sound, watching as Conor lifted Joshua over the rail and sent him tumbling into the dirt with a thud.

"I believe you're trespassin'," Conor told him, leaning over the rail. "Now, get the hell out."

Joshua staggered to his feet. "Irish bastard," he moaned, raising one hand to his face. "You broke my nose."

Conor moved to go over the rail after him, more than happy to break the rest of the other man's face, but Joshua turned and fled, disappearing into the darkness.

Olivia let out her breath in a gasp of relief, sagging against the door.

"Are you all right?" Conor asked, crossing the porch to stand in front of her.

"I'm fine." She started to straighten away from the door, but then she began to shake with reaction, and her knees started to buckle.

He caught her, pulling her against him to hold her steady. Her arms slid around his neck and she clung to him, her face buried against his chest. "I heard a noise," she said, her voice muffled by the front of his shirt. "I thought it was you. He just grabbed me, and I didn't know what to do."

Conor thought of what might have happened had be been only minutes later, and renewed rage pulsed through his body. His arms tightened around her protectively. "Did he hurt you?"

She shook her head. "No. He was just drunk and bein' ornery."

Conor slid one hand up and down her spine in a soothing caress, and all his rage dissolved into something totally different and unexpected. Tenderness. "It's all right now, love," he murmured, his lips against her hair. "It's all right."

"I know," she whispered.

He held her for a long moment, savoring the warmth of her body against him and the softness of her hair beneath his jaw. When she started to pull away, he knew he should let her go, but he didn't want to. He had to force himself to lower his arms and step back, freeing her.

She straightened her apron and brushed at a loose wisp of hair that touched her cheek, looking so flustered and self-conscious, it made him want to smile. "Thank you. I'm fine now." Without looking at him, she added in a low voice, "We thought you'd left for good."

"I did."

She lifted her face. "Why did you come back?"

He didn't tell her why. "Nobody came by to give me a ride," he lied.

"I'm glad you came back," she whispered. "Thank you."

"Who was he? Did you know him?"

She sighed. "Yes, I know him."

"What did he want?"

Wrapping her arms around her ribs, Olivia walked past him to the porch rail and stared out into the darkness. "It's a long story."

"Time is something I seem to have a lot of these days. What did he want, Olivia?"

"He wanted to frighten me. Imagine Joshua thinking he could scare me." She laughed, but it sounded a rather shaky laugh to Conor.

"Frighten you?" He frowned. Crossing the porch, he reached out and laid a hand on her shoulder, turning her to face him. "Why?"

"He works for a rich and powerful man who wants to build a railroad through here and who wants my land to do it. I'm the only one around here whose land he hasn't been able to get on the proposed route."

"He must be willing to buy it from you?"

"Oh, yes." A wry smile touched her lips. "He's made quite a generous offer. But I'm being rather stubborn about this, I'm afraid. I won't sell. So, he's trying to intimidate me into selling. I'm sure he sent Joshua out here just for that reason."

Conor almost wanted to laugh at the irony. He'd spent most of his life watching as people were terrorized, starved, and evicted, all for some piece of land. He'd seen people toil ceaselessly on their little farms until it broke their backs and their spirits, only to pass it down to children who would toil on in their place. He'd traveled halfway around the world, only to watch it all happen again. Didn't any of them see that it wasn't worth it?

"It's just a piece of land, Olivia."

"No!" She looked up at him, a hard determination in her face he'd never seen before. "It is not just a piece of land. It's my home. My family has lived here for over seventy years. Five generations of Monroe folk have been born here, five generations have poured their blood and sweat into this land. My brothers died defending it. Peachtree is my legacy and my responsibility."

"But if they're threatening you—"

"Nonsense. I won't be driven off my land by empty threats from greedy carpetbaggers and scalawags ."

He studied the determined set of her jaw, and he wondered how many faces like hers he had seen in his life. Dozens, maybe hundreds. All of them thinking that roots and family ties were more important than anything else, all of them passing down land and traditions from one generation to the next, all of them believing that someday things were going to get better—if not for them, then for their children.

But Conor knew things never got any better, and that you couldn't fight the battle forever. Tenants got evicted, railroads got built, homeless children went hungry, and life was bloody unfair.

"So, you'll not be driven off your land, Olivia?" There was a hint of mockery in his voice. "Just how are you going to prevent it?"

"I'll ignore them."

"Oh, that's brilliant, that is. Next time this Joshua fellow comes around, I'll just let him manhandle you, and watch you try to ignore it."

She shot him a fierce look that told him she didn't appreciate the sarcasm. "I'll fight them."

"How?"

"I don't know. Somehow."

He looked into her proud, determined face, and he wondered how long she'd be able to hold out against their threats. Men who were rich and powerful wouldn't let one stubborn woman get in their way. She had no idea what she was up against.

He opened his mouth to tell her the bitter truth, but in her face he saw a tiny glimmer of all his own lost ideals, and he didn't have the heart to tell her that the carpetbaggers and scalawags of the world usually won.

Conor awoke the next morning thinking he must have been daft the night before. Just plain daft. There was no way Olivia could fight those land speculators, and he should have told her so.

He decided to talk to her about it after breakfast. She'd said those men had made her a generous offer for her land. If she sold it to them, she could use the money to buy herself another piece of land, complete with a house that didn't have sagging fences and a leaky roof. That was the only sensible solution, and he figured it was up to him to make her realize it.

He found her in the barn, putting down fresh straw in one of the stalls.

She glanced at him over the top of the stall. "Mornin'."

He decided to get right to the point. He crossed the barn to the opening of the stall. "Are you still planning to fight those men?"

She leaned on the pitchfork in her hand and brushed a loose tendril of hair back from her forehead. "Of course."

"I was hoping you might have done some thinking about it and changed your mind."

She shook her head. "No," she answered, and turned away, plunging her pitchfork into the pile of straw by her feet. "Why would I?"

"Because they have money and you obviously don't. Because they have power and you don't. Because it's a losing battle."

"I told you, this is my home. I won't be forced off my land."

"You're not being sensible."

She stopped working and turned toward him. "What would be sensible?" she asked softly. "Take the money and move on? That's what you'd do, isn't it?"

He thought about all the times he'd fought that battle within himself, knowing the sensible course, unable to follow it, rebelling against it. And he always regretted his rebellions afterward.

"Yes," he said. "That's what I'd do."

"Well, I'm not like you," she said, and resumed her task. "I'm not going anywhere."

"So, what are you planning to do? Stand by your front door and tell the bad men to go away?"

"There's no need to be sarcastic."

"For God's sake, woman!" He stepped forward and yanked the pitchfork out of her hand, forcing her to give him her attention. "This isn't a church social," he said, leaning the pitchfork in one corner of the stall. "That man last night wasn't here for a cup o' tay."

"I told you, I've known Joshua all my life. He wouldn't have hurt me. He just wanted to frighten me."

"Right. And what happens if the next time he comes around, he decides to frighten you a little harder?" He watched her lift her chin, and he figured he'd never met a more exasperating woman in his life. "What are you going to do? He's a man. You're a woman. Christ, do I have to explain this in graphic detail?"

She blushed a deep pink. "Well, you're here. He won't get the opportunity."

"I'm only staying long enough to help you harvest those peaches," he countered. "After that, I'll be gone. Then what will you do?"

She pressed her lips together and didn't answer.

"What will you do?" he asked again.

"I don't know!" she shot back, glaring up at him. "But I'm not going to let Joshua Harlan bully me."

"What about the girls? Are you ready to risk their safety?"

"Joshua's not going to do anything to the girls. He's just Vernon's hired gun, and Vernon wouldn't order him to hurt me or my girls."

Conor heard the name and sucked in his breath as if he'd just been kicked in the stomach. "Who?"

"Vernon Tyler. He's the man who wants my land."

Conor raked a hand through his hair. "No, no, no," he groaned, shaking his head. "'Tis a dead man, I am."

She frowned, perplexed. "What are you talking about?"

He turned away, paying no attention to her question. "Of all the insane, idiotic things I've ever done . . . Vernon Tyler. Oh, Christ." He thought of the farmer's wagon that could have taken him out of here, and he wanted to kick himself in the ass for being so stupid. "Should have bloody well kept going."

You ever cross my path again, boy, I'll snap you into pieces like a dry stick and use you for firewood.

"Conor?" Olivia walked to his side and placed a hand on his arm.

He shook it off with frustrated violence. Punching Vernon's hired gun last night would probably get him beaten again, or worse. He'd leave again, he decided, for good this time. Keeping a promise to a woman wasn't worth it.

"Conor?"

Her soft voice broke into his tumultuous thoughts. He turned around and leaned back against the side of the stall. "Vernon Tyler is the man who had me beaten."

"What? In heaven's name, why?"

Conor scowled. "Because I was an idiot. A dumb bastard who didn't like being told what to do."

"What are you talking about?"

He rubbed a hand across his jaw and let out his breath on a sigh. "Vernon was the one who arranged the boxing match I was in against Elroy Harlan."

"Yes, I know. I saw an advertisement for the match in the mercantile."

"Vernon financed the betting, he was the bookmaker. When the odds came in, he knew he'd lose money if I won the fight, so he ordered me to go down."

"I'm afraid I don't know much about gambling. What does that mean?"

"Take the fall. Lose on purpose. I let Elroy get in a really good punch, you see. I fall to the floor, with a few groans and moans to make it look convincing. Elroy wins the fight; Vernon makes a nice profit; I make my twenty-five dollars anyway; and everybody's happy."

"But that would be cheating."

He let out a bark of laughter at her shocked disapproval. "Well, what do you think, that Vernon is an upstanding citizen who would never do anything dishonest?"

Her cheeks burned at his mockery of her naiveté. "But you didn't do what Vernon wanted you to do? Why?"

"I've never been good at taking orders. Like I said before, I was an idiot. So, Vernon's boys decided to teach me a lesson. Sure, it was Vernon himself who told me, if I ever crossed his path again, he'd do worse. Much worse."

She pressed clasped hands to her mouth. "Oh, Lord in heaven."

He nodded approvingly. "When all else fails, pray. Good idea, that. While you're at it, ask Him if He might consider letting me out of this without getting the rest of my ribs broken, would you?"

She made a distressed sound and turned away. "You should leave, then," she said in a low voice, staring at the straw around her feet. "I wouldn't want you to get hurt again because of my fight with Vernon."

"Olivia, be sensible. If you sold your land to Vernon, you could take the money and buy yourself another farm someplace else, one that isn't too big for you to manage on your own. You can't win anyway."

Slowly, she turned to face him, her shoulders square, her spine straight. "I've been refusing Vernon's offers to buy my land for nigh on four years now. I reckon I can keep on refusing them for a few more. Eventually, he'll get tired of asking and give up." She turned and grabbed the pitchfork. "I appreciate your advice, Mr. Branigan, but as you've so clearly pointed out, you're leaving. My land isn't your affair."

So, he was Mr. Branigan again. Conor watched her for a few moments, but Olivia went on with her chores as if he wasn't there, and he knew the discussion was over.

She was right, of course. This wasn't his land. It was none of his business. Leaving now would be the smartest thing he could do.

Conor strode out of the barn. He paid no attention to the direction of his steps, but took the first path he came across. She was fighting a losing battle, but that was her choice. If she wanted to be so damn stubborn about some piece of land, who was he to interfere?

He imagined her facing this alone, without him there to protect her. He knew the pressure on her would only increase. He imagined Joshua coming back around to threaten her, or worse, and his anger at the thought of it churned to the surface. It wasn't his business, he told himself again, firmly pushing that anger down deep inside. He was done with lost causes. He was leaving.

"Mr. Conor!"

Carrie's voice calling his name intruded on his thoughts. He didn't want to see the girls just now. He paused for an instant, then resumed walking as if he hadn't heard, quickening his pace.

"Mr. Conor! Wait for us!"

This time, it was Miranda's voice calling to him. He could hear running footsteps behind him on the hard-packed dirt of the path. "Damn," he muttered, raking a hand through his hair. He came to an abrupt halt and turned around, giving in to the inevitable.

All three of them were coming toward him down the path, Carrie and Miranda at a flat-out run, Becky following at a slower pace, trying to act grown-up and dignified.

Carrie was the first to reach him. "You're back!" she cried, as she hurled herself at him. "I knew you'd come back! I knew it!" She looked up at him, her eyes shining with absolute trust.

"Did you, now?" he murmured, stunned by the child's unshakable faith in him. If only she knew how little he deserved it.

Miranda followed her sister's lead, wrapping her arms around him with a cry of delight. "You came back! We were scared you'd left us."

"I wasn't scared!" Carrie said and grabbed his hand. "I knew you wouldn't leave us."

Oh, Christ. A sudden wrenching twisted his insides, and he felt like a heartless dog. His hand tightened around Carrie's much smaller one.

"Where'd you go?" Carrie asked.

"I went for a walk. I got lost," he lied.

"Next time, we'll go with you," Miranda said, her arms tightening around his legs. "You won't get lost if we go along. 'Specially Becky. She never gets lost."

"That's right," another voice added, and he looked up to find Becky standing in front of him. She smiled shyly. "I never get lost."

He glanced from her to the other two faces that looked up at him. All he'd done was help birth a calf, play a few games of checkers, fix a roof, and tell a few stories—nothing to get excited about. But these girls insisted on looking at him like he was some kind of hero. They had missed him.

So how are they going to feel, boyo, when you hit the road again? When you don't come back?

Abandoned, probably. Betrayed. Terribly hurt. He

felt that irritating prick of conscience again, and he didn't like it one bit. He'd fancied himself a hero once; he'd had a cause to fight for; he'd felt courageous, noble, and all that rot. But it had all been a sham; his courage had crumbled at the crucial moment, and Conor knew he was no hero at all.

This was not his home. These girls were not his daughters. Olivia was not his wife. They were not his responsibility. He had his own life, and there was no room in it for them. He wasn't going to feel guilty about leaving them here on their own. He wasn't.

But he did. He felt guilty as hell.

Conor said nothing more about Olivia's little war. During breakfast, he barely spoke at all; and right after the meal, he began working on her roof. He spent the entire day up there, coming down only for dinner, then again for supper. Right after supper, he went for a walk. Alone.

He had not returned by the time she put the girls to bed. Olivia searched the first floor of the house, but she did not find him. She walked out onto the back porch and noticed light spilling through the open doorway of the barn.

What on earth was he doing out there? She walked down to the barn and paused in the doorway, staring at Conor and the sack of oats that he had hung from a rafter with a length of rope. Stripped to the waist, he was standing in front of the sack, punching it with his fists.

She watched, fascinated. His days of working outside had darkened his skin, and the scars that crisscrossed his back stood out in stark contrast, vivid white against nut brown. The muscles of his arm bunched tight, then stretched taut with fluid, powerful grace as he hit the sack and sent it swinging away.

A vision of the night before flashed through her mind, of how he had lashed out at Joshua with lightning-quick strength, and of how, only moments later, his arms had wrapped around her like a shield, to keep her safe. She thought about that afternoon in her kitchen and the way he had touched her, with hands strong enough to break her in half and tender enough to caress her; and she wondered at the extraordinary dichotomy that made a man.

He caught the sack as it came back toward him. Wrapping his arms around it, he clung to the sack as if too weary to stand on his own and caught sight of her in the doorway. He straightened with a stiff, abrupt movement. His rasping breaths mingled with the rhythmic chirp of crickets that floated through the open door of the barn. "What are you doing out here?"

"I saw the light, and I didn't know . . . I didn't realize it was you."

He shot her a pointed glance. "I came out here to be alone."

She saw the fierceness in his expression; she heard the clear dismissal in his blunt words. "I didn't mean to intrude."

Olivia knew she should leave, but her feet seemed rooted to the spot. She looked at him, one hand toying nervously with the high collar of her dress, and she yearned for him to hold her again.

He exhaled sharply. "Olivia."

He took a step toward her, then another, then another, until he was standing a foot away from her. She watched his eyes turn smoky. His lashes lowered. Instinctively, she swayed toward him, willing him to kiss her.

But he made no move. The sound of the crickets ticked away the seconds as they looked at each other.

"I'll stay until those peaches are in, because I promised

I would," he said, breaking the silence between them, his voice suddenly harsh as a whip. "After that, I'm leaving."

His words sliced through her, laid her open, and left pain in their wake—because they were nothing less than the truth. She reached up and touched the hard, uncompromising line of his mouth. "I know."

He stepped back as if her touch burned him. "Go away, Olivia," he said, and she imagined that there was the tiny hint of a plea in his voice. "Just go away."

She watched him walk back over to the sack. He slammed his fist into it with enough force to send it banging against the wall. Olivia turned and fled.

His honest words followed her back to the house. *I'm leaving.*

He'd said those words several times before. Why did it hurt to hear them now?

Olivia stopped halfway across the yard and stared back over her shoulder at the light spilling through the open doorway of the barn. It hurt because she was in love with him.

She wanted him to stop his wandering and stay with her. She wanted him to be there every morning when she woke and every night when she fell asleep. She wanted to hear him tell stories to the girls. She wanted him to touch her again, kiss her again. She wanted him to find solace here in her Louisiana hills, without wondering what was over the next one.

She didn't want him to stay because of her battle with Vernon. She didn't want him to stay because he felt obligated by a promise.

She wanted him to stay because he loved her. But he did not. Perhaps he felt a bit of affection for her, but no more. That realization was what hurt her the most.

19

Conor began avoiding her. During the two weeks that followed, he found any number of excuses to stay as far away from her as possible. He finished with her roof and started making repairs to her porch, spending all his time on the task. When he finished that, he cut down all the underbrush that choked the gardens around the house, then he began making repairs to the outbuildings.

Their nightly reading lessons stopped. He knew how to read well enough now to manage on his own, but she missed their nightly lessons; she missed the companionship of sitting with him at the kitchen table, sipping tea, and talking.

There wasn't much time left before he would leave, and she wanted nothing more than to spend the few precious days that remained with him. She wanted just to look at him, listen to his voice, be near him, until he was burned into her memory; for, after he left, the memory of him would be all she had. But he didn't want her company. The only time she saw him was at meals, or when she could watch him unobserved as he worked.

Olivia set the iron on the stove and walked over to the kitchen window. She pressed her nose to the pane of glass and stared out at the lamplight that came from the doorway of the barn. He went out there every night, but she never followed him again. He had made it very clear that he wanted to be left alone. Nonetheless, she found excuses to stay awake, working on those dresses for the harvest dance, doing ironing, or cleaning out cupboards—anything to keep her in the kitchen until he came in. She never went to bed until he did, but he always walked past her with a murmured good-night and went straight to his room without another word.

Olivia stared down at the shirt she was ironing for him, a shirt that had belonged to Stuart, who had also gone away. Mama, Stuart, Charles, Daddy. All gone.

In a different way, Conor was going to leave her, too. She thought of all the days that lay ahead, and they seemed very empty. The thought of his departure filled her with a loneliness that made her chest ache. A tear rolled down her cheek and plopped on the white linen.

She heard the sound of his step on the back porch and she brushed away her useless tears with a hasty swipe of her hand. She grabbed the iron and she did not look up when he walked in. She kept her back straight and her eyes on her task.

"Good night, Olivia," he said as he passed.

"Good night, Conor."

But tears blurred her eyes again as she watched him walk out of the kitchen. He rejected all that she held dear, he carried wounds she could never heal.

Make him stay. Please find a way to make him stay.

It was a futile prayer. There was nothing here that could make him stay. Nothing at all.

*   *   *

When Olivia went to fetch the water the following morning, she found a dead cat beside the well. She stared down at the poor creature, which had obviously been shot and placed there deliberately. Another message from Vernon, a very clear one. He could have had his boys drop the dead animal in her well, he could have poisoned her water, but he had not. Instead, he had simply let her know how easy it would be to do so, should she continue being so stubborn.

Olivia's lips tightened to a thin line as she stared down at the stiff, bloody carcass of the dead cat, and she was furious. She thought of Joshua's threat to burn down her orchard and his swaggering attempts at intimidation. She wondered how many other people had given up their land to Vernon because of threats such as these.

Olivia went to the barn to get a shovel and her long, thick leather gloves. She buried the cat in the woods then went back to the house. She marched up the stairs to the attic and rummaged through the trunks until she found the one that contained all the rifles, pistols, and ammunition of her father and brothers. She chose Stuart's army rifle, thinking that it looked more intimidating than any of the others, then she slammed down the lid on the trunk and took the rifle downstairs.

When Conor awakened and went out to the kitchen, he found Olivia standing on the back porch with the rifle in her hands. She turned at the sound of his footsteps across the kitchen and looked at him through the open doorway. He saw her resolute face, and he knew something had happened.

"I found a dead cat beside the well," she said, as if she could hear his unspoken question. "It was shot."

"Jaysus." Conor knew what that meant, and he could tell that Olivia knew it, too. He glanced at the rifle in her hands. "So, it's to be a war, then, Olivia?"

"I'm just taking precautions, that's all."

"Do you know how to use that thing?" he asked.

She shook her head. "Do you?"

He stared at the gun, thinking of Sean and his American rifles. "Aye," he said heavily. "I know."

"Will you teach me how to shoot?"

"Why don't you just sell them the land? It's not worth a fight, Olivia. It's just not worth it."

She set her jaw. "If you don't teach me, I'll just have to teach myself."

He watched as she turned her back to him and hefted the rifle experimentally in her hands, then lifted it as if to take aim. It was plain as a pikestaff she didn't know the first thing about guns. If he didn't teach her how to handle the thing, she'd probably end up hurting herself.

"Bloody hell," he muttered, and walked out onto the porch. He reached over her shoulder and wrapped his hand over the rifle, pushing down until the barrel pointed toward the plank floor.

She turned her head to give him an inquiring glance.

"Are you prepared to shoot somebody, maybe kill him?" he asked. "Do you think you can?"

"If I have to."

He studied her serious face for a moment, then he nodded. "All right, then. You'd best learn how it's done."

He pulled the rifle from her hands and studied it. It was a Henry .44, not great for long-distance shooting, and a bit heavy for a woman to use, but a fine weapon nonetheless. "When's the last time this rifle was used?"

"Sixty-three. It belonged to my brother Stuart."

He verified that there was no cartridge in the chamber or magazine, then he lifted the gun. He cocked it, took a bead on the right pole of the clothesline, and pulled the trigger.

The hammer fell with a hesitant click. "Needs a good cleaning first," he told her, lowering the gun. "I'll need some rags, a bucket of boiling hot water, and a ramrod. Have you any oil to lubricate it?"

"Sweet oil."

"That'll do. Have you any cartridges?"

"Yes, a whole box of them."

"Bring that, too."

She nodded and went into the house.

Conor stared down at the gun in his hands. He shouldn't do this. The smartest thing Olivia could do would be to sell her land, take the money and her girls, and start fresh someplace else. But he knew she wouldn't do the smartest thing.

A few more weeks, and he wouldn't be here to rescue her if men came at her out of the dark. The least he could do was provide her with some means to protect herself. "Damn," he muttered.

After breakfast, Conor took Olivia out to one of the fields that used to grow cotton but now lay fallow with weeds as their only crop. The girls, who had only been told that she wanted to learn how to shoot, insisted on watching her first lesson. She wasn't sure that was such a good idea, but Conor pointed out it was best if they knew exactly where the girls were while they were having target practice.

He had brought along an armful of tin cans, and he set them up in a line on the fence. He instructed the girls to stand about two dozen feet behind them, and he proceeded to give them a lecture on the dangers of guns. "You're not to be thinking this is a toy," he told them sternly. "It's not."

He reached up one hand to unfasten the top button of his shirt, and he bent down so that Carrie and Miranda could see the round scar at his shoulder. "That came from a bullet, lasses, and your man here almost died because of it. Guns can be very dangerous."

Olivia watched him, and she thought wistfully that he'd make a fine father—even if he hadn't taken Becky's kissing episode with Jeremiah as seriously as he should have—a thought which reminded her of her own first experience with that particular activity and sent a tingle clear down to her toes.

"How'd it happen?" Carrie asked, reaching out to touch the scar on Conor's shoulder with her finger.

"A wee lad who thought a gun was a toy shot me by accident." He straightened and buttoned his shirt. "You're not to touch this rifle at all, for any reason. Is that understood?"

"Yes, sir," they answered in unison, wide-eyed.

"Good girls."

He walked back to Olivia's side and took the box of cartridges out of her hand, then bent down to dump them in a pile on the ground nearby. "This is a forty-four caliber, fifteen-shot, repeating rifle," he told her. Grabbing a handful of the shells, he straightened. "That means it will fire up to sixteen 44-caliber shells, fifteen in the magazine and one in the chamber. You load the shells through the magazine here."

She watched carefully as he showed her how to load the gun. He pushed fifteen shells through a tubular opening located in front of the trigger beneath the barrel, then handed the rifle to her and moved to stand behind her.

"Hold it with the butt braced against your shoulder," he instructed, bringing his arms up around her and moving the rifle into correct position as he spoke. "That way, you'll have better control. Relax, love," he added. "You're too stiff."

Olivia tried, she really did, but all she could think of was how nice it would be to lean back against him and enjoy the feel of his arms around her. The idea that she might actually do such a thing made her acutely self-conscious.

His hand closed over hers on the underside of the barrel, making her pull down on a lever behind the trigger and push it back into place. "That cocks the gun," he explained, "meaning it puts the first bullet in the chamber and makes the gun ready to fire. You have to cock the gun each time you take a shot."

She wanted to ask him about aiming the gun, but when she turned her head to look up at him, the question she'd intended to ask went right out of her head. He was close enough that if she moved just the slightest bit, their lips would touch. She tensed and ran her tongue over her suddenly dry lips, watching his smile fade and his eyes darken to that smoky blue.

She said the first thing that came into her head. "Did you really get that bullet wound because of a child?" she whispered.

"Hell, no," he muttered. "I got shot by a Protestant farmer when I was fifteen. I was trying to obtain one of his sheep at the time."

She choked back a laugh, trying to look disapproving. "Obtain? You mean steal."

He grinned down at her. "Well, I couldn't very well tell them that, could I?" he murmured. "What kind of a lesson would that be for their impressionable young minds?"

That comment reminded her that the three impressionable young minds in question were watching them. He seemed to realize it, too, for he lowered his arms and stepped back from her. Olivia turned toward the fence several dozen yards away and forced her thoughts back to the task at hand.

"I use this to take aim, don't I?" she asked, curving one finger around the rifle to touch the brass flange that jutted above the barrel.

"Aye, that's called a sight. All you do now is pull the trigger, but remember, squeeze it gently, don't jerk. And—"

A loud report interrupted him. The force exerted by the shot rammed the butt of the gun into her shoulder and sent Olivia flying backward. She fell heavily against Conor, who was standing right behind her. He took her weight without moving, almost as if he'd expected this to happen, and wrapped his arms around her.

"And," he finished wryly, "a 44-caliber rifle has quite a kick, so be prepared."

Olivia lowered the rifle. She leaned back against him and rubbed her sore shoulder. "I'll remember that next time," she said ruefully and looked over at the fence. She realized that the tin can she had aimed for now lay on the ground. "At least I made the shot," she said with pride.

Conor gave her a nod of approval. "Not bad," he conceded, "not bad at all. For a lass."

She jabbed him with her elbow for that, then straightened in his arms, cocked the rifle, took aim, and sent another can flying off the fence.

Conor wisely made no more teasing comments about her ability to shoot a gun.

    *   *   *

The two weeks that followed were busy ones. After several practice sessions, Olivia put the gun away, placing it on the top shelf of the kitchen pantry, along with two boxes of shells, deciding that would be the handiest place for it. At Conor's suggestion, she removed a second rifle from the trunk and after he had cleaned it, she put that one under her bed and another box of cartridges in the drawer of her bedside table. But thankfully, no incidents arose that required the use of either weapon.

While Conor continued to work on projects around her place, Olivia spent her days getting ready for the harvest. She got out the bushel baskets and brushed off the cobwebs. She hauled out the ladders and checked them carefully to make sure they hadn't rotted since the previous year.

She went into town and made arrangements with Grady McCann to hire two teams of mules and two wagons, with payment to be made after harvest. She'd need the wagons to cart her peaches to Monroe for sale, and Grady owned the livery stable, one of the few businesses in Callersville that Vernon had not been able to buy.

While she was in town, she made a stop at the sawmill to see about getting sawdust and barrels to pack her peaches. Vernon was still away, but Joshua coldly informed her that she could not barter for them. "Vernon's orders," he'd said with a smug smile. So when she sold her calf to Oren Johnson, she used the money to purchase what she needed. She also asked Oren if he would feed her animals while she was gone and keep an eye on her place. Oren promised he would.

While she was at the Johnsons', she cooed over the new baby and visited with Kate, who said that of course the girls could stay at their place again this year while she took her peaches to the cannery in Monroe. When Kate asked her how she was going to get the peaches there by herself, Olivia said she'd found a farmhand to help her during the harvest and left before Kate could ask any more questions.

When she wasn't busy with preparations for her harvest, Olivia spent her time getting the girls ready for school, which would start about the time harvest was over. She let out the seams on all their dresses and added ruffles to the hems for length. She mended all their torn stockings, sold Lila enough jars of spiced peaches from last year to buy new shoes for them, and ironed pinafores and hair ribbons. Vernon might call them orphans and say they had no decent clothes, but Olivia always made sure her girls went to school neat as pins. This year wasn't going to be any different.

She was grateful for the many tasks that kept her busy, because she didn't want to think about the fact that the harvest also meant Conor's departure. The hot, humid days of August slipped inevitably by, and when she walked through her orchard, when she saw how quickly the peaches were ripening, she wished time would slow to a crawl and keep him from going away.

It didn't, of course. The peaches ripened and the day finally came when Olivia knew they had to be picked.

Conor and the girls went out to the orchard with her, carrying baskets and ladders. Chester followed them. When they got to the orchard, the dog settled himself comfortably in the shade of one tree to watch. Becky and Carrie each took a basket and a ladder, chose a row, and immediately set to work, blithely waving aside Olivia's admonitions to be careful.

"Gosh sakes, Mama," Carrie said, pausing on the ladder to frown down at her. "Stop fussing." She looked over at Conor with an expression of long suffering. "We go through this every year," she told him, rolling her eyes.

Conor glanced over at Olivia, but she wasn't looking at him. Her gaze was fixed on Carrie, and he saw the concern in her expression. "They'll be fine, Olivia. They're not going to get hurt."

"I know," she answered, but she continued to watch Carrie until the child had planted her basket firmly between the branches of the tree and settled herself comfortably on a limb, before she turned to Conor.

"Have you ever picked peaches before?"

He shook his head.

Miranda tugged at her skirt. "Mama, can I pick, too?"

"Not this year, honey. Next year, maybe."

Miranda's face fell. "What can I do?"

"Well, let's see." Olivia tilted her head to one side. "First, we have to show Mr. Conor how to pick. After that, we can start packing the peaches in the barrels. How about that?"

"Okay."

She took the child by the hand and looked over at Conor. "Ready?"

He nodded. "What happens once we've picked them?" he asked, as he followed her and Miranda to another row, his ladder under one arm and a basket in his hand.

"You and I will haul them to Monroe," she answered. "It's a full day's drive from here. The girls will stay at the Johnsons' while we're gone, since we'll have to stay in Monroe overnight. I'll pay for your room, of course, and your meals while we're there." Lest he get the wrong idea, she added hastily, "It's the least I can do, since you're helping me and all."

"You don't owe me anything for this, Olivia. I'll pay

my own way. But I do think, while we're there, we should go somewhere nice for dinner."

"That isn't necessary."

"We both have to eat." He leaned his ladder against a tree, and rested the basket on his hip. "Now, tell me about peach-picking."

She opened her mouth as if to argue, but closed it again. Instead, she looked away and gestured to the tree beside her. "The first thing to remember is that you must pick peaches only when they're ripe."

She reached up and her fingers curled around a peach. "This one's ripe. You can tell because there's no green. The skin has a yellow background color and a rosy blush to it. You hold it in your fingers like this and pull it from the tree with just a slight twist. If you have to try too hard, it's not ripe enough to pick, and the fruit will bruise."

Conor thought peaches sounded a lot like women. Innocent women, anyway, he amended, watching Olivia pluck the peach from the tree. He hadn't been all that gentle in her kitchen that afternoon when he'd kissed her, and he felt a twinge of regret. Next time, he'd do it differently—but that thought brought him up sharp. Sure, there wasn't going to be a next time.

Something about her, something about the inexperienced but passionate way she'd moved beneath his hands, the soft sounds of surprise she'd made, had stripped away all his barriers and ignited him like a keg of dynamite. And that night in the barn, when she'd seen him practicing. The way she'd looked at him, her gaze pulling him with some undefinable force that was stronger than chains, her touch sending his senses into a spin more effectively than a jug of poteen. He knew he didn't dare touch her again. But he wanted to. He watched her take a bite of the peach and lick the sweet juice from her bottom lip. Desire clutched his insides. Christ, he wanted to.

She looked up to find him watching her, and he knew she was thinking about the same thing. *Aye,* he thought, watching the rosy blush flood her cheeks, *peaches are a lot like women.* "A nice restaurant," he said firmly. "And wear that red silk dress of yours. I'd like to see you in something that isn't gray or brown, for a change."

That night, Olivia was awakened by the sound of shattering glass and loud barking from Chester. A terrified shriek followed and she knew instantly it was Miranda. She flung back the sheets and jumped out of bed as the sound of loud whooping and shouting began outside the house. Chester's barks and Miranda's screams grew louder. She raced out into the hall and nearly tripped over the dog. At the same moment, all three girls came running out of their rooms.

Miranda was the first to reach her.

"Mama! Mama!" The child flung herself at Olivia, wrapping her arms around her mother's legs. "Somebody b-broke my w-w-window!" she sobbed. "They threw a rock through my w-window."

Olivia lifted her daughter into her arms. "It's all right, honey," she said, hugging the child fiercely. "It's all right."

"Mama?"

She felt Carrie's arm slide around her, and she stroked the child's hair reassuringly. Outside, the shouting continued, and they could hear the thud of stones hitting the house. Chester, still barking, raced up and down the hall as if unable to decide whether to stay close and protect them or go down and tear the trespassers into pieces.

"Who are they, Mama?" Becky whispered.

Before she could answer, Conor's voice shouted to her up the stairs.

"Olivia!"

With Miranda still in her arms and Chester right behind her, she ran to the stairs and saw Conor coming up, a lamp in his hand. "We're all right," she called down to him as he came to a halt on the landing. "But they broke Miranda's window."

"Keep them up there!" he ordered, and turned to go back down.

"C'mon, girls." She hoisted Miranda higher on her hip, grabbed Carrie's hand, and ran into Becky's room. Chester followed them.

"I'm going to go help Mr. Conor," she told her oldest daughter as she set Miranda down. "I want you to bolt the door behind me. Then, I want all of you to get down on the floor, and stay there until I come for you. And don't go near the windows, understand?"

Becky nodded. "Yes, Mama."

Olivia started for the door.

"Mama?"

She turned at the sound of Miranda's frightened voice and bent down to press her lips to the child's cheek. "Everything's going to be fine, honey. I promise. Now you all stay in here."

She closed the door behind her and ran to her own room. She lit the lamp, then knelt down beside her bed and grabbed the rifle, thankful she had followed Conor's advice and put a second gun upstairs.

Through her open window, she could hear the whooping and hollering of the men outside as they circled the house. She could also hear the rhythm of hoofbeats and knew they were on horseback. She rose to her feet and yanked open the drawer of her bedside table to

grab a handful of shells, then sat down on the edge of
the bed to load the gun. She tried to hurry, but her
hands were shaking so badly that she fumbled awk-
wardly with the cartridges, and it seemed to take forever.

The loud crack of a gunshot jerked her to her feet.
Praying that the shot had come from Conor's rifle, she
shoved the last shell into the magazine of her own gun,
opened the French doors that led out of her bedroom
onto the upstairs veranda, and stepped outside.

The moon came out from behind a cloud to illumi-
nate the darkness just as a trio of riders came around
the corner of the house. Too angry to think about what
she was doing, Olivia stepped to the edge of the
veranda, braced herself against the waist-high rail, and
stared down the sight at the riders below. She took a
bead just above the head of the lead rider as he lifted
his arm and tossed a stone toward the house.

The sound of shattering glass told her they'd broken
another window, and Olivia pulled the trigger. The
man's hat flew off, and she smiled, thinking she was
becoming a mighty fine shot.

"Let's get outta here!" a man shouted, and she'd
have sworn on a stack of bibles it was Joshua Harlan's
voice. The riders turned toward the dense woods that
bordered the house as Olivia lifted her rifle again.

She cocked it and took aim, but the moon had vanished behind a cloud, and the riders had already disappeared from view amid the oaks and darkness. She
lowered the gun and slumped against the rail, drawing
air into her lungs in rapid, gasping breaths as she listened to the departing hoofbeats fade into silence.
Sweat broke out on her forehead, and she leaned down,
pressing her brow to the cool wrought-iron railing.

"Olivia?"

She straightened and whirled around with her rifle raised. Conor stood in the arch of the open doors, a rifle in his hands, his massive frame a dark silhouette against the lamplight behind him. Breathing a sigh of relief, she lowered her own rifle.

"Are you all right?" he asked, walking toward her.

She nodded. "You?"

"Right as rain." He pulled the gun from her hands and set it down, then reached out to touch her face, running his thumb across her mouth. "You're bleeding."

His hand fell away, and she touched the tip of her finger to her lower lip, realizing she must have bitten it when she was firing the gun. "Ouch," she said, feeling the sting for the first time.

He remembered the day she'd confessed her fear of heights and how she couldn't even bring herself to walk out on the upstairs veranda. "Olivia," he said gently, "do you know where you're standing, love?"

She glanced over the railing behind her and saw the ground far below. "Oh, Lord," she breathed, looking away. She pressed her hand across her mouth and froze as if rooted to the spot, squeezing her eyes shut. "I think I'm going to be sick," she choked.

Conor set down his rifle and lifted her into his arms, cradling her against him. "I've got you," he said against her hair. "I've got you."

He carried her into her bedroom and set her on the edge of the high bedstead, then stood in front of her. "Put your head down between your knees," he ordered, "and take deep breaths."

"Where are the girls?"

His hand curved around the back of her neck, and he gently pulled her head toward her lap. "They're all right. A wee bit shaken up, but they're all right. They're still in Becky's room. I told them to stay there."

She pushed against his hand, trying to sit up. "They must be scared to death. I'd better go see."

He kept her head down. "You stay right where you are," he murmured, his fingers lightly caressing the back of her neck.

He let his hand fall and started for the door, but she straightened and reached out impulsively to grab his hand. "Thank you," she whispered. "For being here."

He started to pull away, then stopped and instead wrapped his large hand around her smaller one. He couldn't help wondering if tonight's events had changed her mind about selling her land, but he didn't ask.

Finally, he pulled his hand from hers. "Are you sure you're all right?" When she nodded, he turned away. "I'll go and get the girls."

When he brought the girls and Chester to her room, Olivia held out her arms, and they ran to her. She gathered the girls around her with kisses and hugs. "Are you girls okay?" she asked, not reassured until she'd asked the question at least half a dozen times.

Becky climbed up onto the bed beside her. "Who were they, Mama?"

"What did they want?" Carrie asked.

Miranda tugged on Olivia's nightgown to get her attention. "Why did they break my window?"

Olivia opened her arms, and Miranda climbed up to sit on her lap. "Well," she answered, "there are some men who want me to sell the farm because they want to build a railroad on it. And I don't want to sell, because this is our home. So they're trying to make us leave by throwing rocks and breaking our windows and shouting at us." She looked over at Conor. "Mr. Conor and I scared them, and they ran off, but they may come back."

Carrie stood up and patted her mother's shoulder. "Don't worry, Mama," she said, and walked over to where Conor stood in the doorway, an expression of adoration and absolute trust on her pixie face as she looked up at him. She slipped her hand into his and turned to smile at her mother. "Everything's going to be just fine, you'll see. Mr. Conor won't let anything happen to us."

Conor couldn't breathe. The room felt suffocatingly hot, and he had to get away. "It's late," he managed. "You'd best get some sleep."

He pulled his hand out of the child's, and his chest tightened painfully. He turned on his heel and stepped into the hall, closing the door behind him.

He started down the stairs, but on the landing he stopped. He looked down into the darkness of the foyer below, the darkness all around him. He didn't want anyone to rely on him, need him, look at him with trust. He could never live up to it. He didn't deserve it. Conor lowered his head into his hands with a feeling of dread.

20

LUÍOCHÁN
Lurgangreen, Ireland, 1867

The train was late.

Conor moved through the dense cover of underbrush near the railroad tracks until he was at Adam McMahon's side. "Donnelley's ready with the wagon," he said softly, crouching low.

"Lovely," Adam responded. "So where's the bloody train? It's freezing out here."

Conor cupped his hands and blew on his frozen fingers as he glanced up at the sky, grateful for the moonless January night. It would take a good two hours to remove the guns from the false-bottomed hiding place of the train car, load them on the wagon, and get them to Dooley's farm—longer if anything went wrong. Christ, if the train didn't get here soon, they'd be hauling a wagon-load of rifles across County Louth by the light of day.

This was the tenth shipment, the tenth midnight rendezvous. The transfers had been meticulously planned in the tiny room above McGrath's, and what was even more astonishing, those plans had been carried off nine times in two years without a hitch. Conor hoped their luck would hold just a wee bit longer.

Nine hundred of Sean's American rifles—God bless the generosity of their kinsmen across the water for providing them—were safely tucked away in various hiding places all over Ireland. Only Conor, Sean, and Adam knew the exact locations of all the weapons and the exact manner by which they ended up there.

Conor knew the Council was planning something big, perhaps the rising itself, but he had not yet been told what it was. But Conor also knew that one thousand rifles did not make a war, and he was afraid the Council was moving too fast. Training camps had been set up so that Irish farm lads could be taught how to use a weapon they'd never had the opportunity to touch before, but shooting tins off a stone wall was a far cry from staring down the muzzle of a British army rifle.

He'd tried to tell Sean it was too soon, but only two weeks before, nine comrades had been arrested in Belfast, causing Irish patriotic fervor to run high in Ulster—where Fenianism was weakest—and the Council probably wanted to take advantage of it before the incident became only another tragic song and another lost dream. No word yet from O'Bourne on who had informed, but Conor vowed he'd break the bastard's neck with his bare hands when he found out.

Far down the line, Conor saw a flash of light. Finally, he thought, moving closer to the tracks at the signal from Dooley's lantern. Adam followed him. Still concealed by the thick underbrush, the two men waited as the freight train braked, pulling into the tiny wayside station that was nothing more than a bench and a wooden overhang.

Both men ran to the train as it inched to a stop. Conor pulled a wrench out of his pocket, slipped between the train wheels, and began undoing the bolts that fastened the panel of the false bottom in place, as Adam walked to the front of the train to have a word with the driver.

His scream of warning hit the cold air like an icy wind. *"Luíochán!"*

Conor turned his head and saw two pairs of polished British army boots hit the dirt beside him.

"Luíochán! Ambush, Conor! Run!" Adam screamed again, this time in pain. "Oh, Christ!"

Conor tried to slide out from under the car on the opposite side, but the cold steel of a pistol muzzle pressed against the back of his head and froze him in place.

"Don't make a move, Paddy," a low voice ordered. "Unless you want your brains splattered all over the tracks."

Conor let out his breath in a slow hiss. Their luck had just run out.

21

For the next seven days, Conor picked peaches from dawn to twilight. He was glad of the long hours he spent at the task. During the day, he wasn't close enough to Olivia to touch her, and during the night, he was too exhausted to get himself all desperate thinking about touching her. He went to bed every night right after supper and fell immediately asleep. No nightmares about the Mountjoy, guilt over his pending departure, or erotic dreams about Olivia tormented him in his sleep. He was just too tired.

The work was also making him stronger. He knew, when the time came, he'd go back into the ring in prime shape. When he thought about leaving, guilt and relief flooded through him in equal amounts, battling for control with equal force; so he didn't think about leaving. He got through the days like he always had, one at a time. It was his way, the only way he knew.

When all the peaches had been picked and packed in barrels of sawdust, he loaded them onto the two wagons Olivia brought out from town. He had to pile them high in the wagons to fit them all in, and he tied them down securely with ropes. The next morning at sunrise, Olivia took the girls over to the Johnson farm, where they would spend the next two days. When she returned, she went into the house and fetched a small carpetbag, and they started for Monroe, each driving a wagon.

Conor was glad of the arrangement, preferring the comfortable distance that separate wagons put between them. But since she led the way, he spent the entire morning watching her, and by midday, he suspected that about fifty more miles of distance would probably be required before he could truly feel comfortable again.

When she took off her bonnet, the sun shot red lights through her brown hair and made him remember the feel of it in his fingers. When she let go of the reins to raise her arms overhead and arch her back in a languorous stretch, he envisioned her naked amid a tangle of sheets and pillows. When they stopped to eat the dinner of sandwiches she'd packed, sitting in the cool shade of a grove of pine trees, he watched her undo the top two buttons of her dress, with a comment about the heat, and he felt himself coming apart.

He wished now he hadn't offered to take her to dinner in Monroe. That had been a stupid idea, indeed: To sit across from her, wanting her like crazy, and not being able to have her because he seemed to have developed some ridiculous notion of propriety where she was concerned.

Just a few more days, he told himself, as he snapped the reins and started the wagon moving again; it was just a few more days. Then he'd be quit of this place for good. He'd head for New Orleans first, he decided.

He'd go down to the Irish district and take on all comers at Shaugnessey's. With his winnings, he'd go on a binge of whiskey, cigars, women, and card-playing that would shake off any thoughts of Olivia Maitland, and reassure him that he hadn't picked up a permanent case of scruples from her.

He watched her reach back to rub the stiffness from her neck with one hand, and he imagined doing that for her, starting at her neck and working his way down. He imagined it over and over.

It was a very long trip.

They pulled into Monroe late that afternoon. After Olivia had haggled with Silas Shaw, the owner of the cannery, over an acceptable price for her peaches, the wagons were unloaded, and she tucked the precious cash that would see her through another year securely in the top of her high button shoe. Conor drove the wagons to the livery stable across from the Whitmore Hotel and left them to be boarded, then went to the hotel to get them rooms for the night. Olivia went to Danby's Mercantile and bought eight panes of window glass to be delivered to the Whitmore in the morning, then went to the hotel to meet Conor.

She found him in the lobby waiting for her. When she signed the register, Olivia did not miss the speculative look the clerk gave her at the realization that they were obviously not married, but apparently together, a notion Conor did not dispel when he asked where they might dine. Heat flamed her cheeks, and he responded to her reproving glance with a grin. She snatched her key from the clerk without a word, and followed the bellboy who carried her carpetbag upstairs.

Half an hour later, Olivia slid gratefully into the full-size bathtub brought up to her by the maids, who then filled it with water cool enough to refresh her after the heat of the day, and warm enough to wash away the travel dust and sweat. She indulged in a long soak, then washed her hair, wrapped a towel around it, and stepped from the tub.

She rubbed her body dry with the towel, then pulled on the lacy petticoat and chemise, fastened the hooks of the corset, and slipped the dark red silk dress over her head.

She sat down at the dressing table and brushed out her hair, which was still slightly damp and starting to curl, then she put it up in a loose twist at the back of her head, that left several tendrils loose to curl around her face. Conor had told her he liked her hair that way the Sunday she had given him a shave. She secured the style in place with two combs, and she thought of how he'd taken her hair down that day in the kitchen. The memory still made her tingle.

Olivia smoothed down the folds of the dark red silk, glad that she'd brought it. She tried to remember the last time she'd worn a lovely dress or felt the delicious swish of delicate, lacy undergarments beneath, and she could not remember. It had been too long ago. Far too long.

She rose and took several steps back to get a good look. She studied her reflection in the mirror, and she was surprised. She did not look at all like herself. She looked rather pretty.

She stood there, staring at her reflection. Conor had insisted on taking her out to supper, and she decided that tonight she was not going to sit on the shelf. Tonight, she was not going to be drab Olivia Maitland. She stared at the bodice that skimmed her shoulders and dipped into a vee above her breasts. While still more modest than most, it was rather daring for her, but she didn't care. For once in her life, she wanted to be daring, perhaps even a bit shocking. Just this once, she wanted romance, and this might be her only chance. She thought of Conor's smoky blue eyes, and that tingle ran through her again. *Just this once,* she thought, hugging herself. *Just this once.* She'd have the rest of her life to regret it.

When Olivia opened the door of her room, Conor's throat went dry and he was suddenly seized with the overpowering need for a shot of whiskey. His gaze ran down the line of her body, coming to an abrupt halt at the shadow of cleavage above the dark red silk bodice of her dress. Perhaps two shots. How the hell was he going to get through an entire evening of small talk with her when the only thing he could think of was kissing her soft skin?

"Is something wrong?" she asked.

"Wrong?" He shook his head. "I'm stunned," he said with a laugh, trying to be glib about it. "You're so beautiful, every man downstairs is going to envy me."

He could tell by her pink cheeks and hesitant smile that she didn't really believe him. "It's the dress," she murmured.

"No, it's not." He cast another glance over the red silk. "Although, the dress is a definite improvement, I must say."

"You look very nice, too," she said almost shyly, gesturing to the new suit he wore.

He ran a hand over the charcoal-gray waistcoat. After paying for his room, a haircut, and a bath, he'd laid out three dollars for the clothes. "At least they fit. And I think I still have enough left over to buy you a meal."

"You don't have to," she said. "I can pay my own."

"Perhaps you can, lass, but you won't." He offered her his arm. "Shall we, Miss Maitland?"

She slipped her arm through his and they went downstairs to the hotel restaurant. They dined on clear soup, salmon with dill sauce, asparagus, and peach russe. It was delicious, and perhaps a bit more luxurious than the fare from Olivia's kitchen, but Conor decided it wasn't better.

After their meal, the waiter returned to ask if the lady would care for coffee, adding that perhaps the gentleman would require a drink and a cigar. Conor replied without a moment's hesitation. "Irish whiskey, if you please, and a Havana cigar."

"Very good, sir." The waiter departed with a nod, and Conor watched Olivia bite her lip and look down.

"It bothers you," he said.

"It doesn't."

"Olivia, it's written all over your face. I forgot that you don't approve of whiskey. I'll send it back."

"No, don't. Please." She looked up at him earnestly. "Please feel free to drink your whiskey and smoke your cigar, if you like."

Despite her words, he knew she was uncomfortable. "Why does it bother you?"

She hesitated, then looked down at her plate. Her fingers toyed with the napkin across her lap. "My father drank whiskey," she said in a small voice. "Bourbon. Quite a lot of bourbon, actually. He did not handle it well."

She was twisting her napkin into knots, and she seemed to realize it, for she stopped and smoothed the linen across her lap. "When I was a little girl," she went on, "it wasn't so bad. Mama didn't approve of spirits, so he didn't drink in front of her. He had a special hiding place for his bourbon. She knew, of course. Everybody did. But he kept it under control for her sake. After she died, he didn't bother with a hiding place anymore. He drank openly, and as often as possible. It could be rather . . . embarrassing."

Conor suddenly understood a great deal. "That's why there were no balls and parties."

"Yes. My brothers were away at university most of the time, and of course, I couldn't go to any social gathering without an escort. So, I didn't go very often, and when I did, it was usually with my father. After several embarrassing incidents, we stopped being invited." She paused, then added, "My father had a very difficult time dealing with my mother's death. He felt lost without her, and he became very dependent upon me in some ways, almost possessive. Men who approached my father about courting me were turned away."

"Did you ever resent it?"

"Yes," she admitted. "But he was my father."

The waiter reappeared. He set a cup of coffee before Olivia and a tumbler of whiskey before Conor, along with a small silver tray that contained a cigar and a pair of cigar clips. Conor took a sip of the Irish, but somehow it had lost its appeal. He set the glass down.

She took a sip of coffee, then began running the tip of her finger around and around the rim of her cup. "Then the war came, and all the boys went to fight. Many of them didn't come back. The slaves all left, of course, and the plantation went to rack and ruin because there was no one to work it but me. Then we got word that both my brothers had died at Gettysburg."

Her hand stilled, and she lifted her chin to look at Conor across the table. "That, I think, was the final blow for Daddy. I watched my father deteriorate from a

vigorous, strong-willed figure to a bewildered shell of a
man, and there was nothing I could do to stop it. I tried
to take care of him, I tried to help him, but I couldn't.
That's why he fell off that ladder and broke his back.
He was drunk, and I think he wanted to die."

There was no disapproval in her voice, no anger or
resentment. Just tired resignation and an aching hint of
something that tore at Conor because he understood it
well. Loneliness. With their disparate lives, their oppos-
ing values, their completely different experiences, they
had something in common. He reached across the table
and laid his hand over hers in a comforting gesture that
surprised him. It surprised her, too. She looked down
at their hands and, slowly, she turned hers over to
entwine their fingers. "Thank you," she said.

"For what?"

"For listening. I've never talked to anyone about this
before."

She smiled at him, and his desire to comfort her
changed instantly to desire of a different kind.
Something of what he was feeling must have shown in
his face, for her smile faded and she stared at him with
sudden intensity. "Do you really think I'm beautiful?"
she asked.

He froze, staring into her wide eyes, feeling as if he
were drowning in sweet, melting chocolate.

"I think we'd better call it a night." He slowly, reluctantly pulled his hand away. "'Tis a long trip back
tomorrow, and you'll be needing some sleep."

Sleep was the last thing she needed. Olivia didn't know
what to do. She stared at her closed door, confused and
frustrated. Her romantic evening had been cut short
before it had truly begun.

How it had happened, she still wasn't sure. One minute, they were holding hands in a moment of shared intimacy, and the next minute, she was being shepherded to her room and offered a rather terse goodnight.

She'd asked him if he really thought her beautiful. A gauche question, and one she wished she could take back now. But he had looked at her as if she was, and he'd already told her she was, so maybe that wasn't what had brought their evening to such an abrupt end.

Perhaps she shouldn't have talked so much about her father; it wasn't exactly a romantic topic of conversation. But she had no notion of what topics might be considered romantic.

Or perhaps it had been her reaction when he'd ordered a drink. Goodness, the man had the right to have a drink after supper, of whatever he liked. It was only one drink, and she shouldn't have been so silly about it. She wanted to kick herself.

Olivia sighed and turned away from the door to toss her reticule and gloves on the bed. Whatever it was she'd done, it was too late to remedy it now. She was in her room, Conor was in his, and their evening together had come to an end. Clearly, she wasn't suited to seduction. But then, she'd always known that.

He would leave. She had no illusions about that. Her life would go back to the way it had been before, but tonight she wanted so badly for it to be different. From the moment they'd met, she had sensed what he could give her, and that day in the kitchen, he had given her a taste of all that she had missed. She wanted another taste. Could she just reach out and take it? And could she live with the pain afterward, loving him and watching him walk away?

How did one go about seduction anyway? She

couldn't just go to his room and say, "Would you kiss me again?" She just couldn't.

Could she?

Olivia stood there for several minutes in an agony of uncertainty. She was going to feel the pain anyway. But she didn't want to let him go without feeling the passion first, the passion he could offer her, the passion she'd never even known she could feel until he came.

Olivia thrust her room key into the pocket of her dress and reached for the door handle before she could change her mind.

When she knocked, all she could think was that if she hadn't heard the clerk correctly, if this was the wrong room, she'd die of mortification. But it wasn't the wrong room. The door swung inward, and Conor stood in the doorway.

He had removed his waistcoat and shirt. The shirt was bunched in one hand as if he'd just taken it off when she knocked. She'd seen him without his shirt many times, and it should not have unnerved her, but it did.

"Olivia?" He frowned at her in surprise and tossed the shirt aside. "What the hell are you doing here?"

"There's something I wanted to tell you earlier," she said, trying to keep her nervousness out of her voice and failing completely, "but I didn't have the chance."

Footsteps from the stairs at the end of the corridor had him glancing in that direction. He swore under his breath and grasped her by the elbow to pull her inside. The door closed behind her and she flattened against it, looking up at him. He did not look pleased to see her. She felt her courage falter. He did not look pleased at all.

"What is it?" he asked, in a voice that did not sound promising to her intent.

She took a deep breath. "I told you before that I missed many things when I was a girl." She plucked at the sides of her skirt and had never felt more scared in her life than she did right now. But her gaze did not waver from his.

"What I didn't tell you," she went on, in a shaking voice, "was that I wanted all those things. I wanted balls and parties and sneaking away from chaperones for romantic strolls in the garden with beaux. I wanted to laugh and dance. I wanted romance. I wanted . . . I wanted to be kissed, but I never was, at least, not until you . . . until we . . . I lied to you about that."

"Yes," he said. A hint of a smile lifted one corner of his mouth, and his voice was gentler than she'd ever heard it before. "I know."

She left off plucking at her skirt and spread her palms wide between them. "So, that's what I wanted to tell you."

"Olivia, why did you come to my room late at night to tell me this?"

Her heartbeat quickened to a frantic rhythm. She lifted her face, wet her dry lips, and tried to speak, but the words stuck in her throat. She swallowed twice and gathered all her courage. "I want a little piece of what I missed all those years ago, and you told me that afternoon in the kitchen you could show me, and you did—a little. I want you to show me again, Conor. I want to spend the night with you."

"Jaysus." He stared at her, his dismay so clear, she wanted nothing more than to sink through the floor. All her courage fled, and painful embarrassment took its place.

"I'm sorry the idea doesn't suit you," she said, and turned around, reaching for the door handle. She was not going to let him see how it hurt, she was not. She'd already made enough of a fool out of herself. She tried to open the door, but it didn't budge, and she realized the latch was stuck. Her hands desperately worked the handle back and forth, and she heard him come up behind her as she finally managed to yank the door open.

His palm hit the door beside her, closing it. Though he wasn't touching her at all, she felt the heat of his body behind her as if it were a touch. His warm breath fanned her cheek as he bent his head. "Love, I hope you realize what you're really asking for," he murmured in her ear. "You want me to make love to you."

She turned around and looked up at him, meeting his intense blue gaze squarely. "Yes," she said. "That's exactly what I want."

22

Holy Christ. She was serious.

He studied her bathed in the light of the lamp and the shadow of his body, and he could not think of what to do or what to say. She was flat against the door, her face pale, her dark eyes wide with all that wariness that reminded him of a doe in the forest. She looked ready to flee at the slightest danger. She looked completely vulnerable.

Which was exactly what she was. Vulnerable, innocent, and without a clue about what she was asking for. She wanted romance, not sex.

Conor cursed himself for that afternoon in her kitchen and his own damned teasing, his own cocksure words.

He could show her, aye. He wanted to show her, more than he'd ever wanted anything in his life. Hell, his desire for her had been eating at him for over a month now, until he thought sure it would finally drive him mad. But now, when he had her in his sights, when all he had to do was lower his head and kiss her, he found himself unable to move.

It would be so easy. It would not be easy at all.

He would hurt her. There was no avoiding it. He didn't want to live with that. He liked her too much, he respected her too much. He reminded himself yet again that she was not his kind of woman. She needed a man who didn't suffer from terminal wanderlust, a man who didn't have demons lurking in his soul, a man who actually liked farming, families, and going to church. She needed and deserved a man who would marry her, stand by her, cherish her, be a father to her daughters. He was not that man.

"Go back to your room, Olivia," he said before he could change his mind. "I'm no good."

"I don't believe that."

"Then you're a fool." He watched her lift her trembling chin with stubborn bravado. He sighed. "All right, then, let's just say I'm no good for you."

"I think I'm perfectly capable of deciding what's good for me." She gazed up at him with those damnable dark eyes. "I think that's you."

"Tonight, maybe. But not tomorrow when I leave you and move on."

"I'm not asking for tomorrow," she whispered. "All I'm asking for is tonight."

"You don't know what you're saying."

She lifted her hands, and he saw them shake as she hugged herself and rubbed her bare arms as if she were cold. "I know exactly what I'm saying. I want you to make love to me. I may not be . . . experienced, but I know what that means."

Conor thought of that kiss in the kitchen, and he doubted she had the slightest idea.

"Don't . . . don't you want to?"

Did he want to? To lose himself in the softness of her would be a taste of heaven itself. He should turn her down, toss her out, tell her no. He closed his eyes, fighting what he wanted with everything he had.

"Conor?"

It was the way she said his name that was his undoing. She said it like a caress, with an aching, wobbly tilt that wrenched him, turned him inside out, made him into the vulnerable one. He'd lost, and he knew it. So much for being valiant and noble, and doing the right thing. It had been proven to him a long time ago that he wasn't a hero anyway.

He opened his eyes. "Don't hate me for this tomorrow, Olivia," he said, and cupped her cheeks, tilting her head back as he brought his mouth closer to hers. "For God's sake, don't hate me."

His mouth came down on hers before she could reply. Her lips parted freely, and with that first taste of her, he knew there was no turning back. He deepened the kiss, sliding his hands up into her hair.

His hands found the combs, and as he pulled them free, her hair came tumbling down. The combs dropped to the floor, and he tangled her hair in his hands, reveling in the silken feel of it and the warm, sweet taste of her. He brushed light kisses across her lips and her cheeks as he began walking backward, pulling her with him toward the bed. Arousal coursed through him, and he deepened the kiss, plunging his tongue into her mouth.

She made a tiny smothered sound of desire, and she quivered in his hold, a fluttering feminine response that his body instantly recognized. He wanted to take her without the preliminaries, without the tenderness she wanted and the finesse that she needed. He had to slow down.

He tore his lips from hers and buried his face in the curve of her neck. His hands left her hair and slid down to her slender waist. He trailed kisses along her shoulder, and his fingers caressed the small of her back as he forced himself to contain his moves, to be patient, to wait.

He pulled back and looked into her face, watching as she slowly opened her eyes. He had never seen her look lovelier than she did at this moment, with her hair falling in lustrous waves around her shoulders and an expression of dazed astonishment on her face, a look that pleased him more than the practiced smiles or breathy sighs of all the easy women he'd known.

She smiled that extraordinary smile, tilting her head back, and her eyes closed again as she breathed his name on a tiny sigh. Conor had the feeling he was going to see her like this in his mind, hear her soft, drawling voice echo in his ears for many solitary nights to come.

His hands left her waist and came up between them, his eyes never leaving her face as his fingers found the top button of her dress, hidden beneath a silken rosette.

She gasped and opened her eyes again, shying away with the first hint of resistance. "Shouldn't you put out the light?" she whispered.

He shook his head, and slid the button free. He reached for the next one, then the next. His knuckles brushed against her breasts, then her ribs, as he worked his way down, and he felt her tremble with each button he unfastened. By the time he reached her waist, she was pushing against his shoulders.

"Oh, please, put out the light," she whispered, turning her face away, blushing in hot confusion.

"Why?" He bent his head to kiss her neck. "Sure, you've seen me naked," he teased against her ear. "It's only fair that I see you."

That unnerved her even more. She made a small sound of agitation, and he left off undressing her for the moment. He pulled her against him and began nibbling on her earlobe as his hand caressed her ribs. "Olivia, I don't think I'll be able to unfasten all these hooks of yours in the dark," he confessed. "Besides, I want to see you, look at you. Let me do that."

She did not reply. He ran his hand up and down her torso in a slow caress, kissed the velvet skin of her ear, her throat, down to her shoulder and back again, every move designed to coax, to persuade, to make her yield. "Will you let me?"

"All right," she whispered so softly he almost missed it, her body rigid.

He pulled back and gazed down into her face. "Olivia, look at me."

She slowly, reluctantly, opened her eyes and met his gaze.

He shook his head. "No, look at me." He grasped her hand and drew it toward him, placing it against his chest. "Touch me and look at me."

She tried to pull her hand away, but he held it there, against his chest until he felt the pulling resistance stop. Her hand flattened against his chest. "I don't know what I'm supposed to do," she whispered.

He let go of her hand and spread his arms wide. "Do what you like."

Her lashes lowered, and she remained still for a long moment, staring at his chest. Then she leaned toward him, fanned her hands against his chest, and touched her lips to the jagged marks of knives and hatred, her kisses as soft and tentative as the brush of a butterfly's wings. All the defensive walls he'd spent a lifetime building collapsed as if they were made of straw.

Olivia felt a tremor run through him with each touch of her mouth, and it disarmed her to realize that she had the power to do that. Beneath her lips, she felt the raspy softness of the hair on his chest, the hammering of his heart, the rise and fall of his rapid breathing.

"Enough," he groaned, and his hands tangled in her hair, gently pulling her back. "That's . . . enough for now, I'm thinking."

He slid his hands to her shoulders and hooked his thumbs under the neckline of her dress, pulled it off her shoulders, down to her waist, and let it fall to her feet. She stepped out of it, and he pushed it out of the way with one foot.

He tugged at her corset cover, and she knew what he wanted her to do. She lifted her arms, and he pulled the undergarment over her head, then tossed it aside. He lowered his head and trailed kisses along her shoulder, while his fingers worked to unfasten the front hooks of her corset. Finally, that garment, too, was tossed aside, followed by her petticoat.

With each piece of clothing he took from her, Olivia's anxiety grew. She didn't want him to see her without her clothes. It was too embarrassing, too agonizing. He must have seen many other women, far prettier women than she; and she did not want the comparison.

He slid his hands down her spine, reaching for the hem of her chemise. "Lift your arms, Olivia," he said gently. "Let me see you."

Reluctantly, she raised her arms above her head, allowing him to pull the garment away. He dropped it to the floor, and she could feel his eyes on her body. She could not look at him. She folded her arms over her breasts and squeezed her eyes shut.

"Yes," he said.

The one word startled and puzzled her. "Yes, what?" she whispered, keeping her eyes closed.

"Yes, I think you're beautiful."

Astonished, she opened her eyes and found him smiling at her. His eyes had that smoky hue that made her feel weak. She watched his black lashes lower as he reached out and grasped her wrists gently to pull her arms away, spread them wide, and gaze his fill. "So goddamned beautiful, it makes my head spin. It does, indeed."

Relief washed over her. He didn't think she was plain, he didn't think she was disappointing. He thought she was beautiful. He told her so, not just with his words, but with his eyes, his hands, his voice. Her shyness and embarrassment melted away under his heated gaze. "You shouldn't swear, Conor," she whispered and pulled one hand free to touch his lean cheek.

He turned his face into her hand and kissed her palm, then his eyes met hers. They held the wicked gleam she knew so well. "Goddamned bloody beautiful."

He released her other hand, and she watched him sink to his knees in front of her. He unlaced her boots and when he lifted one of her feet in his hands, she grasped the bedpost to steady herself as he pulled the shoe off and tossed it aside. He removed her other shoe, then his hands curved behind her ankles and moved slowly up her calves to her knees, sliding inside her drawers to the garters that held up her stockings.

His fingers lightly caressed the backs of her knees, and that slow, aching warmth began spreading through her. She felt as if she were melting beneath the magic touch of his fingers, and her hand tightened its grasp on the bedpost. "Oh, my," she gasped. "Oh, my."

She thought she heard him laugh softly under his breath, but she couldn't be sure. He pulled the ribbon ties of her garters, then slowly slid the stockings down her legs, his hands gliding over her skin like a warm breeze. She lifted her right foot and he pulled the stocking off.

When he had removed both her stockings, he slid his hands up her legs again, the heat of his touch burning her through the thin lawn fabric of her drawers. His hands moved up her thighs, her hips, to her waist, where he reached for the drawstring and pulled, undoing the bow that held up her drawers. He bunched the delicate fabric in his fists and began tugging it inexorably downward over her hips.

Olivia felt another wave of embarrassment as she realized what he was doing, what he was seeing, and she tensed, fighting off the impulse to shy away.

"Lovely," he murmured as more and more of her bare skin was revealed to his gaze. "So lovely."

He leaned toward her, letting go of the drawers to grasp her bare hips in his hands. She felt the garment slide down her legs to pool around her feet, as he pulled her toward him and pressed a kiss to her stomach.

Olivia gave a startled cry at the carnal pleasure of that kiss, at the quivering sensations that rippled through her. She let go of the bedpost and reached for him instead, her hands settling on his shoulders to keep herself from falling as he traced kisses across her stomach and her ribs, tasting her skin with his tongue.

His hands moved upward along her hips, following the curve of her waist, across her ribs to cup her breasts, his thumbs brushing lightly back and forth across the tips. She tilted her head back with a moan, closing her eyes, and her hands tightened convulsively on his shoulders.

His hands slid to her back, guiding her to bend closer to him. She did, and he opened his mouth over her breast and drew her nipple between his teeth. She felt an incredible pulling sensation that seemed to draw all the breath from her. She lifted her hands from his shoulders to cradle his head, to pull him even closer.

But he did not come closer. Instead, he pulled back and rose to his feet. He grasped the top hem of the bedcovers and pulled them down to the foot of the bed. He turned to her, and lifted her into his arms as if she weighed nothing, and laid her in the center of the bed. She opened her eyes to find him watching her as he began to pull off his boots. She kept her gaze locked with his, unable to look lower while he undid the buttons of his trousers and slid them off his hips.

The mattress dipped with his weight as he moved to lie beside her on the bed. Leaning on one elbow, he gazed down at her for a moment, then reached out to touch her face. She closed her eyes and felt his fingertips lightly graze her cheek, her chin, her throat, then move across her collarbone to brush lightly over her breast. His hand lingered there for a moment, then moved lower, tracing a light, random pattern over her stomach with his fingertips, then lower still. Olivia forgot to breathe as his hand slid between her thighs. When he touched her there, she cried out and jerked against him with a wordless sound, feeling hot little shivers race through her body.

Shocked by the intimacy of it, she thought she ought to push his hand away, tell him to stop, but she could not. She could not think past the tension and heat that rose within her at the touch of his fingers. She clutched at the sheets, bunching fabric in her fists as she began to move with his hand, unable to stop herself. The tension seemed to build inside of her with every stroke of his fingers. "Conor, oh, Conor," she gasped, feeling as if she were hovering on the edge of something glorious and wonderful.

"That's it, love," he murmured. "That's it."

She heard herself making tiny sounds, but she could not seem to stop. She felt as if she must be on fire with the shame of it and the wicked, breathless excitement. Until suddenly, everything inside her seemed to explode in a white-hot flash that sent delicious waves of pleasure through her entire body.

Her body was still tingling with the incredible sensations when he withdrew his hand. She felt him move, felt his weight and strength above her, pushing her into the mattress with sudden urgency, overwhelming her with the power of his body. The air rushed from her lungs, and she gasped as he pressed against her, *into* her. All the incredible, delicious sensations of a moment before vanished as if she had suddenly been drenched with ice water. She had thought herself prepared for this, but she was not. It hurt.

She bit her lip to keep from crying out, but he seemed to realize what he had done. His body went rigidly still, and he bent his head to nuzzle her neck softly .

"Are you all right, *á mhúirnín*?" His voice sounded strained, and she wondered if this had hurt him, too. "Olivia, are you all right?"

"I think so." The sharp, stinging sensation was already beginning to fade. She moved her hips beneath him experimentally.

"Olivia," he groaned against her ear, "don't move. Christ Almighty, don't move."

She tried to keep still, but though the pain was gone, the odd, stretching sensation was rather uncomfortable. She was not at all certain she liked it. She sucked in a deep breath and wriggled her hips again.

"Olivia, no, don't do that. Oh, Christ. Oh, Christ."

He began to move against her, forcefully now, his breathing harsh and ragged, his hips pressing her into the mattress with each thrust he made. As he moved, she began to get used to it, and she was actually beginning to find it rather enjoyable, when suddenly, a shudder rocked him, and he let out a hoarse cry, then he thrust against her one last time and was still.

It was over.

"*Neamh*," he murmured. "'Tis *Neamh*, you are, Olivia."

She did not understand the Irish word, but she heard her name and the tenderness in his voice, and she thought wistfully that it might have been an endearment. Her arms tightened around him, and she felt an overpowering wave of tenderness wash over her. One hand caressed his broad back, the other raked gently through his hair as she felt the tension leave his body and lethargy take its place.

When he rolled to his side, he took her with him, cradling her against his body. Within moments, his breathing deepened into sleep. Olivia reached for the sheet that had tangled at the foot of the bed, and she pulled it over them both, then she extinguished the lamp and snuggled closer in the circle of his arms.

She was a fallen woman now, she supposed. She felt no regret, no shame. Just an incredible, overpowering joy that opened and blossomed inside her like a flower and made her feel alive, vibrant, and beautiful. She wanted nothing more than to lie beside him like this forever. She loved him. She closed her eyes, pressed her cheek against his chest, and listened to his heartbeat; and she pretended—just for tonight—that he loved her, too.

Conor awoke with the scent of her filling his senses. No cloying cologne, just the provocative feminine warmth of Olivia's soft skin and tumbled hair.

Some time in the night, she had turned over to lie with her back pressed to his chest. Without opening his eyes, he recognized every aspect of her form—the exquisite shape of her calf nestled between his legs, the deep curve of her waist where his arm curled around her, the velvety underside of her breast against the back of his hand, the silken strands of her hair beneath his jaw. Her body was perfectly aligned with his, as if she were made for him. Still half-asleep, he breathed a sigh of utter contentment, savoring the unfamiliar pleasure of waking up with a woman in his arms.

He'd slept with her.

That thought doused his contentment. He opened his eyes and lifted his head from the pillow they shared to glance down at the creamy skin of her shoulder and the tangled strands of russet-brown hair that fell across her breast and over his hand, barely visible in the dim light that filtered into the room around the shuttered window.

He'd slept with her.

The realization stunned him. He never slept with women. Kissed them, sure, undressed them, enjoyed them, then left them, and slept alone. Alone, where his nightmares wouldn't wake them, where his weaknesses couldn't be seen or his secrets revealed. Where his shame remained silent and hidden.

He gazed down at her profile, a perfect cameo of long lashes, tilted nose, and parted lips, of tangled hair and tempting disarray. He thought of the night before, remembering everything: the scent of her skin, the taste of her mouth, the touch of her hands, the sounds of her passion that had ignited the lust inside him like a match to black powder, leaving him sated and sleepy and wanting only to hold her close. Hold her. *Christ Almighty.*

Even as he felt the panic stirring inside him, he also felt the desire. He wanted to do it all again; he wanted the intense explosion of pleasure and blessed release; he wanted the peaceful lethargy and the dreamless sleep. Beside her, with her. He'd never felt anything like this with any other woman.

It scared the hell out of him.

He eased away until he was no longer touching her, then turned onto his back, staring up at the ceiling. He could leave. Right now. He could get up, put on his clothes, and walk out while she slept. Leaving a woman was easy. He'd done it dozens of times.

He didn't move.

He lay still, listening to the soft rhythm of her breathing, and thought about all the reasons why it made sense to leave now while she was still asleep. That way, there would be no awkward silences or emotional scene. No bloody tears, no injured feminine pride, no wounded brown eyes to haunt him after he had walked away.

He didn't move.

He hated being tied down. But he'd been tied down two months now. It suffocated him to get close. But he hadn't felt suffocated when he'd first woken, holding her in his arms. He'd felt a moment of contentment, hadn't he? A moment of peace.

He shoved away that fanciful thought the moment it came. To Olivia, land, home, family, and honor were everything. But to Conor, they were all the things that had been taken from him, all the things he couldn't bear to lose again.

It wasn't as if he hadn't been honest with her. It wasn't as if he'd given her any false hopes. She'd come to him last night; he'd given her what she wanted because he had wanted it, too. That was the end of it. He'd promised to stay until her harvest, and her harvest was over. There was no reason to stay with her a moment longer.

He didn't move.

He couldn't leave yet. He couldn't let her make the trip back alone. She needed him to drive the second wagon. Besides, it was dangerous for a woman to travel alone. He had to stay with her long enough to get her home to her farm and her girls where she belonged. Then he'd leave. He hauled himself out of bed and pulled on his underdrawers and trousers, then walked across the room to pick up his shirt. He wondered why it seemed like the longest walk of his life.

Olivia woke slowly. With a huge yawn, she lifted her arms above her head and stretched, grimacing at the twinge of pain that shot through her muscles. She felt stiff and a bit sore, as if she'd been riding horseback too long, but she also felt gloriously alive and incredibly happy. She was a fallen woman, she reminded herself, trying to feel ashamed.

Memories of the night before came rushing back. She smiled even as she blushed, unable to feel properly guilty. She opened her eyes and found him already awake, dressed, and seated in a chair across the room, watching her. To her surprise, her carpetbag was on the floor beside his chair.

She stirred beneath his gaze, feeling shy and flustered and very feminine. "Good morning," she said, brushing her hair out of her eyes and drawing the sheet around herself as she sat up.

"Good morning." He turned his face away, and her happiness vanished.

He was sitting right in front of her, but he wasn't really there. He'd already withdrawn into himself, retreated behind his walls. He was an isolated stranger. Again.

Raw pain ripped through her, but she did not show it. She could not. It would be too humiliating. She lowered her gaze to the sheets and fought to keep her face expressionless, but after a moment she took a peek at him from beneath her lashes and realized it didn't matter. He wasn't even looking at her.

He gestured to a tray on the table beside his chair. "I thought you might want some breakfast and coffee," he said, studying the covered plate and silver coffeepot on the tray as if he found them fascinating.

"Thank you."

"You'll have to eat it quickly," he went on. "It's after seven o'clock and the maid will be bringing water and towels at about half past. We'd best be going, anyway. It's a long drive back." He rose to his feet without looking at her. He gestured to her carpetbag. "I brought your things in here, and put my things in your room. I'll meet you downstairs in an hour."

Her grip on the sheet tightened, and she held it around herself as if it were a shield. "Of course," she said stiffly, and watched him leave, closing the door behind him.

She pushed back the covers and immediately saw the bloodstains that marked her thighs and the sheets. Shocked, she stared down at the dark smears, knowing full well it wasn't time for her monthly illness. It must have come from what had happened last night. She hadn't realized that she had bled; it really hadn't hurt that much.

The physical pain seemed insignificant now, but the emotional pain was a different matter entirely.

She closed her eyes, struggling against the hurt of his withdrawal even as she accepted the inevitability of his imminent departure. She'd known all along he was just passing through her life. It wasn't his fault she'd developed foolish wishes about him; it wasn't his fault she'd fallen in love with him.

When he was gone, she would still have her girls and

her home to get her through the days, and she would have memories of him to get her through the nights. But at this moment, that thought brought very little comfort.

The sewing party for Kate Johnson was already well under way by the time the guest of honor made her appearance. The ladies of Callersville had been arriving at the white frame house behind the mercantile in a steady stream ever since ten o'clock, accompanied by sewing baskets and quilting hoops, until Lila Miller's tiny parlor was filled to overflowing. All of the ladies were working on quilts and clothes for Kate's new baby, of course, but the real reason for any such gathering was to exchange recipes, advice, and gossip. Gossip, most of all.

Cara Johnson and Becky pulled their younger sisters out of the way as all the ladies crowded into the foyer to see Kate and gush over the baby. The universal opinion seemed to be that he looked just like his daddy.

"I see you brought Olivia's girls," Martha Chubb said, with a nod to Becky and her sisters, as the ladies settled themselves back in their chairs and resumed their sewing.

"Peach harvest," Kate reminded them, gladly handing over Robert Thomas to her oldest daughter, who immediately began showing him off to those friends who hadn't yet seen her baby brother. Kate sat down beside Becky on one of the settees and pulled out her knitting. "Since Nate's not here to take her peaches to Monroe, Olivia's gone there herself. The girls are staying with us until she gets back tonight."

Martha frowned with disapproval. "Really, Olivia is becoming quite eccentric, leaving her girls to be cared for by others, to go gadding about the countryside alone. And she'll have to stay in a hotel—unchaperoned, of course. It's shocking."

"Quite shocking," Emily Chubb echoed her sister.

Becky's head shot up at these comments. She glanced over at Miranda and Carrie, who had stopped their game of checkers to listen, and it made her angry that Martha would say things like that in front of her little sisters. She frowned at the woman. "I don't think you should say things like that about my mama. It's rude."

"Shush, child," Martha said with a dismissive wave of her hand. "Young ladies speak only when spoken to."

Becky fell silent at the rebuke and lowered her head, but her cheeks grew hot as Martha went on, "Olivia's behavior since her father's death has been less than decorous, but going to Monroe alone? It's indecent."

"Martha!" Kate lowered her knitting needles to give the other woman a piece of her mind. "That's not fair. How is she supposed to get her peaches to market otherwise? She's been trying to find help. In fact, she told him—"

"And that's another thing," Martha interrupted, with a decisive nod that set the feather of her bonnet bouncing. "Advertising all over the four parishes for a farmhand. Shameless."

"Appalling," Emily added.

Becky pushed her needle through the doily she was embroidering, too furious to notice what she was doing, and jabbed her finger hard enough to draw blood. She winced and dropped her sewing to suck the tip of her finger, wishing she could tell Martha Chubb just what she thought of her, the old busybody.

Kate sat up straighter in her chair. "And how else is Olivia supposed to find a farmhand?" she demanded. "Land sakes, Martha, Olivia's had enough trouble in her life. Leave her be."

Martha started to interrupt, but Kate drew a deep breath and went on, her voice rising as fast as her temper. "The Harlan boys all got drunk the other night and went out to her place. They threw rocks in her windows and scared the girls nearly half to death. Olivia had to use a shotgun to get rid of them. We heard the shots clear over at our place, and Olivia told us about what happened when she dropped off the girls yesterday."

"A shotgun?" Martha lifted her hands in an expansive gesture and sniffed. "That's exactly the kind of thing I'm talking about. Shotguns. I can't think what's gotten into Olivia."

"I think Olivia's a brave woman who's managing as best she can," Kate answered. "Furthermore, I probably wouldn't even be here if it hadn't been for her. She helped deliver Robert Thomas. I was having such a hard time, and she helped me. Why, I might have died without Olivia."

Kate glanced over at Becky, and the girl shot the woman a grateful look for coming to her mother's defense when she'd been prevented from doing that herself. She felt a hand on her shoulder and she turned to look at Carrie, who had moved to stand beside her chair, Miranda right behind her.

"Why are the Chubb sisters saying mean things about Mama?" Carrie whispered.

"Because they're nasty old busybodies," Becky answered through clenched teeth, glaring at Martha and Emily. "That's why."

Kate leaned forward in her chair and spoke again. "We all know it was Vernon who sent the Harlan boys out there, and we all know why. He wants Olivia's land to build that railroad of his with his wife's Yankee money. He's done the same thing to half the folks around here. I say good for Olivia for standing up to him!"

Becky wanted to cheer.

"Need I remind you that Vernon donated a new organ to the church last year?" Martha said acidly.

"That's because Vernon thinks he can buy anything," Kate shot back, with a toss of her blond head, "even a place in heaven."

Lila, as the hostess, tried to intervene and stop the discussion before tempers flared any higher. She grabbed the plate of tea cakes from the table before her and rose to her feet. "Would anyone care for a cake?"

She was ignored by everyone except Miranda, who adored sweets and was close enough to take her up on that offer.

"I hardly think blasphemy is necessary, Kate." Martha settled back in her chair as a queen might on her throne, fully aware that she had everyone's attention. "Olivia shouldn't be trying to run Peachtree herself anyway. She should have sold that land when her father died."

"Balderdash!" was Kate's decisive response.

Other voices began to rise as the point was debated among the ladies present. But when Martha spoke again, her formidable voice rose above the others.

"I realize that, as her friend, you feel compelled to defend her, Kate; but really, this trip to Monroe passes all bounds of feminine decency. Going all that way alone!"

Some of the ladies nodded agreement, and the discussion began again.

"But Mama's not alone," Miranda piped up, reaching for another of the cakes on Lila's tray. "Mr. Conor's with her."

The low murmurs of the ladies faded into silence.

"Miranda, you weren't supposed to tell anybody about Mr. Conor!" Carrie cried, scowling at her sister. "Mama said it was a secret."

Miranda dropped the cake back onto the plate and clapped a hand over her mouth, giving her sister a contrite glance. "I forgot."

Becky glanced around at the circle of horrified faces, with a sinking feeling of dismay.

Martha leaned forward and gave Miranda a hard stare. "Just who is this Mr. Conor, child?"

Becky remembered her mother's words about how easily a girl could lose her reputation just by walking out with a boy, and the ramifications of Miranda's innocent comment about Mama and Mr. Conor suddenly hit her. She lowered her face into her hands. "Oh, no," she whispered. "Oh, no."

23

Because they'd gotten a late start out of Monroe, it was dark by the time Olivia and Conor reached the Johnson farm to pick up the girls. She halted her wagon beside the lane that led to their home, and when Conor pulled his wagon to a halt beside hers, she asked him to wait for her there, then turned her wagon down the lane, the moon lighting her way.

Ever since this morning, Conor had been withdrawn and silent. He had not told her exactly when he would be leaving—she didn't know if it would be tomorrow or the day after or next week—but it would be soon. Olivia knew that he would probably not say good-bye; he would just vanish as he had done the last time, without a word. During the long trip back, she tried to toughen her heart, but every time she thought of the night before, of the incredible things he had done to her, of the extraordinary way she had reacted to his touch, all she wanted to do was fling her arms around him and hold him tight, as if somehow that would keep him with her. She knew it would not.

Oren was on the veranda of the house by the time she pulled into the drive, as if he'd been watching for her arrival. She brought the wagon to a halt, and Oren came down the steps to the wagon before she could climb down.

"Kate and your girls are already over at your place," he told her.

Olivia frowned in bewilderment. "Why? I told Kate I'd pick them up here. She didn't have to take them home."

He pushed back his hat and heaved a heavy sigh. "I'm afraid there's been a bit of trouble."

Olivia thought of Vernon and instantly assumed the worst. "My girls? Are they all right?"

He hastened to reassure her. "They're fine. It's nothing like that. But you'd better get home quick."

"Why? What's happened?"

Oren eyed her with a grave expression. "Everybody knows, Liv. About the Irishman who's been staying at your place."

A sick feeling of dread settled in the pit of her stomach. "Everybody?"

"Everybody in town," he answered, confirming the worst. "Including Martha and Emily Chubb."

The sick feeling of dread was like a stone in her belly. "Oh, heavens."

"It's causing quite a stir. You better get home and straighten it out."

Olivia nodded and snapped the reins without another word, sending the team of mules flying back down the lane. Gravel spun off the wheels as she turned onto the main road and raced past Conor's wagon. She heard him shout her name, but she did not pause for explanations.

She couldn't think; she couldn't feel. All she could

do was stare at the moonlit road in front of her, cold and numb with dread, as she raced the wagon toward home.

When she pulled into the drive of her house, they were waiting for her, just as Oren had said. The girls were nowhere to be seen, but Kate was there, along with Reverend Allen and, of course, the Chubb sisters. Light spilled through the windows behind them, and she could not see their faces, but she could imagine the condemnation in their eyes.

She climbed down from the wagon and moved slowly toward the house, each step a jerky movement that propelled her forward like a puppet on a string, even as panic made her want to run, to hide.

They knew. All of them. She could tell by their silence and their rigid stances and she wondered how she would ever be able to face them in the light of day. She thought of the passionate night before, of what she had done, of what she had let Conor do; and every remembered kiss, every remembered touch seemed to flay her like the lash of a whip. The shame of it caused her cheeks to burn, but she kept her head high.

Her mind began to spin crazily with explanations, excuses, denials. But they would all be lies. She wished she could just sink into the ground and disappear.

Behind her, she heard the second wagon pull into the drive and stop, but she didn't turn and look at Conor. She couldn't. She mounted the steps to the veranda, and the weight of guilt and shame seemed heavier with each one.

Kate stepped to the front of the veranda. She grabbed Olivia's gloved hand and gave it a quick squeeze. "I'm sorry, Liv," she whispered. "They insisted on coming out here. I couldn't stop them."

Olivia pulled her hand out of Kate's and looked

away from the understanding sympathy in her friend's face. She couldn't bear it. "Where are my girls?"

"They're in the house having supper. They don't . . . understand. Well, Becky might, perhaps, but the little ones don't."

She was given no chance to reply. Martha elbowed her way around Kate and studied Olivia with pursed lips and speculative eyes. "So, you're back, Olivia. I'm surprised you can show your face after what you've done."

Olivia tried to tell herself that Martha couldn't possibly know what had actually happened in Monroe, but it didn't matter. She knew, and she couldn't lie to herself. She couldn't act nonchalant and innocent, because she wasn't. Her hands began to shake.

Behind her, she heard the tread of footsteps and knew it was Conor, but she kept her back to him. Martha glanced past her and looked him up and down. "You even had the gall to bring the man back with you," she added. "Have you no shame?"

Conor watched Olivia wilt beneath the censuring voice of the stout woman in the hideous feathered hat, and decided he'd had enough. His jaw tightened grimly, and he started forward to yank her away from that vicious old cat, but he felt a hand on his shoulder and turned to look at the gray-haired man in black broadcloth and cleric's collar who stood beside him.

"Walk with me, son."

It was not a request. Conor let out a frustrated breath and reluctantly followed the elderly man, who picked up a lamp and led him around the side of the house and down to the barn.

When they stepped inside, the man closed the barn door behind them and set the lamp on the floor. "There," he said, sitting down on a dusty barrel and settling himself as comfortably as possible. "Now we can talk freely."

Conor eyed him in stony silence. He could not conjure up the words for polite conversation. All he could think of was defense.

"I'm Reverend Allen, by the way," the man continued in his mild, Southern voice. "I'm the minister of the Baptist church here in Callersville. You, I assume, are Mr. Conor."

The form of address caught Conor's attention, and everything fell into place with utter clarity. "The girls," he said tightly.

Reverend Allen nodded. "The girls, yes."

"What exactly did they say about me?"

"I'm not quite certain. I wasn't there, you see. But I'm told it was during a sewing party in town this afternoon. All the ladies were there." He leaned back against the wall and folded his arms. "The talk now is that you've been living in this house with Olivia, her husband in all but name."

Conor thought of all the frustrating nights he'd spent out in this barn trying to blot out erotic fantasies about her, and wanted to laugh at that notion. If this were happening to any other man, he would have. "What else?"

"They say that you are a drifter, a prizefighter by trade, which of course makes her behavior all the more reprehensible. If you were a local man, it would still be scandalous, but perhaps not quite so shocking. I'm afraid Olivia's reputation is in serious jeopardy."

"Mother of God!" Conor scowled at the minister, despising all men of the cloth. "I was injured, and Olivia, being a softhearted woman—God bless her— took me into her home so that I could get well. For an act of kindness, she is condemned?"

"You don't have to tell me about Olivia, young man. I've known her since she was a child."

"Then you know damn good and well she has nothing to be ashamed of." He thought of their night together, and he hated the way something beautiful could be twisted into something sordid by those who had nothing better to do with their time. "Nothing," he repeated.

"Unfortunately, I cannot stop people from thinking what they will. And Olivia recognized the risk in what she was doing. Evidently, she took great pains to conceal your presence here."

"I can bloody well see why!"

The reverend looked at him with patient understanding, which only fueled Conor's resentment. He swore under his breath.

"I'm not here to debate the right or wrong of Olivia's actions," Reverend Allen said quietly. "Or yours."

"Then why are you here?"

"I'm here because I believe I might be of some assistance in this matter. Believe it or not, I care about Olivia's welfare. I can only hope that you do, as well."

The reverend leaned forward, rested his elbows on his knees, and steepled his fingers together. "It comes down to this," he said. "You have two choices. The first is to leave. You don't have any ties here, I understand, and are free to go."

Conor thought that sounded like a very good idea.

"You could simply walk away and abandon Olivia to face the scandal alone," the reverend went on, in that same gentle, unassuming tone. "Of course, the girls will be taken away from her."

Conor's body went rigid, and he felt as if he'd suddenly been caught by a left hook out of nowhere. "Taken away?"

"Olivia never legally adopted the Taylor children. She never thought it necessary. In fact, I doubt the idea even occurred to her. Martha and Emily have already asked the sheriff to remove them from this house. Most of the ladies in town are in agreement with them, I'm afraid."

"I'll leave," he said tightly. "I'll go tonight. Anything to let Olivia keep those girls."

The reverend shook his head. "It's too late for that now. The damage has been done."

Conor started to reply, but he couldn't speak past the stone that seemed lodged in his chest. He closed his eyes, and in his mind, he saw Olivia in the backyard laughing with her daughters. He saw her arms open to enfold them, heard her loving, gentle voice speak to them.

He opened his eyes and ruthlessly shoved the image away.

The reverend was watching him steadily. "That needn't be your concern," he said. "They aren't your daughters, so they aren't your responsibility." He paused and gave a slight cough. "However, another child might make your choice more difficult."

Conor stared into the mild blue eyes watching him and made a sound of denial.

"She might be carrying a baby."

Now was the moment to lie, to say that was not possible, that their trip had been innocent and nothing had happened, to absolve himself and make a quick exit out of town, to be exactly what he knew he was. A coward.

Reverend Allen was watching him expectantly, waiting for those words of denial. When they did not come, he went on, "You seem to be a man of the world. I assume you've thought of that possibility."

He hadn't. Christ, until now it hadn't occurred to him. And it should have. A babe. He thought of Mary, of the child that had been his, and something fractured inside him, a crack in his armor, a weakness to be exposed and exploited.

Reverend Allen seemed to see it, too. "There is another option," he said carefully.

Conor eyed the other man with caution, knowing the trap. "I'm listening."

"You could marry her."

The trap closed, and Conor clenched his fists, struggling against the mindless panic that surged within him. He could not think; he could not reason. He could only rail against the inevitable, and curse himself for his own stupidity.

He turned away. "Marriage is not an option," he said through his teeth, barely grinding out the words amid the rage and the fear and the desperation within himself.

"You're not already married, are you?"

Conor tilted back his head and stared at the rafters above. He made a harsh sound that might have been a laugh. "No."

"I could perform the ceremony tomorrow at the church. If the two of you married, the scandal would quickly die, Olivia's reputation would be saved, and her girls would not be taken to the orphanage."

The orphanage. *Oh, Christ.*

Conor turned around, unable to believe that after all his running, all his struggling to remain free, his life came to this kind of choice. "You say you care about Olivia. If you knew anything about me, Reverend, if you knew even half of what I've done, you would be running me out of town with a shotgun, you would, indeed, not asking me to marry her."

"I'm not asking you to do anything. I'm simply telling you what your options are. Now, I'm going to leave and let you decide which one to take." He gave Conor a benign smile. "But I'm a meddlesome old man, so I'll give you one small piece of advice before I go."

He paused, and his smile faded to a serious and earnest expression. "Do the right thing, son," he said in his gentle minister's voice. "For once in your life, do the right thing."

He turned away and departed, closing the barn door behind him and leaving Conor to make his choice alone.

Conor glanced around at the walls that surrounded him, hemmed him in, threatened to imprison him in a life he did not want. He looked down, and his gaze caught on the flame of the lamp at his feet. He watched it flicker, trapped in its frosted glass cage like the demons locked inside himself. *Do the right thing, son.*

He slammed his hands over his ears to shut out the words that clanged through his head like the iron bars of the Mountjoy.

For once in your life, do the right thing . . . the right thing . . . the right thing . . . for once in your life.

He could not do the right thing. Slowly, by infinitesimal increments, he pulled logic and reason and reality together, fusing them into the cold, indifferent armor that had protected him all his life. By sheer force of will, he pushed away the vision of Olivia's wounded dark eyes that floated at the edge of his consciousness. He had no intention of doing the right thing.

Olivia watched the vicar's carriage drive away with the Chubb sisters inside. Kate's wagon followed, with her girls in the back. They looked back at her as the wagon bumped down the lane, taking them away. Becky, anguished and silent, Carrie voicing indignant wails of protest, and Miranda sobbing for her mama.

Olivia listened to her youngest daughter's sobs, and they threatened to rip her apart. She bit down on her trembling lip, and a tear rolled down her cheek as she watched the wagon disappear into the night. She wrapped her arms tightly around one of the columns of the veranda to keep herself from chasing after the wagon.

She tried to tell herself it was only temporary. She had agreed to the compromise suggested by Reverend Allen—that the girls would stay at the Johnson farm until things were worked out—only because Martha had threatened to bring the sheriff out here to take them away and transport them immediately to the orphanage in Monroe.

She did not know how long she stood there, but she could not seem to find the will to move, to force herself to turn away and go back into her empty house. Moving meant thinking, deciding, finding a way to go on, and she could not. She remained standing on the veranda, staring down the lane long after the wagon had disappeared into the night, and Miranda's sobs echoed only in her mind.

In any tragedy of her life, she had always turned to her faith; she talked to God and got the answers she needed. But the only prayer she made now was that He would do to her what He had done to Lot's sinful wife—she wanted to be turned to a pillar of salt right here on her own front porch, and cease to exist.

She heard a sound behind her, the opening and closing of her front door and a squeaking step on the plank floor of the veranda. She let go her death grip on the column and turned around. "That spot always did squeak," she said, staring down at Conor's boots. "I always meant to do something about it, but I—"

She faltered, unable to remember what she was saying. She lifted her face and stared at his chest as if she were staring through him to the doorway beyond.

"They've taken my girls," she whispered, looking like a bewildered, lost child. "They've taken my girls away."

Conor sucked in his breath, then lashed out at her with deliberate cruelty, desperate to hide the panic and guilt that churned beneath. "I can't stay here. I can't marry you."

She didn't seem to hear him. Dazed, she continued to stare straight through him as if he weren't there.

"I can't do it, Olivia. Be a husband, a father . . . Christ, I can't." He held out his hands, clenching and unclenching his fists in front of her. "This is what I am! This is what I'm good at!"

He slammed his fist into his palm with a savagery that made her flinch. "I told you I'll not be tied down to a piece of land or a way of life or a woman. I've been to prison. I won't go back into one. I have to be free, damn it. Free. Do you understand?"

She didn't answer. She didn't look at him. She simply stared at his hands. A tear rolled down her cheek. He hated her for that suddenly; he hated himself more. He grabbed her shoulders as if to shake her, as if she were to blame for all the self-loathing that darkened his soul. "Do you?"

"Yes," she choked. "I understand."

She lifted her face, and he saw those dark eyes glazed with pain and tears, her long lashes spiky and clinging together. His carefully welded indifference crumbled into pieces. He was like a china cup that had been broken, glued back together, and shattered again with the slightest pressure.

"Olivia. Oh, Christ, don't look at me like that. Damn you."

He let go of her as if she burned him. He felt the chains of her anguish wrapping around him, binding him to her with inexorable force, growing stronger with each step he took away from her. His back hit the door.

He wanted to crush something, strike out at the fate that had brought him to this. But her tears defeated him, they brought him to his knees, a mightier opponent than any he had ever faced before, and he knew he could not leave her. He straightened with an abrupt move and walked past her, down the steps, and across the weedy, graveled drive. His voice resonated back to her as he disappeared into the darkness. "You win. We'll go into town tomorrow and get married."

Olivia watched him go. She heard his words. But she

also heard the lifetime of bitterness carried with them on the still night air, and she knew she'd won nothing at all.

It rained on her wedding day. Olivia followed Conor into the church just as the storm broke, and she wondered gloomily if the hard summer rain that pelted the roof was some sort of omen. She withdrew to the small alcove beside the door, dismally watching Conor's rigid back as he left her there to go in search of Reverend Allen. He disappeared through the archway that led into the church without a word, and she decided the rain was appropriate to the occasion.

He hadn't spoken to her at all this morning, and his silence told her more clearly than any words how he felt. He was being trapped into marriage, trapped into fatherhood, and she found herself dreading all the days of cold silence that would follow this one. Even if he did not blame her, she would blame herself.

She turned to the mirror. Many Callersville brides had smiled joyfully into their reflections here. As a young girl filled with romantic daydreams, she had once hoped to do the same.

Tears threatened, the tears she had been keeping back through a long, sleepless night, and Olivia closed her eyes to prevent them from falling now. She feared, if she started to cry, she would not be able to stop.

At the sound of footsteps, she blinked the tears back hastily and turned to find both Conor and Reverend Allen standing in the archway. Only one of them smiled at her.

"I'm afraid I'll have to find witnesses," the reverend said. "So—"

The opening of the church door interrupted him, bringing in a rush of rain and Olivia's three soaking-wet daughters, followed by Kate and Oren Johnson, dressed in their Sunday best and equally drenched. In one hand, Kate carried a huge bouquet of gardenias.

"Mama!" the girls cried in unison as they caught sight of her in the alcove. They rushed to her, and Olivia fell to her knees with a sob of relief, striving to hold all three at once.

"We missed you, Mama," Miranda whispered, throwing her arms around her mother's neck.

"I missed you, too, sweetheart." She kissed Miranda's cheek and wrapped an arm around Carrie.

"Are you and Mr. Conor really going to get married?" Carrie asked. "Really?"

She glanced past the nine-year-old to the grim, silent figure watching from the archway. "Yes," she answered. Rising to her feet, she tore her gaze from his and turned to Becky.

The girl looked contrite and miserable. "I'm sorry, Mama. I tried to explain what happened. But Martha Chubb was so awful, she kept twisting around everything I said, and—"

Olivia pressed her fingers to the girl's lips. "It's all right, honey," she said. "Everything's going to be all right."

The reverend gave a slight cough to get everyone's attention. "Now that we have witnesses, we can begin."

Kate Johnson stepped forward. "Reverend, I think the bride needs a minute to freshen up." She glanced down at her rain-soaked skirt. "And so does the matron of honor. Why don't you all go in? We'll be along shortly."

"Of course. We'll begin whenever you're ready. Come along, girls."

The reverend led Olivia's daughters out of the room. Oren walked over to Conor and introduced himself. "We're Olivia's neighbors," he said, holding out his hand.

Conor shook the offered hand. "Conor Branigan."

Oren nodded. "I know. I saw that boxing match. It was something to see, when you swung that punch and sent old Elroy flying. I've never seen anything like it, and that's a fact. Lost a dollar," he added. "But it was worth it."

"Oren!" Kate's voice censured him. "We are in church," she reminded. "You all quit that talk about gambling this instant." She gestured to the archway behind them. "Go. We'll be along."

Oren shook his head. "Women. They get all riled up about the oddest things."

"Indeed," Conor answered, as the two men walked away. "I know just what you mean."

Olivia watched Conor follow Oren out of the room. It would be nice if he and Oren could become friends. It might make settling down easier for him. If he settled down. She wasn't fool enough to think that a wedding vow would be enough to hold him if he decided to move on.

But that did not matter. He was doing this because she would lose her girls if he did not. Because of that, she would be the best wife to him that she could be, for as long as it lasted. And because she loved him.

Kate laid a hand on her arm. "I like your man," she said, and thrust the bouquet of gardenias tied with a blue muslin bow into Olivia's hand. "Thought you'd need something blue."

Olivia stared down at the gardenias. "He's not mine," she said quietly. "At least, he doesn't want to be." She felt Kate's hand tighten on her arm, and the tears threatened again. She blinked them back and lifted her head. "How did you know we were going to be here?"

The other woman smiled. "Oren just happened to be in the south pasture this morning and saw the two of you drive past on your way to town. Wasn't that lucky?"

"Very lucky," Olivia choked.

"We figured you'd need witnesses," Kate went on cheerfully. "Oren will stand with your man, and I'll be your matron of honor."

"Oh, Kate." Overcome by a rush of feeling, she couldn't say more, but she gave her friend a shaky smile of gratitude.

Kate smiled back at her. "You didn't think we'd let you go through this alone, did you?"

"Thank you."

"Honey, there's nothing to thank me for. You brought my baby into this world. Without you, I don't think I could have done it. Nothing Oren and I could ever do will be able to repay you for that."

She removed the small gold cross from around her neck and fastened it around Olivia's. "That's your 'something borrowed,'" she said, and frowned down at Olivia's gray dress. "I suppose the dress will have to be the 'something old,'" she added with a sigh. "Why didn't you wear your mother's wedding gown?"

The tears threatened again, and Olivia blinked, trying to force them away. When she'd been a young girl, filled with dreams of her wedding day, she had always envisioned herself wearing her mother's wedding gown; but when she had taken it out of the cedar chest last night and unwrapped it from its protective layers of paper, she'd known she could not wear her mother's dress. Virginal white satin would have only heightened the hypocrisy of it all. "I couldn't," she mumbled, lowering her head to stare down at the bouquet in her hand. "I just couldn't."

Kate grasped her shoulders and gave her a little shake, forcing her to look up. "Now, you listen to me, Olivia Louise Maitland. You've got nothing to be ashamed of."

Olivia started to deny that, but Kate interrupted her.

"I know what's been said. I was at that sewing party, remember? And I don't care if that man's been living in your house. I don't care if you went to Monroe with him on an unchaperoned overnight trip. I don't care if you slept with him or danced the seven veils of Salome for him. I saw the way you looked at him a minute ago. You're in love with him—it's written all over your face. Nothing's wrong if it's done with love. You hold your head up when you say those vows, you hear me?"

Olivia was dismayed to learn that her feelings were so transparent, but she forced herself to nod.

"Good girl." Kate started toward the archway that led out of the alcove and into the church. "We'd better get started."

Olivia glanced down at herself then back up as she moved to follow her friend. "What about the 'something new'?"

Kate glanced back at her over one shoulder. "The gardenias," she answered. "They opened this morning."

Olivia choked back the hysterical bubble of laughter that rose in her throat as she followed Kate down the aisle to the man who waited for her at the front of the church.

She did not look at him. She kept her gaze fixed on Reverend Allen and followed Kate's advice, keeping her chin high.

But when she saw her girls smile at her as she passed, her tightly reined emotions almost overcame her, and her steps faltered. They looked so happy, as if this wedding were a celebration instead of a sham.

Everything began to blur as the hot tears welled up again, as she struggled again to hold them back.

She had prayed for a man to help her, and a man had been provided. She had fallen in love with the man and prayed for a way to make him stay, and now the man was staying. At least for now. All her prayers had been answered. God had given her everything she had asked for. She ought to be thankful.

But when Kate took the bouquet of gardenias from her stiff fingers and stepped back, when Olivia was forced to turn and face Conor, she looked into the ice-blue eyes of a stranger, and she could not find it within herself to be thankful. She heard him vow to love, honor, and keep her, and she could find no happiness in his promise, for it was a false one. He did not love her, and all the prayers and wishes in the world could not make it so.

But she loved him, and when the moment came to say the vows that bound her to him for the rest of her days, she said them with conviction, for they were true and came from her heart.

I now pronounce you man and wife.

He bent his head, and his lips grazed her cheek. He offered her his arm, and they walked back down the aisle together.

Man and wife.

A blessed numbness came over her. Conor re-leased her arm and stepped away, allowing the girls to gather around her in the alcove. She watched as the reverend shook his hand and led him across the small room.

"Prayers really do work, Mama," Carrie said, throwing her arms around Olivia's waist and hugging her tight. "I promise I'll say my prayers every night now. I will."

Olivia shook her head slowly, trying to think past the numb haze that had fallen over her and listen to her daughter's words. "What are you talking about, Carrie?"

The child pulled back and beamed up at her. "It's wonderful, isn't it? I asked God to make Mr. Conor my new daddy, and He did! I got what I asked for!"

Olivia's fragile composure finally shattered. She burst into tears.

*   *   *

Playing a role was nothing new to Conor. False smiles came easily, even the one he gave the reverend, who probably didn't mean to sound condescending when he said, "I'm proud of you, son," and shook his hand.

But when he looked over at Olivia, surrounded by her girls, with her face in her hands, he knew she was crying. He felt her tears, and he suspected they were not tears of happiness. He thought of the night before, of the tears that had cut him like a knife, and he felt the knife twist again. His false smile faltered.

"I believe this belongs to you."

Conor glanced down at the leather pouch the reverend held out to him. "Sure and it does," he murmured, taking it. "Where did you find it?"

"One of the local men found it and brought it to me a couple months ago. He mentioned at the time that he'd found it in Jackson Field—which I believe was the place where that prizefight was held in July—and when I opened it, I found a crucifix inside." He paused and gave Conor an apologetic smile. "I didn't mean to pry, but I'd hoped to find a name or some other clue to the owner, you see. Amid all that fuss yesterday, I learned that you were a prizefighter and that you were Irish, so I thought perhaps it might be yours."

"Thank you." Conor opened it and began rummaging through the contents, hoping to hell the man who'd found his pack hadn't appropriated the most important item inside.

"Nothing missing, I hope?"

Conor's fingers closed around the bottle of Irish still tucked amid his clothes. "No, Reverend," he said, and closed the pack, then slung it over his shoulder. "Nothing missing at'all."

24

GAOL
Mountjoy Prison, Dublin, Ireland, 1867

Fish guts. For the tenth straight day. Conor's stomach revolted at the raw, slimy mess on a tin plate that he was expected to eat. He couldn't do it, not again. He couldn't smile at the guard who brought it to him as if he hadn't a care in the world; he couldn't eat it as if it were the grandest meal he'd ever had the privilege of tasting; he couldn't even look at it. But he thought of Megan and the offal of the Derry fish market, and with a cry of pure hatred, he grabbed the plate in his chained hands and tossed it, sending fish innards flying against the stalwart body of the prison guard who asked him where the guns were hidden.

Exhaustion. He longed for sleep. They would not let him. They walked him around and around the walled yard of the *gaol*, hour after hour, changing guards at regular intervals. When Conor slowed, they pushed him with their sticks. When he stumbled, they dragged him to his feet. When he closed his eyes, they poured icy water over his head. When they asked him about the guns, he laughed in their faces.

Floggings. They peeled flesh from his back and screams from his throat. He prayed the wounds would fester and he would die, but the doctor was called in to save his miserable life so that he could tell them about the guns.

Hate. Through it all, he thought about the food-laden ships that had sailed out of Lough Foyle. He thought of his mother begging for her home, and his sisters starving in the streets, and his brother being beaten to death. He thought of all the other Irishmen sitting in British *gaols* for treasonous crimes against a government they did not recognize. He thought about all of that, and hate coalesced to a ball of fire in his belly. He sang every republican song he knew as they beat him; he hurled every curse he'd ever learned as they starved him. When they gagged him . . . he hummed the tunes and cursed them in his mind.

He lost track of the days. He began to hear voices in his head. The brawny body that had made him the champion of pub boxing deteriorated to a massive rack of bones. But still, he would not break.

After eighteen days, they took him to the warden.

"'Oh, they're hangin' men and women for the wearin' o' the green,'" Conor sang, his voice a hoarse parody of a once low, rich baritone, as they dragged him into a small, dark cell with a long table, burning coals in a grate, and a thin, anemic man who looked more like a clerk than a prison warden.

They snagged the chains on his wrists to a hook from the ceiling that forced Conor to stand on his toes. "'When we were savage, fierce and wild,'" he went on, trying to keep in tune when his throat felt as raw as the fish guts they insisted on ramming down his throat.

The warden watched him impassively for a moment, then turned toward the grate. He pulled an iron from the fire, then glanced over at Conor, who was still singing. He smiled at him pleasantly, then lifted the poker out of the fire to examine the tip that glowed orange in the darkened room. "We're going to talk now, you and I," he said when the song ended. "And I'm sure you'll have a great deal to say."

Conor kept his gaze fixed on the poker as the man brought it closer to him, then closer still. "Aye," he whispered. "I do have something to say."

"Yes." The man nodded with understanding. "I thought you might."

Conor spit. It hit the warden's cheek and slid slowly down his cadaverous face. "That's all the talk you'll be getting from me, you fucking British bastard. So you might as well stop wasting your time, and kill me now."

The warden wiped away the saliva from his cheek with an unhurried movement of his hand. He lifted the poker and blew on the fiery orange tip, turning it to stark white. Slowly, he shook his head. "Paddy, we're not going to kill you. We're just going to make you wish you were dead."

25

The girls were so excited that it took forever to settle them down enough for sleep. Through the long ride home, supper, and several games of checkers, they had chattered nonstop about how wonderful it all was, how great it was that Conor and Mama were married, and how they couldn't wait to tell their friends about it when school started Monday.

Conor endured all of the attention they showered on him and did not show the least sign of impatience with them. But Olivia noticed that each time they talked about how he was going to stay "forever," Conor's lips tightened ever so slightly, and she knew he was only tolerating their worshipful adoration, not enjoying it.

Finally, the chatter eased into exhaustion, and Olivia was able to put them to bed. Thank the Lord, they fell asleep almost immediately.

When she returned downstairs, he was still in the library. He looked up from the book in his hands as she entered the room. "Girls asleep?" he asked.

"Yes."

This was their wedding night.

They looked at each other, and the awkwardness was a tangible thing between them.

She didn't know the proper etiquette for wedding nights. She wondered if she should sit down, but that would mean conversation, and making small talk seemed unbearably trite. She shifted her weight from one foot to the other, then lifted her hand and smoothed her hair with a nervous gesture. "I thought they'd never fall asleep," she murmured to fill the silence.

He watched her for a moment as she hovered just inside the door.

"Go upstairs, Olivia."

Was he telling her to go away, or was he simply hinting that she should precede him to make whatever feminine preparations she felt necessary? She studied his unreadable expression and did not know. "Of course," she murmured. "Would you put out the lamps before you come up?"

She took a pitcher of water upstairs with her and bathed, remembering how he had looked at her when he'd said she was beautiful. She brushed out her hair and left it loose about her shoulders, thinking that he preferred it that way. She put on her prettiest lawn nightgown and fastened the pearl buttons, thinking about how he had undressed her in that Monroe hotel room. The memories made her shiver with apprehension and anticipation. She turned down the sheets, plumped the pillows, and waited. But he did not come.

She wandered about her bedroom, pacing and fidgeting, trying to banish her growing nervousness. She turned off the lamp, slid between the sheets, and strained to hear his step on the stairs. She lay in the dark and listened to the clock on her vanity table tick away the minutes. But he did not come.

Finally, she could stand it no longer. She put on her wrap and went downstairs. The lamps were out; the house was dark and silent.

She found him on the back porch. He had moved one of the kitchen chairs outside and was sitting in it, staring out at the moon that hung low in the night sky, with his long legs sprawled out before him and his head resting against the wall behind him. In his hand was a bottle.

He turned his head to look at her, taking in her bare feet, loosened hair, and delicate nightgown, without the slightest change in his expression.

Keeping his gaze locked with hers, he lifted the bottle and took a swig. "Ah," he said appreciatively, giving her a wicked smile. "Now, that's what I call a wee drop of the *craythur*."

Although the hand that held the bottle was steady, and his voice was unwavering, Olivia was not fooled. Visions of her father with his bourbon, or later, his cheap moonshine, danced through her mind, and she remembered every anguished line of his face, every cutting remark, every slurred laugh. She remembered all the nights she'd hauled him to bed to sleep it off, all the mornings of profuse apologies and promises.

Heartsick and dismayed, she pulled the edges of her robe together at her throat with a shaking hand as she studied Conor's face. It was harsh and cold in the silver light. "You're drunk."

"I am, indeed." He lifted the bottle and swirled the liquid contents thoughtfully. "I am participating in a fine Irish tradition. Every self-respecting Irishman gets drunk on his wedding night. Did you not know that?"

Wedding night. He said the words with such loathing, she tightened her grip on the collar of her wrap and wondered about all the other nights like this that were to come.

He lifted the bottle in a toast. *"Slainté,"* he said, and downed another swallow of whiskey.

Her father's ghost rattled dangerously again. Olivia stiffened her spine. "I won't have spirits in my house," she said quietly.

He threw her a sharp glance. "Don't you mean *our* house, Mrs. Branigan?"

His voice was as cool and lethal as a knife blade. She swallowed hard and stood her ground. "I will not have spirits in our house."

"But I'm not in the house. I'm outside." He grinned at her, but she sensed the dark undercurrents hidden by the impudent surface.

"That's splitting hairs, Conor. What if the girls saw you this way? What would they think?"

Something in him seemed to change at the mention of the girls. The grin faded, and his head fell back as if he were suddenly weary. "Maybe they'll stop looking at me as if I'm some kind of hero," he said, and shook his head, squeezing his eyes shut. "Hero! God, if they only knew."

Olivia watched him, feeling as if she were missing a very important piece of a very complex puzzle. She felt his pain, she felt his rage, but she saw all the hate he turned inward, and what she knew could not explain that.

I got exactly what I deserved.

He began to hum under his breath a tune she did not recognize.

"That's a song called 'The Bold Fenian Man.'" He opened his eyes and turned his head to look at her. "Do you know what a Fenian is, Olivia?"

"No," she whispered.

He began to sing very softly. "'We may have good men, but we'll never have better. Glory-o, glory-o, to the bold Fenian man.'"

He laughed, and took another swallow of whiskey.

"I was a hero once," he said. "The lads thought because I was a guest of the Crown, because I had the scars of a British whip on my back, because the bastards made me get down on my hands and knees to eat, as if I were a dog—I was a hero. The bold Fenian man. What a joke I was."

She pressed a clenched fist to her mouth at the contempt she heard in his voice. She didn't know if marrying her was what had brought it to the surface now, but it frightened her. "Don't," she whispered. "Please don't do this."

"Don't what? Get drunk? Too late, I'm afraid. I'm three-parts pissed, love."

"Don't torture yourself."

"Not to worry. That's already been done. By experts."

"So, you must continue where they left off? Why?"

He didn't answer her question. Instead, he lifted his bottle in another salute. "'Glory-o,'" he sneered, his voice filled with self-mockery, "'to the bold Fenian man.'"

Olivia couldn't bear it any longer. She turned and left him with his Irish whiskey and his bitter memories.

In her room, Olivia lay in bed with her arms wrapped around her pillow and wondered about the man she had married today. She'd thought she understood, at least a little, what sort of man he was. Now, she knew that she'd barely scratched the surface.

She thought of all the times she had hoped her father would rise above the pit of dark and self-destructive apathy into which he had fallen; but time had proved her hope to be both naive and futile. The idea that her love could somehow heal him had been nothing more than vanity and wishful thinking.

Now, here she was again, in the same situation, stubbornly pinning the same foolish hopes on a different man. Her husband.

The logical part of her knew she did not have the power to heal Conor's wounds. A loving touch and three hot meals a day could not wash away a lifetime of pain and guilt and torment.

But somehow, her heart refused to listen to her head, refused to believe that there was no hope that Conor Branigan would heal. Her heart ached to help him; her arms longed to hold him; her hands wanted to soothe him. She loved him. So, Olivia lay in her bed, awake and alone, silently waiting, foolishly hoping. Of course, he did not come.

The following morning, the congregation of the Callersville Baptist Church was all agog over the news of Olivia's wedding. By the time Olivia arrived, everyone had been informed of her hasty marriage. Even Vernon, who was never the recipient of any local gossip, had been told. He and his Yankee wife had arrived back in town the evening before, Kate informed Olivia on the church steps, and the moment Olivia walked inside, she knew that he had been told of her marriage. He watched her walk up the aisle, and she returned his hard stare with a sweet smile. His thunderous frown was his reply.

She thought of how Vernon had ordered Conor beaten for his refusal to cheat during that boxing match, and she was very proud of her husband.

Her husband.

Olivia's step faltered a moment. She could hear the talk buzzing around her; she could feel the curious stares. Matrons who two days before had condemned her as a jezebel were smiling at her and nodding to each other, clearly pleased that the man had made an honest woman of her, and all was well. Those less forgiving were studying her with speculation, and it was obvious what they were thinking. She knew they had noticed that her husband was not with her in church this morning and were wondering how long marriage to an Irish prizefighter—a Catholic, no less—could possibly last.

Olivia wondered, too. She couldn't help it after what had happened last night. Perhaps someday Conor could come to love her. Given time, he might be able to accept the responsibilities and joys of being a husband and father. But Olivia knew time was not on her side. She could go home today and find him gone, and she wondered how long she could live with that uncertainty.

She paused beside an empty pew and ushered her girls in before her. Her cheeks burned at the whispers around her, but she kept her head high as she took her seat. Yesterday, she had pledged love, honor, and obedience. She was going to do her best to live up to that pledge— well, at least the part about love and honor. She could only hope that Conor would try to do the same.

While Reverend Allen was asking his congregation to contemplate the blessed teachings of Jesus to turn the other cheek and forgive thy neighbor, Vernon was contemplating how he could get rid of Conor Branigan. Permanently.

He fumed with impotent fury as he thought about it. He'd never been good enough for Olivia to marry; but she'd been willing to marry that Irishman. Four years of trying, and he'd never been able to get his hands on Olivia's land, but Conor Branigan had managed it in scarcely two months. He should have killed the cocky son of a bitch when he had the chance.

He should have come back the minute he'd gotten Joshua's telegram about Branigan being at Olivia's place. Damn Alicia and her social whirl for keeping him away so long; damn Hiram for being led around by his own daughter. Vernon knew if he had been here instead of shaking Yankee hands and attending the symphony, none of this would have happened. Olivia's peach crop was in, which meant she had the money to pay her spring taxes. And Branigan had control of her land. It beat all, it truly did.

Until he'd gotten Joshua's telegram, he'd forgotten all about the prizefighter who had defied him. He'd seen a problem that needed solving, and he thought he'd solved it. It had been surprising enough that Olivia had found the man and taken him in, hired him on, but who the hell would've thought she'd *marry* him? A boxer, for Chrissake. Vernon couldn't believe it. Olivia hated gambling. Always had.

His anger simmered as Reverend Allen droned on and on, and he couldn't take it anymore. He stood up in the middle of the sermon, ignoring Alicia's surprised glance. He walked out of the church, fully aware that he was scandalizing the town. Too damn bad. It was his town, wasn't it?

He was going to take care of that prizefighter here and now. After their last encounter, he'd doubted he'd have much trouble; but he decided to stop at the Harlan place on his way. Elroy and his boys loved a good fight.

When Conor awoke, the sun streaming through the window of his room hit his eyes, piercing his skull like white-hot needles. He groaned and pulled the pillow over his head to shut out the light, but it was too late. The pain began to pound mercilessly in his head.

It was the whiskey. Christ, he hadn't felt like this the morning after a drinking bout since he was seventeen. He tried to go back to sleep, but that proved futile. Giving in to the inevitable, Conor slid to the edge of the bed and rose to his feet, grimacing at the pain in his head. Moving with great care, he walked to the door of his room and opened it, but the water Olivia usually set out for him to bathe and shave was not there.

She was angry with him. He remembered the way she had looked at him last night, and the things he had said, and he felt a twinge of guilt. Even though the marriage was a farce, it wasn't her fault. It was his. Well, he was being punished for it now, he thought, and pressed his hands to his aching head.

Aye, she was probably furious with him, but she was so softhearted that when she saw how miserable he was this morn, she'd forget about being angry. She'd fuss over him, of course, but he thought of the gentle touch of her hands and decided he could tolerate a bit of fussing. He was starving, and he knew that even if she was angry, she'd have a hot breakfast waiting for him. She'd insist on making him some of that awful green tea. If it would get rid of the pain in his head, he might even drink it.

Conor dressed and went out to the kitchen and discovered that Chester was the only one there. The dog greeted him with a loud bark that sent a fierce stab of pain through his skull. There was no hot breakfast, no girls, no Olivia. Bewildered and somewhat aggrieved, he looked out the kitchen windows, but he saw no one. He left the kitchen and went into the foyer.

"Olivia!" he called, thinking she and the girls might be upstairs, but his only reply was his own voice echoing through the house.

Then he remembered that today was Sunday, and he felt rather let down by the idea that he was alone, and hungry, and hung over, and clearly wasn't going to get any hot breakfast or fussing.

He went back into the kitchen and took a pail from its hook on the wall. He left the dog inside and went out to the well, then filled the pail at the pump and bent to pour the cool water over his head.

God, it felt good. He straightened to refill the pail for another go, but the sound of wheels grinding on gravel had him glancing up as a wagon came round the side of the house. *Holy Mother*, he thought, tossing aside the bucket and raking a hand through his wet hair, *why this morning?*

He tensed, watching as the wagon came to a halt in the yard, and Vernon Tyler stepped down, followed by Elroy Harlan, Joshua Harlan, and the three men who had turned his body into mush two months ago. Maybe they wouldn't beat him up this time. Maybe they'd just kill him and put him out of his misery.

Conor remembered the first lesson he'd ever learned in life. *No matter what happens, act like you don't give a damn.* He gave them a smile. "Good day, lads. 'Tis a bit early yet for a Sunday call, isn't it?"

No one replied. Vernon paused several feet away and pulled a cheroot out of his jacket pocket. He lit the cigar as his companions surrounded Conor and made it very clear just how outnumbered he was.

"I heard you got married," Vernon said, taking a puff on his cheroot. "I came to offer my congratulations."

Conor thought of the cigar burns the Mountjoy guards had put beneath his right shoulder blade, and wondered if Vernon planned to put a matching set on the opposite side of his back. He thought about that farmer and his wagon of turnips with profound regret. "I appreciate that, Mr. Tyler, I do, indeed."

Vernon studied the lit end of his cigar for a moment, then he looked Conor in the eye, obviously deciding it was time to get to the point. "Seems to me, I told you to get out of my town, boy."

Boy. God, he hated that word. He'd been hearing it all his life. Anger flickered dangerously in his belly. He gritted his teeth, freezing his smile in place. "Yes, I believe you did. But, you see, your lads here did such a fine job waltzing across me ribs that getting out of town wasn't possible."

"I don't take kindly to being crossed." Vernon took a puff on his cheroot. "It took Olivia a long time to get herself married. It'd be a shame if she became a widow. You understand me, boy?"

Steady, he reminded himself. Anger would get him nothing except more cracked ribs. He swallowed the anger down, the way he'd swallowed so many things so many times before, telling himself that was the sensible thing to do. Besides the fact that he had a hellbanger of a headache, he was outnumbered and didn't relish another round of being kicked like a tin can. He met Vernon's eyes. "Aye," he said steadily. "I understand you."

"Good. Now that we've got that straight, I'll move on to what I really want to talk about. You've married Olivia; you've got control of her land; and you're going to sell it to me."

Conor didn't know if he'd heard correctly. He was in control of Olivia's land now, and Vernon wanted to buy it from him? He wished he could think clearly, but there were hammers pounding his skull from the inside out. "Am I? Well, I'm thinking that depends on what you're offering."

"I'm offering not to kill you."

Conor's false smile widened. "I appreciate that, but if you were to kill me, Olivia would have the land again, and you'd be right back where you started. So, I'll be asking again, what are you offering?"

Vernon clamped his cigar between his teeth. "Peachtree is five hundred acres. I'll give you three dollars an acre."

Fifteen hundred dollars. Christ, that was a fortune. If it were truly his land, Conor would take the money in a heartbeat. But it wasn't. His name might be on it now—Vernon would probably know better than he—but it wasn't his land. The question was, how did he get out of this with his ribs intact? Stalling was definitely in order. "'Tis a fine and generous offer you've made, it is, indeed. I'll have to be talking with my wife about it."

To his surprise, Vernon laughed. "Talk? Boy, I don't know how they do things in Ireland, but here, we tell our women what to do, and they do it."

Right. Clearly, stalling wasn't going to work. He couldn't make a run for the house and that fine Henry rifle. Conor glanced at the men who surrounded him, and he braced himself for another round of trays and bedpans. He looked Vernon in the eye and hoped to hell he'd come out of this with all his teeth. "Sod off," he said pleasantly.

The men moved to seize him, but the sound of another wagon rounding the house stopped them. Olivia drove the wagon right into their midst, forcing Vernon to jump out of the way or get run over.

"Hello, boys," she greeted them as the girls jumped down from the wagon and ran to Conor. "Mighty fine day, isn't it?"

The girls surrounded Conor, and he figured it was the first time in his life he'd been rescued by a woman and three girls.

The other men looked over at Vernon, who shook his head and turned to Olivia, tipping his hat. "We just came by to offer our congratulations."

Olivia braked the wagon and smiled. "Why, Vernon, that's right nice of you. I'd ask you stay to Sunday dinner, but I'm sure you all would rather go home to your own families."

Vernon looked back over at Conor. "You think about what I said," he told him, then turned and walked to his own wagon, Elroy and the lads right behind him.

Conor waited until they had driven away, then he said, "Becky, take the wagon into the barn and unhitch the mule, then get him water. Carrie, you and Miranda help your sister. Your mother and I are going for a walk."

He held up his hand to Olivia. She hesitated a moment, then took his hand and allowed him to help her down. Keeping a firm grip on her wrist, he led her through the garden. It wasn't until they were in the dilapidated gazebo that he let her go.

"It's time to give this up, Olivia."

She folded her arms across her breasts. "Seems we've had this discussion before."

"Aye, for all the good it did," he shot back, his voice rising.

"You seem quite out of temper today. Must be all that whiskey you drank last night."

"Whiskey has nothing to do with it," he shouted. "I'm always out of temper when men come to beat me up. And don't you be changin' the subject."

"Then don't tell me what to do with my land."

Exasperated, he glared at her. "Damn it, woman, don't you understand? You can't win."

She glared right back at him. "And don't swear at me. I am winning. We've been fighting this battle for four years, and Vernon still doesn't have my land. I am winning."

He rolled his eyes. "You've won nothing but a wee bit of time. They can wait you out."

Olivia shook her head. "But they can't. Oren told me Vernon's been getting some pressure from his father-in-law, who's one of the major investors in this railroad deal. That means they're running out of time."

"Perhaps, but that only means that Vernon is going to increase the pressure on you."

She started to turn away, but he grabbed her shoulders and kept her there, forcing her to face him, forcing her to face the unpleasant truth. "Listen to me. You can't fight them. If they've bought up enough land to build this railroad, they have a lot invested in it and they stand to make a lot of money once it's built. Do you really think they're going to let one woman get in their way?"

"They'll have to," she said, and jerked free. "I'm not selling."

"Even if they threaten you and the girls? Are you ready to risk the girls' getting hurt?"

"I told you, Vernon wouldn't hurt my girls. Or me."

"What makes you so sure of that?"

"Because he's in love with me," she said simply. "Always has been."

"What?" Her words stunned him, but the violent jolt of jealousy that shot through him stunned him more. It also made him angrier than before. "That piss-poor excuse for a man?"

She frowned. "Don't swear, if you please."

"'Conor, don't swear. Conor, don't drink,'" he mimicked her, scowling. "I'll do what I like, woman. You're the one who promised obedience in that church of yours, not me."

She scowled back at him. "Now, who's changing the subject?"

Conor tried to remember having been more furious in his life than he was right now, and he failed. "Vernon's in love with you," he said again, and the ramifications of such a situation hit him. "Brilliant. This is just brilliant. One more reason for him to hate my guts. One more reason for him to use me as a punching bag."

She turned away and folded her arms, staring out at

the tangle of rosebushes gone wild. "You don't have to stay," she said quietly.

"Thank you, dear wife, but it's a bit late for that now."

She stiffened at the endearment, which carried no affection. "Reverend Allen didn't put any chains around your neck when he married us," she said. "You're free to leave any time you like."

Was she telling him to go? Uncertain, he frowned at her back, feeling dismayed and angry and oddly bereft. He realized he was beginning to care about her far too much, and knowing that made him immediately rebel. "Or, maybe I'll just sell Vernon the land."

"What?" Stunned, she turned and stared at him.

"He offered me fifteen hundred dollars for it. Since I'm now your husband, it seems I'm in control of the land. Fifteen hundred dollars is a bloody fortune. We could live quite well for a long time on that kind of money. I'd be daft not to sell."

A change came over her as he spoke, the rigid still-ness of fear, and he knew she hadn't thought about how her marriage would affect her property. She opened her mouth on a wordless sound and closed it again.

Now was the time to do it, to tell her he was going to take Vernon's offer, but he looked into her face, and damn it all to hell, as angry as he was, as certain he was that he was right, he couldn't do it.

She was looking at him with those brown eyes that melted all a man's good sense and made him do things that were stupid, things that might even get him killed. Vernon was in love with her. He turned away with a curse. "Marriage or no, it's your land, not mine. Do what you want with it."

He kicked the lattice half-wall of the gazebo and put a hole in it to go along with all the holes in his head, then he walked away. Women were the very devil.

26

Reverend Allen was kind enough to give Alicia a ride home, since her husband had apparently forgotten her.

She knew why, of course. Olivia Maitland.

Alicia invited the reverend in for tea, but thankfully, he declined. She went up to her room, pleading a sick headache for the benefit of any callers who might happen to drop by. She wanted time alone to think.

Vernon had always been in love with Olivia. Alicia knew that. She'd known it from the first day she had arrived in this dead little junction, from the first moment she'd seen the woman in faded brown cotton walk into the mercantile Vernon had bought with her Papa's money. She'd known by the way her husband had looked at the woman—with anger and pain. And hunger. The fact that Olivia was now married would make little difference.

Eight years of marriage had given Alicia only the tiniest bits and pieces, for Vernon was not a man who talked about his past, but she knew that her husband was here to build an empire for only one reason: To show *them*. To lord it over all the people who had once looked down on him, including the woman for whom he'd never been good enough.

Alicia sank down on the edge of her bed and wearily pulled off her hat. She fanned herself with the straw boater and remembered wistfully how cool the sea breezes had been at Newport and how wonderful it had been to call on her friends and shop in the elegant stores. She gazed out the window at the rolling countryside that seemed to stretch endlessly into the distance, and she felt as if she were miles from nowhere. Back in Louisiana less than twenty-four hours and she was already miserably homesick.

Why, why, why did Vernon want to build his empire here? When she met him, he had talked about Louisiana as if he hated it. When she married him, she had assumed that Papa would simply bring him into the steamship company, or the garment factory, or any of the other businesses he owned. Never had she dreamed that the two of them would concoct a new venture that would send her a thousand miles from home.

She wished she could just leave him. Leave him to his new Atlanta and his railroad and his memories of Olivia Maitland. But she couldn't. She knew his childish boasting and his bullying ways were only to disguise a lifetime of feeling inferior. She loved him. But she wanted to go home.

Papa was coming down next week to look over the railroad plans and drive the proposed route. She knew his patience with this project was wearing thin, thanks in part to the seeds of doubt she had planted during the weeks she and Vernon had spent with him in New York and Newport, thanks to the subtle hints she'd dropped to the investors at the parties and soirees. She could only hope that her efforts had been worthwhile. If

Vernon didn't get Olivia's land by the time Papa arrived, and if Papa could finally be made to see how miserable she was down here, and if her hints had made the investors concerned enough to put on the pressure, Papa might finally abandon this ridiculous scheme.

Alicia stared out her window at Vernon's cotton fields that seemed to her like a vast white wasteland, and she hoped so.

After Sunday dinner, Conor spent the rest of the afternoon putting in the window glass Olivia had bought in Monroe. Olivia and the girls went down to the orchard and harvested the last of the peaches, the ones that had been too green for picking a few days before. Long before sunset, Conor finished his task, and when he walked into the kitchen, he found Olivia and the girls surrounded by baskets of fruit and glass jars. The air was thick with the scent of peaches, cinnamon, and cloves.

He would have turned around and left the kitchen, but the girls had other ideas. They immediately drafted him into helping. He looked at Olivia, but she said nothing, and he decided to stay. He proved especially useful at carting in buckets of water from the pump and placing the finished jars on the highest shelves of the pantry to cool.

When he was not needed for those tasks, Conor sat at the table and watched, intrigued. Olivia seemed to have the process honed to the efficiency of a cannery and the girls as trained as any factory workers could be. Miranda washed and dried the jars. Becky peeled, pitted, and sliced the fruit. Carrie filled half the jars on the table with peach halves, then poured in the sugar syrup, while Olivia filled the remaining jars with jam. Then she sealed each one with a two-piece metal lid. Sealed jars were placed in two huge kettles of water on the stove to boil while the next load was filled.

When the last jar had been sealed and placed in the water bath, Olivia and Becky made a quick supper, while Conor gave Carrie and Miranda some of his tallest Irish tales, keeping his face as straight as if this were a poker game and he had fifty dollars in the pot and nothing in his hand. The pair of them hung on every word, just as he had done when he was a lad, and by the time the dishes were done, he had them absolutely convinced that leprechauns were real.

They wanted another story, but Olivia declared it was time for them to take their baths and get ready for bed. She held up both hands to halt the flood of protest that followed.

"Kate told me at church today that you didn't have your baths last night when you were supposed to," she said, "and school starts tomorrow, so upstairs you go. You can have another story afterward."

The girls trooped out of the kitchen, and she glanced at Conor. "You'll tell them another story, won't you?" she asked hesitantly.

"Aye, if they want it."

Unexpectedly, she smiled at him, then she took a kettle of boiling water from the stove and went upstairs. Conor went to his room and took a cigar from his pack, then pulled one of the chairs from the kitchen out onto the back porch and sat down.

The night was still and warm, and the full moon cast a glow over the yard. Fireflies—"lightning bugs," the girls called them—occasionally flickered past. Crickets chirped, and frogs croaked, a once-hated chorus that he must be getting used to, since he hardly noticed it anymore.

Through the open window above, he could hear Carrie and Miranda arguing over the soap again. It wouldn't be bath night without that, he supposed.

He leaned his head back against the wall behind his chair and closed his eyes, smiling as he listened. Olivia put up with their fight for about ten seconds.

"Another peep out of either of you," she finally said, "and it's straight to bed. No bedtime story from Conor."

The argument instantly stopped. Conor hadn't realized his stories rated that high.

Miranda was the first one back down, barefoot and dressed for bed, her hair damp from her bath. Chester, her shadow, was right behind her.

She crawled up onto Conor's lap and curled one arm around his neck, studying him with a solemn expression. After a moment, a tiny frown knit her brow as if she were thinking about something very important.

"What's going on in that head of yours, *mó paisté*?" he asked, brushing back a damp lock of hair from her forehead.

She tilted her head to one side. "Since you and Mama are married, does that mean we can call you Daddy now?"

His hand fell away from her hair and everything inside him seemed to explode in a rush of panic. The marriage was a farce, and he wasn't their daddy, but he looked into the child's eyes and could not have refused her if he had tried. "If you want to."

She smiled, pleased, and tucked her head beneath his chin. "Tell me another story," she ordered. "About leprechauns."

"We ought to wait for your sisters, I'm thinking," he said, but the words were barely out of his mouth before Carrie appeared. She saw that Miranda had beaten her to what he assumed by her disappointed face must be the coveted seat of honor, and he shifted Miranda to one knee with a resigned sigh. "C'mon."

Carrie settled herself happily on his other knee, and that was how Olivia found them. She paused beside the door, eyeing them in some amusement.

Conor was reminded of the night she'd come home to find her daughters piled over him, sound asleep, but this time it didn't seem quite as embarrassing. "Becky's not coming down?" he asked.

Olivia's smile widened. "I have been informed that she's fourteen now and much too old for bedtime stories." She brought a chair from the kitchen out onto the porch and placed it beside Conor's. "I, however, am not. You may begin."

This time Conor was able to tell the story of "Cuchulain and the Courtship of Emer" without finding that his audience had fallen asleep, wrapping up the tale with the words, "So, Emer was finally courted as she had desired to be, and that was how Cuchulain won her fair hand and made her his queen. They lived happily ever after," he added. That wasn't quite true, but he didn't think Cuchulain's legendary infidelities were really appropriate for the bedtime stories of little girls.

They wanted another story, of course, but Olivia negated that idea. "It's bedtime," she said firmly, and rose to her feet. "First day of school tomorrow. C'mon."

The girls reluctantly slid down from Conor's lap, and followed their mother into the house.

Carrie's frustrated voice floated back to him. "I don't see why we have to go to bed so early. I'm not even sleepy yet. I'll just lie there and lie there, wide awake, when I could be hearing a great story."

He grinned. Trust Carrie to come up with sound, logical reasons to get her way. It never worked with her mother, but she did keep trying.

Suddenly, he heard the pad of quick footsteps, and Miranda came running back through the doorway. She skidded to a halt beside his chair. "I forgot to say goodnight," she told him breathlessly. "Good night, Daddy."

She stood up on her toes and planted a kiss on his

cheek, then turned and ran back into the house, leaving Conor reeling under the impact of that simple word. It carried with it a host of responsibilities that he was not prepared for. What he had told Olivia two nights before had been the plain and simple truth. He just didn't know how to be a father.

Suddenly restless, he rose and left the porch. He pulled out his cigar and lit it, then crossed the yard and walked amid the dilapidated outbuildings that were silvery gray in the moonlight.

Daddy.

Another man might have been flattered, even delighted, at the prospect. Conor was not. He was just plain scared. How ironic that a child's word could strike more fear in him than all the bullets, prisons, and pain he had ever faced. The desperate need to run came over him, but he could not run. It was too late for that. He was a daddy now.

Perhaps he ought to start thinking about the future, but he could not. He could not think about the endless stretch of days, months, and years that lay ahead. He couldn't accept the idea that he was here for good, that he could never leave, could never find peace. All he could do was what he had always done. Get through the days, one at a time.

When he returned to the house, Olivia was there. She watched him as he came toward her across the yard. He stopped at the bottom of the steps and dropped the end of the cigar into the dirt. He crushed it beneath his boot. "I went for a walk."

"It's a nice night for it." She gestured to the chair beside her own. "Sit with me a spell."

He didn't want to, but he found himself moving toward her instead of away. He sat down. He felt he should say something, but he did not know what to say. He did not know what she expected. He leaned forward in his chair, then leaned back. He shifted, trying to find a comfortable position, but he could not relax.

"Pity we don't have the porch swing anymore," she said. "It would be a sight more comfortable than these chairs."

It wasn't the chair that made him restless. "Porch swing?"

She nodded. "There used to be one out here. My daddy gave it to my mama as a gift. I think, of all the gifts he ever gave her, that was her favorite. It was painted white, I remember, and it had chintz cushions. Mama and Daddy used to sit out here on summer nights, rocking back and forth and holding hands as if it were still their courtin' days."

She smiled. "One night, I sneaked downstairs to get some cookies after I was supposed to be in bed and I saw them out here. They were—" She broke off and smoothed her skirt, looking suddenly flustered. "Mama was sitting on Daddy's lap and they were kissing. It was quite a shock to me. I never dreamed my folks did things like that."

Conor had never really thought about what husbands and wives did on summer evenings, but if they were in love, they probably sat out on porch swings after their children were asleep and kissed. "What happened to it?"

She took a moment to answer. "After Mama died, it was so hard for Daddy to look at the swing every day and know she wasn't ever going to sit in it again. One night, I came out here and found him with his head in his hands, crying. The next day, I took the swing down and gave it away. Perhaps that was wrong of me, but I couldn't bear to watch him suffer like that."

That was love, too. Pain and loss. He turned away and stared out at the moonlit yard. He thought of all the people he had loved. All of them were gone, and the pain of losing them was something he never wanted to feel again.

The silence fell again, but she made no attempt to break it. He realized that he wasn't expected to make conversation, and some of the tenseness began to ease from him. It occurred to him that perhaps she just wanted exactly what they were doing, to sit in the stillness and share it with him. Somehow, as the silence lengthened, it became almost comfortable.

"It's getting late."

Her soft voice shattered the companionable silence. He did not move, but every muscle in his body tensed. He knew what she was saying; from the corner of his eye, he could see her hand pluck nervously at her skirt, pleat the faded blue fabric.

"It's time for bed," she added, and rose.

He was not prepared for the onslaught those words evoked, the sudden, overwhelming need for her, and the need for the aftermath—to hold her, cradle her against him, protect her from every danger there was in the world; but when the dreams came again, who would protect her from him?

"Good night," he said evenly, without looking at her. "Sleep well."

She hesitated, hovering beside his chair. "You aren't coming up?"

He thought about that night in Monroe, and how he had fallen asleep holding her in his arms, a dreamless sleep with no ghosts from the past, no demons to taunt him. But they would come, and he could not be with her when they did. "No."

Still, she did not move away. "Conor, I wish you would come upstairs with me."

She laid a hand on his shoulder, and he stiffened beneath her touch. "I can't," he said. "I'm sorry."

He closed his eyes, breathing deeply, waiting. It seemed an eternity before her hand tightened briefly on his shoulder then fell away, and she walked back into the house.

That night in Monroe was still vivid in his memory, every button he unfastened, every curve of her body, every pleasured gasp she gave, every ounce of his control lost. He remembered drifting into sleep, waking up to the scent of her, the feel of her—all of that almost as pleasurable as the lovemaking itself had been. The peace of it, peace he hadn't known since he was a child, peace he'd never thought to find again.

But peace was an illusion, and it would not last. His dreams would come back when the dark side of him emerged without warning—enraged and snarling, bathed in sweat and screaming, or worse, begging for mercy, pathetic and broken. She'd seen glimmers of that other man, and he knew that man frightened her. He might even hurt her—strike out at her in the dark when he did not know where he was, when he could not recognize her, when he could not separate what was now from what was past.

He imagined her upstairs in her room, lying in bed with her hair spread across the pillow, that nightgown with the pearl buttons down the front tangled around her legs, nothing beneath the delicate fabric but her softness and warmth. Desire pulsed through his body, hungry and hot and needy.

It was unbearable to want her with such intensity, unthinkable to need her with such desperate longing, dangerous to believe that she could somehow keep the demons away. He did not want to need her, for in need, there was dependence. He could not trust, for in trust, there was betrayal. Better never to see heaven at all than to catch a glimpse of it, grab for it, and lose it.

He went to his room. He slept with his demons, and he woke alone.

*   *   *

Monday was the first day of school, and like all the mornings of all the first days of school that had come before, this morning was proving to be a trial for Olivia. Carrie rebelled at the idea of having silly ribbons in her hair and hated her school dress because it now had a ruffle. Miranda was in tears, her excitement about school dissolving into terror when she realized Mama was not going with her. Becky whined that it wasn't fitting to give Miss Sheridan three jars of spiced peaches *again* this year for her first-day gift. Conor proved to be no help whatsoever. He ducked out the back door halfway through breakfast, just about the time Miranda threw up. Obviously, domestic bliss was still an alien concept to him. Olivia watched him go, and she wondered if it always would be.

By the time Oren came to take the girls into town with his own children, Olivia was heartily glad to see them go. She walked back into the kitchen, which looked as if the Union Army had marched through it, rolled up her sleeves, and began cleaning up the mess.

It took about thirty minutes, just long enough to do the breakfast dishes, for her to realize that, for the first time in years, she was completely alone in the house. Miranda had always been at home with her, and that had somehow made it easier to send Becky and Carrie off for the first day of school. But now Miranda was at school with them, she wasn't at home getting underfoot and demanding attention.

Olivia sank down in one of the kitchen chairs, suddenly feeling incredibly lonely. The house was so quiet. She missed her baby.

Chester ambled over to her side. He nuzzled her hand with a whine, as if to say he missed Miranda, too. She patted the dog's head, brushed away a solitary tear with an impatient swipe of her hand, and told herself not to be silly. She had piles of laundry to do, and sitting here wasn't getting it done.

But instead of getting to work as she knew she ought, Olivia rested her elbow on the table and her cheek in her hand, staring dismally at the empty kitchen.

She wondered what Conor was doing. Avoiding her, probably. She couldn't blame him for that. He hadn't wanted to be tied to a farm and a ready-made family. He had only married her out of a sense of obligation. She thought wistfully of that night in Monroe, of how for one brief moment he had let her into his solitary life, and the price he had paid for it.

She was filled with desolation at the idea of spending all the days of her life loving him, knowing he did not love her, knowing he did not want her, knowing he might even hate her for what he had been forced to do, knowing that one day she could wake up and find him gone.

She glanced up at the ceiling, confessing her deepest fear aloud to the only one she knew was listening. "How do I make him forget the past?" she whispered. "I love him so, and I'm so afraid it isn't enough."

But Olivia knew the only thing she could do was keep right on loving him and hope for the best. She was not going to walk on eggshells, or worry about what might not happen, or indulge in any self-pity. She rose from the table and went back to work.

By midday, the laundry was hanging on the clothesline, the garden was weeded, and a pot of vegetable soup was simmering on the stove. She put a pan of corn bread in the oven, and went in search of Conor to tell him dinner was ready. But she did not find him in the yard, or in any of the outbuildings, and she wondered where he had gone.

But she did not go searching for him any farther. When he felt crowded, he retreated to a safe and solitary distance. It was his way, and she wasn't going to go chasing after him. She ate her dinner alone; she did the ironing; and she tried not to think about how quiet and empty the house seemed.

But by midafternoon, she couldn't stand the quiet any longer. She went in search of Conor again. This time, he proved much easier to find. She found him in the old toolshed, sorting through Nate's junk. He glanced up as she entered the dim and dusty shed.

"You missed dinner," she said, striving to sound casual. She wondered where he had gone, how he had spent his day, but she did not ask him. Instead, she asked, "Are you hungry?"

He shook his head. "Thanks, but it's getting too late. I'll wait for supper." He tossed a rusty bucket aside and gestured to a stack of unused lumber in the corner. "Do you mind if I use some of this?"

"Of course not. You don't have to ask my permission, Conor," she said in a quiet voice. "This is your home now, too."

His lips tightened. He turned away and knelt down to rummage through a crate of tools. "Yes, I suppose it is."

He didn't sound happy about that, but what else could she expect? To avoid the painful direction her thoughts were taking, she changed the subject. "What are you going to do with the lumber?"

"I don't really know," he said. "But it seems a shame to let it sit here waiting for the termites to get it." He paused, then looked up at her and added, "When I was fixing the roof, I was thinking how good it felt to hold a hammer again. I haven't done carpentry for a long time."

"Is that what you did back in Ireland?"

He nodded. "I began as an apprentice to a furniture maker when I was sixteen."

She leaned back against Nate's dust-covered work-

bench, which stood beside the door, as Conor continued to sort through the contents of the crate. "Did you
give it up to become a prizefighter?"

"No." He rose to his feet and lifted the crate, then
moved to her side to set the crate on the workbench. "I
gave it up to become a rebel," he said, taking a router
out of the crate to examine it more closely. "A Fenian.
A full-time thorn in the side of the British Empire."

She remembered his bitter, drunken words of two
nights before, and she knew by the ironic glance he
gave her, he remembered them, too. But she was not—
was not—going to become a nag about spirits, or any
other subject, for that matter.

"Fenian," she repeated the strange-sounding word
thoughtfully. "Does that mean some sort of secret
society?"

"Aye. The Irish Republican Brotherhood." He set the
router back in the crate. "Your man had some fine tools."

His words sounded so funny, she couldn't help it—
she burst out laughing.

Conor shot her a puzzled glance. "Did I say something funny?"

She clamped one hand over her mouth and shook
her head, still laughing, unable to speak. "Nate was
about seventy years old," she finally managed. "Black as
coal, with a long, scraggly, white beard and teeth yellow
from chewing tobacco." She made a wry face. "Nasty
habit. He was a sweet old dear, but he wasn't, by any
stretch of the imagination, 'my man,' as you put it."

"It's a figure of speech, love. In Ireland, we say 'your
man' to mean someone you know, or someone you've just
met, or even a stranger who approaches you. Actually,"
he added as her smile widened, "now that I think about it,
the term could refer to just about anybody."

"It's odd the way different people say things, isn't

it? Down here, we say, 'I reckon,' and you say, 'I'm thinking,' but it means the same thing, doesn't it? 'It's going to rain, I reckon.' 'It's going to rain, I'm thinking.'"

"Well, the Irish are known to say things in a way other people find amusing."

"Such as?"

"If I run into a man I haven't seen for a while, I'd probably say something like, 'Why, Daniel O'Shea, is that yourself?'"

She smiled. "Well, down here, we say things that the Yankees find odd, that's for sure."

"That's one of them."

"What?"

"In Ireland, any American is a Yankee."

She lifted her chin. "I am *not* a Yankee. Calling me one is a good way to start a fight."

He grinned at her. "I'll remember that. Or I'll just have to keep ducking when you throw eggs at me."

Suddenly, they were laughing together. She looked at him and remembered what had happened after the eggs. Slowly, their laughter faded into silence.

Olivia felt a tingling awareness radiating through her body. When he moved a hairsbreadth closer, she realized wildly that he was going to kiss her. She swayed toward him.

"Daddy! Mama! Where are you?"

Miranda's voice had both of them jerking back at once. But neither of them looked away. She licked her dry lips, watched his gaze catch on the nervous movement. "The girls are home," she said.

"I figured that," he answered dryly.

"Daddy? Mama? Where are you?"

Feeling almost vexed at the interruption, when she'd been missing her girls like crazy all day, Olivia stepped back through the doorway of the shed and glanced toward the house. Becky and Carrie were coming down the porch steps, but Miranda was much closer. "We're in here!" she called, beckoning to them with a wave of her hand. She also waved to Oren and his four school-age children as he turned the wagon around and headed for home.

Miranda came flying toward the shed, and Olivia smiled, holding out her arms. But the child raced past her into the shed with a perfunctory, "Hello, Mama," and ran straight to Conor.

Olivia turned and watched through the doorway, astonished and somewhat bemused as Conor lifted the child into his arms.

"Look, Daddy!" she said excitedly, holding up a sheet of paper with one hand and wrapping her free arm around his neck. "Look what I drew at school. It's a kangaroo. They have them in Australia. Miss Sheridan told us."

Daddy? Olivia was too astonished to be hurt by the lack of attention. Miranda had called him Daddy, and he didn't seem to mind. In fact, he didn't even seem surprised.

He studied the drawing. "Sure, and it is, lass. A kangaroo. It's a wonderful picture. I think we'll have to frame it and hang it in the house somewhere." He glanced at Olivia. "Don't you think?"

"Of course," she choked, averting her head to blink back another sudden onslaught of tears. But they were not tears of melancholy this time.

Carrie was the next one through the door, and she immediately demanded Daddy's attention as well, showing him her sketch of a castle and explaining to him what a parapet was used for.

Becky came last. She showed Conor the intricate map of Ireland she'd drawn with all the counties and major cities written on it; and Conor read the unfamiliar names aloud for her. *"Sligo, Leitrim, Donegal . . . "*

Through a blurry haze, Olivia watched her daughters

clamoring for Conor's attention, and for the first time, she felt hope for her marriage.

She walked over to stand beside him and have a look at the drawings her daughters had made. After she'd made a great deal of fuss over them, she said, "There's cookies in the kitchen," and watched them race out of the shed. She called after them, "Only two apiece, or you'll ruin your supper! And put your dinner pails away."

She turned her attention to Conor, who was studying Miranda's sketch, still in his hand. He glanced at her. "A kangaroo?" he asked dubiously.

She leaned closer to have another look at the drawing, then she turned it right-side up for him. "Definitely a kangaroo."

The following morning, Conor was awakened by the sound of hurried footsteps overhead, as the girls got ready for school. After he dressed, he went out to chop the wood for Olivia, carried it into the kitchen, and built a fire in the stove. He then took the pail from its hook on the wall and went out to milk the cow for her, knowing she was busy trying to get the girls ready, and thinking she might need a bit of help with the chores.

That was where she found him. He glanced up as she entered the barn, not missing her astonished expression.

"You're milking the cow," she said.

"You don't have to sound so surprised. I do know how." He pulled the filled pail out from beneath Princess, rose to his feet, and pushed aside the milking stool, then turned and handed the pail of milk to her. She took it, but she continued to eye him as if this were the last thing in the world she would have expected. He watched that radiant smile light her face.

He suddenly felt uncomfortable. He didn't want her

thinking this was anything to make a fuss about. "I just thought you might need some help in the mornings now that the girls are in school," he explained, looking away. He pointed to the sack of chicken feed in the corner. "I'll take over feeding the chickens, too, if you like."

"Thank you," she said and started for the door, the pail of milk in her hand. In the doorway, she stopped and turned back. "Conor?"

"Hmm?"

"If you'll bring in the eggs, I'll make breakfast. I've got fresh bread in the oven this morning."

She disappeared through the door before he could reply, but her words eased the tension inside him, and a sense of satisfaction slowly took its place.

That morning created a new routine in the house. While Olivia got the girls ready for school, Conor did the morning chores. After he'd brought in the milk and the eggs, Olivia made breakfast, while he took the water she'd heated for him to his room, where he bathed and shaved. After breakfast, the girls went off to school, and Conor and Olivia went about their own work. By tacit agreement, they divided work into two distinct halves, with Olivia handling the household tasks, and leaving the outdoor work to Conor, along with anything that required the use of a ladder.

To his surprise, Conor found the routine that defined his days did not feel stifling. He was able to choose how to spend his day. He could do whatever work he felt like doing, and that had an appeal of its own. Instead of feeling suffocated, he began to find a certain satisfaction in the hard work that kept him busy until late in the day, when the girls came home and told him what they'd learned that day, when he sat at the supper table and listened to them say grace, when in the cool of evening he sat beside Olivia in an uncomfortable chair on the back porch and enjoyed the quiet and the serenity.

Something deep within him turned toward those moments with her, like a plant turning toward the sunlight. But he could not believe that it would last. And even as part of him began to anticipate it, actually hunger for it, another part of him remained uneasy and tense, waiting for it all to end, to crash down around him in pieces.

He continued to sleep alone, and Olivia made no further attempts to change the arrangement. He knew she did not understand his reasons, and he could not explain them to her. He'd spent the better part of his life on his own; he'd never felt the desire to confide in anyone. He couldn't do it now. But there were times, when they sat on the porch side by side, when he watched her bent over her sewing, her face soft in lamplight through the kitchen window, that he felt the overpowering desire to confide in her. But shame kept him silent.

There were times, too, when all he wanted was to grab her, carry her up those stairs, and make love to her. Just the sight of her hair in the sunlight or the sound of her voice when she said his name were enough to arouse him. But he thought of all the women he'd had who'd woken in the morning to find him gone, and he could not treat Olivia that way. She deserved a man who would sleep by her side when it was over, and he could not.

He still had dreams, and late at night, while the rest of the house slept, Conor would often go out to the toolshed with a lamp and work until the wee small hours, keeping his demons at bay with hammer and saw instead of a punching bag. He was making something special, and he did not want to think about why he was making it.

27

Saturday night was the harvest dance, and that morning, Becky tried on her blue silk dress at least five times, asked Olivia if it looked all right at least a dozen times, and acted so jumpy that her mother finally lost patience with her.

"For heaven's sake, Rebecca Ann, find something to do," she exclaimed in vexation when Becky started to ask her yet another question. "You're making me crazy."

"But, Mama, I just realized something."

Olivia sighed and looked up from the butter churn, exasperated. "Conor took your sisters fishing down by the creek. Why don't you join them?"

"But, Mama—"

"Out." Olivia pointed to the door.

Becky whirled around and left the kitchen, but she slammed the door behind her, making it clear that she thought her mother a most insensitive person for not listening to her. Olivia didn't care. She was too relieved.

But an hour later when she went out to the barn,

Olivia found that Conor and the girls were not fishing. She heard voices from inside the barn as she approached.

"*One*-two-three . . . *one*-two-three . . . "

What on earth? She stepped inside the barn and came to an abrupt halt, staring in astonishment at the sight that met her eyes. Conor was leading Becky across the dusty floor in a waltz, while Miranda and Carrie sat atop the two dusty barrels in the corner and watched.

Dancing. Dumbfounded, Olivia realized that Becky had never learned how to waltz because she had never taught her, and she wondered how she could have neglected something so obvious. Becky had evidently not realized it either, until this morning.

Conor brought the girl to a swirling halt. "Perfect," he told her. "Just count in your head, lass, and after a while, it'll just come naturally. And remember, that lad of yours'll probably be counting, too."

"Thank you, Daddy," she whispered, and wrapped her arms around his neck in a smothering hug. "Thank you."

Conor caught sight of Olivia standing in the doorway. "The lass is going to do well, don't you think?" he said, sounding quite pleased.

Olivia smiled at her daughter. "Yes, I do."

But that night, when they stood beside the refreshment table in the Callersville town hall and watched Jeremiah lead Becky toward the dance floor for yet another waltz, Olivia found Conor wasn't quite so pleased any longer.

"That's four waltzes now," he commented with a frown.

Olivia didn't realize he'd been counting. "Well, she did put his name down for all the waltzes on her dance card."

Conor's frown deepened as he watched them. "They're dancing rather close together, aren't they?"

She caught the disapproval in his voice, and she

glanced at Becky and Jeremiah, who were just far enough apart for it to remain respectable. She slanted a speculative, sidelong look at her husband from beneath her lashes. He was positively scowling.

She turned away, choking back her laughter, and ladled glasses of lemonade for Miranda and Carrie, who stood beside her. He really was the most unpredictable man. "Oh, I don't think it's anything to worry about," she murmured, although secretly she was delighted by Conor's disapproval, which was so obviously paternal.

"How can you say that?" he demanded, still watching the couple. "She's only fourteen. Perhaps I should have a talk with the lad."

With a great deal of effort, Olivia smothered her amusement and handed him a glass of lemonade. But Conor was too busy frowning at Becky and Jeremiah to notice the smile that hovered at the corners of her mouth.

Miranda and Carrie were both fast asleep by the time they arrived home. Becky, still dreamily humming the melody of a waltz, led the way upstairs with the lamp. Olivia followed, carrying Miranda. Conor came last, with Carrie in his arms.

In the hall, Olivia took the lamp from Becky's hand. "Go on to bed, honey."

Becky complied, walking to her room as if she were floating on clouds. Conor turned to Olivia, who was watching the girl with a smile. She looked over at him and whispered, "I think she enjoyed herself."

Conor thought she had enjoyed herself a bit too much for his peace of mind. He'd best be keeping a watchful eye on Jeremiah Miller.

"Will you put Carrie in bed?" Olivia asked, breaking in on his thoughts.

He nodded and took Carrie into her room. Guided by the moonlight through the windows, he carried the child over to the bed. Shifting her weight to one arm, he pulled back the covers, then gently laid her in the bed. He pulled the covers over her and moved to go, but her voice stopped him.

"Daddy?"

Conor sat down on the edge of the bed. "Hmm?"

She opened her eyes and blinked up at him sleepily. "When I'm old enough to have a dance card, you'll be the first man on it."

Conor felt a hard, burning tightness in his chest, a tightness that twisted his heart and left him unable to speak. He watched Carrie's eyes close. Within seconds, her even breathing told him she was asleep again.

He bent down and kissed her brow. "Good night, *mó cailín,*" he whispered, but he made no move to leave. Instead, he sat there for a bit longer, just watching her sleep.

He'd build her a tree house in that massive oak down by the orchard, and when she had a dance card, he'd bloody well check the names of all the lads on it. As for Becky and Jeremiah, Conor decided he wasn't going to let her marry the lad until she was at least eighteen. Miranda would probably want a new doll for Christmas and pudding cake again next year on her birthday. He thought of watching them grow up and knew he'd have to keep a firm hand with them, especially Carrie. But he could do that. He thought of the empty fields to the south and wondered how much cotton seed cost.

He began to build a vision of the future in his mind. He could see himself lying beside Olivia, feel himself falling asleep with her in his arms. He could see them waltzing at every harvest dance that was to come. He could see her playing birthday games in the yard with the girls and the other children they would have. He could hear her laughing with them and singing "Ring-Around-the-Rosy." It was a vision that promised things he hadn't dared to want for a long time.

The moment he realized it, he began to deny it. Instantly, the impossibility of it all flared up in his face, burning away the mist of what he knew was only a fantasy.

He remembered himself as a boy, standing outside a Derry bakery with snow falling over him, staring longingly through the window at the pastries and confections laid out for the rich Christmas shoppers—how he'd pressed his nose against the glass and felt the hunger gnawing at his insides.

Now, he felt like that again; he felt a hunger just as strong. He wanted it so badly. The whole future was laid out before him like those pastries in the window, so close, yet out of his reach.

He shoved away memories of that hungry, lonely child, but could not set aside the realization that, over twenty years later, he was a man just as hungry, just as lonely, just as needy as the boy he'd been.

Conor rose to his feet and left Carrie's room. He stepped over Chester, who had taken up his sentry post in the center of the hall, and walked toward the stairs. He glanced toward Olivia's room and saw the light that filtered out from beneath her closed door. She was still awake.

What was she doing right now? Sitting at the dressing table, brushing her hair. Or lying in bed, reading a book. Maybe she was waiting for him. He reached for the door handle, then stopped, his hand poised in midair.

It was only a fantasy.

He let his hand fall and walked away, closing himself off from what he wanted because he knew he did not deserve it.

*   *   *

The following afternoon after church, Olivia took the girls over to the Johnson farm for a visit. Conor, who wanted to finish the project he was working on, did not go with them.

Conor was in the shed when he heard the rattle of carriage wheels. He walked outside and watched as a sleek black carriage pulled by a matched pair of Morgans came into the yard followed by Chester, who was barking furiously. The driver brought the carriage to a stop, and a man Conor had never seen before, elegantly dressed and obviously wealthy, stepped down. The man started toward the house, but Chester blocked his path, still barking. The man came to a halt.

Conor brushed the dust from his clothes and crossed the yard. "Chester, be quiet," he commanded. The dog obeyed, but gave a low growl before sitting back on his haunches.

The man pushed back his hat with the tip of his ebony walking stick and gave Conor a hard perusal. Conor, never one to be intimidated by any man's stare, studied him with equal thoroughness.

"Conor Branigan?"

"Aye. And who might you be?"

"My name is Hiram Jamison." He did not hold out his hand in greeting, but he continued to watch Conor with a slightly arrogant expression.

Conor raised one brow. "Is that name supposed to mean something to me?"

The man stiffened. "I am Vernon Tyler's father-in-law."

Conor suddenly understood. He wondered how much they were going to offer him for the land this time. "How unfortunate for you. My condolences."

Unexpectedly, the man smiled, but it was a smile

that did not reach his eyes. "Vernon was right about you. You are an arrogant bastard."

"Fancy that. I was thinking the same about you."

Hiram Jamison glanced around. "I'd like to have a word with you, if you don't mind. Is there someplace we could sit down and talk?"

Conor gestured to the house, but he didn't take the man inside. That would be a courtesy, and he didn't feel like being that courteous. He put Chester in the house and brought two of Olivia's horribly uncomfortable kitchen chairs out onto the back porch. Both men sat down.

"Mr. Branigan, I am not a man who likes to waste time, and too much time has been wasted already. I'll come straight to the point. Vernon already offered you three dollars an acre. I'll double it."

Just for sport, Conor pretended to consider it. Then he shook his head. "No."

That surprised Hiram. "No?" He leaned forward in the chair. "That's three thousand dollars."

"Thank you, Mr. Jamison," Conor said dryly, "but I do know how to add."

The man flushed a dark red. From anger, Conor suspected, not embarrassment. "It's the best offer you'll get," Hiram said. "Take it, boy."

Take it, boy. Conor thought of Eversleigh's words of so long ago and the sixpence he'd wanted to spit on. He remembered all the men he'd known in his life who thought they could buy anything they wanted. But he thought of Olivia, and he knew some things could not be bought or sold at any price. He shook his head. "No."

Hiram let out an impatient breath between his teeth. "All right then, how much do you want?"

Conor grinned, knowing he had the upper hand and enjoying it immensely. "You don't have that much money."

"I assure you, I do. Name your price."

"I don't have one." Conor rose to his feet. "Mr. Jamison, this land is not for sale. Not at any price. You'll just have to build your railroad somewhere else."

Hiram stood up, but he made no move to depart. "You obviously don't know who I am. I own three railroads, a steamship company, four Pennsylvania coal mines, two linen factories, and half a dozen other businesses. I have a mansion in New York, another mansion in Newport, and a yacht on Cape Cod."

He cast a contemptuous glance over Conor, his voice rising along with his temper. "And what are you, boy? Nothing but another ignorant Mick off the potato boat, just like all the ignorant Micks who work for me, who load my ships and dig my coal, who shine my boots and bring me my morning coffee."

Conor had been waiting patiently for the tirade to end, and when it did, he folded his arms across his chest, met the other man's eyes, and said, "I'll give you exactly ten seconds to get into that fancy carriage of yours and drive away. Because I'm beginning to lose my temper, and as you know, ignorant Micks have violent tempers."

Hiram whirled around and stalked away, but he halted beside the carriage door and turned. "You will regret this."

"Of that, I have no doubt," Conor answered, watching Hiram Jamison climb into his carriage, knowing he'd once again defied the powers that be. He just never could seem to learn not to do that.

Kate poured Olivia a cup of tea. "So, how is married life?" she asked, sitting down across the kitchen table.

Olivia stared down into her cup, studying her wavy reflection in the black tea, and didn't reply.

"That good?"

Olivia bit her lip and shook her head. "It's not bad, really. He's so good with the girls, and they adore him. I just wish—"

"What?"

"I wish that he could open up a little." She found herself pouring out the whole story, how she found him, what she knew about him, what had happened in Monroe. Everything. "Now, he's so withdrawn," she finished, staring down into her tea. "He won't sleep with me, Kate. He won't even come near me."

Kate started laughing.

Olivia lifted her head. "What are you laughing about?"

"Most married women have the opposite complaint."

Olivia did not find that funny.

Kate sighed, seeing her dismal face. "Honey, married life is never easy. Not for anybody. Every couple has problems, and it takes time to sort them out. Oren and I fought like cats and dogs when we got married. Still do, sometimes."

"I wish Conor and I fought," Olivia said, slumping forward to rest her chin in her hand. "We don't talk enough to fight. He didn't want to be married. He made no secret of that."

"Well, like it or not, he's married now."

"Only because he had no choice."

"Olivia." Kate set down her teacup and eyed her sternly across the table. "A man who can't afford to foot the bill has no business looking at the menu. Of course, he had a choice. No one forced him to sleep with you."

Olivia blushed hotly. She could not look up.

"He's a grown man, Liv, who knew what he was doing. The worst thing you can do is blame yourself."

"What can I do?"

"Give the man time. I think he'll come around."

Olivia looked up. "He doesn't love me."

"Did he say that?"

"Not in so many words, but—"

"You, of course, tell him every day how much you love him."

Startled, Olivia sat up in her chair. "Well, no, actually, I haven't."

"Why not?"

"I'm afraid that'd just make him run for the next stage out of town," she confessed in a small voice.

"When I got married, my mama gave me some advice I'll never forget. Since your mama never got the chance, I'll tell you what my mama said. She said that the most important thing to a marriage isn't being in love, although that's important. It isn't money, although that would be nice. It isn't even children, although they usually come with the territory. The most important thing is trust."

She reached across the table and gave Olivia's hand an encouraging squeeze. "I think you picked yourself a good man. Now, you just have to have faith in him. From what you've told me, he's been through some hard times in his life. A man like that won't wear his heart on his sleeve, but that doesn't mean he doesn't have one."

"Thanks, Kate."

Kate waved her hand in a dismissive gesture. "Nothing to thank me for. Besides, next time Oren and I have a fight, I'll come cry on your shoulder."

In the middle of the night, Carrie had a nightmare. Conor heard her screaming—"Daddy! Daddy!"—and he took the stairs two at a time to reach her. When he got to her room, her sisters and Olivia were already there. Olivia was sitting with her on the bed, rocking her. She looked up as Conor moved into the room, past Becky, Miranda, and the ever-faithful Chester.

He walked over to the bed and sat down. Olivia relinquished her hold, and Conor pulled the sobbing child into his arms. Her frightened sobs tore at his heart—wee Carrie, who never seemed afraid of anything.

Olivia glanced over at the other two girls. "Everything's all right," she said gently. "Go back to bed."

The girls departed, taking Chester with them, and Olivia returned her attention to Carrie, watching as Conor held the child and spoke softly to her.

"*Sha sha,*" he murmured, stroking her hair. "*Sha sha. Bermíd go maith. Tá mé anseo.*" He repeated the soothing Gaelic words over and over until Carrie's sobs faded to hiccups.

He pulled back and brushed tears from her cheeks. "Better?"

She nodded, but when he moved to pull away, she clutched at him. "Don't go, Daddy."

"I'll not go anywhere, lass." He shifted their positions so that he could lean back against the headboard with her on his lap. She rested her head on his chest and closed her eyes. He glanced at Olivia, who sat beside him on Carrie's bed, but neither of them spoke. After a few minutes, he tilted his head to look at the child in his arms.

"Is she asleep?" Olivia asked.

He nodded. Moving carefully, he eased himself out from beneath her, and settled her back into bed, pulling the covers up to her chin. He bent and pressed a kiss to her cheek. "Good night, *mó paisté.*"

Olivia kissed her sleeping daughter, too, then she and Conor left the room together, closing the door behind them. They paused in the hall.

"You'll have to teach me some of that Irish," Olivia said. "It seems to work."

"I've some whiskey left, but I didn't think you'd let me give her that."

She slanted a prim look at him. "You thought correctly. No whiskey in our house." Then, suddenly, she smiled at him. "Oh, dear. I told myself I wasn't going to do this. Mr. Branigan, I'm afraid your wife is a nag."

My wife, he thought. *My wife.*

He touched her face. His palm grazed her cheek, his thumb brushed across her lashes. His fingers slid through her hair. His other hand glided over her hip, pulling her closer.

He couldn't fight this, he didn't want to fight it. All he wanted to do was kiss her and touch her and ravish her. He wanted to please her, keep her safe, make her glad that she had married him. *His wife.*

"Olivia." He wanted to say more than just her name, but he found he could not. He could not form the words to ask for what he wanted. All he could do was take it.

He drew his hand from her hair and reached behind him, grasping for the door handle. He pushed the door wide and pulled her into the bedroom they should have been sharing all along. She came without resistance, and once they were inside, he closed the door. He even remembered to lock it.

In the darkness, he found her lips with his. He kissed her, a long, hard kiss. His hands curved around her waist; his fingers spread across the small of her back to pull her closer. He trailed kisses along her jaw, to the delicate line of her throat, as his hands slid between them and reached for the top button of her nightgown.

Her arms came around his neck. "Oh, Conor," she whispered against his ear. "Yes. Yes."

It took every ounce of will he possessed to stop himself from ripping the gown apart. His hands shook as he fought to keep his desire in check just a little longer. He worked his way down, slipping the pearl buttons free, one at a time, until all twenty-six of them were unfastened. He curled his fingers beneath the edges to pull the gown from her shoulders. It slid down her arms and caught at the flare of her hips.

He left it there and slid his hands up her ribs to the long braid of her hair. He pulled the ribbon away and the braid unraveled in his hands. He twined the thick, heavy silk in his fists as he tasted the heated skin of her throat and felt the pulse beneath her jaw beat a frantic rhythm against his tongue.

He loved her hair, her skin, her breasts, her scent, her heart, all the softness in her that drew him with a power stronger than his will to resist it. It alarmed him, it enthralled him.

He wished they had light so he could see her, but he found the exquisite shape of her with his hands—her breast, her waist, her hips.

He gave the gown a tug. It slipped free of her hips and fell to the floor. He slid his hand between her thighs, and he felt her arousal in the silken warmth he found there. He caressed her, savoring the shivers that ran through her as his fingertips glided back and forth.

Her arms tightened around his neck, and he heard her breathing quicken to tiny gasps as he found the place that pleased her most. Suddenly, her body arched and she cried out, a soft keening wail muffled by his shoulder.

He couldn't hold back another instant. He withdrew his hand, then he lifted her in his arms and took her to the dim outline of the four-poster bed. He lifted her onto the high mattress, then began tugging at the buttons of his shirt and trousers with impatient movements, muttering a curse when he had to stop and pull off his boots. When he was finally out of his clothes, he climbed up beside her, not bothering with the stepstool, which he would only have wasted precious time trying to find in the dark anyway.

"Jaysus," he muttered, "for a woman who's afraid of heights, you've a bed damned high off the ground, Mrs. Branigan." And he kissed her before she could even think about admonishing him for swearing.

He covered her body with his own. Her arms encircled his neck, welcoming him. Her legs parted, inviting him to come inside. He slid his hands beneath her shoulders, his weight on his forearms, and entered her slowly. He'd hurt her that night in Monroe, and although he felt her yield and stretch to accommodate him, he strove to contain the driving force inside himself. But when she whispered his name in that shy, drawling, incredibly erotic way of hers, his control snapped and he forgot all his tender intentions.

Wanting complete possession, he thrust deep, then deeper still. The rhythm caught him in a burning tension that built upon itself, growing stronger, until she shuddered beneath him and made the startled, gasping cries of feminine release. He felt the heat, the flash, and the explosive climax like gunpowder set alight.

He lowered himself onto her and buried his face in the curve of her neck, his arms closing tightly around her. He did not move for a long time, savoring the feel of her fingertips gliding across his back in hypnotic circles, until he felt himself sinking into that blissful lethargy.

He realized it and stirred. "I must be smothering

you," he murmured, and shifted his weight, slipping free of her, raising himself on his arms as if to leave her. But her arms tightened around him almost fiercely, and he knew she guessed his half-formed intention. She lifted her head and kissed him. "Don't go," she whispered against his mouth. "Stay with me."

Her embrace he could have broken with no effort at all, but her voice and her kiss conquered him, and he eased slowly back down, moving to lie on his back beside her. He slid his arm beneath her and pulled her to his side. She settled herself comfortably within the embrace and rested her cheek in the dent of his shoulder with a contented sigh.

"Go to sleep, Olivia," he said. "I'll not leave you, *á mhúirnín*. Just go to sleep."

Conor knew the moment they strapped him down. He felt the leather bands across his body, and he struggled until they broke. Free, he jerked sideways with a savage movement and a curse, rolling to the edge of the table, his only thought to get away, to escape. But then everything shifted, changed, and he was in a darkened room, there were no guards, and what he'd thought was a table was the soft down of a feather mattress. Disoriented, he sat up, blinking at the soft moonlight that filtered in through the window. The only sound was his own harsh breathing.

He turned his head and saw her and remembered where he was.

She sat huddled at one corner of the mattress, knees against her chest, the sheet drawn up around her and bunched in her fists, her long hair tangled around her shoulders—utterly still. She was watching him, her expression one of dismay. And fear.

Oh, Christ.

He slumped forward with a groan, cradling his head in his hands. "I thought they tied me down again. I thought—" He stopped abruptly.

"It was me," she whispered. "I had my arms around you."

He shook his head. "Didn't want you to see me like this," he mumbled, not looking at her. "Didn't want you to see."

The mattress dipped with her weight as she moved to his side. She touched his shoulder. "Conor, I already have seen. I tended you for four nights, remember?"

"I didn't know you then," he cried, anguished, yanking away from her touch. "I didn't even know you were there."

He felt everything crumbling, every illusion, every wish, every vision of a future with her, a future that was peaceful and safe. Nothing was safe. Nothing. "Did I—" He took a deep breath and lifted his head to stare at the closed door across the room. "Did I hurt you?"

"Of course not."

"There's no 'of course' about it, lass," he said, despising himself. "I could have."

"But you didn't." She put her hands on his shoulders and pressed her lips to his back. "I love you," she said against his skin.

Inside, he began to shake. He flung back the sheet, slid off the bed, and retrieved his clothes. "You don't love me."

"Yes, I do."

He began to dress. He pulled on his socks and his linen, then reached for his trousers. He jerked them on. "No, you don't. You can't."

"Conor, I'm not going to argue with you about this. I love you. I can't help it if you don't believe me."

He turned his back to her and buttoned his trousers. "You don't love me," he said and crossed the room. Keeping his back to her, he added, "You can't. You don't even know me."

"I know you better than you think."

The shaking inside him grew more intense, and he took refuge. "Really?" He turned on her savagely, all his defenses rising, wanting to shock her, repel her, push her away. "What do you know? Do you know that I've stolen, I've cheated, I've lied. I've even killed. And you love me, do you?"

She did not look shocked, nor repelled. She did not even look slightly horrified. She just looked at him with patience and infinite tenderness.

He could not bear it. He closed his eyes, refusing to see. She could not know, she could not understand and still look at him like that, as if she loved him. It was impossible.

Shame. No matter where he went or what he did, it was always with him. The taint of it was a permanent stain nothing could remove. He turned away and stared at the moonlit window. "Olivia, you have no idea what I am, what I've done."

"Then why don't you tell me?"

He drew a deep breath and faced her, faced the moment of truth. "All right," he said flatly. "I'll make my *admhaím*."

"Ah-veem," she said, pronouncing the word carefully. "What is that?"

"Confession. It's supposed to be good for the soul, isn't it?"

28

ADMHAÍM

    "It was all because of the guns," he began. "They wanted to know where the guns were hidden. Sean's American rifles. We'd been smuggling them in for two years, right under the noses of the British customs officials. Hiding them all over Ireland, a hundred here, a hundred there. We were planning a war, you see. Training camps and warfare tactics and weapons, all that. We didn't know then it was a war we couldn't win."

He spoke almost tentatively, and Olivia knew he had never talked about this to anyone before.

"We'd smuggled in nine hundred rifles and a thousand rounds of ammunition before they caught us. Adam and I were arrested for attempting to pull guns off a train north of Dublin. They put us in the bridewell. They'd arrested Sean at a safehouse in Dublin. Someone had informed on us—we never found out who it was."

She felt herself being pulled into a world she knew

nothing about; he was leading her into the dark, twisted paths of his nightmares, where there were safehouses and informers, prisons and torture. Olivia bit down on her lip and listened, knowing she had to follow him so that she could bring him back to her world, where there was safety and light.

"They gave us a trial," he went on. "But Sean had gotten word about the informant and managed to get the guns off the train. He tried to let us know the guns weren't on the train, but his man didn't reach us in time. Anyway, because they couldn't find the guns, they could only convict us of attempted robbery. They sent us to Mountjoy Prison."

He sat motionless in the chair, hidden in the shadows.

"It was only the three of us who knew where all the guns were hidden, Sean and Adam and me. But Sean was useless to them. They knew he wouldn't talk. He'd been in many a prison before, our Sean, and the British knew he wouldn't break. So they killed him. Right in front of Adam and me. He was grinning at me when the guard pulled his head back and slit his throat."

Olivia closed her eyes briefly, prayed for strength, and opened her eyes again. She didn't want to hear this; she didn't want to see what he saw in his mind. But she had to. Her fingers curled tightly into the sheets as she listened, bracing herself for the rest.

"The man let him go, and his body collapsed, all the blood pumping out of him. He looked up at me with these dead, sightless eyes and his blood spurting out of the artery in his throat, but he was still grinning."

Suddenly Conor leaned forward in the chair, his arms curling protectively over his head as if he were trying to hide. "Oh, God," he moaned. "Oh, God."

Olivia waited, but he said nothing more. She knew she could not let him stop now, not before he had told it all. His inner torments had to be forced out into the open. It was the only way for him to begin to heal. "What happened then?"

At the sound of her voice, he jerked himself upright, stiffening. "They were so stupid," he said, his voice flat, with only a hint of the contempt that lay beneath. "They thought killing Sean would intimidate us, frighten us into talking. All it did was make us hate them more, if that was possible. They realized then that they'd made a mistake, that one dead martyr was worth a dozen rebels. They separated us, Adam and me. I never saw him again. They put me in a cell, with shackles on my hands and feet, and kept me chained to the wall, except when they brought me food. They made me eat on my hands and knees from a plate on the floor, like a dog. Fish guts, it was. Raw, stinking fish guts, for days and days. But I wouldn't tell them where the guns were hidden. I wouldn't tell them."

He shook his head blindly. "Then they wouldn't let me sleep. They walked me round and round the prison yard, doused me with water if I fell asleep standing up. I saw the sun rise and fall three times before I collapsed. Then they flogged me. But I didn't break. I didn't tell them."

Olivia heard the defiance in his voice, but with his next words, the defiance left him, and his voice changed to one of bewilderment.

"I started to hear voices in my head. My sisters'. *Tá ocrás orm, Conor. Tá ocrás orm,* over and over. It never stops . . . a tide that never ebbs. I still hear it. Oh, Christ," he moaned, curling himself tightly in the chair again, "they're so hungry, and there's nothing to eat. They're begging me to find food. Brigid and Eileen and Megan. I could hear them, but I couldn't help them. There was no food."

He slammed his hands over his ears as if to shut out the voices.

"I knew they were dead," he mumbled, "but I could hear them in my cell, see their faces as if they were there. And Michael, too, screaming for help, and I couldn't help him. And the guards. 'Tell us, Paddy, tell us where the guns are. Tell us. Tell us.'"

He lifted his head, staring straight at her across the room, but she did not know if he recognized her. The anguish was in every line of his face, every movement of his body. She wanted to run to him, soothe him, tell him to hush, to stop, but she knew she could not. She remembered her days at the hospital and the soldiers who screamed about the cannon fire and the blood, and she had learned to let them be, to let them pour it all out.

"I cursed them, I sang, I shouted, but I didn't tell them. I didn't break. So they took me to Arthur Delemere, the warden." He rubbed a shaking hand across his jaw. "I thought I'd already felt all the pain there was in this life," he whispered, "but I was wrong."

Oh, Lord, she thought desperately, *how do I help him? What do I do?*

"They strapped me down on a table." He closed his eyes and a shudder rocked him. "Some things are beyond description. They can't be put into words."

She pressed her clasped hands to her mouth. Deep down inside, she began to shake.

"I would pass out from the pain," he said, "and when I would awaken, the guards would be gone, and Delemere would talk to me. Tell me how he understood what I was going through, and how he would like to help me, but he couldn't unless I told him where the guns were hidden. He'd tell me to think about it for a while, and he would leave. But then the guards would come back, and we would go through it all again. . . . I lost track of time. One moment blended into the next, one day into the next. I would lie there and count backward from one thousand, focusing on remembering the next number, making it the most important thing in the world, trying not to feel the pain. It worked for a while. I even tried to pray, if you can believe that. I said the rosary, but I couldn't remember it all. I couldn't remember."

He raked a hand through his hair. "It didn't matter. God wasn't listening. Not Mary, nor Jesus, nor all the saints heard me screaming. No one heard but Delemere. He became the only thing that seemed real to me. He brought me food and water. He sat beside me after the men were done, and he talked to me endlessly. He bathed my face with cool rags, wiping away the tears and the vomit and the blood. He kept telling me that he was my friend, that if I would help him, he would help me. I don't know how long it took, but I started to believe him. I started to rationalize it all in my mind. I made up places, thinking that wasn't really telling. So, Delemere would have me taken back to my cell, and have the doctor come to patch me up as best he could, while he sent men out to find the guns. Of course, they'd come back empty-handed a few days later, so they'd have me in, and we'd have another go."

He folded his arms across his knees, hunching forward as if he wanted simply to curl into a ball and never move again.

"It took three, maybe four rounds," he said dully, staring at the floor. "I just wanted the pain to stop. I wanted him to kill me; I begged him to kill me. When we were alone, he would whisper to me. He kept promising me that he would make it all stop if I would just tell him the truth. There came a point when I believed him." There was a long pause. "So, I told him."

He lifted his head and the moonlight hit his face as he looked at her, the agony in his expression far beyond memories of physical pain. "He laughed when I told him. Laughed. It was all a joke, you see. They already knew where the guns were; they'd confiscated all of them days before. Adam, Delemere told me, had been much more cooperative than myself. It had taken only two days to break him."

Suddenly, he straightened. His hand slammed down on the tiny drop-leaf table beside him with such force, Olivia jumped.

"They took everything I was!" he cried. "Everything I believed in. They destroyed what I thought myself to be, and remade me into what I despised most. They made me an informer against my own people. I tried to stop them. God, I tried." His voice broke. "I fought so hard. But I couldn't stop them. And it was all for a joke."

He shoved at the table and sent it skidding across the floor. It crashed into the wall. "Delemere didn't care about the guns. He wanted to break me just to prove that he could. And the worst of it was, the bastard didn't keep his promise. He didn't kill me."

All his rage evaporated as quickly as it had come, and Conor sagged in the chair. "Delemere died that same night. There was a riot, some of the prisoners escaped, and one of them got Delemere. Prime Minister Gladstone found out about it and heard about the torture, as well. There was a hue and cry about it; people protested, marched, rioted in the streets, demanded that the Fenians involved be released. It took nearly a year, but I was eventually given amnesty, along with several others. It was too late for Adam. Word had gotten out right after the guns were confiscated that he'd informed, and the Fenian Council had one of their men on the inside execute him. Stabbed him in the prison yard with a piece of a bed frame a week before Delemere died. I wish to hell they had done the same to me."

The mocking cast returned to his face, the same harsh expression that she had seen the night he'd gotten drunk.

"People knew what had happened to me, but no one knew that I had told Delemere about the guns. My friends all shook my hand, and gave me pats on the back, and bought me drinks. I hadn't broken, they said. I was a hero, they said. They cheered me; they boasted about me; they were proud to know me. Proud, for God's sake! I didn't have the guts to tell them the truth, and I couldn't face the shame of knowing I didn't deserve their praise. That's why I left and came to America. That's why I can't go home. I'm not their bloody hero. I'm a sham. And I'm a coward."

Olivia felt his self-hatred and his shame, and she spoke very gently. "You did what any man would have done in your place."

"No. There were men stronger than I. Men who suffered more than I, who had more courage than I. Men like Sean." He leaned forward and buried his face in his hands. "Why didn't Delemere just kill me?"

Olivia did not know what to say. She did not know how to reach him, she did not even know if she could, but she had to try. She rose to her feet and began to walk toward him very slowly, speaking to him very softly.

"Conor, I want you to listen to me. If you were a coward, you would not even be here. A coward would have killed himself long ago."

He wasn't looking at her. He sat with his head hung low, staring at the floor. She didn't even know if he heard her, but she went on. "I'm not sure I know what true courage is," she said as she continued to approach him. "But I think it must be the ability to endure. Perhaps it's selfish of me to be glad those men did not kill you or put you out of your pain, but I am. I'm glad you had the courage to endure. So very, very glad." She came to a halt in front of him. "I love you."

He stiffened and sat up in his chair. He still would not look at her. "Just as well to love a shell then, lass," he said, his voice weary. "'Tis empty I am. I have no purpose, no ideals, no honor. They took all of that from me. I am a shell of a man. I have nothing left to believe in. I have no honor to hold on to."

She reached out to touch him, tentatively laying her hand against his cheek. He flinched, but he did not pull away, and that gave her hope. Slowly, she moved closer to him. With infinite care, she wedged herself between his knees and moved closer still. "Hold on to me, then," she whispered. "Even if you can't believe in yourself, I'll believe in you. I'll be your anchor. Hold on to me."

He took a choked, panicky breath, turning his face away from her touch, and she thought he was going to push her away again, retreat again into his self-made prison. But suddenly his arms came up around her naked hips, and he pulled her toward him. He buried his face against her and held her fast, as if she were a lifeline in a storm-tossed sea.

She felt his massive frame shudder, and his cry of rage and pain nearly broke her heart. She cradled his head and she stroked his hair, as all the anguish of a lifetime poured out of him, and she sought to replace it with all the love she had to give. She prayed it would be enough.

29

Conor knew by the rhythm of her breathing that Olivia was asleep. He listened to the soft, even cadence of each breath and told himself it was impossible. She could not love him. But she did.

She loved him. It was hard to believe it, harder still to trust it.

He had never told anyone about Mountjoy before. By telling her, he'd thought to drive her away, make her see what he was. But he hadn't driven her away. She had seen what he was and she didn't care. She had told him to hold on to her and he had. Then she had led him back to bed and curled up beside him.

He looked down at the small hand spread across his chest in a gesture of complete trust.

She trusted him. After she'd seen him in the throes of his nightmares, he could not imagine how.

She loved him. After what he had told her, he could not imagine why.

He looked at the face so close to his own. By the

moonlight through the window, he could see the dark lashes that swept her cheeks, the creamy skin that was so soft to touch, the silken strands of her hair that spread across the pillow, and felt a kind of peace he'd never known before.

When he'd said that confession was good for the soul, he had said it with mockery, but perhaps there was truth in it, as well. The shame was still with him, the guilt still haunted him, but they seemed lighter burdens now, they seemed easier to bear than they ever had before.

He touched her face, ran one finger down her cheek to her lips, soft and warm and slightly parted in sleep. *My wife*, he thought. *My wife*.

He wanted it. God, he wanted it all. He wanted tree houses and picnics and butter-pecan cookies; he wanted a home and land to call his own. He wanted to tell bedtime stories to the girls—his girls—and he wanted to watch them grow up. He wanted Olivia; he wanted the warmth and softness of her to soothe away all the cynical hardness within himself. He wanted to wake every morning to that radiant smile, that felt like sunlight when it touched him, and let it banish all his dark dreams. He wanted her by his side all the days and nights of his life.

For the first time, the future beckoned to him, a future beyond the next town, the next fight, the next bad dream. A future that had what he'd never thought to find again: love. He wanted that future. He didn't give a damn if he deserved it. He wanted it, and he was going to take it, hang on to it, make it his own.

Conor eased out of the bed, careful not to wake her, and went out onto the veranda. Moonlight sifted between the branches of the oak trees and cast twisted shadows across the gravel of the drive below. He'd prune those trees come spring and those boxwood hedges, too.

He thrust his hands in the pockets of his trousers and walked down the veranda, making plans. The house would need a coat of paint before next winter. The gardens and flower beds needed to be completely redone.

He turned the corner and walked along the side of the house. The gazebo wasn't worth saving, he decided, staring down at the dilapidated structure. The hopeless tangle of roses that climbed up the sides were the only thing that kept the structure from falling down. He'd tear it down and build Olivia a new gazebo, with the honeysuckle she loved so much planted all around it.

He came to the end of the veranda and leaned against the rail, looking out over the backyard. If they tore down the deserted cabins, they could plant an orchard of pears in that spot. The old stable and the barn were all right, but—

A flicker of light caught his attention. Conor frowned, staring at the outline of the barn, and he saw movement in the shadows. He got a brief glimpse of a man running for the woods, then the tiny flicker of light suddenly burst into flame.

Christ. Conor turned around and raced back the way he'd come. "Olivia!" he shouted, as he entered the bedroom. "Olivia, the barn's on fire!"

She flung aside the covers and jumped out of bed, fumbling for her clothes in the dark. "What happened?"

"I don't know," he answered, as he grabbed his boots and yanked them on. "Bring as many buckets as you can. Shovels, too, if you can find any."

He pulled the sheet off the bed and ran out the door. Within seconds, he had descended the stairs and left the house, his only thought to get the animals out of the barn.

The barn was filled with smoke when Conor opened

the door, and a wall of heat hit him. Coughing, he jumped back, took three deep breaths, and entered the barn.

He could hear Cally and Princess making the wild neighs of panic and kicking at the sides of their stalls, trying desperately to escape. Orange flames licked the walls at the other end, feeding on the dry wood with crackling intensity.

Coughing, Conor grabbed the coil of rope that lay in one corner and made for the first stall. He got in with the mule, careful to avoid the animal's kicking hooves, and wrapped the sheet around its head. After looping the rope around its neck, he led the frightened mule out of the barn, as Olivia came running with a bucket of water from the pump, the girls right behind her.

"Grab the mule!" he told her, as he pulled the sheet and the rope away from Cally's head, and ran back to the barn. He could hear Olivia calling after him, but he did not stop.

Smoke stung his eyes as Conor made for the second stall and began to guide Princess out of the barn. The heat seared his skin, and the flames were a roar in his ears. He held his breath against the thick smoke. He got Princess out just as the roof fell in.

Olivia dropped the empty bucket and ran to him with a cry of relief. He let go of the cow and wrapped his arms around her, sucking in great gasps of air. He held her tight against him, thinking he'd never let her go as long as he lived, when suddenly she yanked out of his hold and glared up at him.

"Going back in there for a cow!" she shouted furiously. "Are you out of your mind? You could have been killed. Don't you ever do that to me again—do you hear me, Conor Branigan?"

She loved him. He grabbed her and kissed her, hard, before she could say another word.

*　　　*　　　*

The sun had lifted well above the trees by the time the fire was out. Conor, Olivia, and the girls, along with neighbors and friends who had seen the blaze and come running to assist, continued to throw buckets of water and shovels of dirt over the charred remains, and the flames had finally been extinguished.

It was Oren who found the can of kerosene. He brought it to Conor and said, "I reckon you all must've turned down their last offer."

Conor set aside his shovel and took the tin can. He stared down at it for a moment, then he lifted his head and took a long, hard look at the smoldering remains of the barn. He thought about another fire and a cottage in Derry twenty-five years ago. He thought about Hiram Jamison and Vernon Tyler, Lord Eversleigh and Arthur Delemere, and all the other men who thought everything in the world was theirs to take, theirs to destroy.

He looked up and met Oren's somber gaze. "Would you happen to know where Vernon Tyler lives?"

The other man studied him for a moment, then he said, "About a mile this side of town. Go west on the main road. When you cross the Sugar Creek bridge, it's the first lane to the left."

Conor nodded. "I'm after borrowing your horse, if you don't mind?"

"Sure. I can ride home with Kate in the wagon. Unless you want some company?"

"No. I'd rather do this myself."

"Sure thing." Oren shoved his hands in his pockets and added, "Be careful."

Conor walked away without replying. He knew what he had to do, and being careful had nothing to do with it.

*   *   *

When Conor arrived at Vernon Tyler's estate, he didn't bother to give his name. He pushed his way past the black gentleman who had just informed him the family was at breakfast, and entered the house.

"Suh!" the man cried as he was shoved aside. "You can't come in here. I told you—"

Conor ignored him. He crossed the foyer, and began searching for the dining room. The butler followed him, protesting loudly.

When he located the dining room, he found Hiram, Vernon, and a beautiful blond woman who must be Vernon's wife, seated at a table laid with gleaming china, crystal, and covered silver dishes.

All of them stared at him in astonishment as he entered the room. Conor glanced down at his soot-covered clothes and the stains of charcoal and mud that his boots had made on the plush white rug. "Top of the mornin' to you," he said, and walked to the table.

He faced Hiram Jamison and slammed the can of kerosene down on the table. "Mr. Jamison, I'll make this quite simple for you. The answer is still no, it will always be no, and there is nothing you can do to change my mind. You can threaten me, you can burn down my barn again and again and again, but I'm not selling my land to you. Is that clear?"

"What is he talking about?" The blond woman turned to Hiram with a troubled look on her face. "Papa, you didn't do anything to this man's barn, did you?"

"Of course not, my dear. He is obviously deranged." He gestured to the doorway. "Abraham, remove this man from my house."

Conor turned to glare at the butler, who was coming toward him. "Back off, lad," he said quietly.

The man hesitated, glanced at Hiram, then back at Conor again. Something of his seething rage must have shown in his face, for the man stepped back, shaking his head. Conor returned his attention to the man across the table, hoping to hell he could pull this off.

He pulled out one of the chairs and sat down without waiting for an invitation, unmindful of the black soot on his clothes that stained the ivory velvet upholstery. "Mr. Jamison, let's not waste time dancing around the issue. You want to build a railroad, but I can tell you right now, even if you manage to steal my land, you'll not build that railroad of yours on it. I can promise you that."

Vernon made a sound of contempt and threw down his napkin. "Who the hell do you think you are, boy, coming in here and making threats? You can't stop us."

"No?" Conor turned to look at Vernon. "Who do you think lays railroad track, boyo?" he asked, his voice deceptively soft. "Every mile of track across this great country has been laid with the blood and sweat of thousands of Irishmen. When the Irishmen you hire to lay track find out that you threatened one of their own to get his land, you'll not sink one spike or lay one tie on that land."

Appearing completely at ease, Conor leaned back in his chair. Returning his attention to Hiram, he said, "Trust me, Mr. Jamison, if you force me off my land, you'll never build a railroad on it."

"That's nothing to worry about," Vernon said. "We'll just hire workers who aren't Irish."

Conor smiled. He addressed his reply to Vernon, but his gaze never left the gray-haired man across the table. "Ah, but Mr. Jamison here isn't thinking about this

penny-ante little railroad in Louisiana, now. He's thinking about those steamships of his, and all the Irish longshoremen who load his cargo, and all the Irish navvies
who run the engines. He's thinking what a shame it
would be if some dynamite happened to find its way
onto some of those ships once they're fully loaded with
cargo and ready to move out." Conor tilted his head
thoughtfully to one side. "A few accidents like that
could ruin a shipping company, wouldn't you say?"

Conor did not wait for a reply. He shook his head
and went on, "No, Vernon, your man here's thinking
about those mines of his in Pennsylvania, and all the
Irishmen who go down there every day to haul out that
coal, and all the accidents and wildcat strikes that
might suddenly start happening. He's thinking about
the Irish lasses who put together shirts in his linen
mills, and the Irishman who drives his carriage. He's
thinking about the wee Irish maid who brings his coffee
in the mornings, and he's wondering if he'll notice
when it starts to have a bitter taste."

The other man smiled, leaning back in his chair.
"You're bluffing. You don't have that kind of influ-
ence."

"Don't I?" Conor countered swiftly. "I suppose that
if I were just another Mick off the potato boat—I do
believe that was how you put it, wasn't it?—I wouldn't
be able to rally my fellow Irishmen around me."

He paused, then gave the other man an insolent grin.
"But, you see, I don't happen to be just any Irishman.
Go into any Irish pub along the New York docks, and
talk to your longshoremen about Conor Branigan, and
listen to what they'll tell you. Or, ask those men who go
down into those coal mines of yours. Or, ask the men
who lay your railroad track. Or, ask the Irish lasses who
make shirts in your factories or bring your coffee."

Conor straightened in his chair and the grin vanished. "They'll tell you how I spent two years running guns from New York to Belfast, smuggling them in right under the noses of British customs. They'll tell you how I was arrested and tried for treason, how I was subjected to the cruelest tortures imaginable when I served time in a British prison, of how it was the protests and marches of their sisters and brothers back in Ireland that forced Prime Minister Gladstone to free me."

Conor grabbed the edges of his shirt and tore the linen apart. The woman gave a sharp little gasp. "These are my badges of valor, Mr. Jamison, and with every lash and every burn and every bullet, I earned the respect of another Irish heart. There are men who sit in pubs in New York and lift their glasses in songs about me. There are wee girls skipping rope in Boston and Belfast to songs about me. And there are Irish people who would risk their lives for me if I asked them to. To them, I represent hope and freedom. To them, I'm a hero."

He waited for his words to sink in, then Conor played his last card. "All I have to do is send one telegram to New York, to a gentleman by the name of Hugh O'Donnell. He's the head of *Clan na Gael*, which is the American counterpart to my own Irish Republican Brotherhood. I smuggled many of Hugh's guns into Belfast, and he owes me more than a few favors. If Hugh puts out the word that you're trying to steal Conor Branigan's land, just the way the British back home have stolen Irish land for the last three hundred years, you won't lay one foot of railroad track, here or anywhere else. You'll have so many problems, you won't know which way to turn. I'll cost you so much money, those investors backing this railroad of yours will start asking questions and demanding explanations. You'll be looking over your shoulder and jumping out of your skin at every Irish voice you hear. Your life will be hell for as long as it lasts, and it won't last long."

He stared at the man across the table, and he didn't know if Jamison believed him or not. It was such an outrageous load of shit. He had no idea if Hugh would really do anything to help him, after he'd refused to raise money for the cause when he'd come to America. But bluffing was something Conor knew he did very well, and as long as Jamison believed him, the truth didn't really matter.

The woman laid a hand on Hiram's arm. "Papa?"

Vernon shoved back his chair and stood up, ready to throw Conor out himself, but Jamison lifted a hand in warning, and Vernon sank slowly back into his chair. "Hiram, you're not going to let him get away with this, are you?" he demanded incredulously.

Hiram said nothing. He kept his assessing gaze fixed on Conor, trying to sift through the blarney and find the truth.

Conor gave it to him. "Bigger bastards than you have tried to break me, Mr. Jamison. They're dead now."

"Papa," the woman said in a shaking voice, clearly upset by the threats, "it's not worth it. I couldn't bear it if anything happened to you. Please, abandon this before—"

"Alicia, shut up!" Vernon snapped. He turned to his father-in-law. "We can't let him destroy everything we've worked for down here, everything we've built. We can handle any of his friends who might cause trouble."

"Papa, give this up," Alicia implored, ignoring her husband. "It's not worth it. These people could kill you."

Conor heard the tearful, frightened note in her voice,

and he took full advantage of it. "Your daughter is lovely, Mr. Jamison, but no woman looks beautiful in mourning cloth."

"Papa!" Alicia cried fearfully and grabbed his sleeve. "Please, give this up. Do it for me."

Conor saw a glimmer of fear in the other man's face, and he began to think this was actually going to work. He waited, his face impassive, his gaze locked with that of the man across the table.

Hiram was the one who looked away; he took his daughter's hand. "What do you want, Branigan?"

"Give up this idea of putting a railroad across my land. Stop threatening my family. Take your daughter and your son-in-law, and go back to New York."

"No!" Vernon shouted, slamming his fist on the table and rattling the breakfast dishes. "We can't stop now!"

"Be quiet, Vernon." Hiram considered the situation for a moment, then rose to his feet. "Very well," he said, and his daughter gave a sob of relief. "For my daughter's sake, I agree to your terms. You have my word."

"I'm glad we could come to an understanding." Conor stood up and turned to leave, but in the doorway, he paused.

"By the way," he added, "I've already sent a telegram to Hugh O'Donnell. It's not that I don't trust your word, Mr. Jamison, but I've learned the hard way that it's always best to take precautions. If anything happens to me or my wife or my daughters, Hugh knows what to do." He nodded to the woman. "Mrs. Tyler."

He didn't bother to acknowledge Vernon. He walked out without another word, mounted his borrowed horse, and rode away. At the main road, he didn't turn the horse toward Peachtree, but set off in the opposite direction, figuring he'd better go into town and send that telegram to Hugh, just in case Jamison decided to verify that part of his claim. Hell, if nothing else, Hugh would enjoy the story.

Conor rather enjoyed it, too, but for a different reason. He'd always appreciated irony. He'd spent the past three years avoiding the heroic reputation that was such a sham, and now he was using it to gain the love he'd never wanted and become the hero he'd never been in the first place. He might even succeed. Conor threw back his head and laughed in utter disbelief.

Silence fell in the dining room after Conor Branigan's departure, and both men turned to Alicia. She took the hint and rose to her feet. "I'm sure you two will want to discuss business," she murmured, and left the room.

Vernon spoke the moment Alicia was gone. "I'll go see Olivia. After this business with the barn, I'm sure she'll be much more willing to talk about selling. If I can get her to agree, Branigan will go along with her."

"No."

"What?" Vernon stared at the other man in astonishment. "You're not really going to agree to his demands?"

Hiram did not answer that question. Instead, he leaned forward in his chair and gave Vernon a hard stare across the table. "You had Joshua set fire to their barn, didn't you?"

Vernon opened his mouth to deny it, but Hiram's face told him a denial would be futile. "We talked about this," he said instead, "and you said more pressure might be required."

Hiram shook his head, frowning with displeasure. "Don't try to justify your actions by laying the blame on me. What you have done is appalling, not to mention stupid. Branigan isn't the kind of man to be intimidated. I tried that in my one conversation with him. It didn't work." Hiram stood up. "Tomorrow, you will begin making arrangements to sell our holdings here, so that the investors can be repaid. We are abandoning this venture."

"Hiram, you can't be serious."

"But I am. We'll sell what land and business we have down here. The land ought to bring a decent profit, since prices are rising, and I'm sure we'll be able to sell the businesses, as well, without too much trouble. We won't lose money."

"We've come so close. You can't do this."

The moment he said it, he knew he'd made a mistake. Hiram didn't like being told what to do.

"This has always been your little project, Vernon," Hiram replied coldly, "not mine. I never wanted you to take Alicia so far away from home in the first place. But you wanted the chance to prove yourself, and I have given you four years to do it. That's long enough. You have failed, and I won't back a failure."

Failure. The word cut deep. "What he said was just a lot of big talk, Hiram. You know it was."

"Some of it, I agree, but perhaps not all of it." The other man set aside his napkin and rose. "Branigan might have enough friends in New York to do some serious damage. I've heard of *Clan na Gael,* and I know they could cause trouble if they wanted to. Many Irish people work for me. I can't fire them all. I won't put my other business ventures at risk for this railroad scheme of yours. And I have no intention of ending up dead with an Irish knife in my belly. As Alicia said, it's not worth it."

He walked out of the dining room, leaving Vernon staring after him in shock and fury.

He couldn't believe that everything he wanted was slipping out of his grasp because of that Irish prize-fighter. A hero? Vernon didn't believe that cock-and-bull story for a second.

A sound from the doorway caused Vernon to turn. Alicia stood there, watching him with a somber expression. He knew perfectly well she'd heard every word, and he could almost feel her disapproval. His anger rose to the surface, and he scowled at her. "What were you thinking," he demanded, "pushing your father to abandon this project when you know damn good and well how much it means to me?"

She brushed at an imaginary speck of lint on her skirt and did not meet his gaze. "You heard that man, the threats he made. I was frightened."

"Bull." He shoved back his chair and stood up. "You've never wanted me to succeed."

She lifted her head. "That's not true. I've always supported you."

"Only when it suited you." He stalked out of the dining room, and Alicia followed him as he crossed the foyer. When he reached his study, he entered the room and slammed the door between them, shutting her out.

I won't back a failure. Hiram's words rang in his ears, and his rage escalated. Hiram thought he was a failure. Alicia, too. He saw it in her eyes.

The empire he'd built so carefully was about to fall down around him, and he wasn't going to let that happen. Branigan was to blame for this. If it hadn't been for him, Olivia would have sold the land eventually. If it hadn't been for him, Hiram would not be running like a scared rabbit.

Vernon walked to his desk and opened the top drawer. He pulled out the deed and bill of sale he'd drawn up four years ago and his Colt pistol. He shoved the deed into one pocket of his jacket and the gun in the other. Then he shut the drawer and left the study.

Alicia was still standing outside the door, waiting for him. "Vernon," she began, "I'm sorry if—"

"Save it," he said, and walked past her.

"Where are you going?" she cried, as he headed for the front door.

"I'm not letting that cocky Irish bastard ruin everything I've worked for," he shot back furiously. "I'll get that land, one way or the other."

He walked out of the house, and slammed the door behind him hard enough to rattle the windowpanes. Alicia and her father thought he was a failure. Well, Vernon was about to prove them wrong.

30

Olivia was so tired that by the time all the neighbors left to return to their own farms, she was ready to collapse. Oren and Kate departed last, after Olivia assured them at least three times that she and the girls would be fine and didn't need them to stay. She knew they had their own family to see to. Besides, what she needed right now was not company. She needed a cool bath, a change of clothes, and Conor to hold her.

But Conor wasn't here to hold her. She and the girls had been combing the woods, searching for stray livestock that had escaped the fire, and she had not noticed his departure until after she'd rounded up her few remaining chickens and hogs and put them in the stable with Princess and Cally. He had borrowed Oren's horse and gone to town. Oren had not told her why, but she knew the fire was no accident, and she had realized where Conor had gone.

She leaned back against the wall of the stable and stared at the charred remains of her barn. The idea of him confronting Vernon and what might happen made her sick with worry. Vernon might not do anything to her or the girls, but Conor was a different matter. She closed her eyes and prayed for his safe return. If anything happened to him because of her refusal to sell—

"Mama?"

Olivia turned at the sound of Becky's voice and studied the somber faces of her three daughters, who stood behind her inside the stable, their faces streaked with soot and tears and sweat. Chester, also covered with soot, stood beside them. She remembered Conor's words of a month ago. *It's not worth a fight, Olivia. It's not worth it.* She walked over to them, opened her arms, and enfolded all three of her daughters in a hug. "Everything's going to be fine," she said, trying to believe it herself. "Just fine."

She pulled back. "C'mon," she said, "let's get you girls cleaned up."

She started out the door of the stable, but the sound of hoofbeats brought her to a halt, and she watched as Vernon rode around the side of the house and into the yard, followed by Joshua and Earl Harlan. Chester halted beside her and began to bark.

Fear shot through Olivia, and her first thought was to keep the girls away. She turned to her oldest daughter. "Becky, take your sisters out at the other end of the stable and go to the Johnsons'. Take Chester with you. Tell Oren that Vernon's here, and I need help."

"Why?" Becky leaned forward, trying to see the men who had ridden into the yard, but Olivia grabbed her by the shoulders and turned her around.

"Just do it," she said, giving the girl a push toward the door at the other end. "Run as fast as you can. Go."

Becky grabbed each of her sisters by the hand. "C'mon, Chester," she said. The three girls and the dog ran out of the stable and headed for the Johnson farm. Olivia would have gone with them, but she had to find out what had happened to Conor. She waited until she saw the girls and Chester disappear into the dense woods, then she left the stable and walked across the yard.

Vernon saw her approach. He wrapped the reins of his roan stallion around the porch rail, then moved to stand by the steps. The Harlan boys followed suit.

As she approached, she felt the anger that emanated from him like the stillness before a thunderstorm. There was strain in his face and tense restraint in his movements, as if he were keeping that anger tightly leashed, and the slightest change could start the storm raging. For the first time in her life, she was afraid of Vernon, afraid of what he and his boys might have done to Conor.

He waited to speak until she stopped several feet away from him. "Where's Branigan?" he asked tightly. "He came to see me this morning, but he left before we could finish our little talk."

A blessed feeling of relief washed over her. Vernon didn't know where Conor was, and that meant that her husband was safe.

But her relief vanished when Vernon pulled back his jacket to show her the gun stuck in his belt. He began walking toward her. "I'm here to finish it."

She refused to show fear by stepping back, and he halted a foot in front of her. She stared at the pistol for a moment, then looked up and met his eyes. "Conor isn't here. I don't know where he is."

"Then we'll wait for him." Before she could move, he grabbed her arm in a viselike grip. It would have been pointless to struggle, so Olivia did not, and Vernon hauled her up the steps and into the house. The Harlan boys followed them into the kitchen.

"Earl, go keep a watch on the front window, and tell

me if Branigan's coming," Vernon instructed. "Joshua, you go out and watch the back."

Earl left the room, and Joshua went out onto the back porch, closing the door behind him. Vernon pushed Olivia into a chair.

"What are you going to do?" she asked.

He pulled out a chair beside her and sat down. "I'm going to get his signature on a deed and bill of sale for this land."

"What makes you think he'll sell it to you?"

"He'll sell." Vernon leaned back in his chair, and pulled his pistol out of his belt, and took aim at the door.

That gesture left no doubt of his intentions. Olivia clasped her shaking hands together, and cast a longing glance at the pantry, wondering if she could get to the rifle. She stirred in her chair. "Since we may be waiting for Conor awhile," she said, "I think I'll make some tea."

She started to rise, but Vernon grabbed her and yanked her back into her seat. "We don't need any tea, Liv. You just sit tight."

The minutes went by, and each one seemed like an eternity to Olivia.

She prayed that Oren would be able to do something, but it was four miles to the Johnson farm, and she knew it would be at least an hour before the girls could get there. If Conor arrived in the meantime, Vernon might very well shoot him. He was tight as a bowstring, and anything could make him snap.

She looked at him. "Vernon," she said quietly, "if it's the land you want, we'll sell it to you. There's no need for any of this."

He turned on her. "No need?" he shouted, his anger flaring. "That son of a bitch came barging his way into my home this morning as if he was king of the hill, threatening me and my wife's father, telling us how he was going to destroy us and get his Irish friends in New York to help him do it. And Hiram fell for it!" Vernon slammed his fist down on the table. "Nobody threatens me! Nobody! Especially not some Irish boxer who hasn't got two nickels to rub together."

He looked at her, contempt and rage twisting his features. "And you married him! I wasn't good enough for you, but he was? You wouldn't marry me, but you married *him*."

He shoved back his chair. Rising to his feet, he leaned over her, the gun between them, so much loathing in his face that she shrank back in her chair. "You've let him touch you. You've let him put his filthy Irish hands on you. God, you disgust me."

She stared up at Vernon and realized the truth. "This isn't about the land anymore, is it?" she whispered. "This is about my marriage."

Before he could answer, Earl came in from the parlor. "Branigan's coming up the lane, boss."

Vernon straightened, regaining control of himself with an effort. He grabbed her arm and yanked her out of the chair. "Come on, Mrs. Branigan," he said, pulling her with him out the back door. "Let's go greet your husband."

When Conor rode into the yard, he immediately saw the horses and the four people waiting for him on the back porch. He saw the gun in Vernon's hand and the fear in Olivia's face. He dismounted from Oren's horse and walked slowly toward the porch, but he stopped several feet from the steps, trying to figure out what to do.

Vernon held Olivia close to his side, but the gun was not pointed at her. It was pointed at Conor. "Afternoon, Branigan. We've been waiting for you."

Conor looked at Olivia. "Where are the girls?"

"They're at the Johnsons'."

He nodded and returned his gaze to Vernon. "What's the offer now, Vernon?" he asked, striving to sound casual. "Seven dollars an acre?"

"It's back down to one."

Conor wondered if Vernon would use Olivia as a bargaining chip. He needed to find out, and he slowly shook his head. "No deal."

"I thought you might say that." Vernon glanced at the two men who stood beside him. "Joshua, Earl, I think Mr. Branigan here needs to be persuaded."

The two men came down the porch steps, walking toward him, and Conor had his answer.

"Conor, let them have the land!" Olivia called to him. "It's not worth this."

He heard the plea in her voice, but he could not concede. This wasn't just about land; it was about standing up to bullies and fighting for what you believed in. Well, he had something to believe in now, and unless Vernon threatened Olivia, he wasn't going to give it up without a fight.

Conor backed away, to give himself more fighting room, and assessed the abilities of the two men who came toward him. Joshua he could take down with no problem. But he remembered how it had felt when Earl's fist had smashed his face that night nearly three months ago, and he knew that man might be a bit tougher.

He clenched his fists and waited for one of them to make the first move, suspecting it would be Joshua, who had a personal grudge and very little patience. When the first punch came at him, he was proven right.

He ducked to avoid Joshua's fist, and at the same time, he jammed his elbow backward into Earl's belly. Joshua's fist sailed over his head, Earl doubled over with a grunt of pain, and Conor straightened, bringing his right fist up beneath Joshua's chin and following with his left hook to smash the man's cheek. Joshua fell back and hit the dirt.

But Conor had no time to relish his victory. He turned, hoping he was quick enough. But he wasn't. Earl's punch caught him just below his cheekbone. Conor staggered back from the force of the blow, but he stayed on his feet and managed to lean left as Earl followed through with a second punch that didn't even touch him.

Conor slammed his right fist into Earl's ribs and followed with a clean uppercut to the jaw that stunned the other man long enough for one more right hook. Bone hit bone in a shattered thwack that sent Earl to the ground. Conor whirled back around, but Joshua still lay where he'd fallen, groaning, but making no attempt to rise and continue the fight.

Conor stepped over them and walked to the porch, looking up at the man who stood on the top step. "They didn't persuade me, Vernon," he said, his breath coming hard and fast. "Now, it's just you and me. For once in your miserable life, you'll have to fight your own battle."

Vernon tightened his grip on Olivia, pulling her close to his side, and aimed the pistol directly at Conor's heart. "I'm going to make this real simple for you, boy. Give me the land or I'll kill you."

"No!" Olivia's voice rose on a sob. "Let him have the land," she cried. "It's not worth your life. It's not worth it. Please, Conor."

Conor glanced from Vernon to her and back again, trying to find some other option. Even if he signed over the land, Vernon would probably kill him. "All right, Tyler, you win," he said, lifting his hands in a gesture of surrender.

Suddenly, he moved, so fast that Olivia didn't quite know how he managed it. The gun fired just as Conor knocked it out of Vernon's hand, but the bullet sailed harmlessly through the air, and the gun hit the porch with a thud. Conor grabbed the other man by his lapels and hauled him down the steps. Then he let the other man go and gave him a shove. "All right, boyo," he said through clenched teeth, "let's see how brave you are now."

Olivia ran to the other end of the porch and grabbed the gun. She leaned over the porch rail. She cocked the weapon and pointed it at Vernon. "I've got the gun, Conor."

"Well, don't shoot him yet," he told her. "I'll be having a bit o' sport with him first."

Fear wiped away all the arrogance in Vernon's face. He glanced around as if seeking help, but the only two men who could help him lay sprawled in the dirt, still stunned and dazed, and obviously unwilling to come to his aid.

Conor gave him another push. "What's wrong, Vernon?" he taunted. "Nobody to do your dirty work for you?"

He lifted his fist as if to take a swing, and Vernon cried out, jumping back and shielding his face with his arms. Conor lowered his fist, laughing. "You cowardly bastard," he muttered. "You're not worth hurting my hand."

Vernon lowered his arms, and Conor moved as if to turn away. But suddenly, he changed his mind and swung, momentum adding to the force of the blow that slammed into Vernon's nose and laid him out flat on his back in the dirt.

"I lied," Conor said, wiping blood from his hand.

A carriage pulled into the yard and came to a halt behind the two men, but Olivia spared only one glance at Alicia Tyler and the distinguished-looking gentleman beside her before returning her attention to Conor and Vernon.

Her husband moved to stand over the other man and placed his boot on his throat. "I'm Conor Branigan," he said through clenched teeth. "Now, that name might not mean much to you, so I'd better explain just how things are around here."

He stepped back. Vernon struggled to breathe, sucking air into his lungs in desperate gasps.

Conor gestured to the surrounding countryside and went on, "I own this land and everything on it. This is my farm and my home. You understand me, boyo?"

Vernon nodded and tried to rise.

Conor pushed him back down with his boot. "Good. You've threatened my family, and I don't like that at all. You ever set foot on my land again, you so much as look at my wife, or come within a mile of my daughters, you miserable bastard, and I'll do more than use you for firewood. I'll kill you."

Olivia lowered the pistol in her hand and walked down the steps as she listened to Conor claim what she had thought he would never want. She heard the fierce possessiveness in his voice as he said "my wife" and "my family"—and every word gave her hope. She came to a halt a few feet away and waited, as a wagon came into the yard and pulled up behind the carriage.

"Your girls said there was trouble," Oren said, jumping down from the wagon, rifle in hand. He looked at the three men lying on the ground, including the one pinned beneath Conor's boot. "But I see you've handled it."

Conor grinned and gestured to the two dazed Harlan brothers. "You can do me a favor and dump these two miserable excuses for men in the road on your way home."

As Oren prodded the two Harlan boys to their feet with the muzzle of his rifle, Conor glanced at Olivia and saw the pistol still in her hand. He took it from her, opened the cylinder, and dumped out the bullets. Then he hauled the other man to his feet and gave him a shove toward the waiting carriage. "Get off my land," he said, and tossed the empty weapon at Vernon's feet.

Vernon pressed a hand to his bleeding nose and bent to pick up the gun. Behind him, the door of the carriage opened and Alicia Tyler stepped down. She walked to her husband's side. After removing a delicate linen handkerchief from her pocket, she dabbed it to his nose and spoke to him gently. "I'm leaving, Vernon. The stage departs for Monroe this afternoon, and Papa and I will be on it. You can remain here in Callersville, of course, but you'll have to find a place to live because we will be putting the house up for sale. You'll also have to find a job because we'll be selling the sawmill and the mercantile and all the rest."

"Alicia, you can't—"

"If you wish to come with us," she interrupted, "Papa will make a place for you in one of his companies. You'll have to start at the bottom, of course. A clerk, perhaps. But I'm sure you'll be able to work your way up in no time. Papa will help you."

She let him hold the handkerchief to his nose while she brushed the dust from his torn clothes and straightened his tie as if he were a child. Then she put her arm through his and led him toward the carriage. Before she stepped inside, she paused and turned to look at Conor and Olivia. "I hope the two of you will be happy here. I never was."

She stepped into the carriage, and Vernon followed her inside without a backward glance. The carriage turned around and rolled away, pausing by the porch long enough for the driver to jump down and tie Vernon's horse to the back, then pulled away, going around the side of the house and disappearing from view.

Oren pulled his wagon up beside Conor and Olivia, his bay gelding tied to the back. Keeping his rifle pointed at the Harlans, he watched them mount their horses, to follow Vernon's carriage, and he chuckled. "They both look a bit cross-eyed. Never knew any man could land a punch like you, Conor. I'll bet they never knew what hit 'em."

"I hope they did," Conor answered. "And I hope they'll be remembering it for a long time to come."

"By the way," Oren said, lowering his rifle now that the Harlans had disappeared, "Kate said to tell you that you're welcome to stay for supper when you come pick up the girls."

"Thanks. We'll be along shortly," Conor told him. Oren nodded and snapped the reins. The wagon lurched forward out of the yard.

Olivia looked at her husband, studying his hard profile as he watched the wagon disappear from sight. To Vernon, he had claimed what was his—the land around them, the girls, and her. But she wanted him to claim the most important thing of all: Her heart. "Do you love me?"

The abrupt question caught him off guard. He stiffened. Without looking at her, he said, "You've lost your last chance to be rid of me. I'm staying, with all my bad moods and all my bad habits. I'm not leaving."

"That's not what I asked you."

"I'll try not to swear in front of the girls, but I might slip up. You'll just have to get used to it. And if I have any more nightmares, don't try to wake me. Just promise me you'll keep out of the way until it's over."

"Yes, of course, but—"

"Furthermore," he interrupted, and turned to her, looking almost defiant, "I'm not going to church, so don't be getting any ideas about it."

"I never said you had to go to church, but Conor—"

"I'll smoke my cigars if I want to, and I'll not give up my whiskey. If I want a wee drop now and again, I'll be having it. And there'll be no lectures about it the next morn—"

"Conor!" she interrupted, exasperated, impatient, hopeful, terrified. "Do you love me?"

He opened his mouth as if to answer her, but closed it again. A shadow crossed his face, a shadow of something she could not define, something hungry and fierce. It might have been fear. It might have been love. Perhaps it was both.

Suddenly, he reached out and grabbed her hand.

"I want to show you something," he said, and pulled her across the yard, past the charred remains of the barn, past the stable and the cabins, to Nate's old toolshed.

He halted by the door, and let go of her hand. "There's something in there," he said, and looked suddenly uncertain. He began backing away. "I . . . um . . . I made it for you."

She watched him, puzzled by his sudden reticence. "What is it?" she asked; but he didn't answer. She turned to the door and pushed it open.

Sunlight fell through the doorway, casting her shadow across the wooden bench that stood in the center of the shed. It was painted white, and there were chains attached to the sides as if it were meant to be hung. It was a porch swing.

Olivia stared at it, blinking back a sudden onslaught of tears. She walked over to it slowly, and ran her hand along the smooth white surface. "You made this for me?" She turned to look at him, but the sun behind him made his expression unreadable. "Why?"

He lowered his head, staring down at the ground. A

long silence passed, then he spoke, slowly, as if thinking out each word. "Olivia, I've spent a long time running away from a lot of things. Love, most of all. I convinced myself that I didn't need it, that I didn't want it, even that I couldn't feel it anymore. But the truth is, I was afraid of it. I've lost everything I ever loved, and I never wanted to love anyone or anything again. I never wanted to risk feeling that kind of pain again."

Olivia listened, and with every stilted word, her hope burned brighter. When he fell silent, she took a tentative step closer to him. "And now?"

She held her breath, waiting.

He lifted his head. "Now, I've come to realize that there are some things worth the risk, some things that are too powerful to walk away from, and too valuable to lose. You taught me that. This porch swing is my wedding gift to you, and I want to sit in it with you all the evenings of my life. I love you, *á mhúirnín*."

Words failed her. She wanted to tell him how much his gift meant to her, how much she needed him, how afraid she'd been that he would leave her, how much she loved him. But she could not find words.

So, she ran to him, flinging herself into his embrace with a sob of relief and joy that told him more than any words could have done.

Each of the girls had an opinion about Olivia's gift.

"I think it's wonderful, Daddy," Becky said, as she kissed him good-night. "Jeremiah and I can sit in it next time he comes to Sunday dinner."

"Over my dead body," Conor muttered under his breath, as she walked down the hall to her room.

Olivia made a choked sound that sounded highly suspicious. He frowned at her, wondering if she were laughing about something, but she had already stepped over Chester and crossed the hall to Carrie's room, so he couldn't be certain.

Carrie wasn't as enthusiastic about the porch swing as her sister. "It's okay," she said, yawning. "But, Daddy, couldn't you have made something fun, like a tree house?"

He leaned down and kissed her. "That's next, *mó cailín*. I promise. Go to sleep."

Olivia kissed her daughter. "Good night, sweetie. Sleep tight."

They moved on to Miranda's room, and together, they tucked their youngest daughter into bed.

As they pulled the covers up to her chin, she asked, "Daddy, since you made Mama a swing, can you make me a dollhouse?"

His throat tightened, and he brushed his lips against her cheek. "I can do that, love."

"Good," she said, closing her eyes. "Now my dolls can have a home."

Conor met Olivia's eyes over the bed. "Everybody ought to have one of those," he murmured, and watched his wife smile. He vowed that, every day of his life, he was going to find a way to make her smile. He was going to do everything in his power to see that she was safe and happy. And loved. Always.

She kissed Miranda good-night and turned out the lamp. Then she took Conor's hand, and together they left Miranda's room. As they went downstairs, he said, "I never thought I needed a home and children to complete my life. Now, I couldn't imagine living my life without them. But sometimes, Olivia, it's damned frightening."

Olivia's hand tightened in his. "You'll do fine," she told him. "The thing about being a good parent is not to think about it too much."

The words were familiar. He thought of that day in her kitchen when he'd kissed her for the first time, and he gave her a smile that was deliberately wicked. "Let's go sit in that porch swing."

When they stepped outside, Conor felt the slight chill in the air and recognized the first sign of autumn. He thought of all the things that needed doing before spring, but instead of suffocating him, those things made him realize how much he had to look forward to.

He sat down and pulled Olivia onto his lap, a move that set the swing rocking. "So, Mrs. Branigan," he murmured in her ear, "tell me again what your mama and daddy used to do in this porch swing."

She leaned closer until her lips were an inch from his. "I'll show you," she whispered, her arms tightening around his neck.

When she kissed him, Conor spent a long time enjoying the real reason husbands sat in porch swings with their wives after the children were in bed. In his opinion, it was a fine way to spend an evening. But it wasn't what he had in mind just now.

He broke the kiss and stood up with her in his arms, a move that surprised her.

"I thought you wanted to sit in the porch swing."

"I changed my mind," he murmured hoarsely, trailing kisses along her throat as he started for the back door. "We'll sit in it tomorrow."

He carried her across the threshold and back into the house, up the stairs and into their bedroom. He kicked the door shut. As it closed behind them and the latch clicked into place, Conor Branigan kissed his wife again and knew that he had finally come home.

Glossary of Gaelic Terms

Author's note
Gaelic does not always translate with literal accuracy to English. These translations are given to provide a general meaning, not a literal translation.

admhaím: confession
á mhúirnín: "my love," a term of endearment
bermíd go maith: "all is well"
Clan na Gael: a secret society formed in America during the nineteenth century and composed of Irish immigrants dedicated to the liberation of Ireland from British rule
clochan: a storage shed for crops
craythur: an affectionate term for Irish whiskey
fiabhras dubh: "black fever" or typhus
fuathaím: hate
gaol: prison
luíochán: ambush
mó cailín: my girl, a term of endearment
mó paisté: my child, a term of endearment
Neamh: heaven
seanachaie: storyteller
sha sha: "there, there," a phrase to soothe or comfort
slainté: a toast meaning good health
tá mé anseo: "I'm here."
tá ocrás orm: "I'm hungry," or "The hunger is upon me."
Uilleann pipes: Irish bagpipes

Author's Note

On August 31, 1994, the Irish Republican Army declared a full cease-fire, and Protestant paramilitary groups quickly followed suit. Talks have begun so that a peaceful solution to "The Troubles" of Northern Ireland can be found. During much of the writing of this book, the streets of Northern Ireland have been quiet. Let us all hope and pray that peace has finally come to that lovely, tragic land and its warm, generous people.

Let HarperMonogram Sweep You Away!

※❀❁❀❧

Once a Knight by **Christina Dodd**
Golden Heart and RITA Award–winning author. Though slightly rusty, once great knight Sir David Radcliffe agrees to protect Lady Alisoun for a price. His mercenary heart betrayed by passion, Sir David proves to his lady that he is still master of love—and his sword is as swift as ever.

Timberline by **Deborah Bedford**
Held captive in her mountain cabin by escaped convict Ben Pershall, Rebecca Woodburn realizes that the man's need for love mirrors her own. Even though Ben has taken her hostage, he ultimately sets her soul free.

Conor's Way by **Laura Lee Guhrke**
Desperate to save her plantation after the Civil War, beautiful Olivia Maitland takes in Irish ex-boxer Conor Branigan in exchange for help. Cynical Conor has no place for romance in his life, until the strong-willed belle shows him that the love of a lifetime is worth fighting for.

Lord of Misrule by **Stephanie Maynard**
Golden Heart Award Winner. Posing as a thief to avenge the destruction of her noble family, Catrienne Lyly must match wits with Nicholas D'Avenant, Queen Elizabeth's most mysterious agent. But Cat's bold ruse cannot protect her from the ecstasy of Nicholas's touch.

And in case you missed last month's selections . . .

Once Upon a Time by **Constance O'Banyon**
Over seven million copies of her books in print. To save her idyllic kingdom from the English, Queen Jilliana must marry Prince Ruyen and produce an heir. Both are willing to do anything to defeat a common enemy, but they are power-less to fight the wanton desires that threaten to engulf them.

The Marrying Kind by Sharon Ihle

Romantic Times *Reviewers' Choice Award–winning author.* Liberty Ann Justice has no time for the silver-tongued stranger she believes is trying to destroy her father's Wyoming newspaper. Donovan isn't about to let a little misunderstanding hinder her pursuit of happiness, however, or his pursuit of the tempestuous vixen who has him hungering for her sweet love.

Honor by Mary Spencer

Sent by King Henry V to save Amica of Lancaster from a cruel marriage, Sir Thomas of Reed discovers his rough ways are no match for Amica's innocent sensuality. A damsel in distress to his knight, she unleashes passions in Sir Thomas that leave him longing for her touch.

Wake Not the Dragon by Jo Ann Ferguson

As the queen's midwife, Gizela de Montpellier travels to Wales and meets Rhys ap Cynan—a Welsh chieftain determined to drive out the despised English. Captivated by the handsome warlord, Gizela must choose between her loyalty to the crown and her heart's desire.

Harper Monogram

Buy 4 or more and receive FREE postage & handling

MAIL TO: HarperCollins Publishers
P.O. Box 588 Dunmore, PA 18512–0588
OR CALL: **1-800-331-3761 (Visa/MasterCard)**
YES! Please send me the books I have checked:

- ❏ **ONCE A KNIGHT** 108398-4..........................$5.99 U.S./$7.99 CAN.
- ❏ **TIMBERLINE** 108358-5 ....$4.99 U.S./$5.99 CAN.
- ❏ **CONOR'S WAY** 108402-6 ....$4.99 U.S./$5.99 CAN.
- ❏ **LORD OF MISRULE** 108395-X ....$4.99 U.S./$5.99 CAN.
- ❏ **ONCE UPON A TIME** 108229-5 ....$5.99 U.S./$7.99 CAN.
- ❏ **THE MARRYING KIND** 108399-2 ....$5.50 U.S./$7.50 CAN.
- ❏ **HONOR** 108407-7 ....$5.50 U.S./$7.50 CAN.
- ❏ **WAKE NOT THE DRAGON** 108413-1 ....$4.99 U.S./$5.99 CAN.

SUBTOTAL..$_____
POSTAGE & HANDLING.......................................$_____ 2.00
SALES TAX (Add applicable sales tax)......................$_____
TOTAL ....$_____
Name_____
Address_____
City_____ State_____ Zip Code_____

Order 4 or more titles and postage & handling is **FREE!** Orders of less than 4 books, please include $2.00 p/h. Remit in U.S. funds. Do not send cash. Allow up to 6 weeks for delivery. Prices subject to change. Valid only in U.S. and Canada.

M023

Visa & MasterCard holders—call 1-800-331-3761

ATTENTION: ORGANIZATIONS AND CORPORATIONS

Most HarperPaperbacks are available at special quantity discounts for bulk purchases for sales promotions, premiums, or fund-raising. For information, please call or write:
Special Markets Department, HarperCollins Publishers, 10 East 53rd Street, New York, N.Y. 10022.
Telephone: (212) 207-7528. Fax: (212) 207-7222.